continued . . .

"Another paranormal romance by Ashley is just what the doctor ordered. Her characters are intense and full of passion."

—*RT Book Reviews*

WILD CAT

"Danger, desire, and sizzling-hot action! *Wild Cat* is a wild ride. Jennifer Ashley walks the razor's edge of primal passion . . . This is one for the keeper shelf!"

—Alyssa Day, *New York Times* bestselling author

"A riveting read, with intriguing characters, page-turning action, and danger lurking around every turn. Ashley's Shifter world is exciting, sexy, and magical."

—Yasmine Galenorn, *New York Times* bestselling author

PRIMAL BONDS

"[A] sexually charged and imaginative tale . . . [A] quick pace and smart, skilled writing." —*Publishers Weekly*

"An enjoyable thriller . . . [An] action-packed tale."

—Midwest Book Review

"Humor and passion abound in this excellent addition to this series."

—Fresh Fiction

PRIDE MATES

"With her usual gift for creating imaginative plots fueled by scorchingly sensual chemistry, RITA Award–winning Ashley begins a new sexy paranormal series that neatly combines high-adrenaline suspense with humor." —*Booklist*

"A whole new way to look at shapeshifters . . . Rousing action and sensually charged, MapQuest me the directions for Shiftertown."

—*Publishers Weekly*

"Absolutely fabulous! . . . I was blown away . . . Paranormal fans will be raving over this one!" —The Romance Readers Connection

More Praise for the Novels of Jennifer Ashley

"Ashley demonstrates her gift for combining complex characters; emotionally compelling, danger-tinged plotting; and a delectably sensual romance into one unforgettable love story."
—*Booklist* (starred review)

"Big, arrogant, sexy highlanders—Jennifer Ashley writes the kinds of heroes I crave!"
—Elizabeth Hoyt, *New York Times* bestselling author

"A sexy, passion-filled romance that will keep you reading until dawn."
—Julianne MacLean, *USA Today* bestselling author

"I adore this novel: It's heartrending, funny, honest, and true. I want to know the hero—no, I want to *marry* the hero!"
—Eloisa James, *New York Times* bestselling author

"Readers rejoice! . . . A unique love story brimming over with depth of emotion, unforgettable characters, sizzling passion, mystery, and a story that reaches out and grabs your heart. Brava!"
—*RT Book Reviews* (Top Pick)

"Mysterious, heartfelt, sensitive, and sensual . . . Two big thumbs up."
—*Publishers Weekly*

"A story full of mystery and intrigue with two wonderful, bright characters . . . I look forward to more from Jennifer Ashley, an extremely gifted author."
—Fresh Fiction

"Brimming with mystery, suspense, an intriguing plot, villains, romance, a tormented hero, and a feisty heroine, this book is a winner."
—Romance Junkies

"Wow! All I can say is *The Madness of Lord Ian Mackenzie* is one of the best books that I have ever read."
—Once Upon A Romance

"Fabulous . . . A sensual, gorgeous story that was captivating from the first page to the very last."
—Joyfully Reviewed

MATE BOND

JENNIFER ASHLEY

BERKLEY SENSATION, NEW YORK

THE BERKLEY PUBLISHING GROUP
Published by the Penguin Group
Penguin Group (USA) LLC
375 Hudson Street, New York, New York 10014

USA • Canada • UK • Ireland • Australia • New Zealand • India • South Africa • China

penguin.com

A Penguin Random House Company

MATE BOND

A Berkley Sensation Book / published by arrangement with the author

For information, address: The Berkley Publishing Group,
a division of Penguin Group (USA) LLC,
375 Hudson Street, New York, New York 10014.

ISBN: 978-0-425-26605-2

PUBLISHING HISTORY
Berkley Sensation mass-market edition / April 2015

PRINTED IN THE UNITED STATES OF AMERICA

10 9 8 7 6 5 4 3 2 1

Cover design by Edwin Tse.
Cover art by Tony Mauro.
Art direction by George Long.

CHAPTER ONE

The Shifter groupie was new.

Kenzie had never seen her before, anyway. The woman stood with a knot of friends who'd clumped together for reassurance but turned excited gazes toward the male Shifters roaming the roadhouse tonight.

Kenzie watched Bowman size up the woman while he appeared to be merely leaning on the bar talking to his friends. She saw him conclude, as Kenzie had, that the new girl wasn't a real groupie.

No one but Kenzie would have known, given Bowman's posture, that he'd even noticed the woman. He rested both elbows on the bar as he conversed with Cade on one side of him, Jamie on the other. Even as they laughed and joked, Cade, his second, and Jamie, one of his trackers, kept a little space between themselves and their leader. Bowman dominated the whole damn place without even standing upright.

His casual position stretched his jeans over his great ass, outlining narrow hips and strong legs, one knee bent as he rested his motorcycle-booted foot on the lower rail of the bar. His black T-shirt was smoothed over his broad shoulders, outlining every muscle from neck to shoulder blades and all the way down his spine.

Kenzie couldn't take her eyes off him. She absently held an untasted bottle of beer, half listening to two of her female cousins chatter. Bowman turned his head to say something to Cade, giving Kenzie a glimpse of his strong, square jaw and the nose he considered too large for his face but Kenzie thought just right. He was a wolf, after all.

Bowman's gray eyes flashed at something Cade said, a quick ripple of a smile tipping his mouth. A strong mouth, equally good at snarling orders or kissing.

He was going to teach the fake groupie, whoever she was, a lesson, Kenzie deduced from his quick glance in the woman's direction. Would be fun to watch . . . and painful too.

Bowman pushed himself off the bar, giving a nod to those around him. Cade, a big grizzly Shifter, acknowledged it without moving. Cade and Bowman, in spite of being different species, were so wired to each other that they communicated without words or even gestures.

Kenzie's heart squeezed as she watched Bowman walk in a slow, even pace to the new young woman. The fake ears the girl wore were wolf instead of cat—a signal she was into Lupines—and both she and one of her friends had wolf tails fastened to their backsides. When the friend saw Bowman coming over, she started excitedly patting the new girl's arm.

Bowman could charm. Didn't Kenzie know it? Just by walking toward them, he had the cluster of young women smiling, beaming, melting at his feet, before he even spoke.

The new young woman imitated her friends, but there was something calculating in her eyes, watchful. She might be a reporter, come to dish the dirt on the Shifter groupie scene, or she could be an informer for the human police.

When Bowman gave the new girl a jerk of his chin to follow him, the true groupies dissolved into excited laughter mixed with looks of furious envy.

Kenzie knew how they felt. She set down her beer, told her cousin Bianca she was using the ladies'—alone—and walked away.

She knew she wasn't fooling them. The other two Shifter

women exchanged knowing looks and let her go. They knew way too much about Kenzie—everyone in Shiftertown did.

Bowman and the groupie had reached the darkest part of the parking lot by the time Kenzie emerged. It was cold; a North Carolina winter at its peak. The roadhouse was ten miles from Shiftertown, halfway between Asheville and the Tennessee border, popular on a Saturday night.

Kenzie heard the two before she saw them. Bowman's voice, imprinted on her heart, came to her from a deep shadow between the generator-run lights. "So you want to be with a Shifter, do you?" He was growling, and it was not really a question.

The woman answered nervously, her high-pitched voice grating on Kenzie's nerves. Kenzie didn't pay much attention to her actual words—the woman's tone said she was afraid of Bowman but determined to get her story, whatever that story happened to be.

Kenzie edged close enough to be in scent range of Bowman, which meant the woman's cloying perfume came to her loud and clear. Why did human women douse themselves like that? Made Kenzie want to sneeze.

She knew Bowman would be able scent Kenzie skulking in the darkness, even over the perfume. She also knew Bowman wouldn't care that she was there. Those thoughts hurt, but Kenzie remained in the shadows, watching.

"Shifters are dangerous, sweetheart," Bowman was saying. He leaned against the back of a dusty SUV and stretched out his long legs, crossing them at the ankles. Bowman's arms were folded, both shutting himself off and giving the groupie and Kenzie a view of his sculpted muscles. He hadn't bothered with a coat—Bowman often didn't. "Better be sure you know what you're getting into."

He was angry, even if his slow drawl didn't betray it. He hated anyone spying on his Shifters, and with good reason. The young woman couldn't scent his fury as Kenzie did, but some instinct inside her knew to be worried.

"I've always wanted to do a Lupine." The pseudo-groupie was trying to sound as though she stalked Shifters to have sex with them all the time, but Kenzie—and Bowman—knew better.

Bowman remained silent and motionless for a long moment, while the girl grew more and more nervous. Then Bowman moved—the movement was slow and casual, but all the more devastating for that.

He reached down and undid his belt, the clink of it coming to Kenzie. Next, she heard the whisper of his jeans' zipper.

Kenzie froze, riveted in place, as Bowman languidly slid his jeans and underwear halfway down his thighs and leaned back again on the SUV.

Kenzie couldn't breathe. His half-lifted shirt showed a slice of hard abdomen, and his large Shifter cock stood straight up between his strong, sun-bronzed legs. The brush of dark hair that cradled his shaft was lost in shadow, but Kenzie knew exactly what he looked like.

The young woman made a strangled sound that Kenzie wanted to echo. Bowman erect was a beautiful sight.

"Come on, sweetheart," Bowman said impatiently. "I haven't got all night."

The young woman opened and closed her mouth a couple times and took a few shaky steps backward. "I don't . . . I don't know."

Bowman came off the SUV with a suddenness only a Shifter could manage. One moment he was reclining, ready, and the next he was nearly on top of the woman, his big hands on her shoulders.

"Here's what I know," he said in a fierce voice. "You came to look at Shifters, for whatever reason. So here I am. We look human, but we aren't—not even close." His jeans were still around his knees, his tight backside bare under the lights of the parking lot. But he didn't look ridiculous—Bowman never could. He was as decadent and enticing as ever. Kenzie's mating need, never very far away, flared.

The groupie's words choked in her throat, her nervousness turning to full-blown fear. "I wanted . . . I just wanted to talk . . ."

Bowman shoved her away. "I know what you wanted." He leaned down and pulled up his jeans, taking his time. "You wanted to come here and get all up in our shit and go tell the world about it. I don't know if you're a reporter or a detective or a do-gooder, but I want you out of here, away from my Shifters."

The pseudo-groupie had the presence of mind to point out the obvious. "You don't own this place. This isn't Shiftertown. You can't tell me to leave."

Her breathless groupie eagerness had gone, replaced by the hard, nasally voice of a woman who liked having her own way. Bowman wasn't impressed. His hands clamped down on her shoulders again, and a very wolf growl came out of his throat.

"I might not own the bar." His voice went low, as it did when he was truly angry. "But I know the owner, and he doesn't like people coming here and giving Shifters trouble. Let me give you a tip—I'm way nicer than he is. So get out, or I'll let him and his bouncers take you off the property in a more forceful way."

"Now you're threatening me?"

Bowman said nothing. He only looked at the pseudo-groupie, and Kenzie scented the wolf in him getting ready to come out. Bowman was careful, but he was still pretty close to wild, and he didn't like his authority challenged in any way.

He hadn't said so—the woman wouldn't understand—but Bowman considered this roadhouse to be part of his territory. Humans might have confined Shifters to Shiftertowns and restricted them from owning places like this bar, but true Shifter territory stretched from one Shiftertown to the next. There was another Shiftertown far to the west of them in the middle of Tennessee, and Bowman considered that his territory ended about fifty miles from that, where the other leader's territory began.

By Shifter thinking, Bowman had a perfect right to sling this woman out. Humans wouldn't see it that way though.

The woman started to reach for something in her purse. Pepper spray? A gun? Bowman caught her hand, his growl rumbling across the empty parking lot, vibrating the ground.

Shit. If Bowman hurt the woman, or even scared her bad enough, the human cops would be all over this place in a heartbeat. Bowman would be dragged away in cuffs spelled to contain Shifters, and probably every Shifter in the roadhouse would be arrested along with him.

Only one thing to do. Kenzie hurried out of the shadows, making for the two of them. At the last minute, she slowed and pretended to be out for a nonchalant stroll. She put a sway in her hips as she eased herself up to Bowman and draped her arm around his neck.

The heat of him came to her, along with his wild scent. The strength of him quivering under her touch made Kenzie flush with warmth.

Bowman's entire body went rigid. No one touched an alpha when he was at the height of his anger, especially not when he was this close to shifting.

No one but his mate.

"Hey, Bowman," Kenzie said, letting her voice drawl in a sultry way. "You seeing someone else now? I'm going to get jealous."

CHAPTER TWO

Kenzie, her arm still around Bowman, pinned the pseudo-groupie with a stare that she hoped showed a hint of feral red.

The woman backed a step under their collective gazes, and Bowman, thank the Goddess, released the woman's wrist. Kenzie remained draped over him, pretending not to feel every bit of tension in his body that told her he did not want her there.

The woman opened her mouth to deliver a final word. Her wolf ears had slid back on her head, and her makeup was running with her sweat. But she apparently thought better of speaking, and turned and walked hurriedly away. Her fake wolf tail waved as she went.

As soon as she disappeared back into the roadhouse, Bowman spun around. He did it so fast, Kenzie didn't have time to let go of him.

She found herself holding six-feet-eight of enraged Shifter. Bowman's body was tight, his gray eyes almost white with the suppressed change. The wolf in him was furious and wanted to hunt, to bring down and tear apart prey.

With any other Lupine, Kenzie might laugh and suggest he

needed a beer—she'd buy. But Bowman wasn't going to calm down. While Kenzie didn't blame him—that woman was up to no good and might be dangerous—he had to stand down, or he might do something that would get them all into trouble.

Only one thing could soothe a wolf as dominant as Bowman. The touch of a mate.

Kenzie ran her hands over Bowman's shoulders, the tension in him incredible. He didn't want to calm down. He wanted a run.

Well, he could do that, but not right *now*. Other people were coming out of the roadhouse, paying no attention to them in the darkness. Some got into trucks and cars to drive home or on to the next bar; others lingered to talk and laugh. Bowman was too close to wild not to try to turn one of them into prey.

Bowman glared at Kenzie, but she didn't ease off. She skimmed her hands down his hard chest, feeling his heart beating crazily, his skin hot under his shirt. His growls continued to rumble—if anything, growing louder.

She kept up her massage, moving her hands in circles on his chest, pressing her body against his. He was incredibly warm in the January cold, his mating heat starting to take over the killing need.

Bowman seized her wrists in a grip that would have hurt anyone else. "Kenzie, you need to *stop*."

Kenzie flattened herself against him. She felt him with her whole body now, his heartbeat against hers, his breath on her skin, the hardness of his entire body.

"Not until you can walk inside without throwing people all over the tables."

Bowman's growl rumbled. "I don't like anyone watching my Shifters."

"I get that. But she's gone."

"People like that always come back."

"I know."

If he'd been anyone else, Kenzie might be tempted to get up in his face, wag her finger at him, bean him with sarcasm or bitchy words, but she knew better than to try it with Bowman. She knew *him*, and what he'd respond to.

Bowman's eyes at least had lost their spark of killing rage. Another spark flared in him, though, and Kenzie knew she was in trouble. Not that she minded. It had been a while. Too long.

Bowman's grip on her wrists tightened, his growl returning, but softer now, with a different note. Kenzie responded with a low growl of her own.

That was all it took. Bowman hauled her against him, arms coming around her to scoop her into him. She saw his eyes, still white gray, before he closed them on his way to parting her lips with a searing kiss. Kenzie bent back under his onslaught, curling her fingers against his chest.

She wanted this. Every time they came together, Kenzie was so hopeful, not only for the intense pleasure he could bestow, but for what might come of their mating frenzy. Another cub, maybe. Or the mate bond.

Bowman wanted these things too. He never said so, but she knew.

Kenzie sank into the kiss, but Bowman broke it all too soon and started pulling her toward the darkness at the edge of the parking lot. He nearly hauled Kenzie off her feet, he moved so fast, but he would never slow his pace for her. She was Lupine, and alpha, and he knew she could keep up with him. He expected it, which was both flattering and frustrating at the same time.

The parking lot ended in the beginning of a dense woods of old pine trees whose boles rose a hundred feet in the air before they sprouted branches. Kenzie found the rough bark of one at her back as Bowman shoved her against it.

His mouth came down on hers, his eyes closing again as his kiss turned savage. Bowman jammed his hands to the tree trunk, pinning her in place with his body. His heat embraced her, and his low growls vibrated through her.

Kenzie's mating frenzy rose to meet his. They were always like this, unable to come together without wanting to tear into each other. She clutched the back of his shirt as Bowman kissed her, his mouth opening hers. He had her trapped—she couldn't get away. Not that she wanted to.

Bowman's fingers became claws that shredded her new cropped top, bought today. He never touched her skin beneath, but Kenzie's shirt and bra became so much scrap. She'd be pissed off about that later, but right now, she didn't care.

Kenzie plucked at Bowman's shirt, tight across his shoulders, until Bowman broke the kiss long enough to yank it off.

She and Bowman came together, skin to skin, the heat of his chest burning her bare flesh. Never mind that it was about thirty degrees outside and their breath steamed in the cold. Kenzie and Bowman were already sweating. They'd burn down the woods if they weren't careful.

Kenzie stroked his shoulders and his short black hair, using her touch and her pliant body to soothe him. No one else could touch Bowman when he got this crazed. Only Kenzie. No other Shifter could calm him like she could, which was why they'd ended up becoming mates. They'd done it for the safety of not only their wolf packs but all of Shiftertown.

Bowman didn't want calm right now. He yanked Kenzie away from the tree, and she found herself on the ground, though she'd never felt the fall.

She landed in his arms, both of them now stretched full length on frozen dirt. Snow from last week had melted, leaving mud that had hardened with this temperature drop. The frozen earth pressed against Kenzie's back while Bowman lay over her, his mouth on her neck.

His teeth scraped her skin, then she felt the pain of a love bite. Kenzie arched into her mate, needy for him. Bowman's mouth was a place of fire, hurting and wonderful at the same time. The hard ridge she felt beneath his jeans excited her, and she wanted him.

He wanted it too. Bowman jerked at the button of her pants, ripping the zipper. He'd never fastened his jeans again, and very soon Kenzie felt his cock, bare and hot, against her abdomen.

Right here, right now, in this woods with music thumping in the roadhouse and humans in the parking lot. Never mind soothing him. Bowman always made it so exciting.

He raised his head, his smoke gray eyes light, his breath a snarl in his throat. "Damn you, Kenz," he whispered.

Kenzie's heart thumped in painful and excited need. There was so much between them, and yet so much wrong, that she was never sure how she felt with him.

Sometimes, when they started this, Bowman would stop, jerk himself from her, and walk away. He'd shift into wolf and depart deep into the woods, returning to their home in Shiftertown after many hours. He'd never abandon them completely; she knew that. Bowman was a leader, and he'd never leave his Shifters to fend for themselves, nor would he leave his family, his son.

As Kenzie held her breath, waiting to see what he'd do—thrust himself into her or get off and walk away—a growl came out of the woods, one so menacing that both Bowman and Kenzie froze.

The night around them went deathly still—no rustle of birds or small animals in the undergrowth. It was cold, yes, but animals often foraged for early shoots and overlooked seeds even this late at night. Kenzie had assumed the animals had shut up and hidden because of the two noisy Shifters come to mate on their doorstep.

Now she realized. There was something out here with them.

The snarl came again, like a beast in slow anger. Warning now, rather than attacking. Promising it would stop warning soon.

Kenzie had never heard anything like it before. Shifters made all kinds of sounds—snarling, growling, howling, even shrieking—in anger, fear, mating need, fighting craze. She'd heard it all—Feline, Lupine, and bear.

This was nothing like that. Nor did it sound like a wild animal, a bear maybe, come down out of the mountains to wander in this woods looking for easier pickings.

Bowman, in near silence, released Kenzie and got to his feet. He didn't reach down to help her rise—Bowman knew she'd get up on her own, unhampered, in silence.

Which she did. They stood together, shoulder to shoulder, peering out into the blackness of the woods, their breaths streaming fog into the night.

Bowman's tension said what Kenzie's did: *What the fuck was that?* But neither of them spoke; neither moved.

The growl came again, with a hint of something salivating for its next meal. Something very large.

Bowman's voice sounded in Kenzie's ear, so low it tickled deep inside her, so close that his breath burned. "Go back to the roadhouse. Get everyone inside and have them lock the doors."

And what are you going to do? Kenzie wanted to ask. Bowman knew she did, because he added firmly, "Go. Now."

Everything Shifter inside Kenzie scrambled to obey when Bowman commanded. She'd been programmed to that from cubhood. She was more dominant than most females out there, and many males too, but a true pack leader like Bowman made her instincts want to stand up and snap off a salute.

On the other hand, the mate in her needed to shout at him, *Are you crazy? You want me to leave you here to face whatever the hell that is alone?*

Bowman had his gaze on her, the hard Shifter stare that made the instincts win over the mate's worry. At least this time.

Kenzie also knew that Bowman wanted her gone so that she could look after the others—Shifters and humans alike—while he figured out what this menace was and how to deal with it.

She glanced at herself. "I can't go in there," she whispered, even in the face of his gray white stare. "You tore up my shirt. They have a policy." She fought the hysterical laugh that came up with the words.

In a swift and economical move, Bowman swept his T-shirt from the ground and thrust it into her hands. The cloth still held his heat, and his scent.

Kenzie took the shirt and backed slowly away from him. She didn't run—whatever was in the woods sounded in the mood for a chase.

She made it to the edge of the parking lot, the men and women there having already gotten into vehicles and gone. Tears stung her eyes as she pulled on the black T-shirt that still held Bowman's heat. Once under the glare of the lot's lights, she could no longer see her mate.

This was wrong. All wrong. She had to go back to him, to fight with him. Kenzie couldn't stand by while he stayed to face the danger alone, perhaps to be killed.

Another human couple came out of the roadhouse, the man and woman wrapped around each other, laughing. There was no doubt what they were leaving the bar to do. The noise from the open door spilled out behind them.

A rumbling growl came from the woods and rolled over the ground, sweeping all other sound away with it.

The couple stopped. "Shit," the guy said. "What the hell was that?"

Kenzie's indecision fled, the alpha female in her taking over. "Get back inside," she snapped in her best commanding voice. *"Now."*

The man and woman looked startled, but obeyed her, their eyes wide with fear.

Kenzie took one last look at the darkness beyond the parking lot, scenting both Bowman and something overwhelming behind him. Heart racing and aching, she herded the humans into the bar and shut the door on them, then turned back to Bowman.

She still couldn't see him, but she heard his snarl. "Kenzie, *inside.*"

It was the command of a leader. She needed to help his trackers be his backup, to keep the civilians protected. Bowman knew she'd handle it all better than anybody.

"Do it."

He was no longer trying to be quiet—no point. Kenzie forced herself to stop being sentimental and think like a warrior. She silently offered up a prayer to the Goddess, yanked open the door, and ran into the roadhouse, calling for Cade.

CHAPTER THREE

Bowman knew exactly when Kenzie closed the door to the roadhouse. Her scent cut off, as did the sound of her voice, and the *presence* of her. Bowman always knew when Kenzie was near.

He'd known when he'd dragged the fake groupie out to the parking lot that Kenzie had followed. He'd pulled the stunt of yanking down his jeans because he'd been aware of Kenzie watching from the shadows. He'd wanted to scare the woman in the stupid Lupine ears and tail, but he'd also wanted to challenge Kenzie. He always did. His mate could bring out the worst in him.

But his challenge had backfired, because Bowman's mating frenzy had shot high. His hard-on had been for Kenzie alone. The only way to relieve the frenzy had been to get rid of the fake groupie woman and run into the woods with Kenzie to scratch that itch.

Thank the Goddess for this unknown foe. Best distraction he could hope for.

Which left the question—what was it?

Bowman slid off his boots and shucked his jeans and

underwear. Naked in his socks, he gazed into the woods, his Shifter sight trying to penetrate the blackness under the trees.

Nothing. No shadows moving, no eyes. Just the soft snarling of an animal not afraid of the lone Shifter waiting at the edge of the woods.

Bowman got rid of the socks and let his wolf come. He could shift quickly, though not painlessly, but his tension was so high tonight he barely noticed the ache as his bones changed form.

The edges of objects curved as his eyes became wolf, colors growing muted but at the same time lighter and more precise. Shifters didn't necessarily see *better* than humans, just differently. They could discern things outside the range of human sight, and scent added another layer.

Whatever was out there stank like a sewer. Bad scent could be used to confuse trackers or disgust them so much they abandoned the prey. Or maybe this thing had simply been spawned in a cesspit.

Bowman had no desire to put his nose down and follow its trail, but he had to know what he was dealing with. Was it seriously dangerous? Or just smelly?

The snarl built up into a roar, and something huge charged Bowman. At least, at the place where Bowman had been. He was gone by the time the thing came barreling out of the trees, then he cut back sharply into the woods to draw it away from the roadhouse.

He needed backup, and lots of it. Kenzie would be organizing that, he knew, letting him get on with the fight. She knew her job. His heart warmed at the thought.

The thing swung around, following Bowman unerringly between the trees. The growls increased, and underbrush snapped and broke as it came.

One of the giant trees behind Bowman started to fall toward him. He couldn't see it clearly in the dark, but he heard the breaking branches and pop of roots, smelled the explosion of sap and resin as a pine tree that had stood strong for hundreds of years now rushed at the ground.

Bowman sprang out of the way, and the woods shuddered as the tree came down, tangling in its brothers on the way. The tree never made it to the forest floor, but came to a rocking halt above Bowman, trapped in a cradle of close-growing branches.

Not Bowman's worry right now. His worry was the enormous thing that had pushed the tree aside to get to him.

The animal's stink canceled out the rest of the forest smells, and its shadow cut off all light. Bowman looked up into darkness that contained a flash of red eyes, the glint of giant teeth, and claws that would frighten a feral bear.

He flung himself out of the way of its plunging fist, his wolf moving fast, but not fast enough. One huge clawed hand caught Bowman's hindquarters as he leapt away.

Pain jolted through him—ripped flesh, snapped bone. Bowman's Collar went off, activating the shock implant that theoretically kept Shifters from violence. Bowman tried to ignore it as he let his momentum carry him away from the creature, but the Collar beat pain into his spine. He stumbled toward the edge of the woods, emerging after an agonizingly long time from under the trees into the roadhouse's parking lot.

He realized that if Kenzie brought backup outside, they'd be shredded. He had to warn them. Bowman's cell phone, though, was in the jeans he'd stripped off and left at the edge of the woods, and the monster chasing him had just stepped on it. He had backup phones, but they were at home, and couldn't help him now.

He still couldn't see what the thing was. Hard to when he was running, limping, and trying to look over his shoulder at the same time, all while his Collar sizzled the fur around his neck. He only knew that whatever came behind him was big, deadly, and mad as hell.

Makes two of us, shithead.

Bowman hurled himself at the back door of the roadhouse. Pain and flight reaction took away his presence of mind to shift to human, so he howled and scratched at the door like a pathetic pup.

The door was wrenched open, and two large hands grabbed him by the scruff and pulled him inside. The scent that came to Bowman's pain-crazed brain was bear, and he had just enough functioning thought to keep himself from attacking.

The big hands belonged to a giant of a man who slammed the door and dragged Bowman into the tiny back hall. Bowman collapsed to smooth, cold, polished cement, panting hard, pain blotting out all thought.

"Son of a bitch," Cade said. "What the hell was that? Bowman? Bowman—damn it, stay with me . . ."

Kenzie pushed her way through the frightened crowd, knowing before she reached the back hall that Bowman was hurt. She scented it, she sensed it—she'd suspected it before he'd even made it inside.

Cade was sitting cross-legged beside a big timber wolf, who lay bleeding on the floor. He'd grabbed a towel from somewhere, not a very clean one, and was pressing it to Bowman's back right leg.

The leg was broken. Bone protruded through red flesh, and Bowman's dark gray fur was matted with blood. His Collar emitted one shock, his reaction to Cade touching his injury, then went silent.

Kenzie said nothing. She knew Bowman didn't like wailing females, didn't want her to fling herself on top of him and bawl. He'd expect her to quit whimpering and do something useful.

She made herself kneel calmly beside Cade, who shot her a worried look. Cade's short hair was mottled black and brown—grizzly colors—his eyes a darker brown. He was a huge man, with hands twice the size of Kenzie's and a hard body she knew women liked to climb. A tatt of interlocking Celtic knot designs flowed down his right arm.

"Hold that on him," Cade said, handing her the towel. "I'll try to find something clean."

"How about an ambulance and someone to set his bones?" Kenzie said, even as she pressed the towel to Bowman's wound.

"Not with whatever that is prowling out there. I saw *something* as I hauled his ass inside." Cade's brown eyes were white around the edges, his face stark. Nothing scared Cade, who was bigger than anyone in Shiftertown—bigger than anyone, period. Humans took one look at him and ran the other way.

"What was it?" Kenzie asked him.

Cade hauled himself to his feet. "Hard to say. Huge. Fast. Stinky. Probably could knock over any ambulance that came out here. *If* we can get one to come out here."

"Feral Shifter?"

"No clue. Bigger than a Shifter."

That's what Kenzie had thought too. She felt cold.

Under her touch, Bowman moved, but weakly. He needed a healer. Needed one now. If he could shift back to human, a hospital might be able to work on him, though Shifters were tough for most doctors to treat.

"Touch of a mate," Cade said. He was looking at Kenzie with a mixture of sympathy, worry, and understanding.

"Doesn't always work," Kenzie said irritably. The subject was a sensitive one for her. "You know that."

"We got a choice right now?"

Bowman rumbled something, and Kenzie leaned down to look him in his eyes. His flat wolf face held such beauty, though she'd never say so to him.

Now his gray eyes were filled with vast pain and, behind that, frustration. He needed to tell her something, but he couldn't shift to speak words.

Kenzie stroked his head. "We're going to try to fix you up," she said. "Me and Cade. Don't worry too much."

Bowman's muzzle wrinkled in annoyance. Stupid thing to say, and Kenzie knew it. She might as well have bleated, *There's an unknown monster stalking around outside, you've broken your leg, we can't get medical help, and all I can do is pet you. But don't worry, everything will be fine.*

Bowman rumbled again, holding her gaze. He was willing her to understand, but she followed his body language much better when they were both the same species.

"Hang on." Kenzie rose to her feet, unsteady in the new turquoise cowboy boots she'd bought to dance in tonight. She'd been so proud of the damn things, and the sexy top that was now so much scrap in the woods, when she'd brought them home from her shopping trip today. "Cade, turn your back."

Cade scowled. "I'm Shifter, woman. I've seen naked Shifters before."

Kenzie planted her hands on her hips. "I want to see your back, grizzly. Now."

"Touchy, touchy." Cade swung around and stared at pipes and dirty walls. His well-muscled back in its tight T-shirt quivered, but Kenzie couldn't tell if he were laughing or letting his concern about Bowman get to him.

Kenzie peeled off the shirt Bowman had lent her, not liking to take his scent from her skin. Next, the pretty new boots came off, then her jeans and underwear.

She envied Bowman's ability to shift so easily—it came harder for her. The wolf in her began to growl and protest as her limbs transformed, her skin itching as it stretched and changed. After a few long and painful moments, Kenzie landed on four big paws, shaking out the light gray fur of her wolf.

Bowman's scent slammed into her. She smelled his pain, his fear, his concern that he wouldn't be able to figure out how to fight this unknown menace. The Collar around Kenzie's neck, which had expanded to fit her wolf, wanted to spark to match his agitation.

She tried to calm herself, to block out the waves of complicated worry that came with his scent and his nearness as she lowered herself next to him. Kenzie moved her face in front of Bowman's and touched his nose with hers. No other wolf in the pack could do that—Bowman might touch *them*, but not the other way around. Not without his permission.

Kenzie was wolf enough now to give him a lick. His fur tasted of blood and dirt, and the tang that was Bowman. She whined a little, but when wolves whined, it didn't necessarily mean submission or fear. Right now, she asked a question.

Bowman answered her in a series of rumbles and flicks of his eyes. What came to Kenzie were impressions and images rather than exact words, but they would roughly translate as, *Big. Deadly. Don't know what it is. Can't fight it. Pain. Damn. Fucking pain. Can't think.*

I'll try to help you, Kenzie conveyed back. *I have to touch you. It might hurt.*

You think? Bowman growled.

Kenzie licked his face again. She let her tongue move behind his ears, her mate's pain coming to her through the tiny link they shared. They had nothing like the magical, all-consuming mate bond other pairs developed, but at least they had *something*, even if it was only the understanding between two alphas.

Fifteen years ago, when Kenzie and Bowman had mated to

keep the Shifters in the North Carolina Shiftertown under
control and the humans from closing the place down, Kenzie
had hoped the two of them would form the mate bond. It didn't
always happen right away—a couple could be together for a
year and more before the true bond came. Sometimes it happened only after the first cub. Kenzie had been hopeful once
Ryan had been born. She knew Bowman had been hopeful
too, but still the mate bond hadn't formed.

Hadn't formed *yet,* Kenzie hastily amended in her head.

The way Shifter rules worked, though, if Bowman met a
female—Shifter, human, or otherwise—with whom he *did*
form the mate bond, Kenzie would be expected to step aside
and let him go. Her clan leader, her uncle Cristian in this case,
would officially dissolve Kenzie and Bowman's mating, and
that would be that. Shiftertown would rejoice that a Shifter
had found his true mate, and Kenzie would be expected to
congratulate him.

Likewise Bowman would have to step aside for Kenzie if
she found the bond with someone else, though historically it
had been rare that a male let his mate go to pursue a mate bond.
The whole situation was rare, Kenzie knew, but that didn't
comfort her much.

Knowing she could lose Bowman anytime to anyone out
there made Kenzie jealous and protective, which couldn't make
Bowman very happy. She drove him crazy, and he didn't hesitate to tell her so.

Not that Kenzie stuck her tail between her legs and cowered
under his admonishments. Kenzie's and Bowman's furious fights
could make their neighbors run into the woods—literally—until
the two of them calmed down again.

Now Kenzie smoothed Bowman's fur with her tongue,
gradually sliding her wolf's body on top of his. Cade crouched
behind Bowman, with a cleaner towel this time, sopping up
blood.

Kenzie was dimly aware of others coming into the back,
both human and Shifter. The man who owned the place, who
liked Shifters and didn't mind them filling up his bar, arrived
first. A few Shifters who were high enough in the hierarchy to
see their leader injured followed, along with a human groupie
or two who'd slipped by the bouncer.

One groupie pushed her way past the Shifters. Like the pseudo-groupie Bowman had banished, this woman had decided to douse herself with perfume. Kenzie's nose wrinkled at the obnoxious smell.

"Can I help?" the groupie asked. "I'm a doctor. A vet, I mean."

Cade rumbled something in answer. Kenzie didn't take her attention from soothing and licking Bowman, and her impression of the woman came only through scent. Under the perfume—they should know better than to wear it around Shifters—Kenzie smelled a hint of antiseptic, antibacterial scrub, and competence. How she could smell competence, she didn't question—her wolf sensed things she never would in human form.

When the woman touched Bowman, he growled, and Kenzie did too. Cade put his hand on Bowman's side. "Easy."

Kenzie added an encouraging rumble to Cade's. She did *not* like the woman putting her hands on her mate—not only in a jealous way, but in a primal fear that animals had for danger—but she convinced herself the vet could help.

"The bone needs to be set, and quickly," the woman said. "If we can get him to my clinic . . ."

"Are you kidding?" Cade asked. "You didn't see what was out there?"

"Yes, what *is* that?" the vet asked him. "Escaped animal from a zoo? Bear from the mountains?"

"Your guess is as good as mine. Escaped from a horror movie, maybe."

Kenzie scented the vet's fear, but the woman tried to bury it to do her job. "I can splint it, at least, but it will need serious medical attention. Can you find me a . . . ?"

She started reeling off things she wanted, giving orders to the humans and Shifters standing around. A woman used to being in charge. So why had she decided to be a groupie tonight? Did she like animals so much she wanted to be around people who turned into them?

Bowman was ignoring the vet, or trying to. He'd closed his eyes, grunting a little as Kenzie managed to lie down fully on top of him. She carefully didn't touch his hindquarters, but she nuzzled his cheek, continuing to lick his face. A she-wolf protecting her mate.

The Shifters and the bar's owner returned with what the vet needed, and the woman ordered Cade to hold Bowman down. "Can you get the other wolf off him?" the vet asked.

Cade laughed, even as Kenzie gave a snarl of fury. "She stays. It's a Shifter thing. Her being here helps him."

"All right." The vet sounded doubtful. "Do you have any kind of tranquilizer? Something to knock him out with?"

The bar's owner cut in. "Nothing but some pretty hefty tequila."

"Anesthetics don't always work on Shifters," Cade said. "We need powerful tranqs to keep us down, and we don't carry them around with us."

Well, not to a bar anyway. Bowman had tranq guns at home, in case he needed them for an unruly Shifter, but he wouldn't take them to where humans could get their hands on them.

"Hold him down, then, please," the vet said crisply.

Kenzie had no idea what the woman was doing, but Bowman jerked, his growls turning to ones of rage. Kenzie let herself grow heavy on him, helping Cade hold him in place.

Let her, she tried to convey.

Bowman struggled. He was one of the strongest Lupines around, even injured, and Kenzie felt her hold slip. Cade was swearing at him, telling him to keep his wolf ass down.

No use. Bowman's instincts had taken over, and he was about to throw off Kenzie and turn on the vet.

Kenzie could think of only one thing to do. She shifted back to human.

Cade bellowed at her, "Kenz, are you crazy?"

Kenzie, a human woman once more, leaned to Bowman's snarling mouth and started petting him, putting her vulnerable face close to his and nuzzling him.

The red-hot rage began to fade from Bowman's eyes. He was still angry, and Kenzie would hear about this later, but, as she'd hoped, Bowman started curtailing his reaction so he wouldn't hurt Kenzie in this form. When Kenzie was wolf, she was stronger and could take a lot from him. Her human form was more vulnerable, and Bowman understood that he could hurt her, or even kill her. He rumbled at her, annoyed at her ploy.

"Almost done," the vet said from behind them. "Tell me you have some Ace bandages and that they're clean."

The bar's owner handed her whatever he had from his first aid kit, and she started working again. At the same time, one of the younger Shifters, a cub really, though he was old enough to come to a human bar, came charging into the back.

"Kenzie," he yelled. He stopped short, his scent betraying fear as he saw Bowman with a mangled leg, Cade holding him down, and Kenzie naked on top of him. Kenzie slid off Bowman, though she kept her hand firmly on his fur.

"It's all right," she said in a steady voice. "Bowman's hurt, but he's being helped. He's fine."

Bowman added his growl, trying to reassure, but the cub had stark fear in his eyes. "That thing out there," he said. He couldn't be more than twenty-one, a wolf Shifter who thought he'd be safe at this bar where his pack leader hung out. "It's trying to get in."

A loud *bang* sounded from the front of the bar, something huge pounding on the big metal door that was the club's entrance.

Bowman rumbled at Kenzie, urgent, angry. She didn't need to be wolf this time to know what he meant. *Get out there and make sure everyone's all right.*

"Go," Cade said to her. "I'll join you as soon as she's done."

Kenzie hesitated, hating to leave Bowman, but she knew she had to. Cade was good in a fight, but the pack needed the leader's mate right now to reassure them. She had to hold it together, in spite of her worry for Bowman, so the Shifters would fight alongside her and not scatter in panic.

She got to her feet, earning a startled look from the vet. The vet looked bizarre herself, wearing fake cat's ears, whiskers penciled in across her cheeks. She was competently wrapping a bandage around Bowman's leg, the two aspects of her incongruous.

Kenzie, stark naked, walked by her and into the bar proper. When the Shifters in there saw her coming, they started to relax.

The humans gaped at her nudity, men looking their fill, women blinking in surprise or giving her *how-dare-she?* looks. The only Shifter who gave her the once-over was Jamie, who was probably the highest-ranking Shifter in the place right now, besides Kenzie and Cade. He was the highest-ranking Feline, anyway.

Jamie was reputed to screw anything female, and he didn't pretend not to look at Kenzie. He'd never touch her, though—he wasn't that foolish—but he looked, and later he'd tease.

Tonight, Jamie's expression also included fear. It took a lot to scare Jamie, who was a lithe cheetah and a mean fighter, but his golden eyes clouded as the beast outside threw itself at the solid front door once again, with hideous force.

Jamie reached Kenzie and spoke in a low voice. "What the fuck *is* that?"

"I don't know." Kenzie tried to match his soft tone, but she was in a room full of Shifters who were listening hard. "I'll just say we can't let it get in here."

"Or we're toast," Jamie said, not bothering anymore to be quiet. "You, and you two—over there. You three on the right of the door." Jamie arranged the strongest Shifters where they'd have the best fighting advantage. He was good at it, though Shifters rarely fought as a team. Shifter battle strategy was more like *Don't mess with me or my family, or I'll kill you and walk away.*

But tonight they'd have to fight together. One Shifter alone, even two, wouldn't be enough to make a dent in something that could so easily take down Bowman.

Kenzie and Jamie got everyone organized, the Shifters moving into fighting positions. Jamie's cousin Marcus, another cheetah, put himself in charge of herding the humans well back, and getting the women under and behind pool tables.

Kenzie's battle plan, when she outlined it, brought swearing and protests, but Kenzie remained firm until the Shifters reluctantly agreed. Jamie backed her up. "She's right. Suck it up."

Another enormous *boom* sounded on the front door. The door was heavy steel, the kind that rolled back, and right now it was barred and locked. A Shifter with great strength could break through it, given time, and Kenzie already knew that whatever was out there had great strength.

She became wolf as Jamie shucked his clothes and shifted into a leggy cheetah about twice the size of a non-Shifter one. He snarled a big cat snarl, ready.

At a growled command from Kenzie, one of the bigger Shifters threw the bolt on the door and shoved it open.

Shouts and swearing sounded from Shifters and humans alike as the stench rolled in. But Kenzie had decided it would be better to rush out and attack the thing head-on than to wait to be trapped inside the roadhouse and picked off one by one. If they pushed the creature into the middle of the empty parking lot, together the Shifters could surround it and take it down.

Now that she saw it, though, Kenzie wasn't so sure. She looked up into a horrible face—like a cross between several Shifters rolled into one. Red eyes fixed on her from above the muzzle of a gigantic wolf. The ears, if the things on top of its head were ears, were more like a cat's, its body big like a bear's. A *ginormous* bear, Ryan, her son, would say. Kenzie let herself take a moment's relief that Ryan was far away, at home in Shiftertown with his great-grandmother.

Unless there were more than one of the things out there.

The monster stank like a feral Shifter. Plus it was as crazed as one and three times the size.

Kenzie drew a breath, took strength from the tension of Jamie beside her and the Shifters around her at the ready, and launched her attack.

CHAPTER FOUR

Bowman heard the roar of the attack even through his agony. The vet, though she wore the stupid costume of a groupie, had efficiently shoved his bones back into position and wrapped his leg, but it fucking *hurt*. Bowman's Collar had gone off, the shock trying to keep him from rolling over and gutting her, but had only succeeded in making the pain worse. Cade's weight on his side didn't help either. Kenzie had been so much sexier.

Bowman knew he shouldn't attempt to shift back until he was more healed—he'd risk snapping the bones in the splint apart. But he wished he could communicate better with Cade, find out what was happening.

He snarled as the draft brought the smell of the beast down the hall, not that he hadn't smelled it the instant the front door opened. Even the vet winced, and Cade growled.

Bowman snarled back at him. Cross-species communication was sorely lacking among Shifters, but Cade had known Bowman long enough to understand him. He gave Bowman a nod and left him for the main part of the bar.

Bowman started to push himself up, but the vet said sternly, "No, you need to stay down."

Bowman sent her a growl. He knew Kenzie was out there, in front of the others, leading them. He didn't need a mate bond to tell him that. Kenzie knew what to do. Cade was now with her, and Jamie and Marcus. They had it covered.

Except—every instinct in Bowman told him they didn't. This monster was something new, something they'd never faced before. The screech and boom of the front door giving way, and the howls and cries of hurt Shifters reinforced that conviction.

Bowman dragged himself up. The splint held. Though it hurt like hell, Bowman's natural ability to heal was kicking in. Kenzie lying on him had helped a lot. The touch of a mate, though no one could explain the process, seemed to work.

Bowman easily pushed past the vet, in spite of her protests, and staggered down the hall to the main part of the bar. What he saw made every human thought in him flee and his wolf take over.

His mate and friends were battling the thing that had broken the doorframe it had shoved itself through. Cade had turned bear, the grizzly on his back legs, ears flat, roaring his power. The beast coming at them was three times Cade's size.

Jamie, with the lightning speed of the cheetah, was darting around the creature, trying to get under it for attack in vulnerable places. The beast caught Jamie with a swipe of a giant hand and threw him across the room. Jamie let out a cat screech, more pissed off than terrified. He hit the wall with a crunch, slid down it, and went still.

Bowman dragged himself over to Jamie, who was out cold. Damn it. Kenzie had the right idea, but not enough Shifters to make it work.

He had to do something, or this would turn into a bloodbath, all Shifters down. He snarled at the nearest Shifter, the cub who'd begged Kenzie to come help. The cub was a Lupine, one of Bowman's clan. Bowman made him understand that he should look after Jamie, then Bowman left them and hobbled down the back hall again.

He growled at the bar's owner, who was cowering with the vet against the far wall, until the man got the idea and unlocked and opened the back door.

The rear parking lot was still mostly empty, only a few cars and trucks left. None of the vehicles were what Bowman needed, so he crept around to the front of the roadhouse, keeping to the shadows.

A row of cars in the front lot had been flattened by the attacking creature. The trucks had fared a little better, but most were dented and shoved askew.

The truck Bowman sought rested at the edge of the lot, untouched. The pickup was a giant of a thing with a huge cab, raised body, and oversized tires made for off-roading.

Cade's truck. His baby. Cade had bought it used from a guy who ran monster trucks, and spent his days happily tinkering it into a honed machine.

The beast paid no attention to Bowman as he crept across the lot, making for the truck, which told Bowman the creature wasn't very smart. Even an ordinary animal made sure it knew what threat was behind it.

Bowman reached the pickup and stopped a moment to rest in its shadow. For the next step, he'd have to shift back to human, which he knew was going to hurt.

Shifters usually healed fast. Cuts closed rapidly and bruises vanished as the Shifter's metabolism strove to make them whole again. They'd been bred to be fighters ages ago—battle beasts, they'd been called—meant to fight wars for others without suffering too many casualties.

Nice idea. Hadn't worked. Shifters had died being forced to fight other Shifters, until the Shifters had decided to combine forces and turn on their masters.

Shifter physique had remained unchanged through the passing centuries, though, even if these days Shifters preferred to watch TV, drink beer, and get laid instead of fighting battles to the death for the Fae. Bowman knew his leg had already begun its healing process, bones and muscles knitting. Even so, this shift was going to be a bitch.

Bowman suppressed a howl, then a groan as he moved from wolf form to human. His body protested, sinews not wanting to change and stretch. Pain lanced his broken leg but Bowman ended up human once more, panting against the side of the pickup, holding on to it and fighting not to pass out.

Cade had locked his truck, but it was an older model, with no fancy electronic locks to foil would-be thieves. He'd locked it against humans, anyway; Shifters could easily break in, but they never would. Shifters didn't touch one another's things. They respected territory—violating it was deadly dangerous and bone-headed stupid.

Bowman took a few more breaths, waiting until he could pull himself all the way up, then drew back his fist and punched out the window. He clenched his teeth against that pain, shaking blood from his hand. Then he brushed aside broken glass and flipped the latch to unlock the door.

Another breath as he yanked the door open and used it to lever his body into the cab. He landed on the seat, then clutched the steering wheel and rested his forehead on it, searing pain making him want to pass out again.

Bowman's speculations had been right—when the splint had fallen away as he shifted, his leg had twisted in the setting, and it was broken again. But he'd have to live with it for now.

Cade had the truck's keys, but that fact didn't slow Bowman down. He had the steering column broken and the wires tapped together in a matter of seconds. The truck roared to life.

The beast spun around at the sudden sound, at last taking its attention from the roadhouse. Bowman turned on all the truck's lights—headlights, fog lights, spotlights—every gimmicky piece Cade had bolted to the thing—put the truck in gear, and rammed his good foot to the gas pedal.

The truck's tires spun on the dirt, then caught, and the truck leapt forward. The monster hesitated, red eyes staring, then it snarled and charged at Bowman. The Shifters who were still whole poured out of the bar after it.

The beast rushed the truck, and Bowman drove straight for it, never wavering.

He hit the creature at fifty miles an hour. The truck's windshield shattered as the monster slammed across the hood and onto the cab, crushing the roof under its weight. Bowman dove down onto the seat, his foot coming off the gas, but the truck kept moving of its own momentum, the weight on the cab sending it into a tailspin.

The truck whirled until the bed met the side of the roadhouse. The beast was flung off, but the huge thing gained its feet, and a nightmare horror stared into the broken cab at Bowman.

Someone had engineered a monster, but it was not put together from parts. This thing was whole—born, not made—with the giant claws of a bear, the maw of a wolf, and the face of a lion. And it was very, very big.

The impact with the truck had cost the beast, though. Blood ran down its side, and one of its arms dangled uselessly. It pulled at the driver's-side door of the broken cab with its good hand and managed to rip the door off. Then the wave of Shifters—wolves, big cats, and one huge, angry grizzly—were upon it.

The creature threw the pickup's door at the crowd, then turned around and ran for the woods. Ran *fast*. The Shifters sprinted after it, but they stopped just inside the edge of the trees, sitting on haunches or standing with hackles raised, in both fear and frustration.

The beast had vanished. The stench of it faded on a cool breeze, and the sounds of a normal night started up again. A car drove by on the highway beyond, as though nothing were out of the ordinary.

Cade, now in human form, yanked open the still-intact passenger door. He was naked, smelling of sweat, fighting adrenaline, and fear. "Holy shit, Bowman."

Kenzie came to the driver's side, reaching in through the opening that used to be the door. She was naked too, the parking lot's lights sending golden light over her full breasts and their dusky tips. She had a strong body, skin taut over muscle, and curves Bowman lost himself in whenever he touched her. Curves that hugged him now, swallowing him in softness.

A hell of a lot more appealing than Cade, he thought wryly. Kenzie stroked Bowman's hair, her long-fingered hand moving over his pounding skull, soothing, cutting through pain.

Behind him, Cade slammed both fists on the top of the dented cab. "Son of a *bitch*. Do you know how much work it will take to fix this? If I even can fix it. Hell, if the frame is bent . . ."

"Cade," Bowman said, his voice rasping. He leaned into Kenzie's touch, the scent of her warm over the tang of the dying truck.

"What?" Cade snarled, leaning in to listen.

"Shut the fuck up," Bowman said.

He dropped his head back and slipped into blissful, empty darkness. The last sensation he felt was Kenzie's hand on his hair, and the softness of her body as she bent down to kiss him.

"Anyone want to take any guesses what that thing was?" Bowman lay back against his pillows in his bed, one hand behind his head. He looked awful, his face blotchy, healing cuts all over his exposed skin, but his voice was plenty strong. His leg was in another splint, one for humans this time, sticking out over the covers.

Kenzie knew Bowman felt better. He'd snarled at her when she'd tried to make him eat the chicken soup she'd made, so she'd snarled back at him, plopped herself down on a chair, and ate it herself.

Cade and Jamie had come to report. Marcus, the other tracker, hadn't, and Kenzie knew he'd spent the night with her cousin Bianca, whom he was dating—dating in Shifter fashion, that is. After a crazy night like last night, Kenzie didn't blame the two of them for holing up together and not coming out for a while.

Cade had a bandage wrapped around his muscular arm, and Jamie had one around his middle—cracked ribs. The two were nearly as robust as usual, though, Bowman being the one the most hurt. Kenzie had escaped severe injury by being quick, a fact she absolutely would *not* rub in with the trackers in this room.

No one could answer Bowman's question, so he went on. "Any trace of it?"

"Nope," Cade said. "We've been looking. Disappeared like it never existed. Like we imagined it."

"Nothing that stinks that bad is an illusion," Bowman said. In spite of his injuries, he was still the strongest person in the house, which Kenzie knew with every part of her. Only the presence of Cade and Jamie kept her from sliding out of her clothes and snuggling in beside him. She needed contact with him as a Shifter for her pack leader, as a mate for her mate, as a woman for a man.

And what a man. Bowman's upper torso, exposed above the sheet, was tight, sun-touched skin over smooth cords of muscle. The hard planes of his pectorals were dusted with black hair that curled around her fingertips whenever she touched him in bed. His dark nipples beckoned her tongue—she loved the pebble-smooth feel of them.

More wiry hair covered his solid forearms, fading to smooth skin on the inside of his wrists, where he liked to be licked. One firm, blunt-fingered fighter's hand rested on the covers, while the other braced Bowman's head, making his short dark hair stick straight up on one side. He'd leave the house like that if Kenzie didn't grab him and smooth down the unruly hair. Bowman rarely looked into a mirror.

Kenzie almost bit down on her spoon. Bowman was hurt, and here she was, getting horny simply looking at him, lying there so lazily, his gray eyes holding fire.

She hastily ate more soup. Cade and Jamie would pick up on her mating frenzy if she weren't careful, and tease the life out of her.

"We take it as real," Bowman said. "I want every tracker in Shiftertown in that woods and in the bar, getting its scent—"

"Won't be hard," Jamie broke in. "The thing stunk like the shit of something that's been dead twenty years."

"Not what you *smelled*, catbrain," Bowman said. "Its actual scent, not the one it threw out to distract you."

Jamie growled, ready to snap a comeback, but something in Bowman's face made him swallow it.

"We're on it," Cade said seriously. "We know what you mean."

"Kenzie, go with them."

Bowman was looking straight at her, holding her gaze as he did when he wanted no argument.

Kenzie wanted to protest. *No, I need to stay with you, make sure you're all right . . .*

Bowman must have sensed what was in her head, because he said, "I need someone there to keep an eye on everyone. I'm down, Kenz. I need you."

He did. If a Shifter wasn't strong enough to fight, his mate needed to fight for him. Otherwise, those next in power would sense an opening and try to fill it. In the old days, such a thing happened often, and whoever pushed out or killed the leader would steal his mate and offspring. Hardly ever occurred these days, but this Shiftertown was still divisive, and there were those who liked to challenge Bowman's power. Kenzie knew exactly who Bowman was worried about, and exactly why she needed to keep up a strong front.

She gave him a nod, as though leaving him while he was hurt was no big deal. "You mean keep these buttholes in line?" she asked, meeting Bowman's gaze. "I can do that."

Jamie pretended to look offended, but Cade grinned. He knew what was going on.

Speaking of offspring, Bowman's and Kenzie's decided at that moment to walk in.

CHAPTER FIVE

Bowman's protective instincts went off whenever his cub was near, no matter how much he trusted the other Shifters in the room. It made him cranky, which Kenzie would be quick to point out.

Bowman scented twelve-year-old Ryan's fear, his worry. His extraordinary love for the boy rose up and made him soften his question to only a faint snarl.

"Why the hell aren't you still with your great-grandma?"

"I couldn't stay," Ryan said. His hair was dark, like Kenzie's—in fact, he looked a lot like Kenzie in the shape of his face, and in his eyes, which were golden like hers. He'd also inherited Kenzie's back-talking sass. "Had to come make sure you hadn't been knocked off, because then I'd have to take over Shiftertown. But it looks like you ran fast enough this time, Dad."

Kenzie should have said, *Ryan, don't be a smartass,* but she only gave her son a look of sparkling good humor. "I made sure the monster didn't catch him."

"Yeah, your mom kicked some good ass," Jamie said. "Your dad was down in the first five minutes."

"The other guy looked worse," Cade said. "But not because

of your dad. Kenzie was fighting like crazy. You should have seen her. She didn't even get hurt."

"Didn't get hurt *much*," Kenzie said. She'd been bruised and winded, but she'd recovered quickly. "But, sure, I did pretty good." She huffed on her curled fingertips and rubbed them against her shirt. "Think I should go a few rounds at the fight club?"

"Girls can't fight in the fight club," Ryan said, but he sounded uncertain. "It's the rules."

Cade broke in. "Because they'd all win, and make us big, lumbering males look bad."

Ryan's smile came through. "Actually, I'd like to see that. I bet my mom could beat the both of you."

They all laughed, including Jamie, who prided himself on being the top fighter in Shiftertown.

Bowman shot his son a smile, though his pain was still intense. Ryan's fear had climbed down, and Bowman silently thanked Kenzie and the others for that.

Ryan still needed reassurance, though. He needed touch, a hug, the close confines of family. Ryan was trying to hold it together in the presence of Cade and Jamie. One day, Ryan would become a tracker—those Shifters who guarded the leader and helped him keep an eye on everything in and around Shiftertown.

"So, why are you all still sitting here?" Bowman asked them. "Get out there and start hunting."

"Got it." Cade levered himself to his feet. He was a head taller than Jamie, who was long and lanky, but Cade was just *big*. Bears grew that way. "The sooner we find and get rid of it, the sooner I can start fixing my truck." He threw Bowman a pointed look.

"I want to help track it too," Ryan said. "I'm old enough—"
He was cut off by both his parents' sharp, *"No!"*

They hadn't kept the fact that they'd been attacked by some unknown, huge creature secret, because neither Bowman nor Kenzie believed in protecting their cub through lies. The problem with that approach, though, was that Ryan thought he should be able to join his parents in tracking, fighting, and dealing with anything, no matter how dangerous it might be.

Ryan raised his hands, looking pained. "All right, all right. Don't have a cow, Mom."

"Moo," Kenzie said, frowning at him.

She unfolded herself from her chair, setting down the empty soup bowl, and caught Ryan in a rough hug, ruffling his hair. Nothing that would make him look weak in the eyes of Cade and Jamie, but enough that her closeness would ease his fears.

Bowman always felt a touch of envy for other Shifters, whose cubs climbed all over them—Ryan was always conscious of his position as the alpha's first cub and liked his dignity. He'd run the pack one day, and everyone knew it.

The way pack leaders in the wild had been replaced by their offspring had been a father-son fight to the death. But a few years ago in the Austin Shiftertown, the leader, Dylan Morrissey, had defied convention by stepping down and retiring, letting his son, Liam, take over. No deaths necessary.

The handoff hadn't been as simple as that, from what Bowman had heard, but they'd all pretended it had. The Morrisseys had set a new precedent—sons didn't need to kill their fathers.

Even so, there would come a time when Ryan and Bowman went at it, and both Ryan and Bowman knew it.

Not now, though. Ryan was still a cub—the little wolf he became was adorable—and it might be another hundred or so years before there was need for confrontation. And hell, whatever that thing in the woods was might kill them all in the next week.

"Out," Bowman said. "Ryan, stay here. Someone needs to protect me while I'm healing."

Ryan stood up from Kenzie's embrace, surreptitiously wiping his eyes. "Yeah, that's true. Don't worry, Dad. I got your back."

Kenzie ruffled Ryan's hair again as Cade and Jamie left the room—Cade with the slow, long strides of a bear, Jamie with the lightning-quick moves of the fastest wildcat on earth.

Kenzie gave Bowman a long look, golden sparks smoldering deep in her eyes. Kenzie needed him, and he needed her, their mating frenzy always close to the surface. Healing would speed with Kenzie in his bed, and both of them knew it.

"Go," Bowman said, his voice softer. "I need you out there, Kenz."

"I know."

Her look spoke of promise for later. Any other day, Bowman would reach out, latch his hand around her wrist, and tug her down to him. But he was lying here, injured and out of it, and Kenzie had to go. He meant it when he said he needed her to watch the others.

Kenzie smiled at him briefly, gave a more brilliant smile to Ryan, and left the room.

Bowman knew when she walked out the front door, because their little house seemed suddenly emptier.

Ryan stood a bit forlornly in the middle of the room. He still didn't want to admit to fear, but Bowman again sensed his need for reassurance. It was tough being a cub, and tough being the only cub of the leader. Bowman remembered that well from his own childhood.

"Come on up here," Bowman said, patting the bed beside him. "I'm going to fall asleep, and I need you to be on guard."

Ryan didn't hesitate to kick off his shoes and climb upon the bed. He immediately snuggled down into his father, and Bowman let his arms come around him.

Bowman needed the reassurance too, he realized as he started to relax. Just having his son next to him made him feel better.

Knowing he was responsible for the small lad who warmed his side scared the shit out of Bowman, but father and son drifted off to sleep for now, each of them comforted by the other.

Kenzie wanted to be anywhere but back in the woods near the roadhouse, but she sniffed around in her wolf form without fuss, pretending not to be worried.

The world out here was transformed by daylight. What had been blackness and strange shapes last night were now soft and kissed with sunshine. The woods weren't as dense here as they were nearer to Shiftertown—sunlight reached the forest floor, illuminating undergrowth, mud, and the trampled footprints of what looked like every Shifter in Shiftertown.

They'd been tracking all morning, and now the woods was crisscrossed with wolf, wildcat, and bear tracks. Somewhere in the mess must lie the tracks of the monster that had attacked, but so far, no sign of them had been found.

After a thorough search Kenzie returned to human form again and stood, clothed, her hands on her hips, surveying the scene. When she'd arrived this morning she'd thought tracking as Shifter would speed the search along, but they'd gone over this place with noses to the ground for hours, and found nothing.

"You'd think something that stunk like that would be easier to locate," Jamie said beside her. He was on his two human feet, but naked, having just shifted.

Interesting that while Jamie had a tall body replete with muscle, tatts on his lower back and arms, and eyes of green flecked with gold, he never stirred a heartbeat in Kenzie. Not because he was Feline—she'd grown used to living with different species in the last twenty years, and had even gone out with a Feline for a while. No, she'd never looked twice at Jamie, because her mind and her heart were filled with Bowman.

"I'm realizing we're not going to find it by thinking like Shifters," Kenzie said. "We have to think like humans for this one."

Jamie's frown deepened. "What does that mean?"

"The thing wasn't . . . right, was it?" Kenzie asked. "Not really an animal."

"No? If you're implying it was some kind of machine, you're wrong."

"Not a machine, no. Different smell."

"Then what the hell are you talking about?"

Kenzie waited, sensing Jamie's impatience. She was Bowman's voice while he was down, but she was aware that the Shifters acted differently with her. Bowman was injured. Kenzie wasn't Bowman. Her awareness of their awareness made her skin prickle.

"I'm talking about not running around like crazy, leaving scents all over the woods," Kenzie said. "We need to *think*."

"Fine, then," Jamie growled. "Think about what?"

"How it could have disappeared." Kenzie turned in place, her gaze taking in the space between the trees and the mud and undergrowth around them. "How *do* things disappear?"

"Mostly Cade eats them," Jamie said, his irritation dissolving into a big cat chuckle. He had lightning-swift changes of mood, a bit like Bowman. "People disappear because they run, they hide, they get lost, or someone takes them away."

"Exactly." Kenzie remained still, letting her gaze rove the woods, looking with her human brain instead of her wolf's. "Someone takes them away. There," she finished, pointing.

There was a cluster of trees next to a deer feeder, a wooden trough that provided nibbles for deer in deep winter. Kenzie started for it, her feet squelching through mud. Jamie heaved a sigh and came after her. He wouldn't disobey, not blatantly, but he didn't have to like her decisions.

Cade saw them and came loping over in his bear form. His eyes narrowed as he clearly wondered what they were up to, but he fell into step with Kenzie.

No scent came to her at the feeder except that of deer who'd ventured there a few days ago and the metallic odor of car exhaust. Kenzie moved past the feeder and around the clump of trees. On the other side of the trees, a hill led down to a ditch with an inch or so of water in it, trickling from the thaw this morning. January could be cold and then suddenly give them mild days in the high fifties and up. Today would be one of the balmy ones.

Across the ditch were thinner trees—deciduous, rather than the old-growth pines around her. Beyond that, a road.

The road was paved, one of the tiny forest roads that crossed back here. Tracks of a truck with deep-tread tires had sunk through the mud on the side of it. A big truck, by the looks of it.

Jamie followed her, jumping the ditch with his long-legged stride. Cade remained a bear. No human was around to worry that a woman, a naked man, and a grizzly walked out of the woods together, so they didn't bother to hide. *Like the start of a bad joke,* Kenzie thought with grim humor.

"So that's the answer?" Jamie said skeptically. "The monster caught a ride?"

Kenzie wrinkled her nose. The smell of truck dominated, but over it, she caught a tang of the creature. Cade must have caught it too, because he rose on his hind legs and growled.

"Yes," Kenzie said. "Truck was waiting here, monster got into truck, truck drove off."

"Must have been a fucking big truck," Jamie said.

"Eighteen-wheeler," Kenzie observed. She looked down the curve of the narrow road. "Had to be tough to drive it back here, but whoever it was did it."

Cade sat down on his haunches, growling up a storm. Kenzie didn't know exactly what he was saying, but she got the gist. He was right—this was creepy.

"You're saying someone put that weird Shifter thing together?" Jamie asked Kenzie.

"Or found it and tamed it."

"*Tamed* it? Did you see what it did to Bowman? And to Cade's truck?"

Cade's growl grew louder, the look in his eyes murderous. No doubt about what he was saying now.

"Tamed it," Kenzie answered. "How else would they have gotten it to a designated area and into the back of a truck?"

"Shit," Jamie said softly.

The three of them stood looking down the road. Eventually that road would lead to a highway, which in turn would lead to highways and freeways connecting every city in the state, and then every state in the country. A big truck with plenty of fuel could be many miles away by now.

"Yep," Kenzie answered.

They gazed at the empty road and peaceful woods on either side before they turned around without speaking and made for the roadhouse again. Time to report to Bowman.

Kenzie rounded up the other Shifters who were hunting through the woods, and they all walked or bounded back to the roadhouse, where the Shifters had left their vehicles.

When they reached the parking lot, however, they found police cars surrounding it. The cars blocked the way to the Shifters' bikes and trucks, and uniformed police were everywhere.

CHAPTER SIX

Cade ducked back into the woods. Jamie said, "*Shit*," and slid out of sight as well. He'd left his clothes on Kenzie's motorcycle, which was in the lot, and human cops loved to arrest Shifters for public nudity.

Kenzie walked forward. Her cousin Bianca and Bianca's boyfriend, Marcus, who were already dressed, came with her.

One of the cops broke off from the others and strolled to them, not in a hurry. He wore a black uniform, still clean despite the mud and melting ice, had black hair buzzed short, and wore sunglasses against the glare of the winter sunshine. His badge glinted as bright as the sunlight, as did the rims of the glasses when he removed them to reveal eyes of deep brown. His name tag read "Ramirez." He looked Native American, or as though at least one parent had been.

He approached Marcus first—humans tended to think the males were in charge of whatever Shifter thing was going on, and in the humans' defense, usually they weren't wrong. Kenzie stepped in front of Marcus, who conceded to her without getting pissed off about it. He flanked Kenzie on the right, with Bianca on her left, the three of them facing the cop.

Kenzie met the man's gaze without flinching, and he

immediately understood that Kenzie was in charge. He flicked a glance over the other two before returning to look into Kenzie's eyes.

"What are you doing out here?" he asked in a mild voice. "How many more of you are around?" He indicated the number of motorcycles and small pickups in the lot.

"A few," Kenzie said. "We came for a run. The woods are quiet this time of day."

"Uh-huh." Ramirez's skepticism was obvious. He had a roundish face, his high forehead emphasized by his short haircut. His eyes held all kinds of depths, and the strength in them rivaled that in any Shifter's. He was well-built, obviously working out for his job, and wore a holstered black pistol, though Kenzie didn't know what kind. Like most Shifters, she knew damn all about guns.

"Yeah." Kenzie folded her arms and looked right back at him, but softened her word with a little smile.

"Wouldn't have anything to do with the disturbance here last night, would it?" Ramirez asked. "The big fight? The damage to the bar? The crazed monster the dead-drunk patrons reported to police this morning? One of the people here told me to talk to Kenzie O'Donnell, who'd know all about it. That's you, isn't it?"

Kenzie gave him a nod. "That's me."

"Then come inside," Ramirez said. "Let's talk."

He didn't mean in the still-closed bar. He meant in his patrol car, marked as from the nearby town of Marshall.

Jamie and Cade emerged from the woods, both in their animal forms, as Ramirez opened the door to usher Kenzie into the front seat of his car. He closed the door and went around to the driver's side to get in. He moved the small computer screen attached to his dashboard so Kenzie couldn't see it, then settled in and looked at her.

At the edge of the woods, Cade and Jamie stood tense. Kenzie gave them the slightest shake of her head, indicating they were to watch, but to do nothing unless she signaled.

"You don't have to be afraid of me," Ramirez said, glancing at the bear and wolf, then back at Kenzie. "I really just want to talk." His voice carried a rumble of strength and a hint of darkness. His lashes were jet black, matching his hair.

Kenzie had been thinking she should assure Ramirez *he* didn't have to be afraid of *her*. She wouldn't be stupid enough to attack and kill a human police officer in his own patrol car, but she could do it if she had to. She could grab him mid-change and claw out his throat before he had the chance to unholster his weapon.

Ramirez rested his hands on the wheel. "Tell me what happened here last night."

His scent gave off confidence and the fact that he liked coffee. It wasn't a bad scent, though Kenzie didn't always like how humans smelled.

She shrugged. "What's to tell?"

Ramirez gave her a patient look. "I know what I've heard, and I've heard plenty. But the people who reported the fight were drunk or high, or both. I want the story from someone who wasn't hysterical."

Kenzie had to smile. No one had ever accused *her* of being hysterical. "If you want the truth, I don't know what all happened. This thing came out of the woods and attacked the bar. I led a counterattack, but we couldn't make much of a dent in it. It only ran off when my mate drove into it with a truck."

Ramirez listened, dark eyes on her. He didn't make any notes or tap things on the computer. He simply sat, his hands on the wheel, and watched her.

"Your mate," he repeated. "That's like your husband, right?" He wasn't being sarcastic or derogatory; he simply wanted to know.

"Something like that. He was hurt, but the rest of us got away with only superficial injuries. We were lucky."

"Your mate is all right? Did he go to a hospital?"

"To an urgent care place. He broke his leg; they splinted it. Now he's home. Shifters heal fast, and hospitals don't always make a difference. He's resting."

"What's his name?"

Kenzie didn't like all the questions, but she had no reason to lie. He could look up Kenzie O'Donnell and find out her mate's name.

"Bowman," she said. "He's Shiftertown leader."

"I've heard of him." Again, he was acknowledging information, not disparaging her. "You sure he's all right?"

"So far." Kenzie's heart skipped a beat. She'd never seen Bowman badly hurt before, with a pallor on his hard face, shadows under his eyes. He'd kept up his snarling for the benefit of Cade and Jamie, but Kenzie had known he'd been in profound pain.

"What kind of animal was it that attacked you?" Ramirez asked. "What did you see?"

Kenzie shivered. She'd been doing her best not to think about it. Tracking the monster was one thing—she could do that clinically. Remembering every detail was something else.

"It was horrible," she said in a soft voice. "Like a mishmash of a bunch of things."

Ramirez came alert without moving. Shifters could do that, suddenly grow watchful and ready to spring without betraying it. Ramirez didn't have a drop of Shifter blood in him, though. Kenzie would have scented it if he had.

"Go on," he said.

"The truth is, I have no freaking clue what it was. Big. Ugly. Like an animal, but not real. I've never seen anything like it before."

"So, not a Shifter."

Kenzie shook her head. "No Shifter I've ever seen. And trust me, I've seen a lot of Shifters. More than I ever wanted to."

Ramirez's dark brows lifted. "But *you're* Shifter."

"Doesn't mean I love every Shifter in the universe. Some of them can be unbelievable pains in the ass. I'm Lupine, which means Felines seriously drive me crazy. When I lived in Romania, in the wild, I stuck to my family and clan and didn't see a lot of different species. Never met any Felines or bears until I was moved to the States and into this Shiftertown." Kenzie closed her mouth, wondering why she was saying all this to a human. Though she wasn't telling him anything he couldn't look up on the Internet.

"Mmm hmm." Ramirez made the universal noise of someone showing they were listening. "This animal wasn't any of those?"

"No. Like I said, I don't know what it was."

"Where is it now?"

Kenzie held her hands palms up. "No clue. We came back

here today to track it—you have to have guessed that was what we were doing. We found nothing. It disappeared."

"Disappeared?" he asked sharply. "How?"

Kenzie saw no reason not to tell him her theory about a truck and the evidence they'd found of one resting on the side of the road. Ramirez gazed out over the woods as she spoke, his patrollers uneasily wandering the grounds, the Shifters watching them in return. Jamie and Cade had their eyes on the car— Kenzie knew they could be with her in two seconds flat if she needed them.

"Thank you, Ms. O'Donnell," Ramirez said when she finished. "I don't like stories of giant monsters attacking people. Even if the stories are exaggerated, there's still a threat. Shifters are in a good position to help me stop it. You can do things I can't. So I'd appreciate it if you shared anything else you find out. I want to get this thing as much as you do."

Kenzie listened to him, startled. "Work together, you mean?"

Humans rarely wanted to. Though it was obvious to Kenzie that Shifters would be great in military situations or law enforcement, people had been too afraid of them to put them in positions where they could wield weapons or fight humans.

Ramirez gave her a nod. "Surprised?"

"Yes. I have to wonder why you want to."

"Because I took this job because I like to keep people safe. If Shifters can help me do that, I'm not going to pass up the opportunity to recruit them."

Kenzie believed him. She'd spent a lifetime reading body language, and his told her he put protecting people first, and rules second. "Won't you get into trouble?" she asked.

He slanted her a grin. "I wasn't planning on asking permission, or even mentioning it to anyone." He became serious again. "I'm not interested in office politics. I want to catch this thing and figure out what it is before it does any more damage."

Kenzie turned over the possibilities in her mind. Having insight into what the police were doing and what they'd heard about the incident might help Kenzie and Bowman determine where the monster had been taken, and who had taken it there. Bowman would be less than thrilled to learn he had to trust a human, but Bowman had often told Kenzie he liked that she was resourceful. Well, Ramirez was a resource.

She let out a breath. "All right."

"Thanks," Ramirez said. "I appreciate that. I'd appreciate it too if I could speak to your mate."

"He's kind of cranky right now," Kenzie said. "He's like that when he's healing."

Ramirez laughed suddenly. It was a deep, warm laugh, one that would make others laugh with him. Kenzie wanted to smile in response.

"I'm like that too," Ramirez said. "Ask him if, when he feels better, I can come talk to him."

"You want to come to Shiftertown?" Kenzie asked quickly.

"Better I go to him than he come see me at the station. People would get the wrong idea."

"If Shifters see you roll up to our house in uniform in a patrol car, they'll get the wrong idea as well. Shifters get nervous around police."

Ramirez shrugged. "Then I'll come by after work and not in uniform." He gave her an open look. "I'm asking for help. That's all. I think Shifters can help me do my job better, and I'm happy to work around regs to do it. So what do you say?"

He sounded sincere, but Kenzie had spent the last twenty years being suspicious of everyone. Ramirez might be the exception to the rule, or he might be trying to play Kenzie and the other Shifters for his own reasons. Only one way to find out, really.

She flashed him a sudden smile. "Sure. Come tonight and meet Bowman." That would be fun to watch.

"Thanks, I will. After I'm off duty."

"It's a date. Am I free to go now?"

Ramirez laughed again, that rich, warm sound. "You always were. See you, Ms. O'Donnell."

"Kenzie." She gave him another smile, opened the door, and climbed out of the car. Across the way, Jamie and Cade came alert, but again she waved them off. "See you, Mr. Ramirez."

"Gil," Ramirez said. "When I'm off duty."

"See you, Gil," Kenzie said, and shut the door.

She hated to admit it, even to herself, as she turned away. She liked him.

Bowman woke from a sleep a few hours after Kenzie had gone and found Ryan, who was no longer snuggled against him, standing at the foot of his bed. "Woman's here to see you," Ryan said, his eyes narrow. "Human. Says she's a vet."

"Just came to check on you." The breezy voice of the woman who'd set his leg last night came to him from the hall. "I like to follow up on my work."

CHAPTER SEVEN

The vet swept into the room. Bowman hadn't had a clear look at her the night before—he'd been in severe pain, the back hall had been dim, and she'd been wearing groupie makeup.

Bowman remembered her scent, though. Beneath the perfume, which she'd left off today, she'd smelled clean, like soap. Today she smelled like antiseptic and whatever scared dog or cat she'd been working on.

Cat, Bowman decided, wrinkling his nose. All felines had a distinctive odor, whether Shifters or house cats.

The woman was about thirty, with a pointed face and blond hair pulled into a no-nonsense ponytail. Now that she had no penciled-in cat whiskers and cat's eyes and had taken the black paint off her nose, he could see her cheekbone structure, light-colored lashes, and light green eyes. She wore no makeup at all, in fact, her lips a pale brownish red. She wasn't as tall as Kenzie but she had curves beneath her button-up shirt and slacks. Obviously she'd just come from work.

"So?" she asked. "How's the leg? Got it re-splinted, I see."

Bowman lay still, not bothering to pull the blankets over his naked chest. His lower half was covered, except for the leg stuck out over the sheets.

"I didn't catch your name," he said.

She smiled, revealing dimples. "It's Patricia. Patricia Brookman."

"Dr. Brookman," Bowman said, giving her a nod.

Her smile widened. "Too formal. Everyone calls me Dr. Pat. You don't have to call me anything if you don't want to." Her scent and her babbling conveyed her nervousness. "I don't know what to call *you*. You're the leader of all the Shifters around here. I don't know if I'm supposed to bow or what."

"If you bow, my son will shit himself laughing," Bowman said in all seriousness. "Just call me Bowman."

"Fair enough. You haven't answered me about the leg, you know. How is it?"

She advanced into the room, her gaze on the splint, as though longing to take it off and examine what was beneath.

"A lot better," Bowman said, not moving, though he had the sudden urge to wriggle his toes. They were starting to itch. "I'll be healed in a day or so."

Pat's eyes widened. "No, you'll be healed in about six to eight weeks. Those bones were seriously shattered."

"Shifters heal fast," Bowman said—he kept saying the words, reassuring everyone to also reassure himself. "You sticking them back together last night helped a lot. I thank you."

"Did it help? You were up on it, and you re-broke it running around the parking lot."

Bowman shrugged. "It had already started to set by that time. When a Shifter's fighting adrenaline is up, the metabolism speeds up even more. Hell of a hangover the next day, but we can heal at the same time as we fight." An exaggeration, because he felt like shit, and rebreaking the leg had caused a boatload of pain. But it never hurt to make Shifters seem invincible.

"Interesting." Pat looked thoughtful. "I'd think the adrenaline would hinder the healing process, kind of putting it aside until the danger is over. You might not feel pain, but you shouldn't get better until much later."

"No idea," Bowman said, unworried. This woman was so harmless she amused him. He kept an eye on her and assessed her to figure out what she truly wanted, but for now, she could ask questions. "Healers might understand it, but I'm just a fighter. I fight, I heal. It works—I don't argue."

"There are Shifter healers?" Dr. Pat took another step toward the bed, caught up in her curiosity. "What do they do?"

Bowman shrugged. "They heal Shifters."

Ryan had remained silent the entire time, having taken a seat on the chair Kenzie had vacated. He pretended not to be there, but he watched, and he listened. Smart cub.

"Really?" Dr. Pat asked. "Do you have clinics or special hospitals? I've never heard of them—do you think I could meet a healer?"

Bowman lifted one hand to slow her chatter. "There aren't many around, and no, we don't have our own clinics. We go to human ones. Healers are . . . special. And shy. Don't try to find one."

"Oh." She looked puzzled. "Do they go to med school? How do you become a Shifter healer?"

"You're born one," Bowman said. "It runs in families. Parents train cubs."

"Cubs . . . Oh, you mean kids." She shot a glance at Ryan, who stared right back at her. "So it's like an apprenticeship. Neat. The surgical practice was like that, ages ago, before we had med schools and vet schools. Surgeons historically were looked down upon by doctors, you know, and now surgeons are top of the profession. Strange, isn't it?"

She continued to babble. She didn't need to be nervous, but Bowman wasn't going to tell her that. "Are *you* a surgeon?"

Her flush deepened. "I am. But not for humans. Animals pull my compassion—they have as many hurts and diseases as humans, and they need care too."

"You don't have to explain that to me. I'm surrounded by animals every day."

Her eyes were starry. "Shifters are the best of both, aren't they? Animal and human. The strengths of each. Maybe the weaknesses too? Would be fascinating to study . . ."

Bowman's amusement swiftly died. "Humans like to study us a little too much," he said in a hard voice. "They dragged us into laboratories when we were first discovered and tried to figure out what made us work. Not all Shifters survived the process."

"Oh." Now Pat was bright red and no longer smiling. "I

didn't mean like that. I mean study you to learn how to heal you. Like I studied to be a vet. I didn't mean . . . dissection."

"No, you didn't." Bowman looked her over. Harmless, he decided again. He read her scent, her eager chatter, the look in her eyes. She was interested in Shifters because they were Shifters, not for some ulterior motive.

That was his assessment, anyway. Kenzie would probably get a better reading of her. Kenzie was wise about people.

"Is that why you dress up?" Bowman asked her, letting his voice soften to teasing. She was easily played, this woman, and maybe she could be of use. He'd learned long ago how to quickly classify humans and Shifters into either being useful or dangerous—the hazard of inheriting clan leadership at a young age. "You dress up because you want to know how to heal Shifters?"

"It's fun," Pat said, meeting his gaze, her cheeks still pink. "That roadhouse you go to—the crowd isn't really my scene, but if I dress up like the other girls, I get to watch Shifters. You and your friends think I'm just one of the groupies and don't pay attention to me. I can stand by and observe, which is what I like to do."

Bowman cocked a brow. "You know a lot of the groupies go there hoping for sex with a Shifter. What if one of mine took you up on it?"

She looked suddenly shy, shooting another look at the listening Ryan. Bowman had no problem discussing sex in front of his son—Ryan already knew Shifters enjoyed healthy sex lives. Ryan had no interest in it himself, wouldn't until his Transition, but Shifters didn't shield their cubs from knowledge of sex. Sex was natural—how else would they make more cubs?

"It might not be such a bad thing," Dr. Pat said, flushing. She was a woman who couldn't help being honest, Bowman deduced.

He laughed. A genuine laugh, which was something he hadn't felt like doing in a long time. "Tell you what, Dr. Pat, when I'm better, I'll introduce you to some Shifters. They like to talk about themselves, so you'll learn a lot. Maybe more than you want to know."

And Bowman's Shifters knew better than to impart anything humans couldn't already find out on their own. They'd feed Dr. Pat a lot of bullshit, and Shifter secrets would stay Shifter secrets.

Dr. Pat looked grateful. "I'd like that. Now, would you mind if I had a peek at your leg? As a doctor, of course. I'm very interested in seeing how it's doing."

When Kenzie returned, she knew instantly that someone else was in her house. She caught a whiff of scent as soon as she walked in the front door. Bowman's and Ryan's scents were the most predominant, as well as her own, but woven in with theirs was something female and clinical.

She recognized the scent a heartbeat later—the vet who'd set Bowman's leg last night.

Sounds came next: a woman's laughter and Bowman's rumbling baritone. Kenzie strode down the short hall and slapped open the door to the bedroom she shared with her mate.

Bowman lay propped up on the bed's pillows, covers over his hips, his hair still a mess. Ryan sat cross-legged on the chair, watching in silence. The vet was sitting at the end of the bed, Bowman's bare leg in her lap, her hand on Bowman's calf.

A sheen of red rose before Kenzie's eyes, and a snarl clogged in her throat.

Bowman looked leisurely up at her—he'd have known the moment she walked into the house. His gaze was unworried, and he was completely relaxed, hands resting calmly on the sheets. He was conveying to Kenzie that there was nothing at all in this room to worry about, but Kenzie's Shifter instincts roared to life.

Mine. Her hands started to sprout claws, and her skin prickled, fur wanting to come out.

The vet looked up. "Hey," she said in a friendly tone. "You're Kenzie, right? I just popped by to make sure Bowman was doing all right."

Kenzie couldn't speak. If she did, whatever came out would be unintelligible, or possibly an all-out wolf howl as she went for the kill.

Bowman knew it. He pinned her with his cool stare, the

one he used when he planned to make the world obey. Even Kenzie had to stop in her tracks when he wore that look.

His eyes changed from warm gray to cold, his face so still it might be carved from granite. The damaged leg and the woman petting it didn't exist for him. His world narrowed to Kenzie, his gaze commanding her not to gut the nice vet with the blond hair.

Ryan tensed, sensing the silent battle between his parents. Kenzie saw Ryan shiver, the tiny cub inside him wondering whether he'd have only one parent when the confrontation was over. Which one would it be, and what would he do?

Kenzie's maternal instinct slammed against the mate's instinct, and the mother won. "Ryan," she said, surprised her voice sounded almost normal. "Will you come outside and help me with something?"

She held out her hand. Ryan flashed a glance at Bowman, who gave him the barest nod.

Ryan slid off the chair with the energy of youth and walked to Kenzie. Walked, she noted. A few years ago, he would have darted to her side. Now Ryan wanted to show more self-reliance. Her heart squeezed.

The touch of Ryan's hand in hers calmed her. Ryan must have realized that, so he didn't try to pull away after a brief clasp. Instead, he locked his hand around Kenzie's and walked her out of the room. Who was helping whom, Kenzie couldn't say.

She and Ryan went out into the backyard, where Kenzie dragged in a long breath. Ryan carefully let go of her hand, watching her as though to see whether she'd stay here, calming herself, or run back inside and rip out the vet's throat.

"You all right, Mom?" he asked.

"Yes." She took another breath, letting the serenity of the tall trees soothe her. "I'll be fine." Far down the row of widely spaced houses, other cubs were playing. One waved to Ryan, then stood up and waited to see if he'd come over.

Ryan acknowledged his friend and shot a question at his mother.

"Go," she said, putting amusement in her voice. "I promise I won't kill anyone."

"It's not like that, Mom," Ryan said. "I was watching."

No doubt he had been, and no doubt he was right. Not much got past Ryan. "Thank you," Kenzie said sincerely. "Go. Be back for supper."

Relieved of the duty of guarding his parents, Ryan ran off toward his friend's yard. He ran fast, the strength in his legs, which she swore grew longer every day, apparent.

They were the luckiest Shifters, Kenzie thought as she watched Ryan. Unlike other Shifters around the country, who'd been stuck into the slum ends of cities, their Shiftertown had been built in deep woods, in an abandoned housing project from early in the last century.

The houses were surrounded by old-growth forests, with trees that reached several hundred feet, branches reaching out well above the floor of the woods to provide a roof of green. Pine needles carpeted the ground, inches thick. The air always smelled slightly damp but cool, and wind perpetually creaked in the trees high above.

Clean air, far from giant industrial cities, and mountains rising to surround them in beauty at all times. The small houses had been originally built with a woodsy theme, their walls fabricated to look like split logs rather than actually being split logs from any trees around here. In summer, this area could be hot, the air turning dank and humid. Winters, on the other hand, could be fairly mild, with dustings of snow to keep everything moist.

Shiftertowns were places of confinement, but this Shiftertown had always felt welcoming to Kenzie. She'd been to others that made her uncomfortable, but here she'd found home. Didn't matter that she wore a Collar and couldn't run free— *yet*, Bowman would always add—she'd discovered a sort of peace here.

Her clan had come from Romania, in the wilds of the mountains there, which was perhaps why she liked this Shiftertown in the middle of nowhere. But here, Kenzie was no longer alone. In Romania, she'd been part of the clan run by her formidable uncle Cristian and dominated by her grandmother, Afina. Kenzie's immediate family, however, had all passed when she'd been a tiny cub. Lonely and withdrawn, she'd known no one but her cousins, and since Shifters couldn't mate within the clan, and Uncle Cristian wasn't letting her out of his sight, she thought she'd never find a mate of her own.

Then Shifters had been outed, the clan had been rounded up, and Uncle Cristian's Shifters had been herded to the States and this Shiftertown.

And Kenzie had seen Bowman. She'd first caught sight of him across the gym of the closed school they'd been taken to. She'd seen a tall, tight-muscled Shifter in jeans and a sweatshirt, with tousled, short hair and movements that said he was more comfortable in his wolf form than his human one.

He'd turned his head, as though he'd felt her gaze, and looked at her. A long look that burned the air—it didn't matter how many Shifters or human soldiers moved between them. His eyes were light gray, she remembered; Bowman on the edge of shifting.

He'd stood very still, looking at her, Kenzie gazing right back at him. She'd stared at him, and he at her, until one of Kenzie's younger cousins had called to her, needing her.

Bowman had let her go, but the slight nod of his head acknowledged her and the spark that had danced between them. His nod was also a dismissal, an indication that he considered her submissive to him, no matter that he'd never seen her before in his life.

Arrogant, insufferable . . . Kenzie had muttered to herself, but for the rest of the time they'd spent in those temporary quarters, she hadn't been able to keep her eyes off him.

Bowman had been chosen as Shiftertown leader by the human government's Shifter Bureau. Kenzie's uncle Cristian hadn't liked that one bit, because he'd thought that, being older and from a bigger clan, *he* should be leader of all Shiftertown. But the two other Lupine clans, smaller and less dominant, had conceded to Bowman's authority. The Felines and bears had wanted to challenge Bowman to put one of their own in the top position, but the Shifter Bureau had decreed Bowman leader. In the human government's view, that was good enough.

Uneasy peace had ensued for a couple of years, but Uncle Cristian couldn't leave well enough alone. Cristian was a dominant wolf, and he chafed under Bowman's leadership. He was also a crafty devil, good at stirring up trouble. Kenzie had always been grateful to Uncle Cristian for taking her in, but she wasn't blind to his personality. He could be a total bastard.

It was too easy to return to wild ways out here, and Shifters over the next years had started reverting to clan loyalty above all else. Uncle Cristian had started turning the Lupines from the lesser clans against Bowman, even joining with Felines who wanted Bowman out. Bears always did their own thing, but after a while even they'd stopped agreeing to obey Bowman, even though Cade was already his second.

Bowman kept everything together by his strength and his smarts, and all would have been right after a while, but the humans got wind of the problems. Kenzie had no doubt at all that Uncle Cristian and his most loyal trackers had made sure the humans had heard about the unrest in their Shiftertown.

The humans had come to Bowman and given him an ultimatum. He either calmed things down, or they'd close this Shiftertown. They'd split up the clans, packs, and prides in order to fit them into other Shiftertowns, deciding that the dominant families would cause less trouble if they were scattered.

When they'd gone, Bowman had walked over to Kenzie's grandmother's, where Kenzie had been living, strode straight into the kitchen, ignoring that it was the territory of a rival clan, and told Kenzie that he was taking her as mate.

Kenzie had gotten in his face, saying she didn't simply roll over and obey when an alpha wolf walked in the door.

Never mind that her heart had been hammering like crazy, her breath gone, every need she possessed screaming at her to leap on him. She'd yelled at him—like hell she'd jump to obey him when he'd been fighting her uncle and every other Shifter in Shiftertown.

His eyes had been white gray with rage, his hard face, with its brush of dark whiskers, speaking of years of kicking the asses of every Shifter who confronted him. But Kenzie wasn't afraid of Bowman.

And yet, she was. But her fear was more of herself, of something primal in her that responded to him.

Female Shifters wanted him—human groupies did too. Bowman hadn't been celibate—he'd satisfied his powerful libido plenty since they'd moved to this Shiftertown, and Kenzie had known it. But never with Kenzie.

Bowman had stood his ground in that kitchen while Kenzie shouted at him. He simply watched her, just as he'd gazed at her that first night in the gym, as he'd looked at her every time they'd crossed paths in the five years since.

Not until Kenzie ran out of words had she realized her grandmother and cousins had quietly departed. They'd left the house empty, and Bowman and Kenzie were alone.

Bowman had waited until she'd finished, then he'd caught her around the waist and crushed a kiss to her mouth.

She didn't honestly remember how they'd gotten into the living room, but there she'd been with Bowman on the floor, her mating frenzy kicking into high gear. They'd torn off each other's clothes, barely able to stay in human shape. Kenzie's back hit the carpet, Bowman's strong arms cushioning her fall, and then everything became a blur. She'd heard herself crying out, heard Bowman's voice joining hers, as her body awakened into unbelievable pleasure.

Her hands had gone down Bowman's bare back, raking his flesh. His mouth bruised hers, his eyes, darkening as he'd taken her, not looking away, not letting her look away.

They'd grappled on the carpet until Kenzie's back was raw. Bowman spilled his seed into her with a groan, but he was hard again at once, and began thrusting again without withdrawing.

All afternoon and well into the night they'd made love in that living room, sometimes rolling over so that Kenzie rode Bowman, his callused hands on her arms or cupping her breasts. They'd taken it to a chair when the floor got too hard, Kenzie just fitting into it with him.

In the end, when the sun was rising and neither of them could move very much, Bowman had cupped Kenzie's face in his hands.

"You're my mate," he'd said in a voice broken by their long night.

"Yes, all right," Kenzie had growled, and that had been that.

They'd been mated in the ceremony under the sun that day, and then held the moon ceremony at the next full moon. They'd said prayers to the Goddess in firelight, and then Kenzie had moved in with Bowman.

Ryan had come along a few years later—a few years of almost constant mating frenzy, Bowman determined to produce a son. Ryan had been born robust and healthy, and beautiful. A gift from the Goddess.

Kenzie now watched her son and his friends running together, small and far away, and her heart warmed. Her jealousy was winding down, as Bowman had known it would. Damn him.

Her rage had eased, but the worry hadn't. In spite of their joining for fifteen years, she and Bowman had never formed the mate bond. Shifters had been proving, in the last years, that they could form it with humans. So just because the vet in there was human didn't mean she wasn't a threat to Kenzie, her happiness, and her sanity.

A pair of very strong arms came around her from behind. Kenzie stiffened as a hard body pressed into her back and Bowman nuzzled the curve of her neck.

"Come on inside . . ." Bowman's broken whisper trailed off. Kenzie bent her head to one side and closed her eyes, letting Bowman's heat trickle down her body. He slid open the button of her jeans and eased his hand under her waistband.

He inhaled, then his hand froze, and his whisper turned to a growl. "And who the hell have *you* been with?" he demanded. "His scent is all over you."

CHAPTER EIGHT

Kenzie swung around to face her mate, who was wearing nothing but a bathrobe, with a crutch under one arm, his leg back in the splint, murder in his eyes.

"What are you doing out of bed?" she asked sharply. "You aren't supposed to put any weight on that for at least two days."

Bowman pinned her with the stare that had stopped her in her tracks across the gym all those years ago. "Don't go all caregiver on me, and tell me who you were with."

Rage had him standing straight, the crutch loose. His eyes were light gray, as though he wanted to shift; but if he did that, he'd hurt himself again.

"I wasn't *with* anyone," Kenzie said. "You have a suspicious mind."

"And you weren't looking the kill at Dr. Pat in there. Would not be good if you gutted her, Kenz."

"Yeah, well, I wasn't sitting with a guy letting him stroke my leg," Kenzie returned. "I was talking to a cop, all right? One who stuffed me into his patrol car and asked me about what happened last night. He's smart. He already knew most of it."

Bowman's anger flared. "He *stuffed you into his patrol car*?"

Kenzie waved her hands. "I exaggerate. He invited me to sit in the front seat with him. He was really polite while he interrogated me."

Bowman climbed down a little, but only a little. "What did you tell him?"

"He already knew almost everything, like I said. The humans who were at the roadhouse last night have been talking. For now, the cops are just trying to figure out what happened."

"Trying to figure out how to blame it on Shifters, you mean."

"Maybe. He didn't say." Kenzie tried to relax, but with Bowman standing a step away, bare beneath the robe, she couldn't. She felt the warmth of him through the fabric, smelled the comforting scent of male—of *him*. It made her want to flow against him, put her arms around him, forget this stupid conversation.

"What *did* he say?" Bowman demanded.

"He seemed like he wanted to help." Kenzie's foot moved to take her closer to Bowman. "Smarter than most cops—more common sense. He wants to work with us to figure this out."

Bowman had started to lean to her, closing the space between them, but he snapped upright again. "What do you mean, work with us?"

"Pool information and skills. He thinks it's stupid for humans and Shifters to not be allowed to help one another."

Bowman's lip curled. "And you believed him?"

"Not all humans suck, Bowman. I liked him."

"I know you did. I scent it on you."

Kenzie took the last step to put her directly against him. "Oh, right. And you hated that cute blond vet coming here to feel up your leg."

"She wasn't . . ." Bowman's brows slammed together. "Goddess, Kenzie, I wasn't about to go all mating frenzy on her with my leg in a splint."

"If you're so hurt, why the hell are you up walking around?"

"I'm better," he said tightly.

They were face-to-face, Kenzie rising on her tiptoes so they'd be nose-to-nose. If he'd thought, fifteen years ago, that Kenzie would run to him like a meek little she-wolf, to sacrifice herself for the good of all Shifters, he'd learned better since—starting on day one, when he'd taken her home. He'd realized quickly that she wouldn't simply roll over and expose her soft throat to him.

Although that sounded kind of fun right now. Kenzie's heart was pumping, her fingers tingling, the scent of her mate filling her.

The only thing that kept her from leaping on him and sending them both to the ground was the fact that he was hurt.

Kenzie's anger softened. Bowman so rarely was injured. He had to be feeling vulnerable and hating it. If a dominant Shifter challenged for his position right now, Bowman wouldn't be able to fight him.

That's why he was outside, she realized. To show any watching Shifter how quickly he was healing. And Kenzie had left him alone today, taking his trackers with her.

"Who's been around?" she asked in sudden concern. "Uncle Cristian? If he's bothered you, I'll kick his ass."

"No one," Bowman said. "They're keeping their distance."

Kenzie glanced around. Trees shielded them from the house next door, and she didn't scent any Shifter lurking in the woods around them. She noted the cubs playing down the road, their happy shouting floating to her.

The only incongruous scent was the cloying one of the vet—what had Bowman called her? Dr. Pat. She no longer wore the perfume she had last night, but the woman's scent was distinctive.

And all over Kenzie's mate.

"Did Dr. Pat go home?" Kenzie asked sharply.

Bowman came alert as he noted the change in her voice. "I sent her away, yes."

Of course. Dr. Pat wouldn't be allowed to just leave, not under the jurisdiction of Bowman the überalpha. No one went until he decided.

He didn't get to decide everything.

Kenzie flattened herself against him. "You're still not healed."

"I know that." Bowman's breath was hot on her cheek. "I know that, Kenz."

A ripple of fire spread through her. Kenzie slid her hands inside Bowman's loose robe, finding the tight warmth of his body, the vibrant power of him.

She nuzzled his neck as she worked the robe open, taking

a pinch of his skin between her teeth. Bowman made an *mmm* sound in his throat. Kenzie nipped him again, and licked where she'd bitten. She'd get rid of the other woman's scent the most effective way she knew.

Kenzie slid down his body to her knees, the robe opening on her way down. She paused at his large, bare cock, stiff and straight out, Bowman not oblivious to her attentions.

Kenzie gave him a glance—more than a glance. Bowman hard was always worth a long, long look. Then she made herself focus on his hurt leg, stuck into the binding splint.

The splint was hard plastic, fastened with Velcro, positioned to hold his limb as motionless as possible. The doctor at the local clinic was familiar with how quickly Shifters healed, and knew how to patch them up to not interfere with that healing. Bowman's leg would be knit by the end of the day.

Kenzie loosened the splint's straps. Bowman leaned heavily on the crutch, but he said nothing as she peeled back the bindings so she could touch his bare skin.

The main part of the splint, molded to the back of his thigh and calf, stayed in place. Kenzie skimmed her hands down the front of his leg, tracing the muscles of his thigh, around his knee, down his lower leg. Dark hair, silken yet wiry, curled around Kenzie's fingers.

The strength beneath the warm skin made her breath catch. She moved gently to where his bone had broken and rested her palm there, almost sensing the hurt beneath the muscle. Bowman tensed, his hand tightening on the crutch.

His taut leg was tanned from bright North Carolina summers. The tan petered out around his hip and groin—Bowman wore a bathing suit whenever they went to the coast and the beaches. Shifters were happy being naked, but Bowman was always conscious of not pissing off too many humans.

Thinking about how many women turned their heads when they saw Bowman walk by on the sand, his bare skin kissed by sunshine, the small pair of trunks covering his ass and not much else, made Kenzie growl again.

Don't touch. Don't even look.

She kissed his thigh, then ran her tongue up the tight ridge of muscle. Bowman sucked in a breath, one hand coming down to furrow her hair.

Kenzie smoothed her fingers over his hurt leg again. Gentle, caressing, kneading, soothing. She bent and pressed another kiss to him, running her tongue over his skin. He tasted like warmth, salt, maleness.

Bowman's fingers tightened in her hair. "Damn you, Kenz," he said softly.

Kenzie caressed him all the way down to his ankle, then she looked up at him and smiled.

Bowman growled. He hooked one hand under her arm and yanked her upward. She landed against his chest, his growl still rumbling.

"Damn you," he repeated. "Don't smile at me like that."

"Like what?" Kenzie gave him an innocent look, but she couldn't make the smile go away.

"Like you're the sexiest woman alive, and you know it." His voice broke over her like the soothing waves of the ocean in summer. "Laughing at me, because you think I don't understand what I've got."

Kenzie had no idea what he was talking about, and she didn't care. She only knew the weight of his voice tumbling her as though she were a pebble in the sand.

His arm was hard around her, Kenzie holding on to him to keep herself steady. He was the hurt one, but she used his strength to remain standing.

"House," he said. "Now."

Kenzie didn't want to go inside. Bowman had been badly injured, and moving might hurt him again.

Not that she had a choice. Bowman hauled her around with him and started walking. The crutch dug into the pine needles as Bowman braced himself on it and on Kenzie for the short distance to the kitchen door.

The house was empty and shut out the cold. Bowman leaned more on Kenzie once they were inside, where no other Shifters could see them.

"You need to rest," she began.

"I'll rest when I'm done with you." Bowman hobbled into the bedroom with her and collapsed on the bed, dropping the crutch in the process.

His robe fell all the way open. Kenzie halted at the foot of the bed, her heart pounding swiftly.

Bowman was stretched out full length, bronzed skin and dark hair against the white robe. The scrapes and abrasions he'd obtained last night had faded into light red lines across his skin, and his face was shadowed with new beard. In all this darkness, his gray eyes stood out like many-faceted diamonds.

Something else stood out prominently. The pale splint couldn't take away from the beauty of him spread out for Kenzie, his cock dark and hard, rigid against his abdomen.

She wanted him with a wild longing—she still burned from their interrupted encounter last night.

Kenzie slipped her shirt over her head without a second thought and tossed away the camisole beneath it. A few more quick movements had her out of her jeans and underwear. Now she was as bare as he was.

Even with her wanting, she hesitated. "You sure you're going to be all right?"

"Goddess." Bowman growled again. "Are you trying to kill me, Kenz? Get over here."

CHAPTER NINE

Kenzie obeyed, but only because she decided to. The alpha called his mate, but Kenzie took her time walking to the side of the bed, putting one knee on the mattress. As soon as she was within his reach, he'd haul her to him, and she knew it. She liked the thought, but he was injured.

"I don't want to hurt you," she said.

Bowman didn't wait. He heaved himself up and seized her, pulling her onto the bed. He hooked his hand under her left thigh, and Kenzie landed straddling him, bracing her weight on her knees, hands splayed on his chest.

"I don't want to hurt you," she repeated.

Bowman thumped back down to the mattress, transferring his grip to her wrists. A feral smile spread across his face. "You can't hurt me, Kenz."

His arrogant confidence heated her blood. "Want to bet?"

Bowman rose on his elbows, his eyes glittering. "Give me your best shot."

Kenzie very carefully moved her hips forward. The brush of his cock at her opening made her shake, and she started to lose all her good intentions.

"Come on," Bowman said impatiently. "I can't lie here all day."

He'd said a similar thing to the pseudo-groupie last night. His gruff command had flared Kenzie's anger then, but now that he directed the words to her, it excited her beyond belief.

The feral in her responded to the wildness in him, his need to have her, never mind the pain.

"Touch of a mate, Kenzie," he whispered.

Kenzie lowered herself slowly, the feeling of him sliding inside her blurring all thought. She sucked in a breath, remembering in time to not rest her full weight on him.

"That's nice," Bowman said, his eyes growing heavy. "I feel better already."

Kenzie had no answer. Bowman was big, filling her, finding her empty spaces. Her head went back in silent joy, and he rocked forward and curled his tongue around her nipple.

The heat of his mouth warmed, banishing winter. Kenzie raised her head so she could look at him as he lay back again on white robe and sheets, his warrior's body beautiful despite the incongruity of the splint.

Her innate need to heal him worked through even her lust. She made sure she put no weight on his hurt limb, and she reached back to touch his leg, hoping that would help.

Bowman's growl broke through her fog, his gaze intensifying, the lines of pain leaving his face. He focused on her, and her alone, his eyes gray like the winter sky.

Kenzie's body felt heavy, her breasts full; where he filled her felt stretched and wonderful. Bowman flicked his tongue once more over her nipple, pulling it between his lips, releasing it after one tug.

His powerful hands caught her hips, urging her to ride him. His raw body and intense strength was trapped beneath her, but Bowman wasn't tamed. Far from it. His fingers gripped her thighs, his hips moved in time with hers, his gaze held hers and wouldn't let go.

"I thought you said you could hurt me," Bowman said as he thrust hard up into her. "Not even close, sweetheart."

Challenging her, was he? Kenzie increased her own thrusts, Bowman's words fading as she sped up to meet him. He got up on his elbows again as he thrust into her as hard as he could.

He was proving he wasn't debilitated, Kenzie realized. Kenzie could stagger outside afterward, looking sated and content, and the story would spread through Shiftertown that Bowman's wounds hadn't slowed him down one bit. And, if any of his enemies decided to burst in, hoping to catch him when he was vulnerable, they'd see him servicing his mate at full strength.

They'd certainly get an eyeful. Kenzie's head went back once more, her hair brushing her shoulders, the silken touch of it erotic. Just as erotic was Bowman, now gripping her thighs, his fingers tight on her soft flesh. Her breasts moved with their rhythm, and every time she looked down at Bowman, he caught her gaze in his strong one and held it.

He was holding her with his gaze when Kenzie's climax overtook her. She forgot about being gentle and ground away at him as wave after wave of joy flooded her.

Bowman snarled—a long wolf snarl, the sound tearing out of his throat. The next moment, Kenzie felt his seed flood her, the life of a strong male Shifter filling her and completing her.

Perhaps another cub would come of this, Kenzie thought in hope as she collapsed on top of him. Bowman caught her, his arms coming around her to cradle her and keep her safe. *A cub,* she repeated to herself muzzily. She longed for that most of all.

Kenzie was heavy on top of him, and Bowman's leg itched like crazy, but no way in hell was he going to push her away.

The most beautiful thing in the world was Kenzie stretched out on him, her dark golden eyes half closed in afterglow, her tight body relaxed in a way she didn't relax any other time. She was a fine armful, her breasts cushioned against his chest, their heartbeats on top of each other's.

Bowman held his breath, waiting for the warm spike in his heart that other Shifters had told him about, the almost-pain that meant he and his mate were bound forever.

It didn't come. It never had. Exhaustion was there—he and Kenzie always tore it up in the bedroom—but the mate bond eluded them. The Goddess testing them, maybe? Telling Bowman he wasn't building enough bonfires to the God or meditating hard enough?

Whatever reason the God and Goddess and the wide universe had for denying Kenzie and Bowman the mate bond, it hurt. He knew it hurt Kenzie too—she was simply good at hiding it. Their Shifters also weren't happy that their leaders shared no bond. Instability could come of that, and they knew it.

Kenzie raised her head and looked down at him. Bowman saw the sorrow in her eyes, knowing she was searching for the bond and not feeling it either.

Instead of comforting her with words, which Kenzie wouldn't want—she never wanted to talk about it—Bowman stroked her hair. He loved the color of it—dark brown with golden streaks, like the sun on polished walnut.

"I need your report, Kenz," he said softly. Getting back to business would calm them both. "What did you find out this morning?"

Kenzie snuggled down to him again, which did nothing to help Bowman's continued hard-on. The last thing he wanted was to talk about the terror of last night, but they couldn't blow it off. A danger existed that they had to find and destroy.

His hardness deflated a bit, however, as she described the creature's disappearing scent and her and Jamie's conclusion that it had been shoved into a semitruck and hauled away.

"By other Shifters?" Bowman asked, still smoothing Kenzie's hair.

"We couldn't tell," she said.

"I know. I'm thinking out loud. Or by humans? And why?"

Kenzie pressed a warm kiss to his throat. "I was more interested in the *how*. What was that thing? Was it real?"

"It was real." Bowman flexed his toes and grimaced. "It tore up my leg, smashed Cade's truck, and laid out half the Shifters of Shiftertown."

"You know what I mean. I hear people can build some cool robotics, but it wasn't mechanical. We'd have scented that."

"That leaves something born and bred. Remember what happened to Tiger."

Tiger was a Shifter now living in the Austin Shiftertown. He'd been bred by humans using an experimental process Shifters still didn't understand. The experiments hadn't gone well, however—all the artificially inseminated Shifters had died except Tiger, who'd been the twenty-third attempt. The researchers had abandoned him, leaving him alone in a cage, barely fed, for years, and he'd pretty much gone insane.

But Tiger, while he was big and powerful and larger than most Felines, was still more or less normal size for a Shifter. After he'd been freed, he'd taken a human mate, a woman named Carly, and Carly so far had no complaints.

Shifters had originally been created by the Fae a couple thousand years ago. Genetic engineering had been invented in Faerie far sooner than humans had figured it out, but it had been blended with magic, as everything in Faerie was.

The Fae had merged humans with big, powerful animal predators—Bowman didn't really want to know the details of how they'd done it—and produced Shifters, creatures with human reason and pure animal instinct.

After Shifters had banded together and defeated their Fae masters, they'd walked away from Faerie, choosing to live— covertly—with their human counterparts. Fae had started abandoning the human world by then, hating its cold iron, which for some reason weakened their metabolisms and killed them. Fae loathing for the human world had been the point of Shifters staying in it. No Fae to worry about equaled good times. Peace. Cubs. Life.

Of course, neither the Fae nor the humans could leave them alone. Both were constantly doing something to get in the way of Shifter happiness, such as humans herding them into Shiftertowns and slapping shock Collars on them—the Collars had been invented by a half Fae.

Shifters now had figured out a way out of the Collars, but it was a deep, dark secret. Removing Collars and replacing them with fake ones took a special process and was slow going.

Bowman had tried to get Kenzie out of her Collar, but she was being stubborn about it. She'd argued that it was better to let the cubs and the weaker Shifters swap theirs out first. She could take the pain.

And she could. She was strong, his mate.

"What about this cop?" Bowman asked her.

Kenzie lifted her head, her eyes dark in the sunlight filtering through half-closed curtains. "He seems all right. He wants to talk to you. I told him he could come over this afternoon."

"*This* afternoon?" Bowman half sat up, then ground his teeth as his leg throbbed. "Shit, Kenzie . . ."

"I think he can help us. Cops have resources that we don't."

"I don't want humans in Shiftertown until I heal." He couldn't protect his mate, his cub, and his Shifters from cops with guns while his leg was in a splint.

"No humans except cute veterinarians?" Kenzie asked with a sly look.

"Give it a rest, Kenz."

Kenzie broke into a big, beautiful smile. "I can't. I'm never letting you off the hook for anything, Bowman O'Donnell. The privilege of a mate."

"What is? Being a serious pain in my ass?"

"Hell, yeah," Kenzie said lightly. "I do it better than anyone."

"Not going to argue with you about that."

She looked seriously good too, sitting up and smiling at him, the clinging sheet falling from her. Kenzie had borne a cub, and her breasts were full and mature, her belly marked where it had stretched to carry his son. Bowman traced one of the stretch marks to where it disappeared on her side, then cupped her heavy breast in his hand.

He'd gone through the mating ceremonies with her to keep her unruly clan from battling with his, but he'd have gone to her anyway, no matter what. Bowman couldn't imagine having any mate but her.

The ends of her silky hair brushed his fingers as he cupped her, Kenzie's breath lifting her breast into his palm. Her eyes were half closed, gleaming gold beneath her dark lashes. Her nipple tightened, responding to Bowman's thumb as he rubbed the smooth point.

A knock on the door made Kenzie jump. Bowman slowly let her go and tucked his hand behind his head. "What?" he called.

The door remained closed, but they both knew who it was. Ryan's scent came to them, wrapping them both, completing them.

Ryan was impatient, not distressed, so they waited to see what he needed. Being a Shifter cub, he'd never open the door without their invitation, knowing exactly what his parents were getting up to in the bedroom. He also had zero interest. The fact that his parents—and all adult Shifters—loved sex was to Ryan a character flaw he would put off acquiring as long as he could.

"Dad," he called through the door. "Can I go with my friends to Cade's? He's got the zip line done, and he says we can start riding it today."

CHAPTER TEN

Zip line? Goddess give him strength.

Bowman started out of bed, was brought up short by his splint, let out a frustrated groan, and said loudly, "No!"

"Aw, come on. Everyone's going. Cade's careful. He wouldn't do anything to hurt us little cubs."

No, he wouldn't. Cade was good with cubs, and all Shifters knew it. Bowman also knew that Ryan was playing up the cute cub angle to get his way. At age twelve, he was a master manipulator.

"You're leader's son," Bowman said, dropping back to the mattress. "No one will think less of you if you don't go. They'll think you're smart for not doing something stupidly dangerous."

"No, they won't." Ryan's voice came firmly through the door. "They'll say I'm a coward. Leader's son should be the first one on."

"Leader's son shouldn't be pushed around by a bunch of cubs," Bowman called back.

Kenzie was up, her naked body touched by winter sunshine. Bowman fell silent as he watched her lean over to sweep up her clothes. A stretch of her arms, and her shirt skimmed down her body, Kenzie glancing at him as she settled it over her breasts. Another bend, and her jeans slid up her thighs, over her smooth ass, hiding herself from him.

"I'll walk him over," she said. "He's right—leader's son shouldn't hold back from new things."

"Leader's son shouldn't break his bloody neck on a stupid idea of Cade's."

"You'll be all right by yourself, won't you?" Kenzie asked. She was good at ignoring him. "I can have my grandmother look in on you."

Kenzie's grandmother, Afina, was a clan matriarch, and didn't have a high opinion of Bowman. She let her disapproval of everything he did, said, wore, and thought come loudly out of her mouth. Afina could insult him in Romanian and also Russian, or in English with a heavy accent, every word barbed.

"No." Bowman growled. "I'll be fine."

Kenzie winked at him as she opened the door. Bowman was grateful the sheet had settled back over him, because that wink had him harder than the headboard behind him.

"Of course you will," she said. "Besides, I want to try the zip line too."

Another smile, and she and Ryan were gone, leaving the room empty, Bowman alone and feeling it.

Kenzie and Ryan walked through Shiftertown, which was a widespread neighborhood of small houses. The roads that wound through it were narrow, climbing up and down hills. Clusters of houses, families of clans clumped together, were scattered throughout, with woods and space between the clusters.

Around this bend, it was Felines, Jamie's family. The next, another Lupine clan. Down the hill, the roofs visible from where Kenzie and Ryan walked, Kenzie's clan's homes. The bears lived on the far side of Shiftertown, their houses the largest. Bear clans tended to be small—making up the lowest percentage of Shifters overall—but bears took up a lot of room.

"Kenzie." A muscular man in sweats came jogging up out of the woods to fall into step with her. "Hello, Ryan."

"Uncle," Kenzie said cautiously around Ryan's more friendly "Hey, Uncle Cris."

Cristian Dimitru was Kenzie's mother's much older brother. Kenzie's father had been a lone wolf, clanless, his small pack and clan having been killed during the war the humans called World War II. Kenzie's dad had been in a human army fighting the Nazi regime—the humans had not known they'd had Shifters join them.

All that had proved, Cristian had said, was that bullets hurt Shifters as much as they did humans. Cristian had come across Kenzie's father, wounded and alone, and Cristian had carried him home, his clan taking him in.

Kenzie's father had mated with Cristian's sister, and died just after Kenzie had been born. His injuries and exposure to chemicals used in wartime had sickened him, and he'd never fully recovered. Kenzie's mother, grieving from the broken mate bond and exhausted from bringing in Kenzie, had not lived much longer.

Kenzie therefore had been raised by Cristian and her grandmother, Afina. They'd both loved her plenty, but she'd always known they'd considered her father weak. A fool, Cristian had said, to join the humans. Cristian's clan had hidden out in the mountains during the war, waiting for the stupid humans to grow tired of killing one another.

That war had changed everything, though. Wild lands became fewer and farther between as humans took them over to feed a growing population. Automobile and airplane use became commonplace, erasing the quietude of the wild. It became increasingly difficult for Shifters to hide their true natures, simply because humans were everywhere, even in the lesser populated areas of Eastern Europe. Living behind an iron curtain made things even more difficult. A few of Kenzie's clan had gotten out to Western Europe and the States, but they'd found themselves alone there.

Once the wall fell in Berlin, things had begun to change even more, and Shifters had to make choices. Then Shifters had been outed. Kenzie's clan was rounded up and shipped off to the States. They'd learned English on the fly, and had found themselves dumped in a high school gym in the state called North Carolina, where Kenzie had seen Bowman for the first time.

Cristian spoke English with a thick accent, though his accent came and went depending on who he talked to and how much he wanted to manipulate them. When he was alone with his pack, he ceased bothering with English altogether, as he did now.

"What happened last night?" he asked her in a dialect of the Transylvanian mountains. Ryan, in a hurry to rejoin his friends, slipped his hand from Kenzie's and jogged on down the road toward Cade's place. "My Lupines are giving me garbled accounts, and Bowman's trackers won't talk to me at all."

Probably because they didn't trust him. Neither did Kenzie. She loved her uncle, but Cristian was slippery, had preferred the world when he was leader, and wanted to be leader again. He was still alpha of his pack, but he hated to be subordinate to anyone else.

"You're getting garbled accounts because we don't know what happened," Kenzie answered. "Whatever attacked us was huge and not normal. We don't know what it was."

"And Bowman brought it down himself?" Cristian threw her a skeptical look. His hair was dark, but brushed with gray, the same color as his wolf's fur. His eyes were a deep gold, like Kenzie's and her grandmother's. "Our fearless leader took down an animal ten times bigger than any Shifter? By himself?"

"Yes, but with our help," Kenzie said, keeping her impatience in check. "We attacked it, and Bowman got it after we harassed it a lot."

"Got it with what? His teeth? His claws? His body odor?"

"Don't be a shit," Kenzie told him in English. "With Cade's truck, and I'm betting you already heard the story, so don't mess with me."

Cristian lost his derision as he let out a real laugh. "No wonder Cade snarled at me. He must be in mourning. He worshiped that stupid truck."

"It wasn't as funny as it sounds. Bowman was nearly crushed to death, and even then the thing only ran off." She remembered her terror as she'd rushed to Bowman lying bleeding under glass and bent metal. She'd nearly wept in relief when she found him still alive. "That creature didn't die. It's still out there."

"I know." Cristian stopped, turning a sharp gaze on Kenzie. "What is Bowman doing about it?"

"He's getting over being hurt first." Kenzie returned his look with a scowl. "He doesn't want to rest, but I'm making him stay down for a while. And you'll leave him alone while he recovers."

Cristian gave her an innocent look that Kenzie didn't believe for a minute. "You think I would rush in while he's injured and try to take over Shiftertown?"

"Yes," Kenzie said steadily.

"Give me credit for some honor, please, sweetling. When I fight him, we will do so on equal footing. I would not creep up on him while he is down and take him out." Cristian looked genuinely hurt that Kenzie would think so, but Kenzie knew better. Her uncle would take any advantage he could—he always did.

In his sweats, his skin sheened with perspiration, Cristian looked like any other man out for a jog—any tall man in great shape. Cristian was a hundred years older than Bowman and had a hundred and fifty on Kenzie, but he was at the height of his strength. "My niece, when I do take Bowman down, you must be ready to decide whose side you are on. I will not let you get in my way. And if I defeat him, you must be prepared for those consequences too."

Kenzie glowered at him. "Don't threaten me, Uncle Cris. You know I'm not afraid of you, and you're just pissing me off." Not exactly true—she did worry a lot about what Uncle Cristian got up to.

Cristian knew she did. "You share no mate bond with Bowman. We all know this. If he dies, you will be free, not dead inside yourself. When that day comes, I know you will be strong. I will need you."

"I'll stand by him," Kenzie said, her jaw so stiff it hurt. "He's my *mate*. Unlike some people in this family, I know what loyalty means."

Cristian's lip curled. "If you refer to me killing my father to take over the clan, he was very old and knew it was his time to die. He fought well, and was grateful to go out with some dignity. He smiled at me when the Guardian came to send him to dust. He knew I could well look after the pack and Afina."

Kenzie had heard this version of the tale before. "So you've said."

"Times were different, Kenzie. All clan leaders gained their position by the death of the leader before them. None of this politeness—*Pardon me, Dad, while I take over the clan, and you go live with your girlfriend.*"

Cristian was talking about the Austin Shiftertown, where leadership had recently switched without bloodshed. The understanding the Morrissey father and son had reached was, to Kenzie, much preferable to a fight to the death. She certainly didn't want to think about Ryan and Bowman trying to kill each other.

"It wasn't exactly like that," Kenzie began, but Cristian shook his head, not interested.

"I should lead this Shiftertown by right of hierarchy, not to mention strength and experience. You're a sweet woman to stick by your mate, but don't push me, Kenzie. I'm still your clan leader."

"Not anymore," Kenzie said. "I switched when I left to live with Bowman, remember?"

Cristian's hands went to her shoulders. "You *never* lose your connections, niece. You're Dimitru pack, and always will be. The sooner you understand that, the easier your life will be."

Kenzie's throat hurt. She'd made a pledge to the O'Donnell pack as soon as she and Bowman had been mated under sun and moon. She was the flag of truce between the packs, Ryan their hope of permanent unification. When Ryan was leader, the clans would be one.

But Ryan, at the moment, was an innocent cub who only wanted to play with his friends.

"I have to catch up with my son," she said to Cristian. "Don't talk to me anymore unless you're passing the time of day or telling me how Grandma's doing. I'm tired of you trying to turn me against Bowman." She made a gesture like a baseball ump signaling an out. "Not gonna happen."

Anger flared in Cristian's eyes, making the gold spark. "You're still family, Kenzie. Still pack. I'll talk about what I damn well please. Soon, you'll have to remember who you are." He gave her a long look. "You'll understand, in the end."

Without giving Kenzie a chance to answer, he turned his back and walked away, picking up into a jog a dozen strides down the road.

Kenzie watched him go in disquiet, knowing the abrupt back-turning for what it was. He was telling her he wasn't afraid to show her his vulnerable side, because it made no difference. He was stronger than any Shifter around and always would be.

Soon, you'll have to remember who you are.

Kenzie didn't like the hint, or the implication that he'd oust Bowman sooner or later. Had he anything to do with last night's attack? Had he figured out a way to clear Bowman out of his way? She didn't see how, but, as she'd thought at the beginning of the conversation, Uncle Cris could be slippery.

Damn him. Whatever he'd been on about, he made the crisp winter air oppressive. Kenzie watched her uncle jog away for a time before she quickened her steps down the road the rest of the way to Cade's.

CHAPTER ELEVEN

Bowman didn't like the thought of Kenzie and Ryan out there alone. Not today.

He started out of bed, letting out a grunt of pain when his leg reminded him it wasn't all the way healed. It wasn't agonizing anymore, but very stiff, the muscles pulled all to hell. The break itself would already be fused, or close to it, but the soft tissues were going to ache and annoy him for a while.

He managed to make it to his feet. Bowman balanced on his good leg while the splinted leg stuck out like a white flagpole. Damn doctors.

All right, so they'd been nice and patched him up. He knew he'd have spent a worse night without the doctors in the clinic helping him out, but Bowman wasn't in the mood to be grateful. He just wanted out of the bloody splint.

He managed to swing his leg up to the bed. He reached for one of the Velcro straps that held the splint to his leg and tugged at it. Nothing happened.

Frustrated swearing filled the room. Good thing everyone had left the house, because this was just stupid.

Bowman gave a harder yank. The strap ripped open, but he

lost his balance and fell on his backside on the carpet next to the bed. *"Shit!"*

The front door to the house swung open, sending a draft of cold air inside. Damn it—another Shifter on his territory, and Bowman was flailing around like a bug on his back.

"Bowman? You in here? I know you are—I can smell you."

Bowman let out his tense breath. "Jamie. Get the hell back here."

Jamie entered the room with his usual restless energy. He didn't exactly laugh when he saw Bowman, buck naked and sprawled on the rug, his bad leg stuck up straight, but his mouth twitched and his ferocious eyes looked dangerously near to twinkling.

"Man, you got screwed over." Jamie folded his arms and stared down at his alpha. "Want me to get a crane?"

"Shut the hell up, and help me get this splint off."

"Sure you should?" Jamie asked. His tatts moved as his arms tightened.

"I'm sure. Get me out of this thing."

"All right, but if you hurt yourself because you took it off too soon, it wasn't me who helped you, all right? If Kenzie finds out, she'll tear my balls off."

"Don't worry, she'd be so busy ripping me a new one you'd have time to get away."

Jamie crouched next to Bowman, reaching for the strap around his ankle. "Didn't it occur to you to pick out a more submissive mate?"

"Nope." Bowman tugged on another strap at his thigh. "If I had a mate so meek she obeyed my every command without arguing, I'd be bored out of my mind. Although sometimes . . ." He thought of Kenzie's sparkling eyes and sassy smile. No, he liked her just the way she was.

"Speaking of Kenzie," Jamie said, "I saw her talking to Cristian. They were on the upper road, in a lonely stretch, the two of them going on about something."

Bowman swallowed the anger that built up in his throat. "He's her uncle and pack leader. Of course she talks to him."

"More like arguing. I couldn't hear, but I could see. He was trying to intimidate her."

"Was she intimidated?"

Jamie snorted. He tore open the last strap and helped Bow-man gently pry the splint apart. "What do you think? She looked pretty mad."

Bowman shrugged as though the news didn't alarm him. "If something's up, she'll tell me."

"You trust her that much?"

The splint came away, and Bowman breathed a sigh of relief. Then he dug his nails into his skin as air hit it. Everything *itched*.

"Yes. I do." Bowman bent a fierce eye on Jamie as he scratched away at his leg. "You'd damn well better trust her too, or we have a problem."

"Oh, I trust *her*," Jamie said, stacking the pieces of splint and setting them aside. "But I don't trust that Romanian were-wolf an inch."

Calling a Shifter a werewolf was an insult—Shifters were a living species; werewolves were movie monsters humans turned into after they were bitten. "I hear you. Help me up."

Jamie lent his sinewy strength while Bowman struggled to get his bad leg under him. Jamie pulled him upright, and finally Bowman was standing.

His hurt leg was annoyingly weak, and Bowman made a face as he tried to put weight on it. "Why did you come?" he asked Jamie. "Or did you sense I was going to get out of bed and fall on my ass?"

"Because of seeing Cristian," Jamie said. "I didn't like the idea of you here alone and hurt while he was wandering around."

Jamie backed away, letting Bowman find his balance on his own, but Jamie's touch had helped Bowman some. Shifters needed one another's comfort, strength, the sense that they were part of a group. Being alone was a terrible thing for a Shifter.

"Thanks," Bowman said. Jamie made such a good tracker because he could anticipate his leader's needs without being told, and took initiative with what he thought was right.

"You're welcome." Jamie looked him up and down and folded his arms again. "But if you think I'm helping you get dressed, you can forget about it."

"Just find me some pants," Bowman growled.

* * *

Walking to the landing end of the zip line gave Bowman a chance to stretch out the still-healing leg, as well as show every Shifter in Shiftertown that he was already up and feeling much better.

He and Jamie didn't pass anyone on the way, though. They were all at Cade's, friends and rivals alike.

Cade had rigged the zip line he'd been going on about high up on a hill above his own house, with a platform in the tall trees. The line ran almost the length of Shiftertown, gliding down the long hill to another platform at the bottom, where Bowman and Jamie headed. Cade had tested the zip line extensively on himself, figuring that if it could take his weight, then it would be safe for cubs.

Why the hell Cade had decided it was a good idea to put up a zip line at all, Bowman didn't know. When he'd asked, Cade had given him his straight-faced look and said, "Bears just want to have fun."

A bear was coming down the line now. It was a cub, in its grizzly form. It clung to the handle with its oversized paws, its back legs dancing as it descended in a rush toward Bowman. At the last minute, the cub dropped from the line to land on the platform with precision.

He bounced up and ran to Bowman, jigging around him, making happy little bear noises, which made Jamie laugh.

The cub, one of Cade's nephews by the look of it, circled Bowman again, then Jamie, then sprang off the platform and scampered to the path that led back up the hill.

Ryan was coming down next. "Cowabunga, Dad!" He let go of the bar and leapt the last few feet down, landing in Bowman's outstretched arms.

Bowman steadied himself on his good leg before lowering Ryan to the ground. "There, are you happy now?" Bowman rumbled at him.

"Nope." Ryan wriggled away. "Have to go again!" He scrambled off the platform and ran up the path after the other cub.

Before Bowman or Jamie could say a word, another rider came barreling toward them. This time it was Kenzie, sensibly in human form, her hands locked around the bar, a crash helmet on her head.

She lifted her legs in a perfect right angle to her body, using the momentum to propel her faster. Bowman's libido charged at the sight of his mate swinging gracefully through the air.

"Woo—hoo—hoo—hooooo!" she bellowed.

She was coming straight for Bowman. Jamie jumped well back, but Bowman waited for her. Kenzie loosened her hold and dropped at the last second, and Bowman caught her.

Kenzie was flushed with wind and excitement, her golden eyes sparkling. Bowman felt the chill of the wind on her, but her skin was heated with her own sweet warmth.

She flung her arms around Bowman and kissed his lips, her cold nose rubbing his cheek. "That was awesome," she said happily, pushing away from Bowman. "Better than sex!"

Jamie let out a howling laugh. Shaking his head, he sprang off into the woods, making himself scarce. Bowman growled, and Kenzie gave him an impish look.

"What?" she asked, one hip canted. The crash helmet made her look sexy as hell.

She was still making him pay for the vet sitting on his bed and rubbing his leg, was she? Bowman increased his growl, which Kenzie pretended to ignore.

Two could play at that game, Bowman decided, his heartbeat speeding heat straight to his groin. If Kenzie wanted the payback challenge, he'd meet it. And he'd show her he played to win.

To Kenzie's surprise, Bowman agreed to let the cop, Gil Ramirez, into the house. No arranging a neutral location like the coffeehouse a half mile outside Shiftertown. Bowman gave Ramirez directions when he called Kenzie's phone, and opened the door himself when Ramirez arrived.

But then, this was Bowman's territory. He liked to control it like he controlled everything else.

"Ramirez," Bowman said. He didn't offer to shake hands or make pleasantries; he simply filled the doorway, staring down at the man before he took one step back and moved so Ramirez could enter.

Welcome to my territory, he was saying. *I'll honor you as a guest as long as you leave my mate and cub alone, don't nose in my business, and don't make me want to kill you.*

Ryan was still at Cade's for the cookout Cade was having tonight. Ryan had gone on the zip line a couple more times, and Kenzie had followed to keep an eye on him, leaving Bowman to wait less than patiently for them at the bottom.

Bowman was on edge, and in pain, Kenzie could tell, but he'd let Ryan have his fun when he could have simply grabbed his son by the scruff and dragged him home. He'd agreed to let Ryan stay behind under Cade's and Jamie's supervision, knowing he'd be well looked after by the trackers.

Bowman also didn't want Ryan here when the cop came— Kenzie understood that.

True to his word, Ramirez wasn't in his uniform, wearing jeans, a sweatshirt, and a leather jacket against the increasing cold. The mild day was at an end.

Ramirez gave Kenzie a nod as he shucked his jacket. "Kenzie."

"Gil," Kenzie answered.

She took the jacket and hung it up for him, because that was what humans did. The wife in a traditional human household, she'd gleaned from television, was a hostess who made the guest comfortable and her husband look good—a custom Shifters didn't always share. The male Shifter and his mate stood side by side against any stranger, keeping him from invading their home. They wouldn't care about the invader's comfort.

Bowman shot Kenzie a look, both because she'd taken the coat and because she'd called the man *Gil.* Bowman's gaze burned her as she finished hanging the jacket on the wooden coat rack in the front hall.

"Won't you sit down?" Kenzie asked, gesturing to the couches in the living room. Bowman, behind Gil's back, rolled his eyes.

"Why don't you get him a beer, honey?" Bowman asked, the snarl in the words ruining his imitation of a TV husband.

Gil, oblivious to their tension, shook his head as he sat

down. "Nothing for me, thanks. I have a long drive back, and I don't get behind the wheel after even one drink."

Kenzie walked past Bowman and sat on the end of the couch Gil had taken. "That's wise," she said. "What a good cop would do."

Gil's intelligent eyes fixed on her. "Yeah, that's what I think."

Kenzie only smiled at him. Bowman sank down on the other sofa, hiding his grimace of pain. He pretended to be relaxed, but he was ready to spring at any sign of danger.

Kenzie ran her hand along the sofa's muted brown fabric, taking comfort from it. She'd redone the living room not long ago, finding soft but sturdy furniture in the earthy colors she liked, adding splashes of bright red and deep blue in pillows and pictures for contrast. The two couches were chunky instead of elegant, but they had deep cushions and were oh so comfortable.

Bowman had declared he didn't like them, but the day after Kenzie had found them at the closeout store and had Cade haul them home in his truck, Bowman had fallen asleep on one, Ryan curled on his chest. Both males had been sleeping deeply. Kenzie had snapped some pictures. For blackmail, she'd told Bowman when she'd shown him the printed photos. He'd grown furious, chasing her and pinning her to snatch the pictures away, which had led to some of the best sex she'd ever had.

"So," Kenzie asked, giving Gil a warm smile. "What news do you have for us?"

Gil turned his body to include both Kenzie and Bowman in the conversation. Wise man. "I looked into Kenzie's idea that a truck had picked up the . . . whatever it was . . . and drove it out of there. There aren't any traffic cams in that remote an area, and satellite feed is iffy. But I was able to look at cameras at traffic lights in the towns around there. An eighteen-wheeler rolled through Asheville just after one in the morning, which was twenty minutes after you say the attack was over."

Bowman sat forward, adjusting his leg at the last minute so it would not bend too sharply. "You get a plate? Company the truck was from?"

Kenzie broke in. "Did it say 'We Move Monsters' on the side?"

Gil chuckled; Bowman scowled. "No such luck. I got a partial plate. The truck was black, both container and cab. Hard to see at night, but still distinctive. People remember glossy black eighteen-wheelers. Took me a while, but I think I found it. The owner has a trucking company in Raleigh, but when I contacted them, they said the truck had been stolen about a year ago. They already have the insurance money for it, and didn't care what happened to it, but they did give me the name of the last driver. I checked him out—he's dropped out of sight, but he did own property around here. I went up there to check it out. Found the truck, but no monster, as you probably guessed."

"Where?" Bowman asked, his eyes changing to white gray.

"Around Leicester, outside an old farm. Farm's been abandoned, but some of the buildings are intact."

Kenzie came alert as well. She and Bowman exchanged a long look, their earlier bantering over. The old farm near Leicester was where the Shifters of this Shiftertown held their fight club.

"We need to get up there," Kenzie said.

"Damn right." Bowman came off the sofa and was out the door before Kenzie could catch him.

CHAPTER TWELVE

Bowman had to concede to go out to the site in Ramirez's car. He'd started for his motorcycle, but his stiff leg, and Kenzie pointing out he hadn't quite finished healing, made him realize he couldn't drive himself. He turned around and ordered Gil to take them there.

He had to admit that Gil wasn't as annoying as most humans, and that fact irritated him. Gil had nodded at Bowman and unlocked his car without fuss or argument.

No one locked a car in Shiftertown, Bowman grumbled to himself as he climbed inside, hiding a grunt of pain. Did Gil think one of Bowman's Shifters was going to steal it? But Bowman knew, as he stretched out in the backseat, that he was deliberately finding fault. He didn't want to like Gil, because Kenzie's eyes softened whenever she looked at the man.

Kenzie rode in front beside Gil, talking in her friendly way as they headed out of Shiftertown into twilight. Bowman pretended to doze but kept a sharp eye on Gil.

He'd alerted Jamie before they left the house as to where they were going, and told him to be on standby. He'd talked to Jamie because Cade hadn't answered his phone. Bowman couldn't hear much of what Jamie said over the background noise of music and shouting, but he thought he heard something about "grizzlies tightrope walking." Fucking bears.

"Just don't let Ryan do it," Bowman had shouted.

"What?" Jamie had yelled back. "Oh, Ryan. No, he's fine. I'll keep him with me until you get back." *Click.* The party's noise had abruptly cut off.

Bowman let it go. He knew that his Shifters were partying hard tonight because they'd been scared shitless last night. Reaction was setting in, and they were letting off steam in the relative safety of Shiftertown, which was well-guarded— better guarded than humans knew.

Good thing it wasn't fight club night, since Gil was taking them up there. Shifters used fighting to let off tension as well, but the schedule for this fight club was rigid: once every two weeks, and that was it. Bowman knew the danger of letting it become a free-for-all, anytime-they-wanted-to-fight scene. Shifters needed boundaries, especially in this Shiftertown, where casual bouts could become clan wars.

Kenzie kept up pleasant chatter with Gil as they rode through hills and down into valleys where farms filled either side of the road. Gil talked easily, he and Kenzie behaving as though they were old friends. Bowman suppressed his irritation and remained silent.

The farm Gil drove to had been abandoned long ago, the owner neither bothering to sell the land nor continuing to farm it. Weeds had taken over the fields; the last crop had dried out and was yielding to fierce choking grasses. Sheds around the fields had fallen in, disintegrating on themselves.

The fight club had commandeered the larger, dilapidated barn, now just a flat floor with a large roof over it. Shifters had replaced rotting beams and timbers, shoring up the old place. Now, on fight club nights, it was a teeming arena, alive with Shifters, humans coming to watch and wager, adrenaline, laughter, and blood sport.

This evening, however, it was deserted and derelict. Gil stopped just below the arena, killing his lights.

Bowman got out, wincing when his leg straightened. Kenzie was beside him almost instantly. She'd ceased her teasing and stood at his shoulder, looking with him toward the ring.

An eighteen-wheeler was parked under the huge roof, its

black paint gleaming in the light of the flashlight lantern Gil carried. Bowman didn't need a flashlight to see it, and he didn't need any more evidence to tell him that the monster had been inside it. Its scent came to him loud and clear.

"Damn," Kenzie said softly. "That really stinks."

The smell triggered Bowman's memory of fighting the creature. Pain and rage mixed with fear flooded back to him, along with the adrenaline high that had gotten him into Cade's truck to ram the solid wall of flesh.

He shuddered, his fight-or-flight reaction too close to the surface. Kenzie put her hand on his arm, but he could feel that her fighting need was as wound up as his.

Gil stood beside them, his human scent making only a small dent in the monster's. "Stinks, yeah, but the truck is empty."

"I know," Bowman said. "The scent is strong, but it's not sharp. It hasn't been in there for hours."

Gil flashed his light around the growing darkness. "The question is, where did it go? I didn't feel like hunting for it by myself."

Smart of him. Bowman had no wish to encounter the thing again, but it was a danger, and he needed to deal with it. "I'll have to go wolf," he said.

"No, let me," Kenzie said quickly.

"No." Bowman turned to face her, catching her golden eyes in the dark. "I need you as backup."

Kenzie glared at him, and Bowman gazed steadily back at her, willing her not to argue. Kenzie's chest, under a tight sweatshirt and fleece-lined jacket, rose with her breath. Her eyes held wicked sparks that he loved, flashing in fear and anger. She was trying to protect him.

He wanted to kiss her right now. More than kiss her—he wanted to lean her back on the hood of the car and take her mouth, tasting her strength. He wanted this woman with his entire body, and with every thought he had, every day.

"All right," Kenzie said, still angry. "But if you break your leg again, don't come crying to me."

"I never cry."

Kenzie shrugged, but her body was stiff. "I know. You're the big, bad alpha. You just bitch and moan until we want to gag you."

Bowman let the fantasy of Kenzie tying him down and working a gag between his lips flit through his mind. Then he shoved it aside. He'd never get this problem solved if he didn't calm down.

Without another word, Bowman slid off his leather jacket and laid it on the hood of Gil's car. He didn't bother to find a place to hide or ask Gil to turn his back; he simply started shedding clothes.

Kenzie caught the shirt and T-shirt he threw off, making sure they got folded up all nice. She was like that, going domestic in the most incongruous places and making snide remarks about the messiness of males.

She also looked her fill as Bowman toed off his boots and slid out of his jeans and underwear, the cold air biting his ass. It was getting colder by the minute, but Kenzie's gaze dropping to his cock made his body roasting hot.

Gil was pretending to fix something on his flashlight, not looking at the stark-naked male next to him. Kenzie, on the other hand, didn't have a problem watching, a satisfied gleam in her eyes.

But enough. Time to finish this.

Bowman shifted as quickly as he could to wolf and dropped to all fours. The world took on the curves he saw in wolf form—at the same time, outlines were sharp, colors muted. His sense of smell nearly overwhelmed him, especially with leftover monster stink, and his pricked ears heard plenty in the darkness.

Kenzie's scent came to him even over the stronger smell, pure female goodness. Gil Ramirez contained the too-salty scent of human, overlaid with a subtler scent Bowman couldn't place.

Hmm. He didn't have time at the moment to find out what was up with that, but he realized that Gil was more than he seemed.

Scents of the night—air, cold, coming snow, small sleeping animals—were hideously tainted by whatever had been in that truck. Bowman's nose wrinkled, and he couldn't stop his growl.

"I know." Kenzie's voice, though she spoke softly, was loud to his sensitive ears. "It's awful."

Everything inside Bowman didn't want to approach the

truck, but he knew he had to hunt this threat. Noiselessly, he padded toward the eighteen-wheeler, leaving the light and Kenzie behind.

The truck waited, inert, its polished black glinting where Gil's flashlight brushed it. The truck was an inanimate object, Bowman knew, but it seemed to crouch in the shadows as though lying in wait.

Bowman heard Kenzie coming behind him, ignoring Gil's admonition to be careful. Kenzie knew what she was doing. He padded into the arena, pausing at the edge to listen, sniff, assess.

No one was in or around the truck. His nose told him that. Whoever the human driver or drivers had been, they were long gone. The beast wasn't in it either. So why was Bowman so reluctant to go any closer?

He shut off every human thought running through his head and let himself be guided by instinct alone. That didn't work well, though, because every instinct of his wolf told him to leave that truck the hell alone. Take Kenzie, take Ryan, leave the area, and hole up in a wild place with them, and to hell with the human world.

The weight of his Collar around his neck stopped him. There were no wild spaces for them anymore. They had to try to make it in captivity, to build strength until the time was right for them to be free again. That was the whole point of agreeing to move to Shiftertowns.

The Collar, however, sparked once as Bowman forced his wolf feet forward. It sensed his rising need to fight.

The truck loomed. Bowman made himself sniff its perimeter, but that told him nothing new.

He sat down, waiting for the other two, and looked up at Kenzie when she stopped beside him, her hip pressing his flank. The intimacy and peace of simply touching her flowed into him, quieting the sparks in his Collar, the jangle of his nerves. She stroked the top of Bowman's head, giving him a nod of understanding.

When they'd first become mated, Bowman had told Kenzie never to pet him when he was in wolf form. He wasn't a frigging dog.

So Kenzie, of course, made sure to pet his head at least

once every time he went wolf. She did it again now, smoothing between his ears, scratching behind them. He'd never, ever tell her how much he liked that.

"We need to open it up," Kenzie said to Gil.

She stroked Bowman's head one more time before she joined Gil, who had thoughtfully brought along a large set of bolt cutters.

Gil, who had the advantage of a weaker sense of smell, went right up to the truck. Bowman knew he could smell just fine, though, because he said, "Sheew," as he broke open the door.

The stench that wafted out made all three of them back up rapidly. The monster wasn't inside, but there was no doubt it had been confined in the truck for some time. It had done what all animals do, judging from the wetness on the floor—repeatedly.

"Wait," Kenzie said. She put her hand on Gil's arm, a familiar gesture that any other time might have made Bowman slam Gil into the nearest wall. "Flash the light in the corner again."

Gil, happy to oblige, did. "Is that blood?"

"Sure is," Kenzie said. "Kind of a lot of it."

"Did it kill someone?" Gil asked. His dark face had gone a shade lighter, and the lantern swayed.

"I don't think so," Kenzie answered. "I'm willing to bet that blood belongs to the monster. Bowman must have hurt it more than he thought."

Bowman caught the scent, distinct from the other disgusting odors. Blood, sharp and acrid. Bowman turned his head, a new breeze bringing the exact same scent from a point beyond the arena.

Bowman growled to Kenzie, came to his feet already moving, and loped out into the cold darkness.

CHAPTER THIRTEEN

Kenzie followed Bowman at a rapid pace, Gil's light bobbing along behind her. She knew Bowman was following a new scent, but her human senses weren't honed enough to catch it.

Was the monster out there? Waiting? Was its blood and piss in the truck bait for Bowman to follow? Pretending to be hurt so he'd walk right into it?

Kenzie shivered, from both dread and the drop in temperature. The night was growing rapidly colder.

She couldn't see Bowman anymore, and a quiet call to him produced nothing. He'd disappeared, keeping silent to better hunt.

Kenzie stopped so quickly that Gil almost ran into her.

"You all right?" he asked, his warm eyes holding concern. Gil wasn't very tall, even for a human, being an inch shorter than Kenzie. But his body held strength, his shoulders wide, muscles as powerful as any Shifter's.

"I'm going to have to go wolf." Kenzie dug cold fingers into her pocket and pulled out her cell phone, scrolling through it. "If anything goes wrong, if we have to fight, call this number. This is Jamie, Bowman's top tracker." Her cell phone was a few years old and refurbished—Shifters were not allowed the latest state-of-the-art smartphones. Phone technology changed so rapidly, though, that a phone from even a few years ago had more bells and whistles than Kenzie ever used.

"Are you sure?" Gil said, taking the phone. "About shifting, I mean."

"I need to be able to help Bowman at a second's notice. Don't call Jamie unless we're really in trouble, though. I don't want all of Shiftertown out here because Bowman spotted a rabbit."

The fact that no snarl came out of the darkness at that remark worried her. Bowman was either keeping quiet because he was sneaking up on something, or something had happened to him.

"Do you have a gun?" Kenzie asked, sliding off her boots. The ground was burning cold beneath her stocking feet.

"Yes," Gil said without reaching for it. "But do you think a pistol will do any good against something that can fill a semitruck?"

Kenzie shot him a smile. "Can't hurt."

Gil returned her grin, the expression lighting his face. "Glad I met you, Shifter woman."

"Same here, human cop." She put her hands on her hips. "Will you turn your back, please? Bowman's happy to strip in front of the Goddess and everyone, but I'm a little more modest."

Gil's smile widened, but he turned around, presenting a strong back under a leather coat. "You know I won't peek. Your mate would tear out my throat if I did. I picked that up from him. He wouldn't even stop to ask questions."

"Probably," Kenzie said in all seriousness. She slid out of her clothes, moving quickly so she had to shiver only a few seconds before her warm fur hugged her, and she shook herself out.

Her growl had Gil turning around again, flashing the light in her face. She winced and blinked, sending him a snarl.

"Oh, sorry. Hey, you look good."

Gil gave her an admiring glance, taking in her wolf. Kenzie's fur was dark, streaked with a tawny brown, her eyes bright gold in contrast to the gray eyes of Bowman and his clan. She was larger than but strongly resembled the wild wolves that had traversed Romania and the Transylvanian mountains where she'd lived as a cub. Kenzie always suspected that the Fae had used Transylvanian wolves as breeding stock for the first Lupines.

She'd also long suspected that Romanian Shifters had inspired the story of the shape-shifting, bloodsucking Vlad Dracul. Likely Uncle Cristian had inspired the tales specifically. He'd been around when the first vampire stories had started gaining popularity.

Kenzie gave Gil another low growl, trying to convey that he should stay close but quiet, and trotted in the direction Bowman had taken. She put enough distance between herself and Gil that his lantern wouldn't night-blind her, but went slowly enough that he wouldn't lose her.

The stink of the creature blanketed the land, but she found Bowman's trail winding like a warm ribbon through it. She inhaled the scent of his passing, trying to blot out the sickening stench that overlaid it. *Find Bowman,* she told herself. *Focus only on him.*

Kenzie made her way up a steeper hill and back into deep woods, leaving the farmlands behind. It was harder going up here, and she heard Gil panting behind her.

The stench grew until it finally erased all scent of Bowman. Didn't matter—Bowman was tracking that smell, and all Kenzie had to do was follow it.

She came across Bowman so suddenly she almost ran into him. Kenzie swerved at the last minute and halted next to him, her paws skidding on the cold, loose dirt.

That same dirt fell over a cliff into the river canyon this hill had been rising toward. Kenzie couldn't make out the bottom in the dark, but the stink that blasted from it sent her back on her haunches. She snorted and shook her head, trying to get the smell out of her nostrils.

She couldn't. Kenzie shifted back to human so fast her muscles protested, and she made a muffled noise of pain as she straightened to her full height. But at least now she could clap her hand over her nose.

How Bowman could simply sit there in that wave of smell, she couldn't fathom. He stared downward, unmoving. There was no moon tonight, clouds blotting out all light, but Gil's lantern glistened on Bowman's fur, ruffled by the rising wind.

Gil came up next to Kenzie, carefully not looking at her nakedness. "Holy—" He broke off and coughed. "Holy shit."

"My thoughts exactly," Kenzie said, still holding her nose. Ryan would have laughed at the nasally sound of her words.

"Is that thing dead down there?"

Kenzie glanced at Bowman. He never looked at her as he crouched low on his limbs and started climbing down the side of the ravine.

Kenzie breathed through her mouth as she lowered her hand. "Crap, I do *not* want to do this."

"Then don't," Gil said quickly. "Stay up here, and he'll tell us what he finds."

"Can't," she said, still sounding as though she had a bad cold. "He might need backup."

Gil glanced over the edge, then back at Kenzie, again keeping his gaze on her face. "You're one brave woman, Kenzie O'Donnell."

"That's what Bowman says. Well, when he's not saying, *What the hell do you think you're doing?*" She touched Gil's arm, first to send him gratitude and second to see if she could sense whether he was up to something. She couldn't tell. "Stay here. If I howl, you dial that cell phone."

"Yes, ma'am," Gil said.

Kenzie shifted, more slowly this time. She embraced the fur that warmed her body, but gagged on the punch of smell, which came to her with renewed strength.

Heaving a wolf sigh, she started downward, following her mate, using the footprints Bowman had left to guide her.

It was dead all right. Bowman shifted back to human and waited for Kenzie to catch up. She stayed wolf, but sat on her haunches and let out a whine.

The beast that had attacked the roadhouse sprawled on the only flat stretch of ground next to the cold, rushing river. In the darkness it was difficult to say exactly what it was even now.

Bowman's wolf sight had shown him fur, with enormous bearlike paws, but there was definitely something snakelike about its body, and *that* might be the stump of a wing. Bowman hadn't seen any wings when he'd been fighting it at the roadhouse, but he'd been busy, there hadn't been much light, and a stumpy wing didn't mean the monster could fly.

Bowman put his hand on Kenzie's head, drawing comfort from her presence. She always came to his side. Always.

The crashing and banging behind them meant Gil was coming down. His lantern flashed, showing that the wing stump had some feathering on it. Gil stopped, breathing hard, next to Bowman.

"Damn." The man shone the flashlight around, its thick beam cutting the darkness. "That is one ugly, stinking mo fo. You sure it's dead?"

"Looks dead. Smells dead." Bowman nudged the hairy paw with his bare foot. "Yep. Dead."

"What the hell *is* it?"

"I don't know," Bowman said. He didn't like not knowing. All kinds of dangerous shit happened from not knowing.

"Did you kill it?" Gil asked. "When you hit it with the truck, I mean. Injure it beyond recovery?"

"I don't think so." Bowman remembered the beast crashing into the windshield, and the truck's roof coming down on him. "It ran off, but it wasn't that hurt. Something else happened."

"The truck's driver maybe," Gil said. "Or whoever hired him. Its work was done, so they finished it off?"

Bowman shook his head. "Why bother to create, or find and trap, a huge, terrifying creature only to kill it? I'd doctor its injuries and keep it to fight another day."

"Yeah, me too," Gil said. "I'd love to know what it is and what killed it, though. I'd call my local medical examiner, but I think the guy would have a coronary if he came out here and saw this."

"We need to study it," Bowman said. "Find out everything we can. If not a human coroner, how about a veterinarian?"

"Hmm." Gil pursed his lips. "You know one with a strong stomach?"

"I have one in mind," Bowman said. "Let's get up the hill, and I'll give her a call."

He felt Kenzie move, and looked down to see her glaring up at him. He hid his amusement. He liked that Kenzie grew jealous sometimes, because it meant she wanted him around. Indifference would have been much harder to bear.

Didn't mean he couldn't tease her about it, though. Teasing Kenzie was just too damn much fun.

"Oh my God," Dr. Pat said. She had her hands over her nose, her eyes watering, as she looked at the body in the narrow canyon.

It was the next morning, the sun was high enough to filter down to the river bottom, and everyone at the site was dressed. Dr. Pat had agreed, when Bowman had called her, to come out and take a look at the dead animal, but said she couldn't possibly get there until morning. Therefore Kenzie, Bowman, and Gil had spent an uncomfortable night in Gil's car, pulled up close enough to the ravine so they could watch to see if anyone came for the creature.

At least, Kenzie had been uncomfortable, and now her eyes felt sandy, her muscles aching. Bowman, stretched out in the backseat because of his healing injury, had dropped off into peaceful sleep. Or at least, he'd pretended to.

Bowman hadn't even suggested that Kenzie go home to a soft bed. She wouldn't leave him, not when he was still hurt, and he knew it, not even if they summoned Cade or Jamie to reprieve her. And neither of them fully trusted Gil yet. So Kenzie stayed.

She called Ryan before they settled in and told him to stay with Cade, which Ryan had no problem with. He was getting to be of an age when having friends and fun was more important than clinging to his parents. He'd sounded worried though— about them, not himself. Ryan was also old enough to realize that his mom and dad did a dangerous job.

Gil proved to be a good conversationalist as the night lengthened. He was well-read and intelligent, and knew many things. Not from education, he said. He'd never been to college. He just liked to read . . . everything. He wrote a little too, he said modestly. Nothing anyone would know.

He had way too good of an attitude, Kenzie thought. Sitting up all night babysitting an oversized corpse, waiting for the vet or maybe a villain to show up, didn't faze him. Gil had plenty of topics at the ready to discuss, but he knew when to let Kenzie doze. She awoke in the morning to find him humming a tune in his throat, tapping his fingers on the steering wheel. He couldn't have slept much, but he looked refreshed.

Bowman also looked rested and energetic. He swung himself out of the car at dawn as though he were healed and as supple as ever. Kenzie felt hungover and exhausted, her eyes aching, and she could murder for some coffee.

Dr. Pat arrived shortly after daybreak in a trim white SUV that went with her chirpy personality. Kenzie softened toward the woman a little when Dr. Pat leaned into the passenger side and withdrew a cardboard carrier holding four cups of steaming coffee. Good, expensive coffee, a rich roast whose scent tickled Kenzie's nose and promised wonderful things.

The smell and taste of the coffee as Kenzie drank almost blotted out the decaying smell of the creature. But not quite. Nothing would wipe that out except time.

After they fortified themselves with coffee, the four climbed down the hill to where the creature lay. Kenzie held her breath against the stench; Dr. Pat's eyes were streaming. The males of the group pretended to be able to stomach it, but Kenzie knew better.

"What the hell is it?" Dr. Pat asked.

"We were hoping you could tell us," Bowman said. "Take your time; I know it's bad. If you need to go back up, that's fine."

Dr. Pat shook her head, and Kenzie's estimation of her rose some more. She wasn't a wuss, that was for sure.

When Dr. Pat took another step toward the body, her foot slipped. Two male hands quickly caught her, steadying her on the muddy ground. Dr. Pat gave both Gil and Bowman a pretty and grateful smile.

Kenzie rolled her eyes. *Dear Goddess, save me from all this testosterone.*

She folded her arms while Bowman and Gil helped Dr. Pat move on the slippery ground toward the creature. The woman stopped a few feet from the thing, wiped her eyes, and looked it over.

Its lower body was definitely lion, or at least Feline, but the rest was like nothing Kenzie had ever seen. The big cat body changed abruptly in the middle to something reptilian, and what looked like the remains of a feathery wing poked out of its back.

Then came the head, a mishmash of lion, wolf, and something eagle-like. Its open mouth showed rows of giant, very sharp teeth. The wide, staring eyes had filmed over, but they were protruding and red.

"Huh," Gil said. "Don't tell me we've taken down Godzilla."

"No." Dr. Pat lifted her hands from her mouth. She looked green and sick, but her eyes were alight with interest. "It's not from the movies; it's from mythology. I think this is a griffin."

CHAPTER FOURTEEN

Bowman stared at Dr. Pat, then at the animal, then up at Kenzie, as though she would have the answer. "What the hell's a griffin?"

Kenzie answered him, proving she *did* know. "A griffin is half lion, half eagle. A mythical beast with origin stories from Persia, Turkey, and Greece. Used in heraldry in Europe beginning in the middle ages." She frowned as she studied it again. "This thing doesn't look exactly like the pictures I've seen. It's as though someone threw in a dragon on top of it."

Dr. Pat nodded gravely. "True, but I've never met a mythical beast before, so I'm not going to argue with it."

Bowman fixed Kenzie with a sharp look. "How the hell do you know all that?"

"Books," Kenzie said without inflection. "Ryan likes fantasy."

His brows slammed together. "Ryan reads about fantasies?"

"Fantasy," Kenzie said, pronouncing it carefully. "As in *Lord of the Rings* and the *Chronicles of Narnia.* Ryan liked Narnia a lot when he was younger. Now he's into the *Dresden Files* and the *Iron Druid Chronicles.*"

Bowman kept scowling as he processed the information. Kenzie raised her brows at Bowman until he turned away and resumed his study of the animal.

Gil had taken out his cell phone to snap pictures. "Cool. A real live mythological beast that shouldn't exist."

"But it does exist," Bowman said, his voice going quiet. "The questions are how? And why?"

"And who created it?" Kenzie asked, her voice also controlled. "This didn't spring up naturally."

Bowman put his hands on his hips, closed his eyes, and took a long sniff. Dr. Pat and Gil both stared at him, amazed that he'd want a deeper smell of the thing, but Kenzie knew what he was doing.

After a time, Bowman opened his eyes, glanced at Kenzie, and shook his head.

No smell of Faerie, he meant. The beast had been born here, in this world. Interesting.

"Now what?" Gil asked.

"Now you send me copies of the pictures you took," Bowman said. "And we burn the body."

Gil stared. "You're kidding, right? That could take days."

"Then it takes days. If someone did breed this thing, I don't want them coming back for it. Harvesting DNA and whatever."

"They might have already," Kenzie pointed out.

"I'd like to," Dr. Pat said. "Take some tissue samples, I mean; do as much of a postmortem here as I can. I might be able to find out its origin." She reached into her pocket and slid out test tubes and latex gloves. "But you guys might have to do a few things for me. I'm not sure how much more of this I can stand." She beamed a wide smile at Gil, and then Bowman.

Gil said, "Sure," very quickly and grabbed a test tube. Bowman took a second one and gave Pat a reassuring nod.

Oh, for the Goddess's sake. The two men moved to do as Dr. Pat dictated, while the woman gave orders like a head surgeon, or a little queen. All three were oblivious to Kenzie's scrutiny.

At least she brought coffee, Kenzie thought. *Otherwise, I'd have to kill her.*

* * *

"A griffin," Cade said, heavily skeptical.
   "Seriously?" Ryan asked. "Awesome."
   They sat around the kitchen table at home, Cade's elbows on the table while he sipped coffee. Bowman lounged in a chair next to Cade's, looking relaxed while keeping an eye on everyone in the house.
   Gil and Dr. Pat both had to return to their day jobs, each disappointed they couldn't stay for the discussion. Gil had placed a friendly hand on Kenzie's shoulder before he left, smiling into her eyes. He made Kenzie feel warm, safe—an odd sensation from a human.
   Bowman had observed all, eyes glittering. Kenzie thought he'd retaliate by kissing Dr. Pat on the cheek or something, but Bowman only told her good-bye and thanked her for her help.
   Anyone would think he'd kissed her, though, from Dr. Pat's flush and little smile. She'd go all groupie on him any moment now.
   Bowman caught Kenzie's eye as she sat down with more coffee, the heat in his glance unmistakable. Kenzie pretended to ignore him.
   Jamie was cooking a mess of eggs, bacon, potatoes, and some kind of sauce, all mixed together. Kenzie hadn't had any yet, but it smelled wonderful. She was enjoying the clean scents of food, coffee, her home, and her mate and cub, all the more precious after the horrible stench of the creature.
   "The problem is," Cade said, his huge hands around his coffee mug, "griffins don't exist."
   "So everyone keeps telling me," Bowman said.
   "Do we *have* to burn it?" Ryan asked. "Can I see it?"
   "No!" Kenzie and Bowman said at the same time.
   Ryan gave a small wolf growl, but he subsided.
   Bowman had left trusted Shifters to guard the fallen creature and start piling fuel around it, and then summoned Cade and Jamie to this meeting. Ryan had insisted on joining in, and Kenzie hadn't stopped him. Ryan had a right to know what was going on. That didn't mean she wanted Ryan standing next to the creature from hell and sucking in its sickening odor.
   Jamie shoveled things onto plates and carried two over.

Bowman got served first, because he was leader. Instead of eating, Bowman picked up the plate Jamie gave him and passed it to Kenzie. He lifted the second one Jamie put in front of him and slid it to his son.

Ryan, used to the ritual, grabbed his fork and dug in.

Jamie brought more plates, putting yet another one in front of Bowman. It was Bowman's choice, in his house, who got the food first. Bowman handed the plate to Cade, and finally took one for himself.

"I take it you think that thing wasn't natural-born?" Jamie asked, returning to the stove for his share.

"How could it be?" Kenzie asked. She forked up a mouthful of Jamie's cooking, savoring the myriad flavors. "What would naturally be a mishmash of three and more animals? All of them giant-sized?"

"Shifter," Cade said in his rumbling voice. "A screwed-up one."

Bowman swallowed the large amount of food he'd shoved into his mouth. "The knowledge of how to make Shifters is a secret known only to the Fae. The humans tried it, remember? They came up with Tiger, but it didn't work right. Besides, all that research got blown up."

"And Tiger's a little different from most Shifters," Kenzie said. "When he's on rescue missions, he can sometimes see numbers in front of his eyes, coordinates that tell him where to go. Somehow."

Bowman fixed her with a look. "How the hell do you know that?"

Kenzie shrugged, lifting her coffee. "I talk to people. They tell me things."

Bowman growled softly, but let it go. "This thing wasn't anything like Tiger. Whoever came up with it wasn't trying to create a Shifter; they were creating something to destroy Shifters."

"Because it attacked us?" Kenzie traced the letters on her coffee mug—"World's Greatest Mom." "How do you know it was targeting Shifters, in particular? There were plenty of humans at the roadhouse that night."

Cade broke in. "But half of Shiftertown was there too.

Everyone knows we like the place. And they took the thing back to where we hold the fight club."

"True," Kenzie said thoughtfully. "Or maybe it was a test run, to see if it could stand against Shifters."

"Or if Shifters could stand against it," Bowman finished. "Notice which residents of Shiftertown *weren't* there that night?"

"Dimitru pack," Jamie said at once. "Bastards. No offense, Kenzie."

"None taken," Kenzie said mildly. As she'd told Uncle Cristian, she didn't consider herself Dimitru pack anymore. Bowman and Ryan were her pack now, all she wanted.

Jamie finally sat down and started eating. "So, Bowman, are you thinking Kenzie's uncle Cristian found a way to breed a crazy animal strong enough to kill off half the Shifters? Would he do that?"

"Are you kidding?" Kenzie asked. "He would totally do that. The question isn't would he, but could he?"

"One way to find out," Bowman said, pushing aside his empty plate and rising.

Kenzie jumped up in alarm and went to him. "Don't even think about charging over to Uncle Cristian's and challenging him this morning."

Bowman turned a cold gaze on her. "I'm not going to think about it. I'm just going to do it."

Kenzie put herself in front of him as he started for the door. "You don't have any evidence. If you take him out without proof he did anything, you violate pack law. The others won't let you get away with that."

Bowman faced her. "I'll have the evidence when I beat it out of him." His eyes were crystalline in the morning light, white gray and unyielding. "I'm not going to rush in and kill him, Kenz. I'll ask him first."

"He's not a pushover. He'll use any excuse to topple you."

Bowman's eyes went whiter still. "You think he can beat me?"

"I think he's treacherous enough to find a way."

Bowman held her gaze, his fury burning her. She wanted to latch on to him, tell him to stay home and be safe, to wrap her arms around him and hold him close.

"Come with me then," Bowman said. "Keep an eye on your uncle for me while I'm beating the crap out of him."

Before Kenzie could answer, Ryan got up and came to them. He was half his father's height now, and while he was still on the slim side, he had plenty of wiry strength.

"You need *me* to come with you too," Ryan declared. "Before you yell at me and say no, you know it's true. I can butter up Uncle Cristian to tell us what he knows. I'm not only his bloodline—I'm also a very cute little cub."

Cade roared a sudden laugh that rattled the pots hanging in the kitchen, and Jamie chuckled. "He's got you there, Bowman," Cade said in his booming voice. "Kid, you're going to make one hell of a pack leader someday."

Bowman agreed, Kenzie could tell. He cast his glare all around, but Kenzie saw the flash of pride in his eyes before he slammed out of the house. Kenzie and Ryan snatched their coats from the hooks in the hall and followed.

C ristian Dimitru made his accent extra thick as he faced Bowman. "What you saying? I make . . . what? Griffin—what does this mean?"

Asshole, Bowman growled to himself. Cristian, the shithead, spoke perfect English. But he liked to mess with Bowman, especially when he didn't want to answer questions.

"It's a cool animal from mythology, Uncle Cris," Ryan said. He sounded more childlike than usual, and Bowman narrowed his eyes. Ryan's cunning came directly from his Dimitru blood. "Dad would only let me see a photo of it, but it was humongous."

Cristian's gaze sharpened as he looked at Bowman. "You let your cub see it?"

Kenzie broke in smoothly. "He deserves to know about any threat to Shifters." She was tense, Bowman saw, though she stood easily and looked Cristian in the eye.

"Show it to me," Cristian said.

Kenzie put her hand into her coat pocket and removed the photos she'd printed. Gil had e-mailed them to Bowman as promised, the e-mails arriving as Jamie cooked, and Kenzie had printed them out. She didn't have any photo paper, only plain, so they were gray scale and not very good. But there was enough detail to prove the creature had existed.

Cristian flipped through them. "Where is this thing now?" His accent had mostly gone.

"On a pyre," Bowman answered. "Ready to be sent to the Goddess."

"I want to see it first."

"Why?" Bowman resisted jerking the pages out of Cristian's hands. "So you can make sure it's dead? Make sure I can never tie it to you?"

Cristian gave him an annoyed look. "I'm flattered you think me skilled enough to breed a mythological beast. Do you have any other theories, or did you decide I alone should take the blame for it?"

Bowman didn't answer. He had plenty of ideas about the beast spinning through his head. Cristian breeding it, or causing it to be bred, or knowing who had done it, was only one. He'd come here to cross this theory off his list and move on to the next idea. Or use it as an excuse to kill Cristian. Whatever.

"If I look at it, maybe I can tell where it came from," Cristian said. "It isn't Fae?"

"No smell of Faerie," Bowman said. Anything from Faerie had a distinctive odor—a hint of sulfur and otherworldly fire. The griffin had only smelled like a very large, very stinky, very dead animal.

Cristian handed the photos back to Kenzie. "The thing about griffins," he said to Bowman, "the thing you might not know about, is they always come in pairs. They mate for life, so it is said. So the question is, O'Donnell—where is the other one?"

CHAPTER FIFTEEN

Kenzie did not want Ryan coming with them to the site, but Bowman decided he could, to his son's delight. Ryan needed to know the bad and the ugly about being Shifter leader, needed to understand the responsibilities, even when they weren't pretty.

They took Cristian's car, but Kenzie drove. Best thing. Bowman didn't trust Cristian not to try to wreck the car and make sure Bowman was in the part that smashed, maybe letting Ryan be badly hurt too. Then Cristian could pretend he was helping Ryan heal, maybe adopting him to raise him in Bowman's place.

Then again, Bowman didn't trust *himself* not to give the car a burst of speed along a lonely stretch of highway and push Cristian out the door. Kenzie driving was the best solution.

They arrived at the creature's final resting place within the hour. Branches had been piled around the dead beast, the underbrush cleared, so they could burn the thing without torching the entire woods. From somewhere—the Goddess knew where—Cade had driven in a water truck, ready to pump water over the fire when it was done. Cade had many human friends, and he somehow got them to do him all kinds of favors.

Cristian scrambled down to the pyre, put his hands on his hips, and gazed at the beast. It looked pathetic now, waiting to be sent to the Goddess and the Summerland, but Bowman remembered all its tonnage charging at him, ready to kill.

"How did it die?" Cristian asked. "You killed it?" He shot a look at Bowman.

"We don't know," Kenzie said, before Bowman could take credit. "We hurt it, and it might have died of its injuries."

"Or its master might have put it down," Cristian said. "Maybe up in the arena, and it made it this far before it died."

"Why didn't its master chase it, then?" Bowman asked. "Or get rid of the body?"

Cristian shrugged. "Who knows? Have you found the driver of the truck?"

"Working on it," Bowman snapped. He hated how Cristian could stand around and do nothing, and at the same time imply that Bowman was slow and incompetent. Undermining him at every turn.

"I would question him," Cristian finished.

"Well, no shit," Bowman said, resisting the urge to punch him. One day he wouldn't resist, and that would feel *good*.

Cade had started a small fire with tinder at one end of the pile. At Bowman's nod, he fanned it to life, and a flame went up.

At first, the fire only crackled a little, but then the pyre caught. The fire zoomed around the tinder, staying confined, and caught the body.

Shifters were adept at building funeral pyres. They never buried one of their own; Shifter souls were released to the Summerland by the Guardian. Every Guardian had a sword that had been made centuries before by a Shifter swordsmith and his Fae mate. The two of them had woven spells into the swords so that, when the blade was thrust through the heart of a dying or dead Shifter, the spells released the soul and rendered the body dust.

The swords had passed down through the generations, one for each clan. In the old days, however, whenever the clan's Guardian was too far away, Shifters had burned their dead, which in theory also allowed the soul to reach the Summerland.

A Shifter soul lingering near its body was susceptible to capture, so the legends went, and torment. No Shifter wanted that for his father, mother, son, daughter, brother, sister, best friend, pack mate. Even this ferocious beast didn't deserve that. The Guardian was present today, but where the thing's heart was, and whether the sword would work on it, was anybody's guess. The fire would have to do.

The Shifters stepped back as the pyre burned, ceasing their shouting, growling, snarling, and talking. Even Cristian became quiet.

Bowman stepped close to Kenzie. They gathered Ryan against them, the fire warming the frigid air. Bowman heard Kenzie's whispered prayer to the Goddess as the flames consumed the beast.

He liked the feeling of Kenzie's shoulder against his, her strength answering his strength. Bowman was still weak after the fight and his broken leg—not that he'd admit it—but Kenzie being next to him made all the difference.

The fire burned a long time, but the Shifters watched. The beast had been their enemy, but it had been out of place in this world, like the Shifters, and the least they could do was send it off with respect.

"Dad," Ryan whispered, breaking the trance-like silence. "Who's that?"

He pointed. A woman stood well back from the ring of Shifters, watching them. She was covered with a bulky jacket and wore a knit hat, but Bowman recognized her. She was the pseudo-groupie who'd been at the roadhouse two nights ago, the one Bowman had scared off by daring her to go down on him.

Bowman broke from Ryan and Kenzie and strode toward her. She saw him coming and, of course, tried to run.

No human woman, especially not one hampered by a padded jacket and thick boots, could outrun Bowman. She had a head start, but he grabbed her at the top of the hill and barreled on with her until they reached the arena. Jamie had driven away the abandoned semitruck, hiding it in a place he said was safe. The arena was empty now, and Bowman swung the woman around in the middle of it.

"Who the hell are you, and what are you doing spying on Shifters?"

"I'm not spying," she said, her voice shrill.

"What else do you call following Shifters around and watching what they do?"

Kenzie jogged into the arena, and after her, Goddess damn him, was Cristian.

"I just like Shifters, all right?" the woman said, her fear breaking through her defiance.

"You tried that one already," Bowman snapped. "Didn't work the last time."

She tried to wrench away from him. "Yeah, when you practically stripped in front of me."

"And if you'd been a groupie, you'd have had your hands on my cock so fast it wouldn't have been funny. You failed that test."

"I didn't touch you, because I knew you were mated." The woman looked past him to Kenzie, now a few feet behind Bowman.

"Bullshit," he said. "Groupies don't care. They just want the sex."

"All right. All right. So I'm not a groupie. Doesn't matter. I have every right to be walking around these woods, and you have no right to stop me."

Bowman leaned close to her. The woman tried to look everywhere but at his eyes, but Bowman locked her gaze to his. "I'm leader of this Shiftertown. That means I deal with whatever threat I see to any Shifters in it. You, sweetheart, are a threat."

"What's your name?" Kenzie asked her.

Bowman felt the woman tighten. She wanted to glance at Kenzie, but she couldn't look away from Bowman. "Answer her," Bowman said.

"Serena." The woman swallowed. "I'm a reporter, like you said. I'm doing a piece—on Shifter groupies."

"She is lying," Cristian said. "I scent it, and so do you."

Serena's eyes widened. They were brown eyes, with a touch of green, her hair light brown under the cap. Her face was narrow, her nose sharp, and she wasn't very old. Maybe early twenties, as humans figured things. Still a cub, by Shifter standards.

"No, really," Serena said quickly. "I am doing a piece on Shifters. On all aspects of Shifter life."

"Including following them into the woods to watch one of their religious rituals?" Bowman demanded.

"Absolutely." Serena grew more confident. "Plus, I saw what you were fighting that night. I drove off, but I came back, and saw . . . What was it?"

"We don't know," Kenzie said before Cristian could volunteer any information. Not that he was about to. Cristian disliked humans even more than he disliked Bowman.

Serena sniffled, her nose red and raw from the cold and smoke. "A Shifter? I couldn't make it out, but it was big. One of the bears?"

Her curiosity grated on Bowman's nerves. The young woman could be a danger, or she might not be anything more than a college girl trying to write her way into her first job.

"We don't know," Kenzie repeated. "Bowman." Her voice held the gentling note that meant she knew Bowman was barely controlling himself. "Let her go."

"Only if she walks the hell out of here and doesn't come back." Bowman gave the woman a shake. "I don't want to see you around Shifters anymore, sweetheart. It's dangerous."

"For me?" Serena backed a step as Bowman released her. "Or for you?"

Bowman growled at her. "Just go."

Serena backed a couple more steps then, apparently deciding not to test her luck, turned and ran. She made for one of the cars in the lot, sprang inside it, started it up, and drove off, churning mud in her haste.

Down the hill, the fire burned, and flakes of pristine snow fluttered down to die with a hiss in the flames.

Kenzie waited with Ryan, catching snowflakes in their gloved hands, for Bowman to finish giving orders so she could take him and their son home.

She was aware, even as she kept Ryan occupied, that all this was rattling her mate. Bowman didn't like it when he didn't know what was going on. Uncertainty made him hard and angry.

She heard him barking orders, and the Shifters, knowing he was in a foul mood, simply said, "Yes, sir." No arguing, no bantering.

Bowman ordered a contingent of Shifters, including the Guardian—Pierce Daniels, a Feline Shifter—to remain and finish the cremation, including burying the ashes. Pierce was also ordered to use his resources as a Guardian to find out

everything he could about the human woman named Serena.
Cade and Jamie he put on investigating the truck and driver
and figuring out where the hell that monster had originated.

"Kenzie," Bowman said, walking toward her, still in his
hard-ass mode. "I want you to find out as much as you can
about Gil Ramirez. Who he is, what he is, why he's so interested in Shifters."

Gil had already explained his interest, sort of, but Kenzie
understood. Something was off about Gil. "What do you mean
what he is?" she asked. "He's human. Isn't he?"

Bowman pinned her with a white gray stare. "I don't like
the way he smells."

Kenzie shot him a sly smile. "You can be pretty rank yourself."

Bowman didn't smile back, her teasing bringing a hard
glitter to his eyes. "You know what I mean. He's more than
what he's saying. Get him to tell you."

"How am I supposed to do that?"

Ryan made a huffing noise. "He means flirt with him,
Mom. Make him trust you. Giggle at him if you have to. I've
heard you do it when you're trying to make Dad jealous."

Bowman put a hand on Ryan's head. "That's enough from
you, cub. Don't sass your mother."

"I'm not sassing. Everyone knows you and Mom are trying
to find out if the other is going to run off first chance to find a
mate bond with someone else. The whole Shiftertown knows
it. I don't know why you think it's such a secret."

Ryan ducked out from under his father's hand and ran off
toward the arena, where Shifters were organizing the pumps
on the water truck to hose down the floor.

"Shit," Bowman said, watching him go.

"You can be kind of obvious," Kenzie said. "Trying to see if
I'll care if you pay attention to other women. Like you did with
Dr. Pat, and Serena in the roadhouse parking lot."

Bowman jerked his head around to focus on Kenzie, his
face, which had been lined with exhaustion, becoming less
tired-looking. "I knew you were out there. I wouldn't have
done that if you hadn't been."

Kenzie remembered him sliding down his jeans, the parking lot lights outlining every perfect inch of him. "I know. That's
what I mean."

Bowman somehow was standing closer. "It wasn't for *her*. It was for you."

Kenzie's heart beat faster, her blood heating until the cold around her faded. "You mean you wanted *me* to walk across that parking lot and go down on you?"

Bowman's hint of smile made her burn. "Wouldn't have minded."

Kenzie was aware of him with every cell in her body. She pictured herself completing what she'd wanted to do that night, sliding down him until she was on her knees in front of his thighs. She'd look him over, then lean forward and take the length of his cock into her mouth. She knew exactly what he tasted like, and never grew tired of it.

She wanted to do it right now. Here, in the freezing cold, with snow falling and Shifters striding every which way to carry out Bowman's commands. She wanted to feel the hard ground beneath her knees, his heat warming her skin.

The intense stillness in Bowman's eyes told her he wanted it too. Their shared look smoldered the air between them.

Each knew the other was imagining every second of Kenzie unbuckling Bowman's jeans, Bowman's fingers going slack as he let the waistband drop from them. He'd be backed against one of the cars, his jeans around his ankles, hand in Kenzie's hair as she knelt.

He'd fill her mouth, the taste of him hot and smooth, the tight skin of his thighs warm under her fingers. The hair curling at his balls would beckon her touch, and Bowman would make a faint sound of pleasure as he rocked into her mouth.

Even now, as they stood face-to-face, Bowman's hands closed into fists. His eyes softened with his fire, and his mouth lost its hard line.

"Kenz," he said in a low voice.

Kenzie said nothing. She stood rigid, wanting him, while the snow fell around her, and Shifters swarmed about a little way from them. Her hands ached, and she realized she'd clenched them tightly.

Bowman said her name again, or she thought he did. In the next second, he closed the space between them and brought his mouth down on hers.

CHAPTER SIXTEEN

The kiss burned, but Kenzie didn't pull away. Bowman's mouth was strong, mastering. His arms went around her, hands hard on her back. Kenzie sought him, scrabbling inside his coat to find his warmth. His sweatshirt stretched over his broad chest, outlining what she wanted to see, to touch.

Her knees went slack, but Bowman's strength poured into her and kept her on her feet. Thinking about how Serena had seen him bare in the parking lot, even if he'd only wanted to scare the woman, made Kenzie growl even as she kissed him.

My mate. Mine.

She slid her hands behind his neck and dragged him against her. Bowman bit down on her lip, the kiss taking over her mouth.

Kenzie gasped for breath, but Bowman wouldn't let her breathe. He wouldn't let her move, or go, or do anything but frantically kiss him back, watery need flowing through every limb, as snow danced around them.

"Goddess," came the irritated voice of Pierce, the Guardian. "Would you two get a room?"

His voice jolted Kenzie out of her building frenzy. Almost. She remained plastered against Bowman, feeling the hard ridge of his cock against her abdomen even as Bowman turned his head to glare at Pierce, his eyes hot with anger.

When they'd first moved to this Shiftertown, Kenzie and Pierce had gone out together for a while. Before that, neither of them had ever tried a cross-species relationship, and Kenzie knew that most of what they'd shared had been curiosity.

They'd gone their separate ways by mutual agreement not long after, and Kenzie and Pierce had remained friends. This had been a few years before Kenzie and Bowman had mated, but their past relationship always drove Bowman crazy.

"What do you want?" he snapped at Pierce.

"The ritual is done," Pierce said, giving Bowman a hard stare in return. Guardians were the few Shifters who could look a leader in the eyes without fear. "The creature has already turned to ash."

"So quickly?" Kenzie didn't back away from Bowman, but she blinked in surprise. "I thought something that big would burn for a while."

Pierce shrugged, which moved the Guardian's sword on his back, its hilt rising above his left shoulder. "It's a magical being, like Shifters. Ashes to ashes, very fast."

"Interesting," Bowman said, his body starting to relax. "Save me a sample of the ash, and bury the rest."

"Right." Pierce nodded to Kenzie—not Bowman—and turned and walked away.

Bowman carefully stepped away from her. "Take Ryan home," he said.

Kenzie didn't move. "You can't kill Pierce, you know. You'd have to hold a Choosing for another Guardian, if the Goddess even let you live after that."

Bowman gave her an annoyed look. "I know."

"Seriously, it was over a long time ago. I don't think we had anything to even *be* over."

Bowman had started to turn away, but at her words, he swung back, gripped Kenzie by the arms and pulled her against him again.

"You think I can stand knowing any second you could walk away from me, and I wouldn't be able to stop you?" His fingers bit down. "That if you feel the mate bond with another male, you'll go—and you won't care? Do you know what that does to me?"

Bowman released her to put both his hands to his chest, digging into his sweatshirt. "It tears me up inside, right here. It messes with me until I can't sleep, or think, or feel anything but wanting to grab you and keep you with me no matter what. I'm fucked up because of you, and every time you smile at another male, it fucks me up even more. So have a little pity, all right, Kenz? You're killing me—a little bit every day."

Bowman twisted his shirt while Kenzie stared, open-mouthed, at him, Then he made a sound of disgust at himself, swung on his heel, and left her.

Bowman stayed out until very late that night, on into the small hours of the morning. Kenzie heard him return, entering the house quietly.

He did this sometimes when he couldn't keep his anger down around Kenzie. He'd never disappear for good, she knew, because he wouldn't leave her or Ryan unprotected. He and Kenzie had to present a united front, no matter what they felt in private, so the other Shifters would remain stable and calm.

The Shifters picked up on any dissonance between the two, instincts making them edgy. After a while those instincts would cancel out any good that Kenzie and Bowman's mating of convenience had wrought. Shifters could split themselves again between supporting Bowman's pack or Cristian's, or splinter into individual clans, each species shutting the others out.

As much as the world tried to humanize Shifters, as much as Shifters presented themselves as human in order to reassure the world, they were still animals. As animals, they had a heightened instinct to survive and to protect their immediate families, at any cost.

Kenzie sat in the dark in bed, her knees drawn up to her chest, as she heard Bowman go into Ryan's room. She knew he'd cross to the bed and look down at Ryan asleep for a moment, then smooth his hair or press a kiss to his forehead before leaving the room and softly closing the door.

Bowman entered their bedroom, where Kenzie waited, and halted on the threshold. All the lights in the house were out, but Bowman could see fine in the dark.

"I thought you'd be asleep." He came inside and shut the door, and Kenzie let out her tense breath. She'd worried he'd turn away when he saw her awake, to go sleep on one of the living room couches.

"I couldn't," she said. "I wondered if you found out anything."

"Not much." Fabric whispered as Bowman's clothes slid from him, his belt clinking in the darkness. "The driver for the trucking company did steal the truck, but he sold it pretty quickly. Then he got caught boosting another truck and has spent the last six months in prison." Kenzie heard his jeans hit the floor. "He's not involved in this, as far as I can tell."

Kenzie tried to keep her tone conversational as Bowman approached the bed, though her heart was pounding. "Who did he sell the truck to?"

"That's what we're trying to find out. Pierce is on it, along with all the Guardians, on their network. I also called Eric and Liam." He made a sound like a grunt. "Because you know how much I love talking to other Shiftertown leaders."

Kenzie smothered a laugh. Eric was the leader of the Las Vegas Shiftertown, and a Feline, and Bowman didn't much like Felines. But then all Shiftertown leaders were competitive with one another. They *could* work together, but the heightened awareness in a roomful of leaders gave off a distinctive odor.

"Did they know anything?" she asked.

"Nope. They've never heard of a creature like it. A griffin, or whatever."

Bowman got into bed as he spoke, bashing his pillows into shape as usual. Kenzie knew he wouldn't act awkward, or apologize for his outburst at the arena, or defend himself in any way. He'd carry on as though nothing had happened.

That's what they always did. If they kept their relationship businesslike, all was well. As soon as they moved into emotions, everything went to hell.

"Both Liam and Eric want to send a couple of their Shifters to help us look around," Bowman said. "I told them I'd think about it."

Kenzie adjusted for Bowman's bulk in the bed, the sheet sliding from her bare torso. "An outsider's perspective might be useful. They both have good trackers."

"I said I'd think about it." Bowman resolutely closed his eyes. "Go to sleep. We have a lot more to do tomorrow."

He pulled the covers up over his chest and pretended to drift off.

Kenzie sat still and watched him. Her Shifter sight let her see him in the darkness, his bronzed shoulders and hands against the pale sheet, his eyes closed, hiding their glitter from her. His lashes were thick and very black, curling against his tanned face.

She knew he wasn't sleeping by the rigidness of his hands, which clenched the sheet. When Bowman slept, his fingers relaxed, the powerful grip finally calming. His breathing would deepen, his chest rising and falling in long, slow cycles. Bowman also snored when he slept hard, a fact he fervently denied.

At the moment, his fingers were stiff, his breathing shallow and quiet.

Kenzie slowly and carefully eased herself down beside him. She slid down farther without disturbing the sheets, until her nose was level with the heat of his bare hip.

Before he could reach down and stop her, Kenzie locked her hand around his far hip, raised her head, and did what she'd dreamed of doing out by the arena today. Bowman's cock was already hard, so he had to be thinking about it too.

"No." Bowman jumped, his hands coming down to push her away.

Too late. Kenzie was already rubbing her tongue along the underside of his cock, reveling in the dark taste of him.

The grip that Bowman meant to stop her instead closed on her hair, his fingers threading it. "Kenzie, you little shit," he whispered.

Kenzie smiled as she worked him into her mouth. The sheet trapped her, as did his hands, but Kenzie didn't care. She was nestled in a warm cocoon with her mate, darkness, and the fine feel and taste of his cock.

As she licked, nipped, and suckled, the smooth head bumped her lips, her nose. She nuzzled him, his skin wet from her tongue, and wanted to laugh.

"Goddess and God." Bowman spoke with jaw clenched. "Damn you . . ."

Kenzie kept on him. His hips moved under her mouth, Bowman wanting to thrust. He'd come any minute, and she'd swallow him, the seed of her beloved mate.

But it wasn't meant to be. Bowman reached down, seized her, and dragged her up and out from under the covers. She couldn't fight the strength of him, not when he was like this— needing and angry.

He had her down on the mattress before Kenzie could say a word, his mouth on hers, his knee forcing her legs open. Then he was inside her, every Shifter inch of him. Their hips rocked together, sweat making his fingers slick where he held down her wrists.

Bowman thrust into her, this loving rapid and fierce, until he came, snarling, and fell on top of her, breathing hard.

Kenzie smoothed his hair, her own climax quiet this time, but still powerful.

Bowman's head was cradled on her breasts when sleep finally took him. His grip relaxed, his hands growing slack, but Kenzie never moved, drifting off to sleep in the strong embrace of her mate.

Bowman's cell phone going off dragged him awake before daylight.

He rolled out of bed to grab the phone from the pocket of his jeans, his body protesting. Only a little of his soreness was residual from his injured leg—frantic sex with his mate always took its toll.

Bowman was highly aware of Kenzie sitting up in the dark behind him, the sheet hugging her breasts. Her eroticism was like a stinging slap. He could never ignore her.

Nor could he ignore the insistent phone. Shifters didn't have access to the scores of ringtones humans did, so it gave a shrill, tinny *brr-brr*. Bowman had noticed, as he noticed everything, that humans, given the huge selection of sounds their phones could make, stuck overall with the same few.

Caller ID told him the number calling was private, but no

one would call a Shiftertown leader at four thirty on an icy morning if it weren't important.

"What?" he asked in a rasping whisper, not wanting to wake Ryan in the next room.

"In the woods near the burn site," came a muffled voice, pitched to hide the caller's gender. "Come now. It's important."

"Why the fuck should I?"

"You need to." The caller sounded anxious, and now Bowman knew she was female. "I don't like what he's doing. I thought he was right, but now—this is bad. I need to show you, or you'll never believe me."

Behind him, Bowman heard Kenzie's phone give the faint buzz that said she had a text. Kenzie leaned to the nightstand to grab it, stretching the sheet over the curve of her hips.

"Who is this?" Bowman demanded.

"I'm—" The woman broke off with a gasp. "Oh, shit! I have to—" And the phone went dead.

Bowman slammed his finger onto his recent calls list, but it didn't give him any more information than before. *Private caller.*

He threw down the phone to find Kenzie texting, her thumbs moving rapidly. Bowman could never get the hang of texts. *Either talk to me or go the hell away* was his motto.

Kenzie finished her message, waited a moment, then read the return message when her phone buzzed again. She typed two letters with her thumbs and hit the send key hard.

"Cristian?" Bowman asked.

"Yes." Kenzie looked up from scowling at the message. "How did you know?"

"I can almost smell him through the phone. And no one else can piss you off as much with a text message."

"*You* could," Kenzie said darkly.

"I don't text. What did he want?"

For answer, Kenzie showed him the phone. Cristian had first written, *I found out something about that Serena. Come to me and speak.*

Kenzie had written, *Just tell me.*

The reply: *She has passed on information about Shifters*

that I fear has endangered us. You need to come. Meet me in the woods near where the monster died.

Kenzie's *NO* blazed in response.

Bowman nodded, indicating he was finished reading. The fact that Cristian had written in English meant he fully expected Kenzie to share the message with Bowman and wanted nothing to be lost in translation.

"We have to go out there," Bowman said. As Kenzie opened her mouth to protest, he said, "My call was from Serena, I'm pretty sure."

Kenzie looked at her message again. "Crap, you mean Uncle Cris is hunting her out there?"

"Something's going on. I need to find out."

Kenzie scrambled out of bed, beautiful and naked. The streetlight outside touched her breasts with a misty glow, and Bowman wished he could forget all about human pseudo-groupies, strange mythical monsters, and her pain-in-the-ass Uncle Cristian and take her back to bed.

Kenzie leaned over to retrieve her clothes, not cooling his distracted body. "I'll call my grandmother to come watch Ryan. I hate to wake him."

"He's already awake and you know it," Bowman said, watching her cover her beauty with drawstring sweatpants, a thin camisole and a sweatshirt. Clothes easy to remove for shifting. "But yeah, call her. If Cristian's out rampaging, Afina will be up and worrying anyway."

Kenzie settled her sweatshirt, shutting him out of her body again. Bowman realized he was holding his jeans in nerveless fingers while he stared at his mate.

She gave him a what-are-you-doing? look as she pushed past him, her phone already in her hand. Bowman hurriedly finished dressing and ran out to catch up to her.

CHAPTER SEVENTEEN

The drive back to the arena was dark and cold. Bowman rode his motorcycle, happy to be able to again, his back warmed by Kenzie clinging on behind.

The moon was still in the sky, rendering the world black-and-white. Snow had fallen all yesterday afternoon, but the clouds had cleared as Kenzie and Bowman slept. The ground glittered in radiant silver, the towering trees like cut black silhouettes. The wind was icy, the temperature in the teens. Weather like this was dry rather than damp, air burning inside the nostrils and lungs.

Kenzie had wrapped a scarf around her nose and mouth, but Bowman rode with only his leather jacket zipped closed to keep out the winter. Cold never bothered him.

The road wound through tree-dense hills. They met no approaching headlights, overtook no one. On this January Sunday morning, humans were staying snug in bed before rising for church, or had just crawled home to sleep off their wild Saturday night.

Bowman cut down into the farms and then up another hill to the arena. He parked where they had when they'd found the griffin and dismounted the bike, sniffing the wind.

He smelled decaying monster, overlaid with cleansing fire, the woods at night, and Kenzie, who'd come up close behind him.

Faintly, from a distance, he caught a new scent—that of human death.

Bowman didn't need to tell Kenzie to follow. The motorcycle would be safe enough here, hidden in shadows. He moved off into the darkness behind the arena, following the moonlit trail. Kenzie walked noiselessly behind him.

Bowman veered from the site where the pyre had been. Smoke hung in the air, but the fire was long gone. His Shifters would have made sure it was completely out before they left.

Down another hill, mud frozen beneath their feet. Kenzie gripped Bowman's hand as they climbed down slippery rocks and found their quarry at the bottom.

Bowman wasn't surprised to see Cristian Dimitru sitting in a crouch beside the body of Serena, the pseudo-groupie, possible-reporter. She had been shot twice, her chest black with blood, her eyes staring upward. She was very dead.

Kenzie took a step back and said a quick prayer to the Goddess. She never liked the smell of death—no Shifter did—whether the corpse was human, animal, or otherwise.

Bowman didn't like it either, she could tell by the tightness of his shoulders, but he joined Uncle Cris on the ground, both of them looking over the body.

Bowman pinned Cristian with a hard gaze. "Did you do this?"

Cristian's golden wolf eyes narrowed, the gray streaks in his hair pale patches in the darkness. He looked much like his wolf at that moment, a great black beast with yellow eyes.

"You think I would make this kill?" he asked. "With a gun?"

Shifters disliked guns. They were loud, smelled, and could damage innocent bystanders. Much better to go for a direct, silent kill with teeth and claws.

"You texted Kenzie about Serena," Bowman said. "And now she's dead."

"She was being hunted." Cristian's accent had all but evaporated. "She came here to meet someone, but either that someone turned on her, or another followed her and chased her. She ran a long way, but in the end, the bullets found her."

"Who was hunting her?" Kenzie leaned down, hands on her knees, to join the conversation. She avoided looking into the woman's open eyes.

"I did not see," Cristian said regretfully. "But I smelled. A man. With a gun—as you can see."

"Where did he go?"

Cristian shrugged. "I lost him. He knows these woods, and I do not."

"You're a Lupine," Bowman said impatiently. "One of the best, you keep telling me. You can track anything."

"I know. That's what worries me."

"Did you track as wolf?" Kenzie asked. "If so, you're neatly dressed again."

Cristian gave her an irritated look. "I left my clothes here and came back for them. You know we must alert the human police as to the fate of this poor girl."

Kenzie agreed, but she knew it would lead to awkward questions. "I can call Gil. He might be able to respond discreetly."

Cristian raised his brows. "Who is this Gil?"

"Friend of Kenzie's," Bowman answered, annoyance in his voice. "A cop."

"He can help," Kenzie said. Under Cristian's suddenly interested stare, she looked to Bowman for confirmation, and he gave her a nod.

Kenzie pulled out her cell phone, hoping she could get a signal this far out. She lifted it to the sky, studying the icon that would show her how strong the signal was.

The next instant, the plastic shattered in her hand.

She spent one second staring at the remnants of her cell phone in shock before Bowman tackled her. They went down in a tangle of limbs, another bullet landing in the dirt where Kenzie had been standing.

"Sniper," Bowman whispered, just as Kenzie's stunned brain registered the fact. "Nightscope."

Kenzie shivered violently. A man with a nightscope could sit under cover and shoot, spotting his target many yards away, and never be seen himself. It made her hackles rise, her wolf want to run, run, *run*.

Bowman tugged her to move, and the two of them melted silently into deeper shadow. They wouldn't be able to find cover in darkness from a nightscope, but they might be able to move out of the hunter's line of sight.

Cristian had vanished, he too trying to put distance between himself and the shooter.

Another bullet pinged two feet from Kenzie's boot.

"Go." Bowman's whisper was a hint of sound, but Kenzie got the message. She ran. A bullet hit the ground at her heels, and she dove down a bank, finding a hollow of mud that hadn't frozen.

The mud sucked at her, and Kenzie pulled herself out, losing one of her running shoes in the process.

To hell with that. Kenzie kept going, shedding clothes as she ran. She was leaving a trail, but it didn't matter. She needed to change from hunted to hunter.

She heard Bowman's growl behind her and then a great gray wolf bounded past her, Bowman back at full strength. Kenzie's vision changed in the next seconds as her wolf took over.

She smelled the hunter now, a human who'd been sitting all night in the woods, his faint odor coating the others in the air. She scented the acrid smells of gunpowder and metal, heard the ping of bullets on trees and in the dirt.

Kenzie put her head down and ran. Her wolf could eat up miles before she tired, could run hard without losing breath. Her paws scrabbled for purchase on rocks as she followed Bowman up a hill.

He led her below a ridgeline so that their silhouettes would not be outlined against the sky. The moon was setting, but the sun would rise soon. Their only hope was to find a thick tumble of rocks, or brush so thick their forms would be blurred. Better still would be to take themselves completely elsewhere.

Bowman stopped below a rocky outcropping, his low growl barely discernible from the wind in the trees. He wanted to go up and over.

He sank to his haunches and began to crawl on his belly. Kenzie imitated him. Felines were better at slinking, but wolves could be pretty good at it too.

They slid over the rocks, grit and frozen weeds catching in Kenzie's fur. She wanted to sneeze but didn't dare.

Over the ridge, down the other side. The trees were thicker here, the darkness more complete. Bowman picked up into a run, flowing down the hill in perfect silence.

Where they were, Kenzie had no idea. She and Bowman had explored the wild lands around Shiftertown plenty, but a wolf could only patrol so much, even with trackers. Then again, Bowman might know exactly where they were—he often went off alone, leaving Kenzie to guard Shiftertown.

No more bullets whizzed around them, at least. Bowman slowed after a time and stopped, lifting his head to sniff the air. Kenzie also sniffed, catching unfamiliar scents, both woodsy and human.

Bowman shook himself. He sat down, his tongue lolling, but his ears and eyes alert.

Kenzie lifted her paw to look in annoyance at the thorn wedged deep between the pads. She closed her teeth around it, and found another muzzle against her own. Bowman nudged his way in, licking her paw to soothe it. The gesture was caring, even in the middle of their flight.

Kenzie nuzzled him, and Bowman made a noise low in his throat. They were alone together out here, the two of them against the night. The mate bond didn't matter right now. Their knowledge of each other and mutual trust did.

The thorn dislodged from Kenzie's paw. Kenzie licked Bowman's ear in thanks, and he shook his head, as though embarrassed he'd been caught enjoying licky-cuddles.

He turned from Kenzie and trotted off into the woods. Kenzie came behind him, a few steps from his tail. If this were a more playful time, she might have lunged forward and grabbed his tail with her teeth, just to annoy him, but playfulness would have to wait.

The scent of human grew stronger. Bowman halted, Kenzie swerving to halt beside him. She looked past him and saw why he'd stopped.

They stood on the edge of a clearing. Within it was a small, narrow house—a mobile home that had been fixed on a permanent foundation. A wooden step led to the front door, which was flanked by two windows. A round barbecue with a dirty grill sat quietly beside the doorstep, and the scent of lighter fluid and burned meat lingered.

Kenzie caught another scent she couldn't place. She had the feeling she *should* be able to recognize it, but either she was mistaken, or it was so covered with something else its identity eluded her.

Bowman's nose wrinkled, and he inhaled deeply. He must have noticed it too.

As they debated in wolf language whether they should approach, the screen door of the house creaked open.

"I know you're out there," a man's voice said. A shotgun poked its way out the door, followed by a human bundled in a thick jacket. The gun, as far as Kenzie could make out, had no nightscope attached. "I need you where I can see you."

Bowman rumbled a low growl, which meant Kenzie should remain behind, then he walked slowly into the clearing.

The starlight that filtered down showed a regal gray wolf, ears pricked, head up, unafraid. Kenzie tensed, ready to spring the moment the man's trigger finger so much as twitched.

The shotgun lowered, and spectacles flashed as the man peered more closely at Bowman. "Hello, my friend," he said. "Tell me, are you *Canis lupus*? Or *Canis lupus shifterensius*?"

CHAPTER EIGHTEEN

Kenzie watched from the shadows as Bowman shifted back to human.

He did it slowly, drawing out the process for greatest effect. His back legs grew thick and strong, his body straightening as he changed. By the time he was standing upright, his arms and legs were human, and his fur receding. His head shifted last, his wolf face flattening to human.

His eyes remained the same, gray white and fixed on the man in the clearing.

"It's Shifter," Bowman said clearly. "There's no such thing as *Canis lupus shifterensius*."

"There is now," the man said. "A new classification has been approved by the scientific journals. A new one for your Felines and your bears as well."

His voice bore the faint soft drawl of a Southerner, from coastal South Carolina, Kenzie surmised. He sounded cultured, educated—he should be lounging in his sophisticated house in the city with swimming pool, not roughing it in the backwoods. Why he was out here, she couldn't guess.

"Were you the one shooting at us?" Bowman asked in a stern voice.

"No." The man sounded surprised. "Is someone shooting? Thanks for the warning."

He didn't seem to be at all bothered by Bowman's lack of clothing. Bowman didn't move, assessing the man and his threat level, as did Kenzie from the shadows of the trees.

"Why don't you and your friend come inside?" the man asked. He uncocked the shotgun and slung it over his arm. "I've got coffee going. Also blankets, if your Shifter friend is shy."

"Do you have a phone?" Bowman asked, not hurrying to obey.

"I do. I have to tell you, though, sometimes it works; sometimes it doesn't. But you're welcome to try." He opened the door and gestured Bowman inside.

"Bring the blankets first," Bowman said.

"Sure thing." The man stepped up into the house. When he returned, he was minus the gun and had an armful of thin fleece blankets. He flipped on a porch light, walked to Bowman in its yellow glare, and put the blankets into Bowman's hands. "My name's Turner. Wayne Turner. Would you happen to be Bowman O'Donnell?"

Bowman's hands closed on the blankets. "Do you prefer it if I am?"

"I study Shifters," Turner said. "In a good way. I know that Bowman O'Donnell is the leader of the local Shiftertown. Your picture gets in the papers. So, you are either him or his twin brother, and you don't have a twin brother."

"You're right; I'm Bowman. My mate, Kenzie." Bowman didn't gesture, but Kenzie knew the signal to walk out of the woods. Still wolf, she joined him, sat down next to Bowman, and gazed up at Turner.

Turner returned the look, interest in his blue eyes behind his glasses. "If it doesn't offend you, can I say she's beautiful? A Romanian gray wolf, right? A number of them survived in the wild lands, didn't they?"

"They did," Bowman said.

"Her eyes are different. Tawny rather than blue or gray. Means she's from a different strain, different pack."

"Yes, we know."

Turner grinned. "Sorry, I don't often get the opportunity to see Shifters close up. I've talked to a few, but I know that coming to Shiftertown and grilling you is rude. I'll try to contain my curiosity. Come on in when you're ready."

He turned his back on them and walked away. Bowman bristled, but Kenzie knew Turner didn't show his back to be insulting, like Uncle Cris did. The man had no idea what the gesture meant.

Bowman, carrying the blankets, walked with Kenzie under the cover of the trees, away from the circle of porch light, and waited for her to shift. When she was finished, he wordlessly handed her a blanket.

Kenzie wrapped it around her, glad of its protection in the sudden chill. "Are we really going in there?"

Bowman lifted one shoulder in a shrug. He'd folded a blanket and wrapped it around his waist like a bath towel. With it hugging his hips, he looked good enough to eat.

"I want to see what he's up to," Bowman said. "Why he's staying here. What he has to do with Serena, if anything, or the sniper, or the beast."

"I don't like it," Kenzie said, tucking the corner of the blanket around her shoulder. "And what about Uncle Cris?"

"He can take care of himself. Besides, if he finds the sniper and takes him down, that's one less thing I have to worry about."

Bowman held his hand out to her, and Kenzie took it. She knew the offer wasn't just to steady her, but to share strength and confidence, and for protection. They would stay united, and alert.

Kenzie gave his hand a squeeze, and they walked to the house, up its wooden step, and inside.

The inside of the trailer was not what Bowman expected. It was less like a house, more like an office. Half the front room was taken up with bookcases plus a large, flat desk holding a computer. The other half did have a couch, a rust-colored, utilitarian thing.

A table near the computer desk was strewn with maps and photographs, and dozens of photos were pinned to the walls. Most humans these days kept their caches of information on computers, but this man seemed to like to spread out his research and immerse himself in it.

His research was on Shifters, the history of, it looked like. Many of the Lupines, Felines, and bears in the photos on the walls didn't wear Collars, but Bowman could tell they were Shifter. The photos were older, from the 1950s and '60s, some from the early twentieth and late nineteenth centuries. Some were photos taken in the wild, of Shifters in their animal forms. The oldest photos were of Shifters in human form sitting stiffly in chairs, posed for portraits. Likely the photographer hadn't known they were Shifters, but their eyes and attitudes told Bowman what they were.

Kenzie looked around in disquiet and threw a glance at Bowman. He agreed. The rows and rows of Shifters staring down at them was creepy.

"What's all this for?" Bowman asked, indicating the photos.

Turner had moved to a tiny room at the far end of the living room, which, when he snapped on the light, proved to be a kitchen. A closed door on the opposite side of the living room likely led to a bedroom.

"I discovered Shifters," he called to them. "Well, unofficially, long before it was common knowledge. I'm a professor of anthropology. At Asheville."

Bowman exchanged another glance with Kenzie. *Is he a danger?* Kenzie's eyes asked the question. *Or just a nut?*

"I'm on sabbatical," Turner said, returning with cups of steaming coffee. "Trying to get my book done. It's a never-ending task."

"You're writing about Shifters?" Kenzie asked, accepting the cup he handed her. She took a long sniff of the coffee, trying to detect whether anything tainted it. Apparently, she smelled nothing amiss, because she sipped it. Then her expression changed. "This is *good*."

Turner shrugged. "I live like an absentminded professor most of the time, but I pack the best Italian roast. Yes, my book is about Shifters. Their history, their origins, what they were like before the 'outing.' I'm something of an expert. I think, you know, that if people read about what Shifters were like 'in the wild,' as you call it, they'll lose their fear. That fear has already lessened, but humans need to better integrate you into society."

Gil Ramirez had told Kenzie much the same thing. Bowman wondered if the two men knew each other.

"Please sit down," Turner said, scooping a pile of maps from the end of the sofa. "If you are Bowman's mate, then you must be Kenzie, of the Dimitru pack."

"Yes," Kenzie said. She settled herself on the burnt orange sofa and took another sip of coffee. She looked delectable with the blanket wrapped around her like a sarong, her unfettered breasts moving softly beneath it. Bowman wondered if he'd ever cease lusting after her. Probably not.

"I'm Kenzie O'Donnell now," Kenzie was saying. "I was absorbed into Bowman's pack when we mated."

"In order to calm the challenging tendencies of the Dimitru pack," Turner finished, sounding pleased with himself. "The Dimitrus and O'Donnells nearly came to battle over who would run the Shiftertown, and Bowman took a Dimitru mate to settle the question. Like Henry the Seventh and Elizabeth of York, ending the Wars of the Roses once and for all."

"I hope so," Kenzie said. "Those two came to care very deeply for each other, so they say."

Bowman shot her a questioning look, which Kenzie returned neutrally. He could almost hear the words in her head—*I read books. You should try it.*

"Exactly," Turner said. "A love story for the ages."

Bowman took a sip of coffee as Turner headed back to the kitchen, but didn't sit down. "The phone?" he asked.

"There." Turner pointed behind him.

It was a landline, but when Bowman lifted it, he didn't hear a dial tone. Turner's cell phone didn't get a signal either when the man brought it to him, along with a plate of lemon cookies poured out of a box. Kenzie ate a cookie, but Bowman declined.

"The phone lines get chewed on," Turner said. "Lots of wildlife out here. If the phone lines are down, I can't e-mail either. Doesn't bother me, but you said there was someone in the woods shooting?"

"Someone with a nightscope," Bowman said grimly. He didn't like this place, but Kenzie was right about the coffee.

He took another sip, filling his mouth with the rich, full taste of it.

"I have a pickup, if you think you should go find the police."

"If we get our bearings, we can go cross-country back to Shiftertown," Bowman said. "Where are we, exactly?"

"Here." Turner moved to a map of western North Carolina tacked to the wall, and stuck his finger on a point where no roads were marked. "About there."

"There" was a blank spot north and west of Leicester. Shiftertown was clearly indicated farther to the north, a long way away. They'd have to cross a couple of valleys and skirt hills, or circle miles around to main roads where they might be able to find a phone and call for Cade to pick them up.

"I can drive you," Turner offered again. "I might not have a reliable phone, but I'm not stupid enough to come out here without a four-wheel drive, good tires, and plenty of gas."

"Sure," Bowman said. "I'll think about it."

He moved across the room and sat down by Kenzie. She was tense, and he was too, though Turner seemed harmless. Bowman had come across humans obsessed with Shifters before, although none had gone so far as to write a book.

"You said you knew about Shifters before anyone else," Bowman said to him. "Did you have a hand in outing us?" His voice took on a dangerous note.

Turner laughed. "Of course not. When I first discovered Shifters—in Ireland it was—I got excited and wrote a paper on what I'd seen, but I was considered a crackpot and lost out on an assistant professorship I'd been an inch from getting." Anger gleamed briefly in his eyes. "Men turning to beasts in the mists? Werewolves were real? They dismissed me as a fool." His smile returned. "They had to eat their words in the long run, but I learned to keep quiet in the meantime. I started calling my research 'weird things people in remote villages believe' and told the scientific community they'd misunderstood my first paper."

"Mmm," was all Bowman could say.

"Wise of you," Kenzie put in. "How were you so certain you'd found Shifters? Did you see one shift?" Her voice was warm, interested. She was trying to charm him—a good way to figure out what he wanted from them.

"Not exactly." Turner leaned one hip against his desk. "As I say, I was in Ireland, doing postdoc studies in villages on the west coast. In one, the locals swore that they were protected by 'magic people' who lived in a ruined castle in the hills. Even the villagers who struck me as being practical and modern believed in the otherworldliness of these people. The consensus was that they were Sidhe—their name for the Fae. Good ones, they said, for a change. They kept the village safe; everything had started going right when the magic people came. So they said. They also swore up and down that the people could turn into lions."

Kenzie lifted her brows as she studied him over her cup. "And you believed them?"

"Not at first. I thought they were messing with me, trying to find out how much the gullible anthropologist would swallow. But the story was repeated by so many, and the people in the next village told me the same things." Turner let out a breath. "So I looked for these magic people, but of course I couldn't find them. One night in the little camp I'd set up near the ruined castle in question, I heard them prowling around, watching me. But I never saw them out there. However, in the village one day, I saw a man, about as big as you, Bowman, who had the most amazing blue eyes. He was staring at me from across the high street, and I couldn't look away. It was the wildest feeling. Almost sexual, I'd say, even though I'm not gay. He just held me with those eyes and released me when *he* chose. When I could finally look away, I blinked, and he was gone."

Bowman listened in disquiet. He had no doubt Turner had spotted a Shifter. The description plus the location made Bowman think he knew which Shifter Turner had seen—sounded a lot like Dylan Morrissey. He must have chosen to let the curious American get a look at him, no doubt ready to lead him away from the rest of his pack.

"So you were convinced?" Bowman asked.

"Not quite. But interested enough to pursue more tales, once I'd learned to keep my mouth shut around my colleagues. I set off on a worldwide quest, looking for more 'magic people.' Eventually, of course, Shifters were revealed as real, I was offered a position at Asheville, and here I am. I'm now one of the leading authorities on all things Shifter."

He finished, smiled at them, and walked to the kitchen to refill his cup.

Kenzie held her coffee away from her, frowning a little.

"What?" Bowman asked her under his breath.

"I smell something."

Bowman smelled coffee. Strong, filling the cabin. He moved the cup from his nose, as Kenzie had, and rested it in his hand on the sofa.

He began to breathe deeply, pulling air into his lungs, forcing himself to sort out odors. He processed them for a long time before he found what had instinctively troubled him. The faint but unmistakable odor of Faerie.

Not strong at all; barely discernible. He glanced again at the map, which was marked with mountains, rivers, valleys, farms, towns. He knew a ley line ran alongside Shiftertown—a ley line was a sort of magical artery of a network that stretched around the globe, near which magic was enhanced and gateways to Faerie could be found. If Bowman was right, that same ley line snaked down to cross near here.

The scent didn't come from Turner. Bowman surreptitiously inhaled when the man came back to refill their cups. Nope, Turner was human. He was not half Fae; not even one quarter. Anyone with Fae blood had a distinctive odor.

A Fae might have been here though. While Fae had difficulty in the human world, with all its iron, Bowman had heard that they could take magical precautions against iron poisoning. But even then, their spells didn't last long.

Not that Bowman knew a lot about the Fae. He had experts like Pierce for that information, and he tried to think about Faerie and the Fae as little as possible.

He exchanged another glance with Kenzie, but she gave him a slight shake of her head and looked up at Turner again.

"This book on Shifters," she said. "I'd love to read what you have so far."

Turner flushed with sudden pleasure. "Really? I'm flattered. Would you? And maybe . . . give me some pointers? I want to get it right."

"Happy to," Kenzie said. "Do you have a copy I can take with me?"

"Why not read it right here?" Turner asked, giving her a

hopeful smile. "While you enjoy some more coffee and stay warm?"

"I'm afraid we should be going," Kenzie said, shaking her head. "Our son will be worried, plus we should report the shooter."

"It's still pretty dark," Turner pointed out. "Dangerous out there until full daylight. And as I say, I'll give you a lift."

He returned to the kitchen without noticing the two Shifters' discomfort. "Do you think he's harmless?" Kenzie whispered into Bowman's ear. "Or not?"

Bowman liked the way Kenzie's breath tickled him, but he didn't know how to answer.

Kenzie quietly put her coffee aside and moved to the front door. She stopped, stymied, and pointed at the keypad that took the place of a doorknob. There was no other latch, bolt, or keyhole; no other way to open the door.

"Oh, that has a code," Turner said, coming back out of the kitchen. "Keeps squatters out when I'm not here."

"What about the windows?" Bowman asked. "They don't look very sturdy."

"Looks are deceiving." Turner smiled. "They're wired to give an intruder a nasty shock when the alarm is on."

"You booby-trapped your own house?" Kenzie asked him, still at the door.

"You'd be amazed at the people who come out here," Turner said, with a quiet sigh of disapproval. "Drug dealers and pot growers, gangs, people trying to hide from the law. Or just hunters. After someone trashed the place once, I got wise."

"Why do *you* come out here?" Kenzie asked. "If it's so dangerous?"

He shrugged. "I like the quiet. I can think better. My dad left this house to me, and the property—why should I give it up because of scum like that? Besides, when I'm here, I can visualize how it used to be for Shifters in the wild. You lived pretty close to the bone, didn't you?"

Kenzie had, in Eastern Europe. Bowman's pack, which had lived north of the Great Lakes, had been hunted, first by Native Americans, then by colonials.

"Yes," Bowman said.

"Ever miss it?"

Bowman shook his head, his look deadpan. "I like indoor plumbing."

Turner laughed. "So captivity is better?"

"I didn't say that. But we almost died in the wild. Our females stopped having many cubs. Now everyone is healthier, and more cubs are born."

"But you and Kenzie just have the one?" Turner asked.

Bowman saw the pain on Kenzie's face, and his voice turned to a growl. "Yes."

Turner continued, not noticing the warning. "But maybe if you'd all remained in the wild, she might have been infertile altogether. So you're right, you have benefited."

"How about you stop talking and open the door?" Bowman suggested. He rose, putting his bulk between Turner and Kenzie. "Enjoyed the coffee. Now it's time to go home."

Turner looked blank. "Sure, if you truly have to. Let me by so I can put in the code. Before you go, though, I want to fix up a time to talk to you, Kenzie. You can come back here, or if you'll let me go to Shiftertown . . . ?"

"We'll discuss it." Bowman stepped aside and pulled Kenzie next him.

Turner touched numbers on the keypad, but before he could push the door open for them, it was wrenched out of his grasp from the outside. Cristian stood on the doorstep, completely dressed, his breath fogging in the dawn light. His large motorcycle was parked in the clearing behind him.

"There you are," Cristian said, his accent thick. "My mother is calling, calling, and every time I'm sure the sniper is going to hear. What are you doing? We need to go."

CHAPTER NINETEEN

Kenzie gave a shiver of relief as she walked into her own house in Shiftertown. She was dressed again, Cristian having thoughtfully rescued all their clothes. They'd ridden triple on Cristian's big black machine back to the arena, where Bowman's bike still waited.

Ryan bounded into the kitchen in his wolf cub form as Kenzie and Bowman walked in the back door. Ryan sprang from the floor into Kenzie's arms and began licking her face.

"Stop that." Kenzie laughed and held her son close, burying her nose in his fur. "What are you doing up so early?"

Ryan kept licking, his tail wagging like a big puppy's. He yipped happily at his father but snuggled down in his mother's arms, not ready to leave her. Though Ryan was twelve in human years, in Shifter terms, he was still a little cub, though his wolf body was getting bigger by the year. He had long legs and big ears and huge paws the rest of him hadn't yet grown into.

Bowman slammed the door. He dumped the manuscript Turner had given them on the table and made for the refrigerator.

Kenzie's grandmother, Afina, came out from the hall that

led to the bedrooms. Though she'd reached her three hundredth year, Afina was tall and strong, with barely any gray in her dark hair. Humans sometimes mistook her for Cristian's sister rather than his mother.

"You are back then?" she asked. "And Cristian? You left him alive?"

"For now," Bowman said, a carton of orange juice in his hand. "Can't say that for everyone out in the woods tonight. I need to make some calls."

Bowman tumbled Ryan's fur, and Ryan's tail whacked against Kenzie's side.

"Ask Cristian for his version of things," Bowman said to Kenzie. He dropped a brief kiss on her cheek and was out the door, his cell phone already at his ear. "Cade," she heard him say, "Wake the hell up already . . ."

Then he was gone.

"Adventures?" Afina asked in Romanian.

"Too many. Ryan, honey, go clean up, and I'll make us breakfast."

"*I* will," Afina said as Ryan squirmed out of Kenzie's arms and scampered away. "You have had too much happen to you. Which you will tell me all about."

Talking to her grandmother did help Kenzie calm down a little. It always had.

Grandmother Afina could be a ruthless fighter, and she was Shifter to the core, but she could also hold Kenzie until all the bad things went away.

After Kenzie had lost her immediate family, Afina had been the only person that had kept her going. Shifters *could* die of broken hearts or terrible grief. They stopped caring about eating or sleeping until either the wild animal in them went feral—pretty much forgetting about the human part of themselves and reverting to living on crazed instincts—or their neglected bodies simply ceased working. Kenzie, just a cub and wanting life, had nearly gone feral, but Grandmother Afina had pulled her back from that edge. Kenzie would always owe her for that.

She saw Cristian walk toward them from up the road, but

he stopped at the edge of the snowy yard, not coming up the walk. This was Bowman's territory. While Afina had been coming here to check in on Kenzie from the moment she moved in, Cristian refused to stand anywhere so infused with Bowman's scent.

Kenzie and Afina left the house and crunched through the snow to talk to him. Ryan banged out after them, still wolf. He ran around and around the three adults, trapping them inside a furrow in the two-inch snowfall.

Cristian watched Ryan play for a moment, then raised a troubled gaze to Kenzie. "What was that stink out there? At that trailer house? Humans are crazy."

Kenzie folded her arms against the cold. "We're not sure, but we thought we smelled something Fae. Or Fae-born."

Cristian gave her a brief nod. "I smelled it too. We should investigate."

"I'm sure Bowman is already doing that."

Cristian's expression turned weary. "I know you think your mate is a superhero, but he can't be everywhere doing everything. He was caught off guard with that shooter and the man in the trailer, and so was I. We need to learn more."

"That's why he has trackers," Kenzie said, but without conviction.

Cristian gave her a sharp look. "Bowman cannot investigate the murder of the young woman, the monster and its death, the sniper, the odd professor, and whatever other things are going on all at the same time." His brows drew down over his wolf-gold eyes. "I want to discover who was shooting at me and almost hit me. And who was shooting at my niece. You are still Dimitru pack at heart, Kenzie, one of mine. I refuse to let this sniper get away with trying to kill you."

Kenzie raised her hands. "If you'll stop talking, I'll tell you I agree with you. We should check it out."

"Not *we*." Cristian pinned her with a stare as intense as Bowman's. "Me."

"Uncle, you can't go running around out there with a shooter on the loose. And you can't without talking to Bowman first—why don't you two work *together*? That was the whole point of my mating with him, wasn't it?"

Kenzie heard the rising pitch in her voice, and she tried to suppress it. She was running on lack of sleep, too much adrenaline, worry for Bowman, and irritation at Cristian for trying to use any excuse to undermine her mate.

Cristian stepped to her and laid his hands on her shoulders, his touch surprisingly gentle.

"Kenzie, child," he said, reverting to his native language. "When I was a young Shifter, my territory was caught between that of Ottoman Turks and the Austrian Empire. Trust me when I say that my life has calmed down a great deal since. Survival then meant to stay alive at any cost—here and now surviving is simply following a set of rules. Humans, especially in this country, are more—how do you say it in English?—touchy-feely. I can deal with one man and his rifle."

"Huh. Are you sure it was only one?"

"I think so. And it was not the man inside the cabin. Different scent."

Kenzie had decided that too. She also knew she had this snowfall's chance in hell of stopping Uncle Cristian doing whatever he wanted.

"If you go back out there, you be careful," Kenzie said sternly. "We don't need to be searching for your dead body on top of everything else."

Cristian gave her a smile that warmed his eyes. He could be a handsome man, when he let the ice crack. "Look at it this way—if I am shot, Bowman will have his victory. None of my nephews will be ready to fight for leadership for some time. Perhaps it would be better for everyone."

Afina scowled. She was half a head shorter than her son, but her glare could have knocked over a building. "Not better for me," she snapped. "I refuse to lose another child before I am old enough to call for the Guardian. This Shiftertown will not be better without you. If nothing else, your antagonism of Bowman helps him be a stronger leader. He'll do *anything* to keep you out of power."

Kenzie hid her smile. Cristian might rule the clan, but Afina never let him forget who'd raised him.

Cristian and his mother exchanged a long look before Cristian let out a sigh. He stepped away from both of them, pretending he hadn't just let his mother win another argument.

"Fine then," Cristian said to Afina. "You can come with me."

Afina blinked, surprised at the turn. "All right, I will," she said.

"*I'm* driving," Cristian said. "The Ottoman Turks were less frightening than you on a motorcycle."

Afina only smiled.

"Wait, now I have to worry about *both* of you?" Kenzie asked, annoyed. "This isn't trading up."

Cristian became serious again. "You worry about your mate, Kenzie-love. He is perhaps too furious, too obsessed with what is happening. One reason I did not oppose him taking you as mate is I knew you could keep him calm. That is what you must do, or Shiftertown will suffer."

Kenzie had known this for years, but Cristian's words gave her a qualm. "Sure. No pressure."

Cristian's smile made his eyes crinkle, and he pulled Kenzie to him for a hug.

Kenzie wrapped her arms around him, remembering how, when she'd been a child, his strength had bolstered her. Her uncle could be a total shit, but he'd also saved her life, time and again.

"Keep in touch," Kenzie said, releasing him. "I mean it."

"I will make him," Afina said. She also enfolded Kenzie in a hug, hers scented with woods, coffee, and cinnamon rolls. "You look after your mate. And your cub." She gave Kenzie a kiss on the cheek before letting her go. "And get some sleep, granddaughter. You look terrible."

"Aw, thanks."

Afina gave her a big smile, then turned and walked away with Cristian. They started arguing about something before they even hit the end of sidewalk, then they turned the corner, their voices fading.

Kenzie let Ryan play a little more before she called to him to return with her to the house. Once inside, he raced to his bedroom to shift and dress—he was getting too modest to shift to a naked human in front of his mother. Kenzie warmed up the cinnamon rolls Afina had made. The good kind—huge and dripping with icing.

She licked icing off her fingers, took out the new cell phone she'd picked up on the way home, and called Gil. She knew Bowman would probably have already talked to him, but Gil's warm voice when he answered lifted her spirits. Kenzie ran her finger through the bowl of icing and told Gil everything.

"Are you going to shut down the fight club?" Jamie asked. He walked beside Bowman with his restless Feline energy, pissed off because he'd missed the excitement in the woods early this morning. Around them, Shifters were starting the day, sweeping snow from porches and driveways, the cubs playing in the winter wonderland.

Bowman pondered Jamie's question. "We might have to move it. The human cops are all over the place up there now, investigating Serena's murder. Poor woman." Death was a waste. Serena had annoyed and worried him, but she'd not deserved to be murdered.

"Yeah." Jamie whispered a brief prayer to the Goddess to look after Serena's soul. "So you think the sniper shooting at you and whoever got her are two different people?"

"Two different guns," Bowman said. "She was shot close range with a pistol. The sniper had a high-powered rifle that could pick us off from a long way away. Though it might have been the same person using a different weapon."

"Great. A killer is out there who could shoot us before he's in scent range, *and* he has no qualm pulling the trigger point-blank." Jamie glanced around, as though the sniper could be lurking behind any tree. "We should keep the cubs inside."

"Agree. That's why we're going to give the cops as much cooperation as they want."

"I hear you. How much will you bet that the cops try to accuse one of us?"

"Nothing," Bowman said dryly. "I don't want to lose." He looked around, but not for the same reason as Jamie. "I haven't seen Marcus for a while," he said, naming his third tracker, from Jamie's pride. "What's with him?"

Jamie made a derisive noise, his tatts rippling as he stretched his hands. "Sex. Frenzy. Scent of a female. He's relieving his stress with Kenzie's cousin."

Bowman envied the man. He wanted nothing more right now than to be holed up with Kenzie, the two of them naked, not leaving the house for days. "Well, maybe he's better off than the rest of us." He let out a breath, suddenly tired, wanting to be done with this. He was coming to understand why Shifter leaders often welcomed the challenge by a younger member of their pack, knowing it was time to lay down the burden.

"If you can pry the two of them apart, tell Marcus I need him," Bowman said. "I'm going out to talk to that Turner guy again. I want you and Cade with me for that, and Marcus needs to guard the fort. And my mate and cub." Who were *not* coming with him.

The only way to make sure of that was to sneak off with Cade and Jamie, and so he did.

CHAPTER TWENTY

Before Bowman made for Turner's cabin, he led Cade and Jamie up into the woods toward where he was sure the sniper had been sitting.

They found indentations in the earth where someone had set up a camp stool or chair to wait. Near a rock, which would have made a good blind, they picked up shell casings. Bowman plucked them from the mud with the end of a twig and put them into a bag Cade had brought with him. With any luck, the casings might carry fingerprints—then again, would the shooter have left them around if they did?

"Why was he shooting at you?" Cade asked as they wandered the area, looking for more evidence. "Or was he just shooting anything that moved, for fun?"

There was nothing to tell them which.

They did at last find prints of thick-soled men's boots leading up a trail toward a road. Not much of a road—rough dirt and only wide enough for one vehicle. Tread marks showed that a pickup had sat here for a time last night. Snow had piled into its tracks, but the truck had left deep enough ruts in the mud that they were easy to read.

"Looks like it was a pickup about the size of mine," Cade said, a regretful note entering his big voice.

There was nothing sadder than a bear mourning the loss of his truck. "You sacrificed it for a good cause," Bowman said. "You know I'll make it up to you."

"*You* sacrificed it," Cade answered darkly. "But I'll hold you to the making-it-up part."

Jamie let out a laugh. "Are you going to build a funeral pyre to send it to the Goddess?"

"Maybe." Cade didn't smile. "I love that truck."

"You'll have as much fun fixing it up the second time." Bowman followed the tire tracks down the road a few yards before he stopped. This road, if he remembered from studying a map of the area this morning, led to a paved one that fed into an east-west highway. But so what? The shooter could have driven here from anywhere.

"Let's visit the strange professor in the trailer," Bowman said, coming back to them.

"Goody," Cade answered. "Just what I wanted to do today."

"I'll be the only one meeting with him," Bowman said. "I want you two to investigate the perimeter, find out all you can. I can't believe he wants so much isolation. No one could love that; I don't care if his dad left him the land and he's sentimental about it. He has to be up to something."

"Felines and Lupines couldn't love that, you mean," Cade said. "Bears like solitude." He grinned, his grief over his truck momentarily forgotten. "Although we'd prefer solitude with a hot female."

"Then it wouldn't be solitude," Jamie pointed out.

"Yeah it would. The best kind of solitude." Cade chuckled, then grew serious. "What I mean is, it's hell for Felines and Lupines to be on their own. You love being part of the group, even when you pretend you don't. But humans are different. Some of them, like bears, prefer being alone."

"Then why do humans use solitary confinement as a punishment?" Bowman countered.

Cade shrugged. "I don't know everything there is to know about humans. I'm speculating. But maybe Professor Turner is the kind of human who prefers to be on his own. You said that others laughed at him and made things hard for him before. Maybe that made him prefer his own company."

"Mmm," was all Bowman would say.

He'd had Pierce look Turner up on the university's website last night. The man did exist. Wayne Turner, associate professor, department of anthropology, University of North Carolina, Asheville. His photo appeared on the site, along with his campus office and phone number, his bio, and his educational background. BA from the University of South Carolina, meaning Kenzie had been right about his accent. PhD from the University of Virginia. Turner specialized in the history and culture of Shifters and their parallels to human culture. He'd published a number of articles in journals Bowman had never heard of, and had been interviewed on local television and on local and national radio.

Bowman was automatically distrustful of humans with too much interest in Shifters. He didn't need humans sniffing around Shiftertowns, finding out more than necessary. Shifters preferred to keep themselves mysterious. Safer that way.

Bowman also hadn't liked the remark Turner had made to Kenzie, observing that she and Bowman had only one cub. He hadn't missed the pain that had flared in Kenzie's eyes when he'd said it.

Ryan had come along after three years of trying, when Kenzie had been about to give up hope for a cub. Ryan had been big and healthy, with no problems at all, and they'd celebrated. For days. Kenzie and Bowman had assumed they'd have several more cubs quickly after that—a big family.

But they'd never conceived again. Not for lack of trying. They had plenty of mating frenzy, but no more cubs came. Bowman knew Kenzie blamed herself—in the past, low fertility among females had led to declines in Shifter population. But Bowman knew it could be his fault. He'd read that stress could lower sperm count, and leading this Shiftertown caused plenty of stress.

When they spied the trailer, Bowman signaled Cade and Jamie to fan out and explore. The two trackers faded noiselessly into the trees, and Bowman strode out into the clearing.

He arrived at the trailer, stepped up on the wooden stair to knock on the door, and found Cristian Dimitru already inside with Turner.

Kenzie and Ryan polished off the cinnamon rolls, Ryan eating most of them. They'd left none for Bowman, but Afina had stashed a second batch of dough in the freezer, the rolls formed already. All Kenzie had to do was bake and frost them.

Afina was like that—hard-edged, but then . . . cinnamon rolls. She could be thoughtful, kind, and loving, exactly what Kenzie had needed as a scared and lonely cub.

As Kenzie contemplated what she'd learned from her phone conversation with Gil, someone pounded on the front door. Alarmed and wary, Kenzie went to answer it.

Her cousin Bianca stood on the doorstep, bringing in the scent of winter plus a flurry of snow that had started to fall again.

Bianca was much younger than Kenzie, having been only a cub when they'd moved to Shiftertown. She'd gone through her Transition here, which was never easy on a Shifter, but she'd been able to do it surrounded by love and support. Bianca was actually a distant cousin, the daughter of one of Cristian's cousins. Her hair was lighter than Kenzie's, a shade of butternut, but she had the golden eyes of the Dimitru pack.

She was smiling at the moment—radiant. Not worried about snipers or murderers or monsters. Happier than Kenzie had ever seen her.

"Kenz, Bowman isn't here, is he?" Bianca asked, looking around the empty living room and into the kitchen.

"No, he's out with the trackers." Kenzie folded her arms and gave Bianca a severe look. "He's been trying to call Marcus, you know. Where is he?"

"Outside. Hiding." Bianca waved her hands, flustered. "I know. Marcus was afraid to come in—he knows Bowman is mad at him. So he sent me in to ask you to ask him. Bowman. I mean . . ." She broke off with a laugh. "Goddess, listen to me. I don't know where to start."

"Take a deep breath . . ."

Bianca took a big one, her chest lifting her sweatshirt. "We came to ask you to ask Bowman if he'll do the mating ceremony

for us," she said in a rush. "For Marcus and me. We know . . . I
mean." Bianca put her hand over her heart. "We *know*."

"You've formed the mate bond," Kenzie said, excited.

"Yes," Bianca answered, laughing and crying at once. "Oh,
Kenzie, it's so wonderful. I've never felt anything like it . . ."

Kenzie's throat closed up abruptly as she whirled between
several emotions at once. One was gladness—Shifters mating
and forming the bond was the most joyful event in Shiftertown.

The second emotion was stark envy. Then grief. The mate
bond came so easily for some. But for Kenzie and Bowman . . .

Bianca's face fell. "Oh, Kenzie, I'm sorry. I didn't mean
to . . ." Bianca enfolded Kenzie in a sudden embrace, her flowing
tears wetting Kenzie's cheek. "I didn't come here to make you
feel bad. I just . . . It's so exciting . . . I've never felt so happy, and
I don't know what I'm doing. I'm crying again. Marcus says I'm
the biggest crybaby. 'Course, he keeps doing it too."

"No." Kenzie took Bianca by the shoulders. "Mate bonding
is a *good* thing. I'm so happy for you. Bowman will be too—
even if a Lupine is mating with a Feline. He'll tease your asses
off, but he'll still be happy. I know he will."

"I've always loved you, Kenzie. You're the big sister I never
had." Tears streamed down Bianca's cheeks again, and she
broke from Kenzie to wipe them away. "I have *got* to stop crying. But I'm so emotional. We think . . . We hope . . . No, we
really do think . . ." Bianca slid her hand down to her abdomen, her eyes shining with joy.

Kenzie forgot about her envy. Cubs were the best things of
all. "Goddess, that's wonderful." She placed her hand on Bianca's belly. She felt nothing, but a mother always knew when a
cub was there. The spark was unmistakable.

"Are you having a cub, Bianca?" Ryan asked, interrupting
the female tears. He punched the air, then danced around in a
circle. "Woo-hoo! That's awesome. Hey, when he's big
enough, I'll teach him how to ride the zip line!"

"You want to know the attractions of living out here by
myself?" Turner looked unperturbed by the question
Cristian so bluntly asked.

They were seated in his office-like living room again. By the light of day, Turner seemed nothing more than an ordinary man. His thinning hair was partly gray, his blue eyes clear, though he peered nearsightedly at things through his thick glasses. He wore a sweatshirt, jeans, and running shoes—casual clothes for a casual setting.

Turner had given them cups of his excellent coffee before settling in on a chair and drinking one himself.

"I'll tell you why," he said. "I am finishing my book, remember? I need to have it done soon. I have soft money, you see. That means grant money," he explained. "I have a grant from the NEH—National Endowment for the Humanities—for my research into Shifters, their social history as far back as I can take it." Turner relaxed into his chair, crossing his legs comfortably. "When you accept grant money, however, you agree to produce something with it, like a book or articles published in peer-reviewed journals. That's so the grantees don't simply take the money and run. You have to account for every dollar spent and produce something that contributes to your field. With me, that means a thick tome with all my findings, charts, maps, and so forth. I only have a few months to finish the book and get it to the press that's publishing it." He heaved a long sigh. "So this year, I took a sabbatical and moved here to get away from phones, research assistants knocking on my door, endless committee meetings. You wouldn't believe how many committees I have to be on, and how many meetings each one generates." He looked pained.

"So this is your hideaway," Cristian said. He set his cup on the table next to him. "And we are disturbing it. Our apologies."

"Not at all," Turner said pleasantly. "I always have time for Shifters. You're my subject matter, after all." His eyes twinkled with his smile.

Bowman had said little, letting Cristian ask all the questions. Cristian, he had to admit, was much better at dealing with humans than Bowman was. For a man who hadn't seen a city until he was a hundred years old, Cristian could be urbane, and people liked his accent. Humans thought him cultured and cosmopolitan, when in reality, he'd been raised in a cave in Transylvania.

Bowman continued to sip coffee and let Cristian and Turner talk while he watched. And sniffed, covertly. He still couldn't figure out the scent layers here.

"And you knew nothing of the large animal in the woods?" Cristian asked. He hadn't brought it up—Turner had—asking them what all the fuss and distant fire had been about.

"I thought I saw something skulking around, but we get bears back here, so I didn't investigate. I leave bears alone and hope they leave me alone. Wild bears, that is. I've met one or two Shifter bears, but they were not keen to talk to me. Scary fellows, but fascinating."

Cade would be flattered by the description, Bowman thought.

"We do not yet know what the beast was," Cristian said. "But it is dead, so it is not likely to, as you say, skulk, any longer."

"Well, that's a relief, in a way. But I'm a softy about animals, so I can feel sorry for it. I suppose that's why I'm so interested in Shifters—an offshoot of my being an animal lover. A girlfriend in college told me I'd decided to study other cultures and how they interact because I was bad at interacting myself." Turner wheezed a laugh. "She was no doubt right. I'm going to ask you what I've been dying to, but I'm trying to be polite. I'd love to interview one or both of you for my book. A chapter straight from the Shifter's mouth, so to speak, would be just the thing. You're so long-lived you must have seen amazing changes in human history."

Cristian gave him an indulgent smile. "No asking our ages, please. It is impolite. I will say that I danced the waltz in Vienna when it was first introduced. I watched Napoleon march across Europe, and Hitler do it again a hundred and more years later. Making many of the same mistakes, I would like to point out. But mostly, Shifters kept to themselves and let humans live their own lives."

Turner listened, his eyes filled with the same kind of eagerness that fired the women and men who came to the Shifter bars. Turner was just another groupie, Bowman decided. Except he wanted knowledge rather than sex. Well—hopefully he didn't want sex.

"If I could get some stories from you, it would round out

the book," Turner said. He switched his gaze to Bowman. "Have you read the part I gave you?"

Bowman stilled. He'd caught, as Turner moved his eyes, a flash inside them, of something Bowman couldn't decipher, an emotion he couldn't pinpoint. Turner hid it well, and in the next second, it was gone. But the flash made Bowman come entirely alert.

Cristian also had seen it, Bowman could tell, though Cristian was more skilled at hiding his reaction. "My niece has the manuscript," Cristian said, pulling Turner's attention away from Bowman. "Kenzie—you met her. She will read and let you know."

"Good. Excellent. I look forward to it."

Cristian took this opening to rise to his feet. "Then we will leave you to it. Thank you for the coffee, Dr. Turner."

"Wayne, please." Turner stuck out his hand.

Cristian pretended to not quite know what to do with the offered hand, then become delighted that Turner was including him in the human custom. He looked hard into the man's eyes as he performed the handshake. Trying to read him, Bowman knew, but Turner didn't seem to notice.

Bowman drained his cup and gave Turner a polite thanks and good-bye, then he and Cristian left the house when Turner opened the door for them.

"I don't think you sucked up to him enough," Bowman said once they were well into the woods. "Sure you don't want to go back and sniff his ass?"

"I was, as you say, *buttering* him up, not sucking up," Cristian said, not offended. "I wanted to know what he knew. He is, on the surface, harmless."

"On the surface, sure. What about underneath? What did you get from him?"

"I don't know." Cristian looked troubled. "A very evasive man. He didn't lie to us—we would have scented that—but he did not provide the entire truth."

"That's what I got. That this whole setup is a lie." Bowman shook his head. "But it's not. He really is a professor at Asheville. Associate professor, whatever that means."

"It means he is tenured—he has a secure position at the university—but has not achieved the rank of full professor, which would give him great status and higher pay. It is my guess that with this book and all his research, he seeks to move up the next rung in the ladder."

Bowman shot him a look. "You know a lot about it."

"I research humans as much as this Dr. Turner researches Shifters. The Internet is very useful, the Guardian Network even more so—when I can convince the Guardians to look something up for me. I very much wish to read his book."

"Do. And tell me what's in it." They'd made it to the rendezvous point to find Cade waiting. Jamie jogged up as they stopped, and behind him came Kenzie's grandmother.

Cade pinned Cristian with a glare. "What are *you* doing here?"

Cristian gave him an alpha stare in return. "Have a care, tracker. Be courteous to your elders."

"I found Cristian grilling Turner," Bowman said. "He's good at it, so I let him. He's useful."

Cristian should have bristled at being called *useful*, but he was too experienced to react to Bowman's insults. "What did you learn?" Christian asked the other three.

Jamie had his hands on his hips, looking annoyed. "There's all kinds of Shifters out here today," he said, glancing at Afina. "Look who I ran into."

"He nearly did run into me," Afina said. "I thought cats were graceful." She smiled when Jamie hid a snarl. "I will be gracious and let you, the important male, tell your leader what we found."

Jamie gave her another irritated look. He'd never openly be hostile to a venerable female like Afina, but he was not happy. Bowman had to wonder what had happened between them out there.

"We found buildings," Jamie said. "Small ones. Shacks, to the naked eye, but shored up and well kept. Two of them, about a mile from Turner's house. We sniffed around, but they were empty. No smell of Shifters, or Fae, or . . . griffins. Might be used by pot farmers."

"I found one like that too," Cade said. "About half a mile from here, maybe a little more. Empty, unused, but well kept. Didn't smell like much of anything."

"If they'd been used to store drugs, the smell would still be there," Bowman said. "To Shifters, anyway."

Jamie broke in. "Don't drug dealers use coffee grounds or whatever to hide the scent from sniffer dogs?" He wrinkled his nose. "Not that I smelled coffee grounds either."

"Turner uses a distinctive blend of coffee," Cristian said. "You'd have smelled it if it had been him out there. It's very good. I will have to ask him where he acquires it."

"There was much mist under the trees," Afina said, her voice going quiet. "I do not trust the mists."

Cristian frowned at her, but uneasily. "It's winter. Of course there is mist as the air warms and cools."

"That is not what I mean, and you know this."

Cade watched both of them. "What are you two talking about?"

Cristian gave his mother another scowl and shook his head at Cade. "Romanian folktales. It is of no matter."

"So you say," Afina returned. "But you'd do well to avoid the mists. You don't know everything, son of mine."

Cristian bristled. They would launch into one of their famous arguments any second.

Bowman was grateful for the soft buzz of his cell phone. He again hadn't found a signal in Turner's trailer, but now that they were higher up the hill, the phone worked fine.

It was Kenzie. "You need to come home," she said, her voice sounding too bright. "A couple of our Shifters are asking to be mated."

CHAPTER TWENTY-ONE

Kenzie took her place near Bowman that afternoon as the Shifters gathered for a mating under full sun. The ceremony had been thrown together in record time, but Shifters were always ready to party.

Streamers had been tied to the trees by females and cubs. Bianca's sisters had rushed to a flower shop in the nearest town and then wove Bianca a garland that was a bit lopsided. Amid the laughter and excitement, though, no one cared how makeshift anything was.

Bad things were happening outside Shiftertown, but the Shifters were eager to put aside fear and embrace this celebration of love, life, and continuity. Because the moon was in one of the three days of the full, Bowman would conduct the sun ceremony now and the full moon ceremony tonight. The moon ceremony was the more important of the two and would seal Bianca and Marcus's mating in the eyes of Shifters and the Goddess.

The mate bond the two had already found would seal them more permanently than any ritual. The mate bond was older, a spiritual joining that had no material form. The link would keep them together through thick and thin, good times and bad, and couldn't be broken. Only death severed the bond, and sometimes the second of the pair didn't survive the grief.

Kenzie didn't necessarily have to participate in the mating ceremony. She could simply stand by while Bowman gave the blessing and be a silent symbol of a successful mating. She chose to give a blessing herself today—Bianca was special to her.

Bowman faced the couple in the woods between the houses, under a tree full of streamers. Friends and family formed a circle around Bowman, Kenzie, Marcus, and Bianca, while the rest of Shiftertown ringed them in ever-widening circles.

Though it was cold, the snow had ceased, and the sun poked through the clouds. When a beam touched Bianca, Bowman lifted his hands.

"Under the light of the sun, the Father God, I declare you mated."

A cheer went up, nearly drowning Kenzie's words. She had to shout them. "The blessings of the Father God be upon you!"

The cheer renewed. Ryan leapt into the air on youthful legs and did a handspring when he came down. Bianca laughed, and Kenzie pulled her into a hug. Kenzie hugged Marcus next, the long-limbed Feline nearly crushing her in his happiness.

After a marathon of hugging, fire flared high, in both bonfires and barbecue grills, and music boomed out of speakers Jamie had wired up in the trees. It was late afternoon, and as soon as the sky darkened and the moon rose, the second ceremony would commence.

For now, there was plenty of food and drink, music and dancing. Kenzie found herself drawn into a circle dance with Bianca and her sisters—all the cousins who had grown up together. They joined hands and swayed in the eternal dance of love and fertility.

The males circled in the opposite direction outside them, always interested in fertility. The men might stay calm until the moon ceremony, but after that, no female Shifter would go without a male tonight, unless she was very fast and good with her claws. Looking at the eager faces of her female cousins and Bianca's girlfriends, Kenzie knew they wouldn't try to run very fast.

Bowman didn't join the dance, though Jamie did, celebrating his cousin's joy with him. Bowman stood with Cade outside the circles, Cade grinning, loving the ceremony. Bowman didn't smile, but Kenzie could tell he was glad of this mating.

Matings meant more cubs, stronger Shifters. The cubs born of the mating frenzies tonight would never wear Collars, if Kenzie and Bowman could help it. That thought made the occasion even brighter.

Bowman caught Kenzie's gaze and held it as she danced. His eyes were smoke gray, the sunlight bringing out the sparkle in them.

He was virile, strong, his sweatshirt and jeans showing off his honed body. More than one woman looked his way in longing. He might be mated, but Bowman hadn't formed the mate bond, and there was always a chance he'd find it with one of *them*. A cub born of a Shifter leader was powerful indeed.

No, Kenzie decided after watching the women watch Bowman awhile. It wasn't just the prospect of a strong cub that made all the unmated females look at him. Bowman was in-your-face, body-clenching hot. Simply touching him made Kenzie ripple with fire, and the fact that she could touch him whenever she wanted made her tighten in satisfaction.

Kenzie shot him a smile, one that said she didn't care how many women followed him with their eyes. Bowman was *hers*.

Bowman frowned back at her, his look becoming fierce. He had no idea what wild fantasies were flitting through her head, and that made her smile widen.

More scowling from Bowman. The expression made his face hard, his mouth tight. Kenzie would soften it with kisses later.

Bowman held her gaze until the dance took her around the circle and too many Shifters got between her and him, and he was lost to sight.

The sun sank, the winter night closing fast. The clouds parted and the moon rose. Another cheer went up, this one holding a wilder note. Voices turned to howls as clothes were shed and Shifters assumed animal forms.

Those who stayed human began a chant to the Goddess. Circles formed. The moon shone down, brushing the woods with silver, rendering it an enchanted place.

The cries, howls, and ululations were shrill with bacchanalian excitement. Bianca and Marcus stood in the middle of the circle again, Bianca's garland slightly squashed, Marcus's wildcat eyes glowing soft gold.

Bowman raised his hands for silence, and mostly got it. The chanters continued, the circles moving slowly as the dancers shuffled their feet in the halting rhythm.

"Under the light of the Mother Goddess," Bowman said, his words booming over the crowd. "As your Shifter leader . . ." He broke off, his eyes sparkling with mirth. "Are you sure you two want to do this?"

Around him Shifters shouted and screamed, crying out in rising frenzy.

Kenzie draped her arm around Bowman's shoulder. "Get on with it, sweetie. Marcus is about to explode."

Marcus winked at Kenzie. Bianca giggled, looking as though *she* wanted to jump Marcus's bones any second.

"All right then." Bowman drew a long breath. He raised his arms again, playing it up, then he threw his head back and howled.

The sound, even from his human throat, cut through the night. The wolves of his pack, attuned to their leader, took up the howl. Those in wolf form let it rise in crazed joy, celebrating the Goddess, and her symbol, the moon.

Kenzie felt her wolf respond. Her fingers slid into claws, and her throat wanted to take up the howl. Only great effort kept her from shifting all the way.

Bowman's howl wound to a close. He brought his arms down slowly, but the Lupines' cries went on. Joining it were the yowls and roars of the Felines and the rumbling growls of the bears.

Bowman spoke in a loud voice. "Under the light of the Mother Goddess, as the leader of the O'Donnell pack . . . and Marcus's boss . . ."

"He acknowledges this mating," Ryan yelled from his father's feet. "Like Mom said, get on with it, Dad."

Laughter burst out, softening the crazed screaming and howling. Bowman's face split with a grin, and he said loudly, "What *he* said. I acknowledge this mating!"

Kenzie was laughing at her son and mate so hard that she

could barely get out her words. "The blessings of the Goddess be upon you!"

Another long whoop went up, followed by more screaming, roaring, howling, shouting. Kenzie had once gone to a concert with Bianca and her cousins, in a crowd that had filled an arena. The noise had been crazy, but it was nothing compared to what the entire Shiftertown could do when they were rejoicing. Shifters knew how to *party*.

Bianca and Marcus were lifted away on shoulders, carried through the chanting crowd. Kenzie found herself lifted as well, passed over heads from hand to hand while she laughed.

Ryan was being bounced around too, and loving it. Bowman, everyone left alone.

The cubs ran around like crazed streaks, paying no attention to the adults. Clothes began to come off, Kenzie's female cousins throwing off their shirts as they were lifted by the crowd, moonlight touching bare breasts.

In her younger years, Kenzie had joined them, but as leader's mate, she kept her clothes firmly on. No use tempting males to come after her, which would make Bowman have to discipline them. She had enough sense, even on a night like this, to keep from that kind of mess.

Cade enjoyed it plenty though, as did Jamie. Cade was already half unclothed in the cold, his jeans sagging around his hips. Jamie had shifted, dashing around in his cheetah form so fast his spots seemed to blur.

Cade jumped onto a tall tree stump, putting himself above the crowd. "Hey!" he shouted. "Up at my house. *Zip-line streaking!*"

About half the Shifters cheered and followed him, the other half too intent on dancing, disrobing, and seeking mates for the night.

The elder Shifters started to round up the cubs to herd them indoors, the cubs protesting all the way. But Afina and the others were firm. In they went, but for a big slumber party involving lots of hot chocolate. The cubs had the right to celebrate too.

Bowman's arms came around Kenzie from behind, as she stood on her feet again, catching her breath. His body vibrated with tension and need as he kissed her neck. "You all right?"

"I'm fine," Kenzie said, closing her eyes to feel his heat. "It's a happy time."

"I know." Another nip to her neck. "But . . ."

"No buts." Kenzie turned in his arms and cupped his face in her hands. "No regrets, Bowman. Not tonight."

Bowman regarded her steadily. She saw raw pain in the depths of his gray eyes, but also vast hunger.

"I agree." He turned his head and kissed her palm. "No regrets tonight."

Kenzie shook her head. The other Shifters faded into the distance as they followed Cade or the cubs, or found the nearest soft thing to land on with a partner.

Bowman gave Kenzie a hot smile, completing the river of fire inside her. "You want to go zip-line streaking?"

"No," Kenzie said softly. "Not right now."

Bowman touched his forehead to hers. "Kenz."

The one word was filled with longing, need, heartache, and frustration

The next thing she knew, Kenzie was against a tree, its bark digging into her back, Bowman's strong hands tearing at her clothes.

CHAPTER TWENTY-TWO

Kenzie smelled and tasted like the night. Her breath was hot, her skin chilled from the winter cold. Fire and ice, that was Kenzie.

Her scent had Bowman wound high. He'd been hard since she'd wrapped her arm around him at the ceremony, giving him the sassy admonishment to get on with it.

His howl had been for Kenzie, for the night and the powerful wanting inside him. For his need, and the longing to be with her forever.

Bowman fumbled with the zipper of her jeans, working it open to find her bare beneath. She never bothered with underwear when there was a possibility she'd be shifting. Fine with Bowman. He grasped her smooth bottom and dragged her close, capturing her mouth in a firm kiss. Kenzie dug her fingers into his sweatshirt, hanging on, while their tongues stroked, lips and mouths seeking.

Her frantic hands tugged his shirt upward, her cold fingers landing on his hot skin. Bowman broke the kiss to strip his shirt from his body, then he pushed her jacket from her and skimmed her shirt off over her head. With her shirt gone and her jeans sagging down her hips, Kenzie was an erotic sight.

The beauty of her in the moonlight made his breath catch. Her breasts were touched by silver, the nipples dark and tight. She shook out her hair, the rumpled brown and gold brushed by moonlight.

Her jeans fell, and now she was bare. Kenzie clung to Bowman while she wrapped first one leg, then the other around his hips, the heat of her planted exactly over the ridge inside his jeans. She began to rub him, while Bowman held her against him, the friction driving him wild.

He bit her chin, then her neck. He loved the scent of her, her beauty only for him.

Kenzie. *Mate.*

Her look turned to one of pure pleasure as she worked herself against the solid denim of his jeans. His cock pounded beneath the cloth, wanting something less tame than simply rubbing against her. Any other night he might slow down and enjoy the myriad sensations, but tonight was electrifying, blotting out all but his rawest needs.

He unlocked Kenzie's legs from him and set her back down, her small noise of protest making him nearly lose all control. Then he unbuckled, unzipped, and kicked his way out of his pants. He was bare beneath as well, also for ease of shifting.

He had Kenzie against the tree again before she could draw a breath. He lifted her, wrapping her legs around his hips, positioning himself at the spread of her.

She leaned back, his strong mate, and Bowman held her behind her waist, her hands locked around his neck. His cock brushed her opening, then slid inside, until she was taking all of him.

Their first mating, long ago, had been primal, so full of torn clothing and rug burns that Bowman hadn't had time to register the pleasure of it. It had been the most intense sex of his life up until that point.

But every time since then had been even better. Tonight was no exception. Those who believed coupling with the same person palled over time, or that the sex could never be as good as the first time, had to be insane. Or maybe they just weren't very good at it.

Kenzie made each experience amazing. Just when Bowman thought he'd never feel more explosive pleasure, Kenzie showed him he was wrong. She knew exactly how to touch him, how to stroke him. Even Kenzie running light fingers across his chest could have him hard and ready in an instant.

When she'd crawled under the covers last night to take him in her mouth, Bowman had thought he'd die. He'd wanted to pin her down and make love to her and never stop.

Now he turned in a circle with her, buried deep inside her. She moved against him, her eyes softening as she found pleasure, which she was giving back to him tenfold.

Goddess, I love you, Kenzie. How could I ever be without you?

Moonlight bathed her face in radiance. Her breasts moved with their rhythm, her breath quickening to gasps of delight. Bowman didn't dampen his groans and the growling laughter in his throat. This was a mating ceremony night, when Shifters gave in to their carnal desires, answering that most basic instinct—to mate, to make cubs.

The Goddess be blessed for making this instinct pure joy.

Bowman held her. "Kenzie, love . . ."

Kenzie answered with wordless cries, their love ringing through the woods. Nothing mattered in the world—not the Collar that gleamed on Kenzie's throat, not the threats outside Shiftertown, not even the problem of the mate bond.

Only *this* mattered, joining with Kenzie, loving her, being one with her. And at the same remaining two, because no way could one single being feel *This. Damn. Good.*

He was coming. Bowman heard words leave his mouth. "You're beautiful, Kenz. You've got the finest ass, the hottest . . ." More phrases, from poetic to filthy came in time with his thrusts. She was hot and slick, and embraced him with her whole body. "I want to be inside you, and never . . . come . . . out."

Kenzie's hips rocked with his, her strong arms steadying herself and, at the same time, him. She was Bowman's anchor, his reality. His necessity.

He loved her, and the hell he'd ever let her go to some asshole who claimed he had a mate bond with her. Screw the fucking mate bond.

Bowman's cries turned to howls. Kenzie's joined his. Their wolves, buried deep within them, rejoiced in the moonlight, for this mating, this joining of bodies and twining of souls.

Bowman found himself on the ground, still inside Kenzie, tears stinging his eyes. Kenzie's face was wet too, but her smile was wide.

She put up her hand and wiped a tear from Bowman's cheek, then they collapsed together into the soft pine needles with warm kisses and touches, murmuring things to each other that weren't really words at all.

B owman often left Kenzie directly after loving, especially when they shared an intense coupling. She lay quietly under him now as he stilled, and braced herself for him heaving to his feet and walking away.

She was surprised, then, when Bowman remained on top of her, gently kissing her neck, licking where he'd bitten her. Kenzie didn't want to move much, in case it reminded him to go, but she couldn't help running her fingers through his short hair, liking the silken buzz of it.

Dappled light touched Bowman's shoulders, brushing the sculpted beauty of his back, his legs, the rise of his buttocks. Kenzie thought she could lie here under him forever, his strength surrounding her.

He raised his head and kissed the tip of her nose, then her lips, with slow tenderness. The sweet kiss led to something deeper, going on for some time.

Bowman lifted his head. His eyes were the same color as the moonlight, his Collar a black streak against his sun-kissed throat.

"We're good together," he said in a soft voice. "You and me."

Beyond the darkness, Shiftertown was lit up, music blaring, Shifters yelling and carrying on. Kenzie couldn't see them from where she lay, but she could definitely hear them. Probably half the county could.

"Yeah," Kenzie answered, smiling up at Bowman. "We are."

She touched his face, feeling the burn of whiskers, and traced his lips. Bowman caught her fingers with his teeth. He drew her forefinger all the way into his mouth, working it the same way he would her nipple. He did so for a time, until Kenzie moved beneath him, fires stirring like the leaping flames of the bonfires.

"The Goddess made us for each other," he said when he released her finger, licking it one more time. "I knew when I first saw you. I looked past all those scared Shifters, and you were standing there, straight up and take-no-shit, helping the cubs, getting in the face of the human guards who tried to mess with you. I never wanted to look away."

"I couldn't look away from you either." Kenzie sent him a grin. "But we had to, or we'd still be there."

"When I knew I had to take a mate, there was no question who it would be."

Kenzie drew her hand through his hair again. She knew he'd come to her to keep Uncle Cristian off his back, but Cristian had other nieces. Bowman could have made a different choice.

"I'm glad you picked me," Kenzie said softly.

Bowman started to laugh. The sound was warm, low, and made her shiver. "Seriously, Kenz, if I'd tried to mate-claim anyone else, you'd have come after me and killed me."

"Possibly." True, Kenzie had never bothered to hide her interest in Bowman. She hadn't chased him, but when she'd seen him around Shiftertown, or at the roadhouse, she'd made sure he looked at her. She'd flirted, swayed her hips, contrived to be wearing the tightest clothes she could when she knew he'd be at the bar. When she'd danced with other men—human or Shifter—she'd look over at Bowman and give him a challenging look.

Bowman's laugh went low, as though he remembered the same things. "No 'possibly' about it. You drove me frigging crazy. I remember once, you mooned me in the roadhouse parking lot. I thought I was going to die. If we'd have been alone, I'd have grabbed you and taken you right there."

"Yeah?" Kenzie slanted him a smile. "I remember you shaking your head and walking away with Cade and Jamie."

"And keeping Jamie from running after you like the horny Feline he is. Of course I wanted you, Kenz. You have the best ass I've ever seen. And being Shifter, I've seen a lot of naked asses. Trust me, yours is the prettiest."

"Are you trying to get into my pants, Bowman O'Donnell? Thinking you have a right to any female you want?"

"Your pants are way over there, Mrs. O'Donnell. The only female I want is *you*. You and your great ass." He looked down at her chest, her skin pearlescent in the moonlight. "Your tits aren't bad either."

"Watch it," Kenzie said. "My evil uncle will make you mate-claim me."

Bowman's voice went low, all teasing gone. "Way too late for that."

He growled as he kissed her, hungry, savage. Kenzie tried to kiss him back, but Bowman broke away, seized her by the hips, and rolled her facedown.

Kenzie pretended to try to scramble away, but she shivered in happiness when Bowman caught her and dragged her back to him.

Bowman plunged inside her from behind, thrusting with the power that would join them, body and soul. Kenzie laughed into the cold, crisp air, loving him, until her laughter wound into joyous cries.

B owman walked with Kenzie back to the heart of Shifter-town later that night, hand in hand. Kenzie was sore, her knees scraped raw. Bowman moved a bit stiffly himself.

They found Ryan at the cub slumber party, watched over by Afina and other older Shifters, including Cristian. Ryan begged to stay the whole night, and Bowman gave the okay. As long as he didn't go to the zip line, not at night—and not without him or Kenzie.

"You mean because they're all starkers up there," Ryan said. "It's only unmated Shifters, Dad." He made a face. "They're just trying to have sex. Like you and Mom. *Not* interested."

One of the girl cubs laughed, but she looked sublimely unin-terested as well. Cubs had no hormonal urges until their Transi-tions in their twenties, and then—watch out. Kenzie would have about another fifteen years before she had to deal with Ryan going through his, but she knew those years would fly by.

Kenzie kissed Ryan good night, then Bowman did, and they walked out into the darkness.

"I'd better go up to Cade's and make sure there's no mate Challenges," Bowman said, sounding regretful. "They're drunk on beer and frenzy. I don't need Shifters trying to fight each other to the death while hanging from a zip line."

Kenzie laughed, but she understood his worry. Shifter rules said no Challenges on mating ceremony night, but when feral needs flared, rules got flushed.

Bowman stuck his hands in his jacket pockets, looking like a wild animal trying to wear civilized clothes. Whiskers were stark black on his face, and his was hair rumpled, his eyes slightly bleary with all the lovemaking they'd enjoyed.

"Check on the Shifters *not* trying to get some tonight," Bowman said. "Make sure they're all right."

"That won't be many, but I will."

Kenzie should turn and walk away now, businesslike. They both had jobs to do, keeping Shiftertown safe. They'd meet up later at home, compare notes. Like always.

Tonight, Kenzie didn't want to look away from Bowman. She kept her gaze on him as he stood a few feet from her, his breath steaming in the cold. His eyes caught hers, the silver gray piercing her to the heart.

Finally, Bowman gave her a nod, turned around, and walked up the street, heading for the end of the zip line. His boots crunched in the loose stones on the asphalt, then darkness swallowed him, and he was gone.

Kenzie sighed, wishing they didn't always have to be Shiftertown leaders. If they were ordinary Shifters, they could lock themselves away and continue what they'd enjoyed in the woods, not emerging for days.

Making herself do her job, Kenzie looked in on the indoor Shifter parties going on, making sure that Shifters who needed to go home got there. She left the parties behind, ignoring the slurred pleas for her to stay, and finally went back home. A few hours in the quiet wouldn't come amiss.

Not meant to be. A car sat in the narrow driveway of the O'Donnell house, and when Kenzie walked inside, she found Gil Ramirez in her living room.

CHAPTER TWENTY-THREE

"Sorry," Gil said, when Kenzie paused on the threshold. "I let myself in. When I called him tonight, Bowman said it would be all right to wait here for you."

"Bowman said . . ." Kenzie trailed off and slammed the door, sliding out of her jacket. "Bowman so needs to learn to text me."

Gil chuckled. "He's an old-fashioned guy. I can respect that."

Kenzie made an impatient noise and walked through the living room to the kitchen. "Did he tell you to help yourself to beer? Or did he want you to wait for me to be the gracious hostess again?"

"If it's a bad time, Kenz, I can talk to you later."

Kenzie turned around with two bottles of beer to see Gil standing in the living room looking apologetic. She flushed.

"No, it's fine." She came back in and handed him a bottle. "Bowman just drives me crazy. Not your fault."

Gil accepted the opened beer, gestured to the sofa, and waited until Kenzie had seated herself before sitting down beside her. Human courtesy.

"So a mating ceremony today?" Gil asked, sipping beer. "Celebrations in my family can be pretty wild too."

"Your family is from here?" Kenzie said. "North Carolina, I mean?"

"No, I'm not native to the Carolinas. Most people think I'm Cherokee, but my family are from far away, and we left there a long time ago."

Kenzie eyed him in curiosity. "From where?"

Gil shrugged. "You wouldn't know it. You're from what's now called Romania, right?"

"I am. Bowman's from Canada. Did you come here to talk about where we're all from?"

"No, I came here to talk about our case." Gil set down his beer and pulled a manila envelope from the inside of his jacket. "I found out about Serena Mitton, the girl who was shot. You interested?"

Of course she was interested. Kenzie noticed that Gil had turned the questions about him neatly aside, but she said nothing as he pulled out papers and photographs.

"Death was from two gunshots to the chest," he said, scanning a sheet, "from a nine millimeter. She died quickly, the report says. Her name was Serena Mitton. She grew up in Baltimore and moved down here to attend UNC at Asheville. She stayed and became a research assistant while she worked on her master's degree, in the anthropology department."

Kenzie's eyes widened. "Did she work for Dr. Turner?" She'd told him all about Dr. Turner when she'd called him this morning.

"Nope. She was an RA in the lab of one Dr. Jane Alston. From what Dr. Alston told me, Serena did no work for Dr. Turner, and didn't interact much with him either. Nodded to him in the hall, maybe, but that's it."

So why had the woman been found dead within a few miles of Turner's trailer house? Near where the beast had been killed? After she'd called Bowman saying, *I don't like what he's doing.* "I don't believe in coincidences," Kenzie said.

"Well, they do happen, but in this case, I agree with you." Gil gathered up the photos: a head shot of Serena and one of the entire department staff. Turner was in that one, at the other end of the row from Serena, looking geeky and professorial, as he'd been when Kenzie had met him. "I checked out the shell casings from the sniper shooting too," Gil said, "but forensics couldn't find any useable fingerprints on them." He closed up the envelope but left it on the coffee table.

"So you don't know who shot Serena, or who shot at us in the woods, or whether the two are connected?"

"I do not. But I'm working on it." Gil leaned forward, his elbows on his knees. "What I *do* know about is that thing you were calling a griffin. Dr. Pat, the nice veterinarian, shared her findings with me, plus I studied some tissue samples. It's an animal all right, but magic went into its making. That much was obvious."

Kenzie blinked and tried to look surprised. "Magic?"

Most humans didn't know anything about magic, or at least, not the real kind. There was magic deep inside Shifters, and in the Collars, and in the Guardian's sword. None of it was stage-magician, make-things-disappear magic, but it was there, and it was powerful.

"Yes, and I know you know what I mean." Gil's dark eyes held seriousness. "There is no way that creature could have lived, not in this world, without a boost of magic. Fae magic, I'm betting."

Kenzie got to her feet very fast. "What the hell do you know about Fae magic? Are you Fae?"

Gil rose to meet her, looking offended. "Hell no, I'm not Fae. But I know about them. I know about the ley lines that run through this Shiftertown and all the way to where you found the thing dead. I'm a bit of a shaman, myself." He contrived to sound modest.

Shaman. So that was why he'd seemed off. Shamans were human, not Fae, thank the Goddess, but they were able to sense and use magic that was inherent in this world.

"I see," Kenzie said cautiously. "What does your shaman knowledge tell you about the creature?"

"That it wasn't born here. Poor thing. Probably bred and raised beyond a gate to Faerie and shoved through to be set on you. The questions are—by whom? And why?"

"By the Fae." Kenzie's anger rose. "In their never-ceasing quest to kill off Shifters or enslave us again."

"No," Gil surprised her by saying. "I'm not sure a Fae did

this, or at least, had control of the beast on this side of the gate. The smell was wrong, and the tissue samples were definitely animal. But the Fae bred Shifters, right? This was the same kind of thing—breeding with magic thrown in. As though someone was trying to redo what the Fae did with Shifters, only making it bigger and stronger."

Kenzie felt ill. "Not anything I want to hear."

"I bet you don't. But look on the bright side. It didn't work. Bowman hurt it with the truck, sure, but the thing died of natural causes. Had heart failure, Dr. Pat thinks. Its body couldn't sustain its size and broke down. Whoever bred it didn't succeed."

"*This* time." Kenzie's blood grew cold. "What about next time?"

"If we can find out who did it and stop them, there won't be a next time."

"We hope."

Gil looked unworried, which was irritating of him. Then again, he wasn't a Shifter, target of every Fae vendetta.

He gestured her to the sofa again. "This isn't all I came over to tell you, or I'd have waited until I knew Bowman would be here. I wanted to talk to *you*."

Kenzie let out a breath and resumed her seat. "What about?"

Gil sat down again, facing her, his beer untouched on the coffee table. He cleared his throat. "I wanted to ask you about the mate bond."

Kenzie started. "The mate bond? Why?"

"Is it true that a human can form one with a Shifter?"

"Yes." Kenzie's heart beat faster. "I know several human and Shifter couples who have it. The humans, after the mating ceremonies, get a dose of Fae magic to extend their lives to match Shifter lifespan. That's from a treaty from the Shifter-Fae war. Fae are shits, but they honor treaties. A pride thing. Why?" She heard herself babbling, but Gil watching her closely with his warm eyes was making her nervous.

"What does it feel like?"

Kenzie swallowed, and her eyes stung. "I don't know. Unfortunately."

"I heard you don't have one with Bowman." Gil leaned forward and touched her knee, a gesture not of sexual need, but of sympathy. Friendship. "I know it hurts you, and I understand why. I'm asking you this for an important reason."

Kenzie's fingers moved restlessly, her throat hurting. "I hear that it's a warmth in the chest, in the heart. There's an answering warmth in the mate. That's how it starts, but then you *know*. You know with your whole being."

"A warmth, here?" Gil pressed his closed fist to his heart. "You sure?"

"As sure as I can be without feeling it myself." Kenzie's gaze went to Gil's hand, her attention sharpening. "Why?"

"Because I think *I'm* feeling it." Gil dug his fist into his sweatshirt. "It's there, and it won't go away."

Kenzie rose abruptly. What was it about Gil that had her jumping up and down like a jack-in-the-box? "Maybe you have heartburn. You should go see a doctor."

Gil was up beside her. "I don't, and you know it. Are you sure, Kenz, that you aren't feeling it too?"

He curled his other fist and pressed it to her chest, right between her breasts. Again, the touch wasn't erotic or suggestive, but a gentle press, a friend helping a friend.

The tingling in Kenzie's heart she'd been trying to ignore blossomed into heat. Not sharp heat, but an agreeable warmth that tried to loosen and relax her.

"No." She jerked back in panic, breaking the contact. The tingling receded but didn't go away. "You're a shaman, you said. You're tricking me."

Gil stepped close to her, and Kenzie found herself looking into the eyes of a very strong man, an alpha in his own right. He hid his power behind smiles and a self-deprecating manner, but it was there.

"It's not a trick," Gil said. "It's real. Look inside yourself, Kenzie. You'll see it's true."

"No!" Kenzie backed another step, starting to shake. "I don't have a mate bond with you. I can't have. I *can't*."

Gil only stood there. The light in the living room was suddenly garish, hurting her eyes. Another being seemed to transpose itself with Gil, looking like him but stained with harsh magic she didn't understand.

"What are you?" Kenzie shouted. "You're one of the fucking Fae, I *knew* it!"

Gil's face darkened. "I told you I wasn't. Don't insult me. Call me any name you want, but for the Goddess's sake, not *Fae*."

Kenzie pointed a rigid finger at the front door. "Get out of my house!"

"You've been in denial since the day I met you, Kenzie. Open your eyes and look around." Gil came to her, and Kenzie couldn't move. He smelled of the woods and the night, and a faint tang of magic. "I know it's a lot to take in." He touched her chest again, and Kenzie's breath caught. She felt the heat, and she couldn't pull away. "Think about it awhile. I'll be around when you want to talk."

Kenzie's throat closed up. "Please, go away."

"I'm going, don't worry." Gil leaned forward and gave her a light kiss on the cheek. The little smile he sent her broke her heart.

He left then, disappearing out the door so quickly she barely saw him go. Kenzie was left alone with two mostly filled bottles of beer, a wrinkled manila envelope, and confused thoughts whirling through her brain.

She couldn't have formed the mate bond with Gil. She *couldn't* have. She barely knew him. He wasn't Shifter.

Cold reason made her discard the arguments as quickly as they came. Shifters could form the mate bond the instant they met their true mate. They could form it with humans and half humans—hell, the Guardian of the Austin Shiftertown had mate bonded with a Shifter who was half Fae.

Kenzie loved Bowman. He was her mate. It would kill her to leave him. It would kill Ryan.

No. She couldn't. It couldn't happen. Not like this.

Gil had said she'd been in denial since she'd met him, and maybe she had. Kenzie had felt something when she'd sat in Gil's car, a feeling that she could talk to him as though they were old friends, even though she'd never seen him before in her life.

Of course Kenzie denied the mate bond with him. It was all wrong.

Her thoughts went to Bowman, smiling at her in the darkness. *We're good together, you and me.*

The memory of his rumbling voice, the warm weight of him as he lay on her in the woods, broke her. Kenzie collapsed to the sofa, all strength leaving her, and she cried as she'd never cried in her life.

Cristian wandered Shiftertown, both irritated and amused at the carryings-on of the Shifters around him. A person would think Shifters never had sex except on mating ceremony nights, but this was not the case. Shifters used any excuse to do the deed.

Cristian was no celibate, but he chose his partners carefully. He was pack and clan leader, and female Shifters were always looking for a high-ranking male to give them cubs. Cristian was older than many of the Shifters in this town, but it didn't matter. To a mate-seeking female, he was a walking target.

But since his mate had gone, so long ago now, taking half his heart with him, Cristian had kept his relationships physical, nothing more. The animal in him needed to relieve basic needs, but he never let things go beyond that.

His beloved Melita had been his life. They'd had forty years together before she'd been shot by a human hunter, mistaken for one of the wolves that had been attacking livestock on nearby farms. She'd died in his arms, and Cristian had kissed her lips before the Guardian had sent her to dust.

Cristian had taken his vengeance on the humans who'd killed her, then disappeared into the wilds for a long time to grieve. Kenzie had found him out there and persuaded him to come home.

She'd been a cub, orphaned, alone, a leggy little wolf with rumpled hair. Adorable. Cristian had followed her back and tried to continue his life.

Now Kenzie was in pain, and he knew it. Bowman was a good leader—Cristian hated to admit it—but Kenzie hurt whenever she looked at the asshole. Cristian would have to do something about that.

And about all the crap that was going on around here. If Bowman didn't get it done, and fast, Cristian would do it for him.

In fact, he'd start now.

CHAPTER TWENTY-FOUR

Bowman returned from patrolling Shiftertown once the sun was rising and Shifters were crawling home. Some slept where they dropped. Lumps of fur littered the ground, Shifters snoring it off.

Bowman had realized long ago that being leader meant he didn't always get to join in the revelry. He protected the perimeter so that his Shifters could let loose and enjoy themselves.

Kenzie often patrolled with him, the two of them sharing the quiet while Shiftertown partied behind them. Now that the party was over, Bowman headed home, intending to make up for missing out—with Kenzie. Ryan was safely with Afina, and they'd have the house to themselves.

When he entered the kitchen through the back door, all was silent. The old-fashioned percolator coffeepot sat on the counter, its lid off, the scent of cold coffee lingering in the room. The coffee table he saw through the open space to the living room held two open bottles of beer, but no one seemed to be around. Bowman did a quick inhale and scented human male over the familiar scents of the house. A particular human male. Gil.

The door to the bedroom he shared with Kenzie was

closed. Bowman strode immediately to it, his killing instincts flaring high. His Collar bit a warning spark deep into his skin, but he ignored it.

He was sick to his stomach as he reached for the doorknob. He did *not* want to open that door and find Gil with Kenzie, but at the same time he needed to let the world know that any man who touched his mate would be ripped in half.

Bowman swallowed bile, ignored a second spark from his Collar, and entered the room.

Kenzie sat cross-legged in the middle of the unrumpled bed. She was dressed in jeans and a tank top, her arms bare, though the room was cool. She had a wad of crumpled tissues in her hand, and she didn't look up when Bowman came in.

"Kenzie, what's wrong?" he asked, his heart pounding. His Collar quieted, but his fears surged. "What happened?"

Kenzie raised her head. Her eyes were red, her nose swollen, her cheeks tear-streaked. "Gil." She started to say more, but a sob caught in her chest.

Bowman came all the way into the room, to the bed. "What did he do to you? Did he touch you? I'll kill him." He felt faint surprise that Kenzie hadn't turned a man who assaulted her into so much raw hamburger, but he waited for her to explain.

Kenzie shook her head. "It's not his fault. Killing him won't help."

"*What* isn't his fault?" Bowman put his fingers under Kenzie's chin and forced her to look up at him.

She didn't want to. She tried to turn her head and avoid his gaze, something Kenzie simply did not do. She always glared Bowman down, and be damned to him.

Kenzie finally looked at him, her eyes red with weeping. "Bowman, do you feel the mate bond?"

She'd never asked him straight out before. When they'd gone through the mating ceremonies and spent their first night together as mates, they'd watched each other closely, to see, even teased about it a little. Which of them would be the first to feel it?

As days stretched to weeks, and then months, they'd stopped talking about it. If it happened, then it would happen. The Goddess bestowed blessings in her own time. They'd stopped talking about having cubs as well.

Bowman stilled at Kenzie's question, not daring to think anything. He focused his awareness to the inside of his chest, which others, including Marcus tonight, had told him was where the feeling started. A burning or itching sensation, they said, which then brought on a stab of joy.

Bowman felt nothing, only the wild beating of his heart. Terror clenched his gut, and he slowly shook his head.

Kenzie let out an anguished sob. She pounded at her chest, her fingers curling, tearing at her shirt. "I want it to go away. I want it to go *away*."

Bowman's insides roiled. He sat on the edge of the bed as his legs went weak.

"What are you saying, Kenzie?" He made himself get the thought out. "You feel a mate bond? With someone else?"

"I don't know." Her words were hoarse, her tears clogging her voice. "I want it to be with *you*. I don't want it with anyone else."

Bowman's hands clenched so hard his nails creased his flesh. "Gil was here. Is it him?"

Kenzie was silent except for her quiet crying. Tears streamed from her eyes, her face twisted in sorrow.

Gil. Bowman would kill the fucker. He was a dead shithead walking.

"Not his fault," Kenzie choked out. "He doesn't understand."

"He understands a hell of a lot more than he lets on. Why'd he come here tonight? To tell you he felt a mate bond with you?"

"To leave information on Serena and the monster." Kenzie's voice shook, then dropped to a whisper. "And to ask me about the mate bond."

Bowman let out his breath. Son of a bitch. Gil had come here to find out what he was feeling inside, to have Kenzie explain it to him, and Kenzie realized . . .

Bowman wanted to fold up into a little ball and never come out. At the same time, he wanted to howl his misery.

Kenzie and Ryan were the joys of his life, the constants that kept him from saying *screw this shit,* pulling off his Collar, and running away into the wilds again. He'd become leader young, having to be convinced to take up the mantle of leadership by lesser members of his pack. Bowman had preferred tearing through the woods as wolf to going to pack meetings.

He'd never really settled down, and he'd nearly gone insane when they'd first put a Collar on him. He'd have preferred to kill Cristian in a battle to the death over Shiftertown, but Bowman had known that if he gave in to that impulse, all the other Shifters would have been rounded up and punished for his deed.

The better solution had been to storm to Afina's house, grab hold of Kenzie, and convince her to become his mate. He'd never regretted the choice, and Kenzie hadn't either.

Kenzie grounded him. Her touch, her kiss, her scent, made everything bad go away. The wild animal in him calmed with Kenzie, allowing him to think, to feel things besides ferocity and frustration.

Now, because of some stupid instinct they couldn't control, he could lose her.

"No." Bowman got to his knees on the bed, cupping Kenzie's face in his hands. Her tears tracked over his thumbs. "I won't let you go to him. I can't. I *need* you."

Kenzie tried to answer, but she gulped on sobs instead. She shook her head.

Panic welled up inside him. "I can't do this alone, Kenz. I'll keep you with me, I swear it, even if I have to chain you to the bed."

Kenzie managed a watery smile. "Please do."

A sound of anguish came from Bowman's throat. He caught her in his arms and buried his face in her neck, his body shuddering.

He wanted to go on arguing, to plead with her, to command her, but he had no words left. He was shaking all over, his face wet. Dimly he felt her hands in his hair, soothing, but Bowman would never be soothed again.

"What are we going to do?" Kenzie whispered.

"I don't know." There was no solution to this, no precedent. He'd never known anyone in his hundred and fifty years of life who'd successfully fought the mate bond. No one had ever tried to fight it—no one had ever wanted to.

No one except Kenzie. That must mean something,

Bowman thought. But he was afraid to hope, because he knew how devastated he'd be if even that little hope was dashed.

They ended up sleeping curled together on top of the bed. Kenzie woke with her nose in Bowman's warm chest, his sweatshirt soft against her skin.

The morning had advanced, sunlight trickling through the windows. Kenzie was sore, from both the crazy lovemaking in the woods and lying on the bed tucked against Bowman.

She tried to unfold herself, to slip out without waking him, but when she raised her head, it was to see Bowman's gray eyes looking into hers.

They gazed at each other for a long time, neither speaking. Kenzie had hoped that with their waking, the bond she'd felt inside her would have faded, would have been a mistake. *Heartburn,* she'd told Gil. They'd feasted on barbecued ribs after the sun ceremony yesterday—could have been the food.

As she studied Bowman, though, she felt it, unmistakably warm, waiting to flood her with happiness. Bowman must have read that in her eyes, because pain rose in his.

Kenzie felt tears coming again. Bowman shook his head. He gently kissed the top of her head and got himself off the bed, coming to his feet. He folded his arms as he looked down at her, shutting himself off.

"If you have to go to him, Kenzie, don't say good-bye. Just go."

"I don't want to leave," Kenzie answered, her voice weak.

"You might not have a choice. But Ryan stays with me."

Kenzie felt as though someone had stepped on her with a large, heavy boot. "I know."

Shifter law dictated that a leader's son remained with his father, unless the son would be in mortal danger if he did. That wasn't the case here. Bowman would never hurt Ryan.

Kenzie wasn't sure where she'd go. Human law dictated that she couldn't simply leave Shiftertown, and Gil wasn't Shifter. He lived somewhere in . . .

Kenzie realized she had no idea where he lived. Well, he'd just have to move to Shiftertown, if this were real. She didn't want to be too far from her cub.

She could simply refuse the mate bond altogether. As she'd just told herself, Gil wasn't Shifter. He didn't understand the implications. She'd talk with him and tell him that humans didn't have to live by Shifter rules, and she was staying put.

Kenzie's head liked this idea, but her body, she knew, would rebel. The mate bond wasn't logic or reason, and it wasn't quite the same as falling in love. Similar, but not the same.

The mate bond was a basic compulsion left over from feral days, when they'd been bred as fighting beasts. A mate bond ensured that two Shifters latched on to each other and didn't let go. They'd fight for each other, protect each other to the death, give in to the mating frenzy, and raise plenty of cubs. To deny the mate bond brought physical pain, relieved only when the couple surrendered to it.

There was magic in the bond, not just a chemical reaction. Gil might not be affected as much, being human, even with his shaman magic, but it could tear Kenzie apart.

She would fight it as hard as she could, regardless. Her mating with Bowman had been more than the two of them deciding to keep Shiftertown together. They'd needed each other—they'd both realized that.

If Kenzie left him, Bowman would have to find another mate, one who would help him keep Shiftertown stable. There were plenty of female Shifters who would be delighted to take up the position. Kenzie had seen that during the mating ceremony yesterday.

The burn of that thought threatened to combust Kenzie right there.

She rolled off the bed, grabbed clean underwear from her drawer, and strode into the bathroom. "I'm not leaving," she called over her shoulder and slammed the door.

When she emerged, clean and damp, Bowman had gone. She found no trace of him in the house, though a coffee cup was now in the sink, the pot emptied and rinsed. The envelope of photos Gil had brought was gone too, as were Bowman's leather jacket and motorcycle.

Kenzie blinked back another flood of tears, found her phone, and called Gil. He wasn't there.

"*Please* call me back when you get this," she said to his voice mail. "We need to talk."

CHAPTER TWENTY-FIVE

The last person Bowman wanted to see this morning was Cristian, fearless leader of the Dimitru pack. But as soon as Bowman pulled up at the makeshift arena where they'd found the truck, Cristian was there.

Bowman had intended to do two things here—first, go over the ground again and find some answers. Second, shift to wolf and run until he dropped.

He knew damn well he was using the first as an excuse to do the second. He was breaking inside, and he needed to give in to his wolf, which was urging him to run until he could feel no more grief.

Bowman's skin itched, his human form barely containing him. Having to face Cristian and his not-so-thinly veiled hostility wasn't what he needed.

Bowman didn't trust himself to speak, but Cristian was already talking, even as Bowman swung off his motorcycle.

"Have you come, as I have, to see if there are any more of these creatures wandering about?" Cristian asked, his breath fogging in the cold morning air. "The second monster, I mean. I speculated that they came in pairs."

"Yes, I remember," Bowman snapped.

"I have been here since the dawn. I have found many things."

"Yeah?" Bowman made himself focus. "Like what?"

Instead of answering, Cristian peered at Bowman's motorcycle, then behind him to the dirt road. "Where is my niece? She would be helpful in this."

Bowman turned his head abruptly so Cristian wouldn't see his face, and pretended to scan the area. "She's busy. So am I. Just tell me what you found."

"Tracks. They tell a story."

"What tracks?" Bowman made himself pay attention. He had a job to do; hurting would have to be pushed aside for later. "We checked all over the place and didn't find any tracks, except the ones the sniper made, but they were way over there." He pointed.

"That is because they weren't here then. These are new."

Bowman faced Cristian again. "Someone's come back? Why?"

"Who can say? It may be innocent, or it may not. Until we find out who brought the monster here, whether there are any more, and why all the shooting is going on, we should not rest."

"I know." Bowman clenched his jaw.

"We have been lucky so far that the monster did not live, but someone shot at us to keep us from discovering things."

"I know," Bowman repeated, louder this time. "But I don't want you going behind my back, digging into things without telling me. *I* make the decisions about this. Me. Don't forget that."

"So then, make decisions." Cristian's look was steady. "We cannot sit around and wait for you to discover the answers. The danger is too great—"

Bowman gave up on control. He slammed himself to Cristian and grabbed him by his leather coat; screw being diplomatic. "And you undermine me at every chance—that's just what you want, isn't it? To charge out here to make it look as though I can't handle it. Then you can go back home and tell the Shifters *you* fixed everything, not me." Bowman gave him a fierce shake. "You keep it up, and I'll kill you. I'll do it now if I don't like what you say to me, and dump your body in a ravine."

Rage flared in Cristian's eyes, but as Bowman's rapid speech ended, his golden gaze narrowed. "Something has happened to you. What is it? Is Kenzie all right?"

Bowman shook him again. Cristian brought his hands up hard against Bowman's wrists, and with a single jerk, broke his hold. Bowman went for him again, but at the last minute, spun and walked away, clenching his hands at his sides.

"Kenzie *is* all right?" Cristian's voice took on a note of deeper concern. "Tell me."

"She's fine," Bowman said, back still turned. "This is between her and me; none of your business."

"She is Dimitru pack—it is my business."

Bowman swung around. "She *was*. Now she's . . ." He trailed off. If Kenzie walked away from him, following the mate bond, he'd have to get the mating annulled—by Cristian. And Kenzie would no longer be O'Donnell pack.

Cristian watched him. The trouble with the asshole was that he was smart. He was long-lived, experienced, and knew too damned much.

"She has felt the mate bond with another," Cristian concluded.

Pain flared. "I said, it's none of your business."

"But it is. She is my niece, my blood." Cristian pressed his hands to his chest. "She is also my foster daughter. I raised her. Everything about Kenzie is my business."

"It doesn't matter," Bowman said in a hard voice. "Yes, she found it with someone else. She'll go. End of conversation."

"It is not that simple."

"Yeah? No shit. Now, can we get on with looking for whatever it is you found?"

Cristian continued to hold his gaze. Bowman finally growled and stalked away, across the cement floor of the arena and out the other side.

"Not that way," Cristian said at his shoulder. The man could move *fast*. "What I found is here."

He pointed down a hill and started in that direction. Bowman gritted his teeth and followed.

They came out into a flatter part of the woods, where the trees thinned slightly and mud proliferated. The snow of the day before had only dusted the ground here, and today's thaw had turned it into a mess.

Cristian pointed out two sets of footprints, both in boots with heavy treads, good for traction in the cold. Two people had stood here talking to each other, then they'd parted ways. The larger set of prints went up the hill to the right, the smaller set down to the left.

"The larger set belonged to a heavier man," Cristian said. "His boot prints, you see, are deeper, much deeper. Or he was carrying something heavy. The second man is lighter, and walks more quickly, with a longer stride."

"Good observation, Holmes," Bowman said dryly. He might not be up on the latest literature, but he knew *that* character.

Cristian did too, and slanted Bowman a look. "I am trying to help. What are *your* deductions?"

"Two men met and walked away from each other. Hunters. Hikers. Friends with a fetish for screwing in the woods."

"Human, by the scent," Cristian said. "Which set would you like to follow?"

"The larger man." He was likely the greater danger, and as much as Bowman wanted Cristian out of his life, if Cristian got himself shot, Kenzie and Afina would make Bowman's life hell—more than it already was.

"Very well," Cristian said. "We will look and meet back at the vehicles in one hour."

"Fine." Bowman didn't bother with more formality. He turned his back and walked off, following the boots up the hill.

B owman made it back to where they'd parked the motor-cycles before Cristian did. He contemplated taking off and leaving the older man behind, but he leaned on the seat of his Harley and waited.

The forest was quiet, the tall trees regal against the half-clouded sky. The scent that Bowman simply called *woods* tried to soothe him, but Bowman's nerves were jangled. Hurt lingered behind where he'd pushed it, wanting to come out and batter him.

Cristian didn't keep him waiting long. "My trail, perhaps not surprisingly, went to Turner's," he said as he approached

Bowman. "Something is very wrong in that clearing, and I would like to know what."

So would Bowman. "Mine went to a road," he said. "Someone had parked a pickup there. Something like an F250 by the spread of the tires and depth of the tracks."

Cristian gave him an ironic smile. "Impressive, Holmes. Anything else?"

Bowman took what he'd found on the trail out of his pocket and wordlessly handed it to Cristian.

It was a charm, a large one, from a necklace or some such, made of solid silver. The design looked Celtic—not the same as the Celtic knot that adorned Shifter Collars, but similar. The silver was old, softened by time; not tarnished, but not bright and shiny either.

Cristian sniffed it. "This is Fae."

"Yep." Bowman folded his arms against the cold. "Just lying in the woods, in the mud, about halfway up to the truck."

Cristian continued to study it. "I would swear that the two men standing in the clearing were human."

"They were. No scent of Fae anywhere. And yet, the guy in the big boots dropped it. I found it right beside his footprints."

"Or it was lying there and had nothing to do with him."

"The ley line is over there." Bowman pointed to the left, away from the arena. "But I've never heard of any gates in it. No standing stones in this woods." Standing stones often contained an entrance to Faerie. "I doubt a Fae popped out, went for a hike, dropped a piece of silver, and ran back home. We'd smell a trail like that."

Cristian scowled at him over the charm. "Then what are you suggesting?"

"That a human had this thing in his possession."

"A human, meaning Turner?"

Bowman nodded. "Why not? If he has studied Shifters as thoroughly as he says, he's come across the ley lines and the Fae."

"What is your idea, then?" Cristian asked. "Turner, in his zeal to find out about Shifters, stumbles across a piece of Fae jewelry and passes it to a large man who drives a pickup? Who drops it along the way as he leaves the woods? I think you had not enough sleep last night, Bowman."

Bowman reached for the charm. He wanted to yank it away, but as much as he'd wanted to hit the man earlier, he knew that starting a fight with Cristian wouldn't help anything. It might make him feel better, but it wouldn't do any good in the long run.

Cristian relinquished the silver piece without fuss. "Maybe Turner does not know exactly what it is," he said.

"And maybe gave it to the other guy as payment for something—like shooting at us the other night? Or killing Serena?" Bowman studied it. "Nothing a Fae makes is free of magic, is it? This thing could have leapt out of the other man's pocket, trying to stay near the ley line, maybe."

"And you picked it up?" Cristian asked, eyes wide. "I am wrong—you *are* a very brave Shifter."

Bowman ignored his needling and shoved the charm into his pocket. "It's important. I want to ask"—his throat closed up—"Kenzie what she thinks about it."

Damn it, he couldn't deal with this. He couldn't let her go. Life without Kenzie would be one long road of emptiness.

Bowman closed his fist in his pocket, the charm still inside it. It burned his hand, calling to the tiny piece of Fae magic all Shifters had inside them.

"We should take it to Turner," Cristian said, watching Bowman. "To see how he squirms when he lies about it."

"Kenzie knows a lot about the Fae. I want her opinion." Bowman smiled a feral smile, taking refuge from pain in thoughts of violence. "Then, yes, we'll go make Turner eat it."

"Damn it, Gil, will you call me?" Kenzie growled in her tenth voice mail at him. "You can't drop a bombshell like this on me and then not answer." She closed her eyes, taking a tighter grip on her phone. "I wanted to say this face-to-face, but I'm just going to tell you. I don't care what you said. I'm staying with Bowman, even if it kills me. You're not Shifter, so you should be all right. I'd appreciate it if you'd just forget all about the mate bond."

The buzz in her ear told her the connection had cut off before she'd finished the message. Kenzie banged the phone to the counter in frustration.

Gil must be at work, patrolling the roads, catching suspects, bringing them in to jail. He had a job, after all. He might have turned his phone off so he could get on with it.

No, this was too important. Kenzie looked up the number of the police station in Marshall, where Gil worked, and called the main switchboard.

"I need to speak to an officer there, Gil Ramirez," she said to the woman who answered. "Is he there? Or can I leave him a message?"

"I'm sorry," the woman answered. "Who?"

"Ramirez. First name Gilbert. I don't know what rank he is, but he's a uniformed officer." Surely the police department wasn't so large that the operator wouldn't know who Gil was. He was pretty memorable.

The woman sounded hesitant. "There's no officer by that name here. Are you sure you called the right police department?"

"Yes. No. Do you know where I can find him?"

"Ma'am, I know every officer in Marshall, Mars Hill, and all towns in this area. There's no one named Gilbert Ramirez. I'd know."

"Oh." Kenzie stilled, cold flowing through her. "I guess I made a mistake."

"Mmm-hmm. Well, you take care of yourself, ma'am. I have another call."

She hung up, leaving Kenzie standing in the middle of her kitchen, stunned, clutching the phone in her slowly lowering hand.

If Gil Ramirez wasn't a police officer in any town around here, why had he been in a Marshall patrol car at the roadhouse the day after it was attacked? Wearing a name tag that said "Ramirez"? With access to the computer database linked from the car? How had he gotten all the information on Serena? And the reports on the forensics on the shell casings found in the woods?

Shit.

Kenzie had always realized Gil was more than an ordinary human. She'd thought his explanation that he was a shaman answered her questions.

But now her heart squeezed in chilling worry. Who the hell

was he, really? And why had he come here last night giving her all that crap about the mate bond, making her insane with heartbreak?

Her thoughts whirling, Kenzie flung herself out of the house, forgetting to grab a coat against the cold. But who cared? She strode along the main road through Shiftertown, breaking into a run as she headed for the bottom of the hill and the small house there.

Pierce Daniels, the Guardian, opened the door to her knock. "Kenzie?" His golden Feline eyes widened. "You all right?"

"No, I'm not. I need a favor. Can you get into the Guardian Network and look someone up for me?"

"Sure," Pierce said, surprise changing to concern. "Come on in."

CHAPTER TWENTY-SIX

"What do you mean, he's not there?" Kenzie sat cross-legged on the chair next to Pierce and pretended she could understand the cryptic script scrolling up the dark screen of his computer.

Shifters weren't allowed the top-of-the-line, state-of-the-art computers, but that didn't stop the Guardians. In any case, they preferred old-style, no-frills boxes that booted up to show *C:\>* and nothing else.

The Guardian Network encompassed all Guardians across the world and contained a database so vast and detailed it would make any spy network have a nervous breakdown. The Guardians programmed it in an ancient Celtic-Fae language, so though Kenzie could now see a screenful of writing, she couldn't read it.

"He's not there." Pierce touched the screen, tracing lines of flowing script. "We have no record of a Gilbert Ramirez—not your Gilbert Ramirez anyway. There are plenty of humans with the same name, but none claiming to be police officers in Marshall, or even living in the area, and no one who matches his exact description."

"Son of a . . ." Kenzie rubbed her temples. "I liked him. I

trusted him. I invited him into our home, for crap's sake. Bowman's going to shit a brick."

A small voice said from the front door. "Well, we knew he wasn't human."

Ryan stood on the front porch, peering in through a crack of the unlocked door. He wouldn't barge in, even though most cubs were given leeway to go wherever they wanted, as long as they were courteous. Ryan already understood enough about territory to not try to enter until invited.

"Come on in, Ryan," Pierce called. "What are you talking about, kid?"

Ryan wiped his feet as he'd been taught and walked into the house, shutting the door against the cold. He came to Kenzie's side to study the computer screen with her. Kenzie draped her arm around him and gave him a quick, fierce hug, deliriously happy she wouldn't have to leave him.

Ryan didn't mind the hug, and he patted Kenzie's knee. "I was walking home, and I saw you run in here. The man who calls himself Gil isn't human," he told Pierce. "Pretends to be, but isn't. Smells all wrong."

"He's human with something else in him, you mean," Kenzie said. "He told me he was a shaman."

Ryan rolled his eyes. "He's playing you, Mom. Or is using a glam. I guess it didn't work on me. He's not right."

Pierce's red-brown brows went up. "Really? Wow. Out of the mouths of cubs . . ."

Ryan patted Kenzie's knee again. "Want me to tell Dad for you? He might get less mad at me."

Kenzie shook her head, her emotions spinning. "No, I'll do it. It has to be me."

Ryan opened his hands in a very grown-up gesture of resignation. "All right. If you must." He looked up at Kenzie. "You look terrible, Mom. Are you feeling okay?"

"I'm fine." Kenzie caught him in a hug again, crushing him to her. Nothing could be wrong as long as she was holding her cub; the adorable boy who was the joy of her life. "I'm fine," she repeated. "Thanks, Pierce. If you find *any* information on this guy, will you get in touch right away? Come on, Ryan. Let's go home."

* * *

Bowman stopped the motorcycle in front of his house and killed the engine, but remained in place, straddling the bike.

He knew Kenzie was home. Her Harley was in the driveway, complete with her helmet. He could also feel her presence inside—he knew she was in there, waiting for him.

The thaw today had rendered a stunted snowman Ryan had built in the yard into shapeless lumps of white. Bowman's feet were damp and cold, the only thing that made him haul his leg over the bike and walk up into the house.

Kenzie was cooking, humming as she stirred something on the stove. Bowman realized, with a start, that it was lunchtime. After his strange night and little sleep, he'd lost track of the hours of the day.

Ryan was setting the table. Three plates, three settings of silverware, three glasses. It was to be a family meal.

"I made my grandmother's stew," Kenzie said without turning around. "Nice and warm on a cold day."

Her voice was bright, but Bowman heard the tremor in it. He was tempted to back out of the house and go elsewhere, but Ryan grinned at him. "Better stay and eat it, Dad. Mom's been cooking up a storm, and if you don't stay, she might throw it at you."

She would, and Bowman knew it. He slid off his jacket and dropped it on one of the sofas in the living room.

"It's almost ready," Kenzie said, still not looking at him. "Make sure you wash your hands, Ryan."

"I will. You too, Dad."

Bowman leaned on the post between living room and kitchen, feeling as though he'd just stepped into a stage production of a family play. He had no doubt Kenzie was doing that on purpose.

Ryan came to Bowman, grabbed him by the hand, and towed him down the hall to the bathroom. Ryan kept up a running talk as they bent over the sink about what he'd done during the sleepover with his friends. Bowman listened in silence, liking to hear his cub rattle on.

Ryan handed his father a towel, and they went out together to the kitchen table.

The food did smell good. Kenzie dished it out at the stove, her grandmother's recipe for a spicy beef stew and dumplings. She'd told Bowman once that humans in Romania had a similar dish with about twenty different vegetables in it. Kenzie's grandmother didn't include all the veg, because Shifters preferred meat, and a lot of it.

Kenzie carried the steaming, shallow bowls to the table and handed each to Bowman, who, following his usual ritual, passed one to Ryan, then to Kenzie as she sat down. Bowman reached for his fork to start on his, but Kenzie held her hands over her bowl and closed her eyes.

"The blessings of the Goddess be upon us and this meal," she said.

"Blessings of the Goddess," Ryan echoed.

Bowman said nothing. Kenzie opened her eyes and smiled at him.

It was a shaky smile, but one that hit him in the gut.

"Mom has some news," Ryan said as Bowman at last picked up his fork.

Bowman skimmed the tines through the thick stew. He'd use a spoon later, to slurp the last of the juices.

Only, today, he wasn't sure he could eat. He didn't want to hear any news—he still hadn't processed the last piece of news Kenzie had given him.

"Later," he said curtly. He dug into his jeans pocket and drew out the silver charm. "What do you make of that?"

He slid the charm to Kenzie, and Ryan looked at it with interest.

Kenzie lost her artificial smile. "It's Fae."

"No shit," Bowman said. "So what do you make of it?"

"Old." Kenzie turned it around in her hands, her food forgotten. She lifted the charm to catch the light. "Looks like it has some runes scratched on it, but I can't read Fae. Pierce might be able to."

"What about your uncle? Could he read it?"

Kenzie pursed her lips, a pucker that made him want to leap across the table and nibble on her mouth. "Doubt it. Uncle Cris loathes everything Fae. He only puts up with the Guardian's sword because it's necessary. But don't ask him to read the runes on it."

"I'll learn Fae," Ryan broke in. To Bowman's frown he said, "We should know as much about them as we can, right? The Fae bastards are plotting to drag us back to them to fight their battles again. I don't think they'll stop trying anytime soon, even if they lose out on controlling us through our Collars."

Bowman stared at his son, feeling shock. Had *he* been that perceptive at twelve years old? Bowman couldn't remember, and he doubted it. He'd only wanted to run and hunt—who cared about pack problems? Ryan, on the other hand, was already thinking like a leader.

Ryan reached for the charm, and Kenzie handed it to him. Ryan examined it as Kenzie had, but shook his head. "Not enough information to form a definitive conclusion."

"Who have you been hanging out with?" Bowman demanded as Ryan handed the charm back to his mother. "To be talking like that?"

Ryan shrugged. "Uncle Cris. And Pierce. They know a lot. And Mom. She's pretty smart."

"Well, warn me before you start using words like that again," Bowman growled. He picked up his fork once more and this time shoveled stew into his mouth. It was good, and spicy enough to make his eyes water.

"Yes," Kenzie said. "Your father will need time to look them up."

She gave him a look so sly, so Kenzie-like, that Bowman dropped his fork. He wanted her with all the intensity mating frenzy brought, wanted her *now*, and here they sat at the dinner table with their son. Ryan ate happily, uncaring that Bowman burned for his mate.

"I bet Gil would know what the words on the silver say," Ryan said after a time. "If we could find him and figure out who he really is."

Bowman's rising appetite encountered a wash of chill. "What do you mean, who he really is?"

"Mom found out he doesn't exist. At least, that Gil isn't his name, and he's not a human cop. Or maybe not even a human at all."

Bowman's glare sliced across the table at Kenzie. "Tell me what the f—" He slapped the word aside. "Tell me what the . . . what he's talking about."

Kenzie sent a severe look at Ryan—Bowman bet that she'd told Ryan to keep his mouth shut. Good for Ryan. He knew better than to obey that kind of order.

Kenzie then launched into a tale that made Bowman forget about food, and almost about mating. "We need to find him," Bowman said when she finished. "Why the hell are we having stew instead of hunting for him?"

"Because you haven't eaten in nearly twenty-four hours, and you haven't slept much either," Kenzie said. "If Gil doesn't realize we're onto him, he might contact me again, answering the twenty messages I left for him."

"You're saying we should sit here and wait to see if he calls?" Bowman scraped back his chair and got to his feet. He swayed, exhaustion catching up to him. "Not after he came here and f— messed with me, and fed you that bullsh— bull crap about the mate bond. I'm going to make him pay for that."

"We don't know what he is," Kenzie said calmly. "He might be powerful. We need to find out more about him before we hunt him."

"Yeah," Ryan said. "He might be a zombie."

"There are no zombies," Bowman said, struggling to hang on to his patience. "There's no such thing as the walking dead."

Ryan raised his brows. "Uncle Cris says vampires are real."

"They are," Kenzie answered in a serene tone. "But they're not dead. They have to drink blood to survive, but they're as alive as we are. I met a couple in Romania."

"Will you two stop talking about vampires and the walking dead?" Bowman shouted. "You're trying to distract me. Don't tell me you're not."

Kenzie picked up a glass of water and touched it to her lips. "Do you want me to tranq you instead? I can."

"Tranq . . ." Bowman broke off and stared at the stew as she gave him a knowing smile. "Kenzie, you did *not* put tranquilizer in my bowl of stew."

"No," Kenzie said. "But I could have. I stuck a needle into your thigh as I served you the food. You were busy looking at my chest as I bent over you. It's a slow-acting tranq, and you have a lot of body weight. It should be taking effect right about now, though."

Bowman's rage flared as warm relaxation flowed through him. "Kenzie, damn you . . ."

A breeze rushed past as he started to fall, and he was out before he hit the floor.

*B*owman.
    Bowman woke, or thought he did. Everything was hazy, and a faint breeze blew in the open window of the kitchen. It was warm, summer, but the stew was still on the table. Ryan was gone, off to play with his friends probably. That was the beauty of Shiftertown. Ryan could run anywhere he wanted, do anything he wanted within its confines, and they never had to worry for his safety.

These were happy days, and Bowman would do anything to hang on to them.

"Hey, Bowman."

The voice belonged to Kenzie. She turned around from the stove to face him, wearing a tight dress that bared her thighs and showed him a deep shadow between her breasts.

This was Kenzie younger, before they'd mated. Shifters aged slowly, but fifteen years could bring a change. Kenzie had borne a child since then, and her breasts were fuller now, but they'd been plenty sweet when she'd come to him in the roadhouse, where she'd been dancing with her friends.

Dancing, letting her ass sway in that tight, short black dress, drawing the eyes of every male Shifter in the place. Bowman's anger had wound high as he'd watched her being watched. He'd already decided she was his.

She came to him in the dream as she'd done that night in the bar, arms overhead, body undulating slowly to the music. "Hey, Bowman. Come dance with me."

She'd been slightly drunk, and he'd figured her friends had dared her to flirt with him. Whatever the reason, his cock had flared to life, not that it had been very flaccid while watching her enjoy herself.

"I don't dance," Bowman had said in a harsh voice.

Instead of blushing and stammering, as a submissive wolf would, Kenzie only gave him a wide smile. "Too bad. I love it."

She walked away from him, giving him another smile over

her shoulder. Walked away on those long, strong legs and mile-high shoes. The little shit.

Bowman had kept his eyes on her the rest of the night, and when she'd waved her hand in front of her face and told her friends she needed some air, he'd followed her outside.

She'd let out a little yelp as he caught her and pulled her around the corner to the back of the roadhouse. This side faced no parking lot, just weeds and the beginnings of woods.

Bowman had pushed her into the wall, curving over her, one fist planted beside her head to brace himself.

Was she afraid of him? Intimidated? Cowed? No, she said, "*Bowman,* this is a new dress," and tried to shove him away.

"You want to dance?" Bowman had said, his voice going guttural. "This is how *I* dance, Kenzie."

Kenzie's irritation had fled, her golden eyes softening. "Yeah?"

Bowman leaned in to her, thrusting his knee between her thighs. "Exactly like this. Do you want to dance with me now?"

Her whispered "Yes" had almost made him lose it. Bowman was very careful about what females he had sex with, and how much he let himself go. He couldn't afford to drop illegitimate cubs here, there, and everywhere.

With Kenzie, he didn't care. He wanted her to carry his cub, wanted to put his hand on her abdomen and feel the cub kicking there. Needed it.

How he didn't have complete sex with her that night, Bowman never knew. He must have had massive self-control, which he seemed to have lost lately.

Very quickly, he had his hands up her skirt, her panties down, her slick heat in his hands. She'd arched against him, the sounds from her mouth uncontrolled, her hips moving against his fingers. Bowman pleasured her with his hand, using one finger, then two, then three. At the same time, she'd fumbled open his jeans, her palm cupping his aching hardness.

They'd pulled at each other, rubbing, sliding, grinding together. Kenzie's breathless climax had opened up spaces inside Bowman he'd not known were there. Her honey had poured over his hands, her teeth on his earlobe had made him come himself, his seed flowing against her fingers.

"Don't stop," she'd moaned. "Please."

Bowman, shaking, had brought her to pleasure again. Their kisses after that had been hot and savage and, at the same time, needing and loving.

It had taken a long time for both of them to calm down. Then they'd leaned against the wall, side by side, breathing hard, taking in the peace of the night.

They'd cleaned up with paper napkins Bowman had stuffed into his pocket from his fast-food lunch earlier in the day. Kenzie had straightened her clothes and given him a wide smile.

"I gotta go," she said. "Thanks for the dance."

"Anytime," Bowman thought he answered. He watched her walk off, as graceful as ever in those high heels, tossing her napkin into the nearest trash can. She'd gone back into the bar, calm and uninhibited.

Bowman hadn't been able to keep still. He'd torn his clothes from his burning body, shifted to wolf, and gone for a long, long run.

He wanted to do that now. Then again, he wanted the woman he found in the kitchen, who said, "Hey, Bowman," and wrapped her arms around his neck. "Want to dance?"

CHAPTER TWENTY-SEVEN

Bowman didn't bother to ask where Ryan had gone. This was a dream—Ryan would be well, and Kenzie and Bowman were alone.

Kenzie kissed his lips, then she took a step back, unzipped the dress, and let it fall, showing him what he'd suspected that night at the roadhouse—she wore nothing underneath but a pair of black lace panties.

This Kenzie was not from his past. She was his Kenzie now. Her body showed new lines, her breasts were rounder, her nipples large and dark.

Her attitude hadn't changed, though, even after fifteen years of being mated to him. She canted her hip and smiled up into his face. "Now, what about my dance?"

Bowman snarled. The haziness had gone, and he saw everything sharp and clear—the table empty of dishes, one light on against the growing dusk, the smile of his mate.

He caught her by the shoulders. Kenzie's lashes swept down, but not in shyness. Her hands, strong and competent, landed on his chest.

She let out a laugh when her butt bumped the edge of the table. Bowman was still growling, the animal in him needing release . . . Who was he kidding? *Everything* in him needed release.

Kenzie was gorgeous, her strong legs lifting under his touch, her soft hips pressing the table, her look growing languid. Bowman skimmed the panties off her and tossed them aside. Stepping between her legs, he leaned down and kissed her abdomen, then her navel, making her laugh.

He kissed his way lower. Kenzie stopped laughing as he brushed his lips over the tender place between her thighs.

She groaned. "Oh, *no.*"

Oh, yes. Why not? Bowman licked her, tasting the beauty of her. Salt and sweet rolled together on his tongue, the scent of her arousal heightening his own.

Kenzie rocked beneath him, moving with what he did. Bowman hooked his arms around her knees, lifted her hips, and slid his tongue all the way inside her.

He loved the sounds she made of pure pleasure. No coy protests, no timidity. Kenzie enjoyed making love and had no qualms about letting him know.

Bowman appreciated that. He knew that if he pressed his fingers *there*, she'd jump and hum in pleasure. If he licked *there,* the hum would turn to a sharp cry. If he thrust his tongue into her like *that*, she'd go crazy, her hands in his hair, begging him for more.

"Love," she gasped. "Love you."

Fire flowed with the words, erasing every restraint Bowman put on himself. He licked and suckled her, playing with her as she lifted to him, her coming sweet.

He was wearing too many clothes. Bowman yanked off his shirt and jeans, hearing something tear, but he didn't care. He threw thc clothes from him and pressed Kenzie back down as she started to rise from the table.

His cock was thick and hard, hot with wanting. Kenzie glanced down at it and sent him a tiny smile.

Bowman lost his last shred of control. He lifted Kenzie's hips, pulling them off the table, positioned himself, and slid swiftly inside her. All the way. Kenzie's eyes widened, and she rose on her elbows.

She was used to him, and yet she watched him in wonder,

as though this was their first time together. The same joyful discovery, the same burst of mating need.

Kenzie was tight, wonderfully tight, but she knew how to take him, how to rise to him so they fit perfectly. She clung to his arms, his skin slick with sweat, the cold of the winter evening nothing. Her cries of joy and the sound of their bodies against the table wound him into white-hot pleasure.

She was his. Only his. Not Gil's or whoever the hell he was. Kenzie belonged to Bowman. Always.

"Love you," he said, the words hoarse. He found it difficult to speak when they made love—he always struggled to put his profoundest emotions into words. But this was a dream, and he could let the words pour forth. "Loved you from the first day I saw you. It doesn't matter about the mate bond, or the Goddess, or any of that shit."

Kenzie's eyes widened, the gold of them glinting in the dim light.

"It's you and me that matter, Kenz," he went on. "You're my mate, the love of my life . . . My everything."

"Bowman . . ." she whispered.

Kenzie reached for him. Bowman's climax grabbed him at the same time, his coming twisting him like a tornado wind. He threw his head back, groaning, shouting words—no idea what he said, but *mate, mine, love* were all in there somewhere.

When he looked down at Kenzie again, his breath coming fast, she tucked one arm behind her head and smiled at him. "We *are* good together," she said softly.

"Yes," Bowman answered. "Damn it. Yes."

Then the dream rushed away—Kenzie, the table, the kitchen, and the light swirling like watercolors on oil—and all was darkness.

Bowman opened his eyes. He was lying on his side on the bed in their bedroom, still in his clothes. His eyes were sandy, his mouth parched.

He rolled himself off to land on his feet, then sat quickly back down, his head spinning. He put his hands to it, groaning.

Time had passed. The room was dark, the clock on the nightstand telling him it was nine P.M. Damn it. He was supposed to have met Cade and Jamie at seven to compare notes and discuss what Bowman and Cristian had found up in the woods.

Kenzie opened the door and walked in. She was in a sweatshirt and jeans, but she looked as good as she had in that slinky black dress—though maybe her standing in only the panties had been a little better. She carried a big glass of water, which she wordlessly handed to him.

Bowman took it, a tingle running through his fingers as their hands brushed. He gulped the water, eying Kenzie over the glass. She watched him, a little smile on her face.

"Why'd you tranq me?" he asked when he'd finished, his voice a croak.

"You'd been running on adrenaline and no food. You looked terrible." She wrinkled her nose as she took the empty glass. "You don't smell that good either."

Bowman ran his hand through his hair. It did feel dusty and lank. "Thanks."

"If you want the truth, there was hardly any tranq in the stew I gave you. A couple drops, that's it."

"Wait." Bowman rubbed his hair again, trying to clear his head. "You said you stuck it in my thigh with a needle."

"I fibbed. Shows you how far gone you were. You believed you hadn't felt the needle stick, and you believed me when I told you an untruth. You never let me lie."

"Kenzie, you're a—"

"Total bitch, I know. But I'm your mate. I take care of you, bitchy or not."

"I was going to say a pain in my ass." *I was going to say you're an amazing woman, and I love you.*

Kenzie's smile widened. "How about a shower?"

Bowman's need jumped to life, the dream lingering. His imaginings hadn't sated him, not physically.

"Take one with me?" he asked, voice going low.

She put her hand on her hip, the sassy Kenzie returning. "You know how to wash yourself."

Bowman came off the bed, his strength returning. He ended up next to Kenzie, in her personal space, which was pretty small for Shifters. "Why are you so chirpy all the sudden?"

"Because Gil is a fraud," Kenzie said, eyes sparkling. "He tricked me into thinking I was forming a mate bond with him. He lied. He was trying to drive a wedge between you and me—I get that now. When I see him, I'm going to kill him."

"That's the spirit." Bowman gave her a grin, then sobered as he laid his hand on her chest. "But you felt something, right?"

"I told you, heartburn."

Bowman shook his head. "You really believed you felt it. You know you did."

Kenzie lost her smile. "It was a trick of Gil's. Must have been."

She didn't believe it had been, not exactly, Bowman could tell. He read uncertainty in her.

He leaned to her and kissed her neck. "Come wash my back," he whispered.

Kenzie flushed. "I'll think about it."

She'd say no more than that. Bowman stepped back from her, peeled off his clothes, and left them in a heap by the bed. He watched Kenzie's gaze rove from his bare shoulders to the hard-on he couldn't dampen down. Not with Kenzie in the room, looking at him like that.

He walked, naked, into the bathroom, and turned on the shower. He stepped into the cold stream, not bothering to wait for the water to warm, and reached for the soap.

A slender hand took the soap out of his grasp and began to rub it on his back. Bowman faced the tile wall, holding himself up on it with balled fists.

Kenzie slid her soap-slicked hands down his spine, over his buttocks, down his thighs, and along his legs to his ankles. Bowman looked down between his legs to see her concentrating on his calves, scrubbing the soap over them.

"I thought you said I could do that," he observed.

She shrugged, her hands slick with suds. "Changed my mind."

Kenzie looked like the best wet dream, with her hair heavy with water, the light streaks in it darkened. Water beaded on her back and trickled from her breasts. She bumped his cock as she worked on his legs, every jolt killing him.

"Kenz." Bowman's hand snaked through her hair. "Don't be a tease."

Kenzie flashed a hot look up at him. "I thought that's why you like me."

No, that's why I love you. He caressed her wet hair, a shiver of need curling inside him as she slid her hands up to his dark cock.

She soaped it up, every stroke of her fingers making him crazy. He sucked in a breath, his heels coming off the tiled floor, as she washed him all the way to his balls.

Kenzie rinsed her hands, cupped them to gather water, and poured it over his cock. She cleaned him off well, then, before he could help her to her feet, she closed her mouth over him.

A wordless sound came from his throat. Bowman's hips were moving, thrusting his cock into her before he could master himself.

Kenzie had learned over the years exactly how to take him. How to shape her mouth to give him maximum feeling, to lick under the head where he was especially sensitive, to cup his balls and tickle behind them. Bowman could only stand, his hands in her hair, rocking into her, all thoughts gone. Sensations ruled, blotting out all else.

He had enough presence of mind to haul her upright, lift her against the tiles, and enter her before he came.

Kenzie laughed in delight as Bowman crushed her between himself and the wall as he made love to her. In the early days, when he'd tried to gentle himself for her, she'd urged him on, goading him to master her, to give way to his most basic needs. They'd only grown more beautifully familiar with each other ever since.

Bowman's seed found home in her, Kenzie slick, tight, and hot. She kissed his face as he dragged in harsh breaths, her own pleasure peaking. She tumbled his hair as the shower's water poured over them, washing them clean.

"Better than the dream," Bowman said, kissing her lips, her face, both of them shuddering with release. "I dreamed I was taking you on the kitchen table. This was better."

"It wasn't a dream," Kenzie murmured.

Bowman lifted his head. "What?"

"You really came out and did that," she said, her voice

languid. "You were half asleep, but you did it. I told you, I didn't tranq you that much."

He stared at her, eyes tightening at the amusement on her face. "I woke up in my clothes."

"You put them back on. I don't know why." She gave him a lazy smile. "Then you hauled yourself into the bedroom, fell facedown on the bed, and started snoring away."

"So it was real?"

"Yes." Her eyes darkened. "I haven't decided whether that or this was better."

"Kenzie, you little . . ."

She laughed, which moved her sleek and warm body against his. She laughed even more when Bowman snapped off the water, carried her swiftly back to the bedroom, and landed, dripping wet, with her on the bed.

The third time that night proved to be best of all.

When Kenzie opened her eyes again in the darkness, Bowman was gone. She dimly remembered him waking, pulling her close to kiss her face, neck, shoulder, before he slid from the bed and dressed. He had things to do; she understood that.

As she drowsed, her cell phone rang on the nightstand. She grabbed it, always worried about Ryan, though she knew her grandmother took good care of him. "Yeah?"

"Kenz?" Not Afina but Pierce, the Guardian. Kenzie let out a breath of relief. "Sorry," Pierce said. "Were you asleep?"

Kenzie ran a hand through her hair, still damp from the impromptu shower. "Doesn't matter. I need to haul my ass out of bed anyway. What's wrong?"

"Nothing. Or . . . Maybe something. I think I found that Gil guy. Can you come over? Easier if I show you."

"Sure." Kenzie swung her legs over the edge of the bed, coming fully alert. "I'll be right there."

CHAPTER TWENTY-EIGHT

Kenzie strode to Pierce's in record time. On the way, she called her grandmother to make sure Ryan was all right, and was reassured. She heard Ryan in the background saying, "Is that my mom *again*?"

"Kiss him good night for me," Kenzie said. "And give him my love."

"Take care of yourself, Kenzie," Afina said in her commanding tone, and she hung up.

Pierce was waiting for her. He ushered her into the house and shut the door against the chill of the night. Pierce was a definite bachelor, with the cluttered house to prove it. His abode was tiny, housing only himself, which was unusual, but Guardians were often treated differently from other Shifters.

"I went back over what you told me about Gil Ramirez and tried to match it to anyone with his description," Pierce said, leading her to the corner where his computer was set up on a desk piled with papers, wires, router boxes, switches, and other bits of electronics Kenzie couldn't identify.

"Like I said before, I didn't find anyone who fit," Pierce went on. "Then I had the idea of going back a few years, looking for his father or other family, or something. And I found him. Gil, I mean. The same guy, same name, different town."

"Good," Kenzie said, sitting down on the chair she'd occupied to watch Pierce's first attempt to locate Gil. "Where's he really from? Do you have an address, so I can go pound his face?"

"There's a catch," Pierce said, tapping keys. The screen split into several segments, rapidly opening photos and documents. "The guy I found lived in a little town called Fayboro, but a hundred years ago."

As Kenzie's mouth popped open, Pierce pointed out a photo.

It was Gil. Or at least a man who looked remarkably like him. He was dressed in the tight, muffling clothes of the mid-1800s, his face darkened by the sun and the rudimentary photography. But in spite of the stiff pose and fading photo, the face that looked out at her belonged to Gil Ramirez.

"Are you sure that's him?" Kenzie asked. "I mean, I can see that it looks remarkably like him, but maybe Gil bears a striking resemblance to one of his ancestors."

"Don't know." Pierce shrugged. "I saw him out at the arena, when we started building the pyre for the monster, but I didn't memorize him. But would anyone look exactly like their great-great-great-whatever-great grandfather? Resemble them, sure, but a perfect copy?"

Kenzie didn't think so. The man in the portrait had the same warmth in his brown eyes that Gil did, the same ironic tilt to his mouth. People hadn't smiled for portraits in the early days of photography, but this man had a definite look of amusement on his face. Laughing at Kenzie.

"Any more information about him than that?" Kenzie asked.

Pierce tapped the keyboard, his movements betraying the restlessness of the big cat within him. "There's a record of *this* Gil Ramirez—place of birth, town he lived in. House, even." He brought up a map and pointed to a dot about thirty miles west of Shiftertown, deeper into the Great Smoky Mountains.

Kenzie sucked in a breath. If Gil or his family had lived there a hundred and fifty years ago, someone connected with him still might. Towns prided themselves on their heritage, and records of this man's descendants might exist. That Gil was some sort of supernatural, Kenzie had no more doubt. She wanted to find out what kind.

"Up for a road trip?" Kenzie asked.

Pierce gave her a slow blink. His golden eyes in his handsome face, his close-cropped brown red hair, and his air of hardness against the world had attracted Kenzie to him when she'd first moved to this Shiftertown. They both had known any relationship they began wouldn't be permanent, but Pierce was still a good friend.

"And have your mate hunt me down?" he asked. "I'll pass."

"I'll tell him. Bowman can come with us, and if he can't, he'd rather have me protected by you than going alone." Kenzie stood up. "If you don't want to, I can't force you. I'll ask Jamie or Cade."

"Now, wait a minute." Pierce unfolded himself to his feet. "You have me curious. Let me shut down here, and we'll go."

Kenzie grinned to herself and called Bowman. He didn't answer, which was typical when he was patrolling, but she left a message. She called Afina again and told her as well, talking to Ryan and explaining that he needed to stay put. Ryan sounded resigned, used to staying the night with Afina when Kenzie and Bowman got involved with things. But the quicker Kenzie finished this, the quicker she could spend more time with her son.

"Let's go," Pierce said. He grabbed a heavy leather jacket and followed Kenzie out into the night.

Not long later, the two of them were rolling through Asheville, then out the other side and onto a smaller highway, continuing west.

They reached the town called Fayboro after midnight. The streets were quiet—most people here went to bed early. The historic downtown drew both tourists and artists, but in the cold months, tourists migrated to the ski resorts. The pointed steeple of a church stuck up into the night, the church sitting on a square lined with neatly trimmed rosebushes, bare now for winter.

Pierce led the way around the square and down the street behind it. They rode slowly—in this tiny town, the police would be itching to nab any outsiders speeding through. They might get stopped simply because they rode motorcycles, and when it was discovered they were Shifters . . .

Pierce killed his light, and Kenzie followed suit. There proved to be no need to sneak up on the house in question, however, because when they stopped in front of it, it was lit up. All the downstairs lights were on, the porch a bright beacon to the Victorian mansion, and the trees in front were strung with tiny white lights.

The house was a Queen Anne–style Victorian, with round towers, peaked gables, and dainty gingerbread trim. Kenzie had become familiar with the house styles of the area since she'd moved here, by riding around the countryside and collecting brochures of historic places.

In the area of Romania where she'd grown up, ruined castles abounded, as well as villages with half-timbered and stone houses. The open, airy styles of the nineteenth-century American wealthy had come as a pleasant surprise to her. Kenzie had already determined that, the day Shifters got free of Shiftertowns, she would live in a house like this one.

Parked cars lined the street in front of the place. A wooden sign planted in the yard said, "Worthington House, Historic Hotel." The smaller sign hanging beneath the larger read, "Vacancy."

Kenzie lifted off her helmet. "Are you sure this is right?"

Pierce's helmet was under his arm, wind ruffling his hair. "Yep. It was turned into a bed and breakfast about twenty years ago. According to the records, Gil was hired help for the family when he first came here, but later they adopted him. When the last of them passed, they left the house to him. Everyone liked him, from what I read."

Of course. Gil was likable. Why wouldn't he have been a hundred and fifty years ago as well? He'd probably charmed his way into the family's hearts. How many lies had he told *them*?

"Looks like the bar's still open," Pierce said. "Want to go in?"

"I do. Let's see if they don't throw out Shifters."

The patronage of the bar was sparse—an older couple, the bartender, and a young couple obviously on honeymoon. The honeymoon couple were absorbed with each other and never noticed Pierce and Kenzie come in, but the older couple glanced up in alarm.

Kenzie knew she and Pierce looked scary—Pierce was a giant of a man compared to humans, and Kenzie was plenty tall. With their leather jackets, rumpled hair, and Collars, they must present a frightening picture.

"I can serve you drinks," the bartender said. "But the hotel doesn't have accommodations for Shifters."

Kenzie wanted to snap that Shifters used the same kind of bedrooms as any human, but she restrained herself. No sense riling the natives.

"We're just passing through," Pierce said smoothly, moving to the long, polished wooden bar. He'd always been more diplomatic than most Shifters. "We'll each have a beer, the best you have on tap. We're wondering if you've seen this guy." Pierce pushed a print of the photo of Gil from long ago across the bar's top.

The bartender glanced at it as he pulled the tap and filled a glass, tilting it to let out a stream of foam. "Of course I've seen him. Most people who work here have, and so have some of the guests."

"Great," Pierce said. "Do you think we could talk to him?"

The bartender shrugged. He placed the filled glass, expertly topped with a small head, in front of Kenzie, and started on the next one. "Depends. Sometimes he shows up; sometimes he doesn't. It's been hit or miss lately. Too bad, because some of the guests drive miles for it. If he appears tonight, it will be out in the lobby, on the old staircase. Was there last night, though before that, he hadn't shown himself for about a week."

Kenzie gave him a blank look. "Shown himself?"

The bartender put the second glass down in front of Pierce, printed out a slip from the register behind the bar, and put the paper facedown by Pierce's hand. "You know, manifest, or whatever it's called." The bartender tapped the picture. "He's our resident ghost. Famous. This is the most popular haunted hotel in the Smokies."

"Ghost, my ass," Kenzie muttered to Pierce as they sat at a table in the corner. The older couple had sidled out, but the newlyweds had their arms wrapped around each other, their mouths meeting and parting, meeting again.

Kenzie had stepped out into the cold on the porch to call Bowman again while Pierce settled the tab. She'd explained to him where she and Pierce had gone. "Seriously?" Bowman had asked. He'd been slightly out of breath, as though he'd been running.

"We're going to wait and see if he manifests," Kenzie said. "Then I'm going to kick his ass."

"Be careful." Bowman's rumbling voice warned her. "If he's been lying to us, it means he's dangerous. I'm coming out there."

"No need," Kenzie said. "Pierce is pretty good in a fight." An understatement—he was one of the best fighters at the fight club, next to his cousin Jamie. "I promise if things go bad, we'll back off."

Bowman hesitated. She could tell he was torn—he wanted to come, but it was clear he was involved in things on his side. "All right, but keep in touch."

"What are *you* doing?" Kenzie asked, worried.

"Stuff I should have done days ago. I'm taking over Turner's house, holding him, and searching everything he's got. He's going to give me some answers."

"*You* be careful," Kenzie said, echoing his warning. Chasing Gil suddenly seemed like a picnic—a Shifter one, with plenty of food, drink, and sex. "I've read parts of Turner's manuscript. He seems to know a lot about Shifters, I mean, back when they first appeared out of Fae gates. He speculates pretty close to the truth about how the original Shifters were created. He knows a lot about it, Bowman. More than anyone should."

"Good. Then he'll tell it all to me. I'll wring the truth out of him."

"And if you hurt him, he'll call the police, and you'll be arrested, caged, and probably killed."

Bowman laughed with the snarling laugh he used when he was at his most angry. "In that case, I'll let Cristian wring him in half for me. Don't worry, Kenz. Turner will talk to *me*, not the police."

Kenzie hung up, not reassured.

She and Pierce waited, restless, and sipped beers. They didn't talk much. The honeymoon couple remained entwined, oblivious, their drinks untouched.

At around one, the bartender sent them a nod. "If you want to see the ghost, he usually shows up about now."

Kenzie was on her feet and leaving the bar. She heard Pierce drop a tip on the table and follow her.

The hotel's main staircase folded into the wall to the right of the front door. At the other end of the lofty main hall, however, behind the check-in counter, another set of stairs rose to a balcony. This staircase had an open balustrade with carved spindles and a polished railing. The gallery above it encircled the hall, with several doors opening off it.

Those were rooms in the original house, the woman who introduced herself as the innkeeper explained, and dated from 1840. The rest of the mansion had been added starting in the 1870s, with renovations continuing into the first decade of the twentieth century. The man who was now the ghost had lived here in the 1860s, adopted by the family when he was in his teens. He now returned to check on the place, it was said, to make sure the house his adopted family had left him was doing well.

Sure he does. Kenzie trained her glare on the balcony.

The older couple from the bar had been joined by two younger ones, and even the honeymoon couple emerged. All turned eagerly toward the staircase and gallery.

They waited. The large case clock in the hall struck half past one, then ticked on toward two.

One of the men behind her let out a long sigh. "He's not going to show. I'm going to bed."

He started to move, then his wife gasped, and Pierce said, "Whoa."

Gil was there, on the balcony at the far end of the hall. He hadn't been a second ago, but Kenzie blinked and then saw him in the shadows.

He was dressed in the old clothes he'd worn in the photo, including the rather battered hat, and stood so that the indirect light made his outline a little fuzzy. His smooth face was blank, his eyes strangely still as he gazed straight ahead, not looking down into the hotel. For a ghost reputed to be checking on his adopted family's home, he seemed not to notice it.

"He's really here," a woman whispered. The click of a phone's camera went off. "He's so lifelike."

Kenzie hid a snort and cupped her hands around her mouth. "Hey, Gil," she called.

He was good. Gil never looked at her, never moved his ghostly hand from where it rested on the railing, but Kenzie saw him start, saw his eyes flicker.

With a suddenness that had the rest of the guests jumping, she launched herself down the length of the hall, past the polished check-in counter, and up the gallery stairs.

"Shit," Pierce said, and banged out the front door.

The innkeeper trotted futilely after Kenzie. "Wait—you can't go up there."

Gil performed to the end. He slowly lifted his hand and took a step back . . . and vanished.

Gone. Just like that. Kenzie blinked. Was he really a . . . ?

No. Ghosts didn't exist, just as zombies didn't. *There's no such thing as the walking dead,* Bowman had growled.

Gil had to be using magic. Some kind of shaman magic that confused the eye, maybe, or a glam, as Ryan had speculated. Kenzie's skepticism helped her see a flutter of movement at one of the doors, and hear a *click* as a latch caught.

Kenzie ran down the gallery to the door. It was locked. The manager came behind her, her voice distressed. "You can't go in there!"

Kenzie could go anywhere she wanted. The door was solid, but Kenzie was strong. A few well-placed kicks, and she was through. The manager shrieked and headed back to the stairs, no doubt to call the police.

The room Kenzie found herself in was old, dusty, and used for storage. The only light came from behind her—the yellow glow of the downstairs chandelier, dimmed for the night—but her Shifter sight let her see well enough. French doors on the other side of the room were closed, but a cold draft told Kenzie they'd been open moments before.

She dodged haphazardly placed furniture and boxes and flung open one of the doors. Modern ones, she saw, with shiny brass fittings. Someone would need a new key to get in from the outside.

The French doors led out onto a balcony. The night was so quiet she easily heard a thump below as someone landed on dirt, then the sound of feet running away.

"Ghost, my ass!" Kenzie shouted after him. "When I catch you, Gil, you *will* be a ghost."

She leapt to the balcony's railing, balanced on it a moment, and sprang off into darkness.

CHAPTER TWENTY-NINE

Cade watched Bowman, a worried look in his bear-brown eyes. Bowman growled in irritation and continued to shove Turner's books to the floor.

They'd reached the trailer house in the woods to find no one home. The front door had been locked—Bowman remembered the keypad on the inside—but the doorframe was weak enough for a Shifter to pull off. Cristian had done that, in fact. Bowman also remembered Turner boasting about electrifying the windows, but Jamie found the junction box and made short work of the wiring.

Most of the papers fluttering out of books and folders—charts with such labels as "Diaspora," colorful bar graphs, and what looked like mathematical equations—meant nothing at all to Bowman. Cristian kept picking things up, saying, "Interesting," and not bothering to explain why.

Bowman searched for something he could use, such as a recorded payment to a sniper, or receipts for supplies to breed a monster, but he found nothing. Turner's desktop computer booted up without a password, but there was nothing on it—according to Jamie, who was clicking away with the mouse.

Pierce would be better at determining that, but right now Pierce was looking after Kenzie.

Who was haring around after Gil. Kenzie would get him— Bowman knew she would—and Pierce would help her. *That's my girl.*

He hated the thought of Pierce out there with her. Once upon a time, Pierce had touched Kenzie, kissed her, listened while she laughed at him in her dusky, sultry voice . . .

"Bowman?" Cade asked. "You all right?"

Bowman found himself standing in the middle of the room, the papers in his hand shredding under his twisting fingers. He cleared his throat.

"I'm fine. Keep going. I want everything he's ever written gone through. Then we track him down."

"Yeah." Cade's concern didn't go away. Bowman's rage had mounted to a place where he'd soon lose control; one spark from his Collar confirmed that.

He needed to find Turner and beat answers out of him, then find Kenzie and let her soothe him down. She was the only one who ever could.

Kenzie landed on her feet, the impact jarring, but she was up and running in seconds. She might not be as graceful as a Feline, but out of all the Shifters, Lupines made the best hunters. Or so Uncle Cristian always said.

The back of the hotel gave onto a small empty lot. Kenzie dashed across it to an alley that led between stores in this touristy part of the town. She scattered a clump of cats who were investigating trash cans in the shadows and ran out into the street beyond.

A flash of movement took her attention to the right. Gil was still trying to cloak himself, to blend into the white mist that was rising in the dark. He couldn't hide from Kenzie's Shifter sight, though, and she wanted to laugh as she sprinted after him.

The road Gil ran down ended in woods, which Gil plunged into. Kenzie dashed after him.

A motorcycle roared up behind her, Pierce's back tire skidding as he stopped. "Kenz, wait."

Kenzie flung off her jacket. "I'm going after him. Either stay here and guard my clothes or come with me."

"Damn it, if anything happens to you, Bowman will take my head off."

Kenzie ripped free of her sweatshirt, kicking off her boots. "Tell Bowman you tried to stop me, and I fought you. He'll believe that."

She started running even as her jeans slid away. She tossed her underwear behind her, becoming wolf before she went another three strides.

The woods here were so thick snow hadn't made it to the forest floor. The carpet of old pine needles and mud was frozen, cold and slick under her paws.

Kenzie had been raised in dense woods in the Transylvanian mountains—wild country, and remote. She'd roamed far and wide as a cub, fearless in her innocence.

Even now, she was more at home in woods than in towns. She craved clear air; to feel the ground, not concrete, beneath her feet; and untainted wind rushing through her fur.

Gil's distinctive scent lay in a clear trail before her. Foolish man—or whatever he was—to think a Shifter couldn't track him. Out here it was even easier, with fewer human scents to get in her way.

Gil could run, though, Kenzie gave him that. He was moving almost as fast as a Shifter could. But not quite.

She burst through the trees, terrifying smaller creatures who huddled in the night, and caught sight of Gil ahead of her. Kenzie rejoiced, the wolf in her ready to land on the man and tear into him. The human part of her that abhorred murder and wanted answers was almost as furious.

Gil was pounding along a narrow trail, nothing ghostly about him . . . until he disappeared again. Kenzie put on a burst of speed, determined not to lose him.

She slid to a halt on the edge of a ravine, her paws backpedaling, dirt and pine needles raining over the edge into the darkness.

Crap. Had Gil gone down this? Fallen to his death? Or did he know a secret path?

Kenzie howled. Partly to let Pierce know her location, partly in frustration.

She could still see and scent pretty well, so she started picking her way along the edge of the cliff, testing ways down into the ravine. She heard water below, one of the many rivers and creeks that crisscrossed the mountains. Rushing water, not frozen, meaning a fair-sized stream.

She sniffed, catching a tang of scent that might be Gil's. But it was confused now, damn him. He'd known exactly where to go to elude her.

After a few false starts, Kenzie found a path that was solid, somewhat dry, and led downward. She had no way of knowing how far she could go before the trail petered out, but she took the chance. If she turned back now, she might never find Gil.

Mist rose as she descended. The ledge on which the path ran widened, keeping her from having to walk too close to the edge, which was fine with her.

The mist was clammy rather than cold, as though she'd left winter behind as she descended. That made no sense—the mountains here were in the five- and six-thousand-feet range, not like the Alps, or the Rockies or Sierras. The change in climate from top to partway down shouldn't be that radical.

A thicker mist suddenly engulfed her. Kenzie sneezed as warm air flowed past her nose.

She heard her name. "Kenzie!"

It was Gil, shouting at her, his dark voice suddenly near. Kenzie whirled around, but she couldn't see him in the mists.

"Kenzie! Shit, *don't* . . ."

Don't what? Kill him? Drag him back to Shiftertown so Bowman could play jump rope with his guts?

"Kenz." Gil's voice was softer, breathless, but Kenzie still couldn't find him. The mists obscured everything.

She tried to retrace her steps, to move toward his voice, but she couldn't see a damn thing. Her paws slipped in mud and she fell.

"Aw, crap," Gil said. "I can't . . . reach . . ."

His voice faded, and the mists cleared. Kenzie could see the woods again, but the trees were different, deciduous rather than evergreen, the forest floor covered with dead leaves, not pine needles.

But this was all wrong. It smelled wrong, felt wrong, looked wrong. Kenzie's throat closed up in sudden panic. The stink around her, the magic squeezing her, made her dizzy and sick.

"I think he meant *don't go in there*," a cool, crisp voice said in the clearing mists. A female voice, speaking English but with an accent Kenzie couldn't place. "Did not your grandmother in Romania always tell you to keep away from the mists?"

"What do you mean, you *lost* her?" Bowman heard himself roar in fury and fear.

Pierce gave him the steady-eyed stare of the Guardian. They were in the clearing at Turner's place, the trackers still going through his house and the small sheds on his property. Cade and the others paused to listen, uneasy.

Bowman's gut clenched in his growing fear. Pierce wouldn't have come to find him unless something very bad had happened to Kenzie.

"She went down into the ravine, gone before I could get there," Pierce was saying. "You know Kenzie. She wouldn't stop. She wanted Gil. And then she just . . . disappeared."

"Show me where. *Now*."

"You won't find her," a man's voice said. "Not like that."

The now-familiar timbre and smooth inflection had Bowman's Collar going off, snapping pain into his neck. Gil stood not six feet from him, his expression quiet, the surprised trackers quickly surrounding him.

Bowman bellowed. He grabbed Gil by his shirt and had him up against the wall of Turner's house before Gil could say another word.

"She was hunting *you*." Bowman cracked Gil's head into the wall. "*Why* won't I find her? What the fuck did you do with her?"

"I didn't do anything with her." Gil's words were choked, his eyes wide, the man finally showing fear. "There are bad places in that woods. I never meant for her to fall into one."

"Bad places? What bad places?"

"Ancient passages. Gates."

"Gates?" Bowman hated the sound of that. "You mean gates to Faerie?"

"Faerie, yes. And other places even worse."

"*What* other places? There's here. There's Faerie. There's the Summerland, where you are very close to heading. That's it."

"Not true," Gil struggled to say. "There are places even the Fae are afraid of. They open on the ley lines, but not on every ley line. They flick in and out. There's evil there, and people can be trapped."

Bowman sensed his Shifters closing around them, Cade now in his grizzly form, his warm bulk reassuring. Jamie next to Pierce, the two looking much alike with their brown red hair and lithe bodies, Pierce's sword glittering on his back. Cristian, quivering in anger as he listened to Gil explain that his beloved niece was lost.

Kenzie. My mate.

"Trapped," Cristian said when Bowman was unable to speak. "You mean in a pocket?"

Gil's gaze flashed to him, and he nodded the best he could with Bowman's hand on his throat.

"What the hell is a pocket?" Jamie asked.

"A piece of a world beyond," Cristian said, "where anything might be. Or so my mother claims. She's always telling me to never go into the mists. Romanian folktales, as I said."

"The pockets are real," Gil broke in. "They open and close. One can lead to many different places or to other pockets. Some are stable, most are not. Even the Fae are afraid of the mists."

Bowman's voice was harsh. "You're saying Kenzie is in one of these?"

"Maybe," Cristian said, at the same time that Gil answered, "Yes."

Bowman yanked Gil from the wall by his frayed shirt. "You will show me exactly where you lost her. And if you're lying, and if she's dead, you will come to understand the meaning of pain."

"That means no more haunting for you," Pierce said with cold humor. "Your mutilated body would scare all the guests in your little hotel away."

CHAPTER THIRTY

"Who the hell are you?" Kenzie called.

She peered between the trees and wet leaves of fern-like plants, searching for whoever had spoken. She'd turned human as soon as she heard the voice, but her sight wasn't as good in this form, and Kenzie strained to see. It was lighter here, as though the sun were rising, but that couldn't be. It was still the middle of the night.

A woman stepped onto the path in front of her. She was as tall as Kenzie, had a sharp, rather pale face, very dark eyes, and many braids of white blond hair that fell to her waist. She was beautiful—in a frightening sort of way.

The clothes she wore had once been rich—velvets, brocades, and fur, cut to flow with her every move. But the brocade was fraying, the velvets torn, the fur damp and matted. The entire ensemble—long tunic and cloak over breeches and soft leather boots—was stained with mud and what looked like dried blood. Kenzie also noticed that though the woman's voice was cool, her scent broadcast her fear.

"Who the hell are *you*?" the woman returned. "More fodder for the trials? I have told him, I'm a hunter, yes, but not a killer. A clean hunt for food and feasting is one thing. Murder to harvest organs is something else entirely."

Kenzie's mouth sagged open. The woman was angry, scared, and arrogant. She was also Fae.

"Harvest organs?" Kenzie repeated.

"To create the mythological beasts. Why stop at Shifters? Why not the griffins, unicorns, and manticores of legend?"

Kenzie folded her arms, suddenly cold, though the air here was warm. "Who wants to create them? Gil?"

The woman frowned and shook her head. "I know not this Gil."

"Who do you know? Who are you? And why is a Fae in the woods in North Carolina?"

"I know not this Northern Carolina either. My mother warned me of the mists, but I forgot in the excitement of the hunt. If I had been a fine young lady and followed the rules, I would be at home weaving tapestries instead of trapped in the mists." The corners of her mouth turned up a little. "I might be, as you say, bored out of my mind, but I'd be safe."

Kenzie had to smile. She'd feel the same. "I'm Kenzie," she said. "And you are . . . ?"

The woman shook her head. "You Shifters. So quick to give away names."

"We don't have a big hang-up about them, no. Though I understand the idea about true names being used for magical control. You have a name you let people call you, don't you? Even if it isn't your real one?"

She conceded this with a nod. "Brigid. You may call me that."

"Good. So, Brigid, where the hell are we? And why are you here? Instead of home weaving tapestries?"

Brigid gave a little shiver. "That I do not know. I was hunting with my sisters. I chased my prey into a misty dell and quite suddenly found myself in this wood. I called for my sisters, but they never heard me."

"Are we in Faerie? Not someplace I want to be."

Kenzie's voice was steady, matter-of-fact, but inside she was tight with worry. A Shifter stumbling through a gate into Fae realms might never get out again. She could be hunted, captured, killed, her wolf skin hung up like a trophy. Or she could be enslaved as Shifters had been of old, used as a fighting and hunting beast.

The best thing Kenzie could do in Faerie was get out. Fast.

"I do not know where this place is," Brigid said. "It might be the inside of a gate between the real world and another place, perhaps many places. I am stuck here, released only when he comes for me."

"He?" Kenzie asked. "He who?"

"Human names make no sense to me. I don't remember. But he likes my skills. I am a—I don't know how to translate to your language, but I breed and raise animals. Hunting dogs, hunting cats, hawks. My father does, that is. I assist him, but I am plenty good at it myself." She ended with pride, a touch of Fae arrogance.

"A breeder?" Kenzie asked, taking a step back. "You keep the animals in cages and take away their cubs?" So the Fae had done to Shifters in the old days, the stories went.

Brigid shook her head. "No. Young taken from a mother too fast can decline and die."

"Hmm, sounds like things have changed. Or maybe that was only special treatment for Shifters." Cubs had been ripped from mothers' arms, never seen again, families torn apart. Humans could be cruel to Shifters, but they had a long way to go to surpass the Fae.

Brigid's frown deepened. "There are no Shifters in Faerie anymore. Breeding them is forbidden, and those secrets are lost. I have tried to tell him that, but he doesn't listen."

Kenzie's focus sharpened. "A human is trying to get you to breed Shifters?"

"Not Shifters. Fae beasts, as I have said. But in the human world, they become monsters."

"Yeah. Seen one. Didn't like it."

"But he is a fool," Brigid said with scorn. "The animals are not viable. They might perhaps be if we were in Faerie, but the magic does not appear to hold in the human world."

"You made the griffin," Kenzie said. "Or what passed for one."

She inclined her head. "I attempted. The beast did not last."

"It lasted long enough to tear into a roadhouse full of Shifters and humans and hurt a lot of people." Kenzie glared at her. "It was on a rampage we barely contained. It almost killed my mate."

Her heart wrenched at the thought of Bowman lying half-crushed in Cade's truck, his body a bleeding wreck. He'd been lucky to escape with only a broken leg.

"Why did you do it?" Kenzie asked angrily. "How could he *make* you create something? I even felt sorry for it when we found it dead. It was as much a victim as we were."

"As am I. He had begun the experiments himself, but he needed Fae magic to make them work. And he has ways—threatening to trap me here forever, threatening my children. He has agents in Faerie, it seems, or so he says. If I do not help him, he sends word, and my daughters die."

Kenzie went silent. Gil was certainly magical, maybe enough to get through to Faerie, but she'd never sensed such cruelty in him. Then again, he'd been skilled enough to make her believe he was a human cop and a fairly normal human being, not a mysterious, hundred-and-fifty-year-old whatever he was.

But then, Gil had been astonished by and interested in the griffin. That interest had not been false, she was sure.

If not Gil, then maybe Turner? But . . .

"If we're talking about the same guy," Kenzie said, "I don't see how he can threaten your kids. He's a university professor, not a mage or a half Fae. He's human, and not even magical."

"He has found a way. Or he has minions who do his work for him. I do not know. He showed me a picture." Brigid's arrogance gave way to fear and sorrow. "Of my wee ones tied up and locked away, their eyes bound. I do not know how he made this picture, but it looked so real. He had it on a human device." She shaped her hand as though holding something the approximate dimensions of a smartphone.

"Oh," Kenzie said. "The picture might be real. I'm sorry."

"He takes me out of here at times and locks me into another place, a human place, a shed he calls it. It smells terrible, and the human world has so much iron. It hurts me."

She shuddered. Kenzie stepped to her. "I'm sorry," she said again. It was a strange feeling to have sympathy for a Fae, but the woman's fears were understandable.

Brigid lifted her shoulders in a shrug. "It is what is before me, the challenge I must meet. I will obey him and breed the beasts—I can't risk the life of my daughters. But all the while I wait for a chance to kill him and return home."

"I like the way you think. We'll gut him together." Kenzie went so far as to lay her hand on the woman's arm. The acrid, sulfur scent of Fae curled in her nose—but she didn't pull away. Touch was comforting, soothing, even for non-Shifters.

"I have no weapons," Brigid said. Her smile returned. "Though now I have you."

"True." Kenzie looked around, seeing only trees, mud, and leaves, encircled by mists. "Are we really trapped in here? Why can't we just walk back out through the mist?"

Brigid gave her an amused look. "Of course, I would be standing here mourning my children if I could simply walk through the mists and be home. I have tried. Many times. You go through, and end up back here."

"Then how does Turner—or whoever it is—come and get you?"

"That I do not know. He appears, locks me in cuffs, and leads me out. Then I am in the human world, in tall woods, and he shoves me into the small building and locks the door. When I am finished, he walks me back again. I have tried again and again to discover the gate to the human world when he is gone, but always I find myself here again. I thought that if I could get to the human world, perhaps I could find another way to Faerie, through the standing stones I have read about. Are there standing stones near where you came in?"

"Not so you'd notice," Kenzie said. "Other powerful places, though." She continued her study of the area. She'd never been to Faerie and had no idea if the trees were like this. Uncle Cristian would know—he had an uncanny amount of knowledge stored in his brain.

Brigid's arrogance left her. Her face settled into lines of resignation, of one who knew her choices were limited.

"Wait." Kenzie frowned. "Bowman found a silver charm. Did that have anything to do with getting through the gate? It might have been a magic device."

"Silver charm?" Brigid came alert. "In the shape of a knot?"

"Yes? You've seen it?"

"It's mine. He took it from me. It was my mother's—has been in my family for generations."

"Oh." Kenzie deflated. "Might not be the key to the gate, then."

"No, it is simply an ornament. He liked it, because it is heavy silver, but it is common. In my home, that is." Brigid let out a sigh. "It is strange, is it not? We are enemies, you and I. I should feel great distaste that you stand here unclothed, so barbaric, but I do not. If I am to escape, I will need your help. But that is not all of my feeling. I am grateful for your presence. I had grown lonely."

She looked wistful, this lovely woman with her certainty that Fae were the greatest creatures in the universe.

"Don't write us off yet," Kenzie said. "I'm getting out of here and back to *my* wee one. I say that when Turner comes back in for you, we jump him, take whatever magical device he's using to get in and out, and go."

"It may not be so simple," Brigid said, sounding skeptical. "He uses some kind of spell that freezes me into place, keeps me from overpowering him and fleeing. He is not a warrior, and I have trained to be, so I should be able to best him. But I cannot get near him."

"Great." Of course it couldn't be that easy, could it? "Will this spell freeze me too?"

"I do not know. You are not Fae, and he might not know you are here."

Kenzie drew a breath. "Well, we'll have to take our chances. If I can pin him fast enough and tear out his throat, that will probably cancel any spell he has on you."

"I am willing to try," Brigid said, giving her a solemn nod.

"Then we'll get the hell out of here. Sound like a plan?"

Brigid's brows drew together. "Why would that not sound like a plan? It *is* a plan."

Kenzie grinned. "It's our way of saying *Is it a good plan?*"

"Better than rotting here." Brigid wrinkled her nose. "This world stinks."

"I'll drink to that."

Brigid looked wistful again. "Aye, a good flagon of mead would go down well. We shall overcome this man and raise a glass."

"Kick his ass and go out for pizza." Kenzie laughed at Brigid's bewildered expression. "Means the same thing."

"Then that is what we shall do." Brigid settled herself on a damp, fallen log. "Now we wait."

"Yeah," Kenzie said, letting out a breath. "We wait."

CHAPTER THIRTY-ONE

Gil led Bowman to the mountain trail where Kenzie had disappeared. "There," he said, pointing down the hill. "But it doesn't mean you can get to her."

Bowman didn't bother arguing. He signaled to his trackers to start searching.

A few hours later, Bowman's hope was dying. Kenzie was nowhere, and the mists were dispersing with the coming morning.

He'd walked into every pocket of mist he could find, until his human hair or wolf's fur was dripping wet, and he still found himself in the familiar wilderness of western North Carolina.

"Where the hell is she?" he snarled at Gil.

"The pockets move," Gil said, shaking his head. He'd gone to a cabin he owned nearby to change out of his nineteenth-century clothes, and now wore jeans and a UNC sweatshirt. He'd been heading to this cabin, he said, to hide from Kenzie when she'd chased him from the hotel. "I tried to go in after her, but most of the gates are locked to me."

"Why are they?" Bowman demanded. "What does that mean?"

"It means I was kicked out of Faerie a thousand years ago, and anything that smacks of Fae magic is barred to me. The Fae made gates to lots of worlds back in the day, though most of them have vanished, disused. The pockets are what's left. I can't traverse them."

"A thousand years ago?" Bowman stared at him.

"Yeah," Gil said. "I'm older than I look."

"Don't be a smart-ass. Why the hell didn't you tell me all this before? About the gates? About you being from Faerie? You don't look Fae."

"Because I'm not. And I had no idea there were pocket gates in this part of the world, or that your professor was breeding monsters. He shouldn't be able to."

"I shouldn't be able to turn into a wolf, but I do." Bowman slung him away, tired of arguing. "Where else can we find these gates?"

"Everywhere. Anywhere. They come and go. A Fae talisman can make them easier to find and use, instead of hit or miss, but working talismans are few and far between. I'm sorry it's not what you want to hear, but there it is."

Shit. Bowman swung from Gil and walked away, deeper into the woods, where all was silence. The trackers didn't follow him, knowing he needed to be alone for the moment.

Bowman stopped and let out a long, steaming breath. *Kenzie, where are you?*

He wouldn't accept that she could be gone forever. Magic happened, yes; but magic could be undone. If Kenzie had gone into a gate, she could come back out of it. Logical.

Bowman didn't want to admit that magic could be more complicated than that. People vanished all the time, never to be found again. Magic had created the beast that had attacked them in the roadhouse—a beast like that shouldn't have been able to exist.

Gil shouldn't be alive after a thousand years, but there he stood. Kenzie shouldn't be gone. But she was.

No. Bowman clenched his fists and pressed them to his stomach. He wouldn't let her be gone. He'd find her. She was his *mate.*

Ryan didn't know yet. Bowman would have to tell him—he deserved to know.

Damn it. Bowman straightened up, his eyes burning.

The others were waiting for him, expecting him to give them orders, expecting him to be leader, no matter that he was dying inside. Even Cristian, as impatient and volatile as he was, was taking his cues from Bowman tonight.

Bowman should know what to do. But he didn't.

He strode back to the waiting group and took a deep breath, the cold mountain air washing into him.

"Pierce," he began. "Take Gil home with you. The two of you will find out all you can about these pockets and how to get into them. Pull in every Guardian out there to help you if you have to. Cristian, you, Cade, and Jamie keep looking for Turner. I want him alive and able to talk. I'll join you after I contact some resources of my own." He pointed at the other Shifters who'd come to help. "The rest of you will keep looking around here for Kenzie or any of these gates. No one go in, just call if you find anything." He swept them in a collective glare, ending at Cristian. "And no one is to blab any of this to my cub. *I'll* be telling him. Got it?"

The Shifters didn't stand around and argue. They dispersed to their tasks without a word.

Except Cristian, of course. He could never let himself be seen simply obeying Bowman. Oh, no. Cristian regave orders to the Lupines in his pack to search for Kenzie, then he joined Bowman.

"Where do you think you're going?" Bowman asked him as he strode for his motorcycle.

"Back home to my mother," Cristian said. "She deserves to know what's happened to her granddaughter. From *my* mouth."

He had a point. Bowman mounted his Harley, kick-started his engine, and took off down the rutted track, the slice of Cristian's light close behind him.

It was forty or so miles back to Shiftertown, the first part of the trip slow through dirt roads that had frozen over. The highway was a little faster but full of icy patches. An hour later, Bowman rode into Shiftertown, not stopping until he reached Afina's.

Bowman dismounted and strode up to the house, not

worrying about territory and courtesy today. But once Afina let him into the kitchen, and Ryan ran in to meet him, Bowman halted, his feet suddenly unable to move.

"Ryan." Bowman's mouth was tight, words dying in his throat.

He heard Cristian enter the house behind him. Afina went to her son and asked him something in Romanian. Cristian shook his head, and Afina put her hand to her chest.

Ryan was looking up at Bowman. His back was straight, his head high, the wisdom in his eyes too old for his twelve years. "Just tell me, Dad."

"Your mother." Bowman swallowed, a world of pain inside him. "She's gone."

"Gone where?" Ryan's question held no panic, only need for information.

"Don't know." The words rasped. "Lost her."

Cristian quickly filled in about the idea of the pockets Gil had told them about. "We think Kenzie stumbled into one of those. But the way was closed when we tried."

Afina's face had lost color as he explained, her hands balling. "The mists?"

Cristian nodded. "I thought they were legend. Stories to frighten children."

"No," Afina said, her words hushed. "They are holes to other places, some of those places worse than Faerie."

"*Worse* than Faerie?" Ryan said, worry entering his voice. "And Mom's in one of these?"

"I have all my trackers looking for her," Bowman said, "and the Guardian and Gil are working on how to get in . . ."

His words ran out, his mouth too dry to continue. The idea that Kenzie was no longer in the world took the air out of the room.

Ryan came to him and took Bowman's big hands where they dangled uselessly at his sides. "You'll find her, Dad."

His words rang with conviction. No doubts, no hysteria. Ryan believed.

Bowman wished he could. "Everyone has told me that because Kenzie and I don't share the mate bond it would be easy for me to let her go." He shook his head. "They're wrong. I won't let her go. I won't stop until I've found her."

"Screw the mate bond," Ryan said, scowling. "You and Mom are madly in love, and everyone knows it. You'll take the world apart looking for her. All the worlds. Doesn't matter about the frigging mate bond."

"He is an intelligent lad," Cristian said with warm approval. "I have raised him well."

Ryan rolled his eyes. "Seriously, Uncle Cris? I'll help you find her, Dad. I love her too."

"And I," Afina said. "Kenzie is as my own daughter. We will, as Ryan says, take the world apart."

Cristian nodded his agreement. "If she can get into these mists, she should be able to get out. Gates to worlds work both ways. We need to discover the key, as it were. And where the gate opens out. They might not have a two-way door in the same area, and some can lead to more than one place."

Bowman looked at Cristian, his vision fuzzy around the edges. "You're saying she might come out in this world again, but in a different place?"

His breathing became slightly easier as Cristian explained that was exactly what he meant, and began outlining plans to find the second gate.

But Bowman's heart was like a stone in his chest as Afina fetched a map of North Carolina and spread it over the dining room table. This world was vast; the one Kenzie had stumbled into might be just as vast. The odds of finding her among all those possibilities were slim.

Bowman, however, never let odds mess with him. He'd allow his wolf to take over and solve this with a finality only a wolf could. He'd clean up the mess later—*after* Kenzie was back home with him, alive and well.

Wherever this place was, it was boring. Kenzie yawned as she sat curled around herself on the ground.

Brigid, in an act of generosity Kenzie would never have associated with the Fae, had removed her cloak and spread it across a dry patch of earth so Kenzie could sit down. When Kenzie had thanked her, Brigid shrugged it off, saying it was too warm here for a cloak anyway.

The mists around them thickened, but they were clammy,

not chilled. Kenzie peered into them . . . and sprang up in delight.

"Bowman!"

She saw her mate raising a hand to her, grinning his Bowman grin. Ryan was next to him, waving as well, his smile wide.

Kenzie darted forward. "You found me!"

"No!" Brigid shouted at her. "Kenzie, stop!"

Kenzie made for Bowman and Ryan, who watched her, still smiling. Brigid caught her with strong hands and jerked her back.

Kenzie snapped around with a snarl. "Let go of me!"

"It's a trick," Brigid said, her face rigid. "They aren't really there."

Kenzie swung away from her. The mists had thinned again, but her mate and cub had vanished.

"I saw them," she said, anguished. "What happened? Did the way close? Why did you stop me?"

"They were never there," Brigid said. "It's a glamour. Giving you your fondest wish. When I first came in, I saw my sisters and my daughters, calling to me. They held out their hands, imploring me to come to them. When I drew closer, the mists boiled up, and I swear the ground tried to suck me down. I extracted myself with difficulty and ran back here. I've seen the images many times, but it is a trap. You must resist."

"Damn it!" Kenzie spun on her feet and brought her fists down. "I hate just sitting here. Why doesn't he *do* something?"

"He will come for us," Brigid said. "He is greedy, and he wants what I can do for him too much to stay away."

"Greedy? For money? Or . . ."

"Power, it seems. Position. He is gambling all to raise himself."

"I'll raise him," Kenzie growled. "And then throw him back down."

"Ah, Shifters," Brigid said, as Kenzie settled herself on the cloak again. "Always so violent. I believe I will like that about you."

Bowman had reached out to his contacts before, and he reached out again. Eric was in the process of sending one of his trackers to North Carolina, but it was always difficult to transport Shifters, as they couldn't travel from state to state without permission. They had to move covertly, and that took time to set up. Las Vegas was on the other side of the country, Austin eleven hundred miles away, so the process was slow.

Bowman called Eric in Las Vegas first for a reason. "Get that dark Fae you have—Reid, that's his name—to answer some questions," Bowman said, after he explained the situation.

The next thing he knew, the phone was pulled from Eric, and a woman's voice came to him. "Bowman? You all right?"

The smooth tones belonged to Iona, Eric's mate, a half human, half Shifter. She and Kenzie had met last year when Eric had paid a brief visit to Bowman to discuss Shifter business. The two women, though one a Feline and the other Lupine, had bonded. They had a common fate—being mated to pain-in-the-ass alpha males—or so they said.

"Kenzie's smart," said Iona, a woman who wasn't lacking in brains herself. "She's resourceful. She'll figure out how to get back to you."

"And I'll figure out how to get to her," Bowman said. "We'll meet halfway."

"What about Ryan?" Iona asked. "How is he?"

Over her words, Bowman heard the soft gurgle of a cub Iona and Eric had brought in a few months ago, a boy they'd called Callum. Callum was already tough, Eric had boasted when he'd last spoken with Bowman, a blue-eyed leopard like the rest of the family. Shifters with human blood were usually born human, not changing into their animal form until age three or so. Callum, though born in human form, had shifted into a leopard within a month. Eric was very proud.

"Ryan's fine," Bowman snapped. *Never let another Shifter know your offspring might be weak,* was Shifter reflex. In this case, Bowman wasn't lying. Ryan was being stouthearted, refusing to crumple.

"Make sure you don't keep him in the dark," Iona said. "I know you'll want to protect him, but let him reassure *you.* He's stronger than you know."

"Yeah," Bowman said. "Thanks."

"Hang in there, Bowman," Iona said. "Trust Ryan."

"I will," Bowman said, his heart tight.

Iona gave the phone back to Eric. "I'll give you Reid if you think you'll need him," Eric said. "And Graham. They're two of my best. Might take a bit of doing." Eric meant he'd have to contact the man who flew his Shifters where they needed to go, but didn't want to say so on the phone. Eric chuckled. "Graham definitely."

Graham hated to fly. Eric liked to send him places in the cargo plane because of this, part of Eric's battle of wills with Graham, the head Lupine in his Shiftertown.

"Thanks," Bowman said. "Keep in touch."

He put down the phone and turned to find Cristian two feet away. "This Eric will send help?" Cristian asked.

Bowman nodded, his neck stiff. "Some. An expert on Faerie. I've met the guy. He's weird, but he knows a lot."

"Good. Let them get on with what they do. And we will get on with what we do. Which is find out everything we can, by interrogation when necessary."

Bowman scowled at him. "Turner's *mine*."

Cristian studied him for a moment, then gave him a nod. "Yours first. Then I want a go at him. If he is still alive after you are finished."

Bowman said nothing, only pushed past Cristian—who moved before Bowman could touch him—and out of the house. For once, he and the crazy Romanian Lupine agreed on one thing: Get Kenzie back, by any means necessary.

CHAPTER THIRTY-TWO

The mists rolled in and rolled back again. When they cleared, Turner was standing a few yards away.

Kenzie was on her feet, shifting as she rose. She landed in her wolf form and charged, intent on killing her enemy. Turner watched her come without worry and held up his hand.

Kenzie hit him full force, and they went down in a tangle. Her Collar went off at the same time as the Taser in his hand.

A cross between a yelp and a scream left Kenzie's throat. Pain flashed around her neck and down her spine, then through every nerve in her body. Her fur crackled, her eyes burned, and a high-pitched *eeeeeeeeeeee* tore through her ears.

She managed to roll away and landed on her belly a few feet away, panting hard, her Collar shocking her. Turner climbed to his feet, still holding the Taser.

Brigid hadn't moved. Not because she didn't want to, Kenzie realized, but because she couldn't. She must be under the influence of the spell she'd told Kenzie about. Brigid struggled to take a step, her booted foot inching in the dirt and then stopping. Her dark eyes burned with frustration and hatred.

"You know you can't touch me," Turner said to Brigid,

sounding far too calm. "I learned a trick from a half Fae," he told Kenzie. "I have taken some of her blood"—he nodded at Brigid—"which I used in a binding spell. I have some of yours now, and some of your fur." He held up his hand, showing Kenzie a tuft of wolf hair between his fingertips. "Thank you. Though Tasers coupled with Collars are excellent at stopping Shifters."

Kenzie snarled. She longed to leap up and tear his face off, but the double shock had robbed her of strength. Her Collar continued to snap curls of electricity through her—it knew her aggression and wanted to stop her. She'd arrogantly told Bowman she'd be among the last to have her Collar removed, taking the pain so others could be freed first. *Way to go, Kenzie.*

Turner waved a hand at her. "Shift back. I can't talk to you when you're like this."

"Don't," Brigid said. Her voice was strained, teeth clenched.

Kenzie had no intention of shifting, but she felt her fur receding, her limbs changing shape against her wishes. That scared her more than anything.

Kenzie came to her feet, naked and breathing hard. She had enough strength of will to snatch up Brigid's cloak from the ground and wrap it around her. She never minded being nude after shifting in front of male Shifters, but the way Turner gazed at her with frank interest made her skin crawl. Kenzie pulled the cloak around her, finding it surprisingly warm for fabric so thin.

"You have no need to be afraid of me, Kenzie," Turner said, his blue eyes innocent behind his glasses. "My work can benefit you. Can benefit everyone, really. The Fae were trying to make a race of skilled fighters to conquer their enemies, and it worked. It cut their casualty rates in half. Think what a contribution you can make to national security."

Kenzie struggled to speak. Her Collar had calmed down, but the pain remained. "*Fae* casualties were cut in half, you mean. Shifters still died. Now you want Shifters for national security? Like joining the military and so forth? We tried. They won't let us."

Turner shook his head. "Not Shifters necessarily. Beasts stronger than Shifters, which the military can control. I am very close to making a breakthrough."

"You mean that poor thing you let loose near the road-house? It was strong, sure, but didn't last very long."

Turner roved his cold gaze over her. "That 'poor thing' nearly killed you all. I was conducting an experiment that night, admittedly, to see how well my creation stood up to the fighting prowess of Shifters. You handled yourself very well, I was pleased to see."

"You were there?" Kenzie adjusted the cloak. She and Bowman had been climbing each other just before the thing attacked. The thought that he'd been watching was repulsive. "I thought you hired a lackey to drive the truck."

"I did. I can't drive a rig. But I rode along, and yes, I watched." His smile made her know he'd seen everything she and Bowman had done. "I wanted to see how my baby performed. Doesn't a mother wish to watch her child's first steps?"

Brigid threw him a look of haughty disgust. "You do not know the first thing about being a mother."

"Yes, women can be so superior about children," Turner said. "My mother never was—if she had been, maybe my father would have been nicer to her. Not that I knew anything about that until after he died. My father was a complete bastard."

Kenzie had little interest in Turner's family and problems at the moment. "Why the hell am I here?" she asked.

"You being here is not my doing. I have found a way to stabilize this gate, yes, but you blundered into it all on your own, chasing that cop. The mists opened to you, so they must have wanted you here, for whatever reason. The gates can be very powerful. But I am glad to see you. Brigid I trapped on purpose. She has the equivalent of what we would call a doctorate in genetics. She's amazing. You are a strong Shifter, an alpha female. Your DNA will be of great use to me."

Turner's words indicated he knew nothing about Gil not being a human cop. Interesting. "If you already have my blood and fur, you have my DNA," Kenzie said. "I'd like to know how to get out of this place, whatever it is."

"It's a world out of time," Turner said. "Or something like that. I'm not sure. It's a different plane of existence anyway. I haven't explored it much—I only know how to access it. A good place to keep you and Brigid—much better than a cage or a locked room, and much harder for anyone but me to find."

"*I* found it," Kenzie said. "That means my mate or my friends could find it too."

"No, you chanced upon it. That cop is very interested in you, Kenzie, in a sexual way, I'd say. You know, it was once thought that Shifters and humans couldn't produce viable offspring, but that idea has been proved wrong many times in the last twenty years. A professor from Chicago presented a paper on it at the last symposium I attended."

"Shifters don't exist for your entertainment," Kenzie said irritably.

"Ah, but you know, entertainment was another reason they were first created. To fight and hunt, yes, but also to perform tricks—Fae would boast to each other how clever their Shifters were. Fae also used them as sex partners, sometimes in their animal forms, if they had such a fetish."

Kenzie hoped to the Goddess Turner didn't. But he spoke with only clinical interest, a curious side note he'd found during his studies.

"Such a thing might be strange to you and me," Turner went on, "but Fae are almost as fascinating to me as Shifters. Not quite." He sent a smile to Brigid that looked apologetic. "I didn't even know of their existence until after I figured out that Shifters were real. Even though my first findings were scorned, I continued hunting for evidence of Shifters. Found other places with similar stories to the ones in Ireland and traveled to them. During my journeys I met a man—I thought he was a man at the time—who believed me about the magical shape-shifting people. He promised to show me more. He took me to Morocco, in the Atlas mountains, up to where a small pack of wolves lived. There were two mated pairs, a few cubs, and an older male who was the obvious leader."

He relaxed his stance, warming to his story. "We hid and watched as they milled around, doing whatever social things wolves do, then, before my eyes, the older leader suddenly turned into a *man*. I couldn't believe it. All this time—I'd been right. I missed the actual transition, I was so amazed, but I photographed the Shifter man talking to the other wolves, being nuzzled by them, acting as one of them.

"This fellow who'd brought me up there at last revealed that he was half Fae. He helped me. He taught me much about Shifters, and also about the Fae and their magic. He gave me talismans and showed me how to move through the mists. He has passed on now, sadly, but I believe his son is helping humans understand and control Shifters. I've learned so much since that day in the mountains, and at last, I am being recognized for my expertise on Shifters. I'm up for full professorship, finally, after all these years. This last research is going to make me famous."

He paused for breath, and Kenzie asked cautiously, "What research?"

"The creation of Shifters. For human purposes. How wonderful to have an army of the beasts at our fingertips. We could breed select soldiers with them to produce the best of both, half Shifters with human savvy as well as Shifter strength."

"That's already been tried," Kenzie pointed out. "In Area 51, years ago. It didn't work."

Turner nodded. "Yes, I know. I even helped start up that project, but they were on the wrong track, and I left. They were attempting to create Shifters by scientific means alone, breeding them in petri dishes." He made a noise of disgust. "Of course it didn't work. They were missing the ingredient they didn't believe in: magic. More specifically, good old-fashioned Fae magic from the dawn of time."

"Hardly the dawn of time," Brigid broke in. "Humans had already created far-flung military empires in the places you call Rome and China by the time we perfected the spells and techniques to produce the battle beasts."

"What you're doing won't work either," Kenzie said to Turner. "Unless that half Fae taught you the magic."

Turner gave her a chill smile. "He did. It is difficult for me to work it myself, but then I caught a Fae. She is quite good at it."

Brigid remained stiff with scorn. "I have no choice but to help him," she told Kenzie. "Though I would rather lay out his guts and bathe in his blood."

Kenzie would rather she did too. "So you're trying to create mythical monsters in order to get a promotion at work?" she asked.

"What an amusing way of putting it," Turner said, his eyes like cold glass. "The large beasts are proving to be difficult to control and physiologically unstable. I've been trying to find a true Shifter for my breeding program, but Shifters protect themselves and their cubs so rigidly you're difficult to get near. But now, a Shifter has tumbled into the mists, and I have her."

Kenzie shivered, but she forced herself to remain stoic. "One female?" she asked, lifting a brow. "Maybe not a fertile one at that. I've only managed to bring in one cub in many years of trying. And believe me, Bowman and I have been trying."

"I know you have," Turner said. "You and your mate are a fascinating study in Shifter fertility. I am pleased to have the opportunity to study you further. In fact, I will go report to O'Donnell that his mate is well and in my care."

Something flashed in his hand, and the mists thickened around him.

Kenzie found herself released from her near paralysis, and rushed him. She could move fast, but she managed only to grab a corner of his padded jacket before he vanished. A bit of cloth tore off in her fingers, but Turner was gone.

CHAPTER THIRTY-THREE

Bowman finished tearing the last floorboard out of Turner's trailer. He'd found nothing there—at least, nothing that told him where Kenzie was.

He and Cristian had rejoined Cade and Jamie here to continue the search for Turner and what he was up to. Between them they'd found plenty of papers and materials on Shifters, which Cristian thought fascinating and Bowman tossed aside. He didn't give a crap about Turner's opinions on the innate maternal instincts in Shifter females. He was interested in only one Shifter female—Kenzie.

"He has a unique mind," Cristian said, scanning a printed-out page. "A brilliant man, in fact, if one looks at it a certain way. He could be useful to us."

Bowman yanked the paper out of Cristian's hands and let it flutter to the floor. "Pay attention. We need to find Kenzie."

Cristian regarded him calmly. "By studying our enemy, we learn more about him; enough to destroy him. This is what he has done with Shifters, apparently, for many years. Not a man to be underestimated."

Bowman knew that Cristian had a point, but right now he wanted only to find Kenzie, and kill anyone who got in his way.

A shout came from outside—Cade. It was nearing dawn, the sky a faint gray. Bowman could see Cade in the clearing, yelling something into the woods.

Bowman pushed past Cristian and headed outside. Jamie, in his cheetah form, came leaping out from the shadows under the trees, his fur on end.

"Something going on out there," Cade said, gesturing to where Jamie had emerged, in the direction of one of the sheds. "Not sure what."

Jamie shifted to human, breathing hard, his eyes wide. "Stinks," he said, his voice tinged with the yowl of a spooked cheetah. "It got super cold all of a sudden, and darker. Nasty."

"Did you smell another of those beasts?" Cristian asked, coming up behind Bowman.

Cristian spoke matter-of-factly, but a chill washed over Bowman. The first monster had been almost impossible to beat, and he'd had half of Shiftertown to help him.

"It's might be another gate," a voice said from the path up to the arena.

Bowman turned in anger to see Gil, who'd spoken, walking toward them. Pierce, his sword prominent on his back, came behind him. Ryan was walking close to Pierce, looking both scared and curious.

"What's the matter?" Bowman asked Pierce, meeting them. "What the hell did you bring Ryan for?"

Pierce gave him a pained look. "You think I could leave him behind? I tried. He stowed away in the back of Gil's car."

Bowman growled at his son, but he'd have to deal with Ryan later. Pierce wouldn't have come here in person if he hadn't discovered something of great importance, too important to trust to a cell phone.

"Guardians around the country have reported gates opening along the ley lines," Pierce said, a worried look in his eyes. "They've rigged a way to sense them, sort of the way seismographs work for earthquakes. A lot of gates have been popping up around here lately, especially tonight. Something's going down, but no one knows what."

A Fae attack—or an attack from something else that used these pockets Gil talked about—would be just perfect right now. But that was not Bowman's immediate concern. "Do any of them know how to open the gates? From this side? Or where they lead?"

Gil answered before Pierce could speak. "You need a talisman. A Fae one. Something permeated with magic."

"Like the silver thing we found?" Bowman asked. He pulled it out of his jacket pocket.

Gil took it and studied it. "Doesn't have that magic tingle, but who knows? Worth a shot."

"Hold up," Cade said, inserting his bulk between Gil and Bowman. "If you're telling Bowman to hang on to that silver thingee and march into the mists, on your say-so, think again. We don't exactly trust you."

He glared down at Gil, and Gil actually looked intimidated. But then, Cade was huge, his buzzed hair emphasizing his hard face, his tatts black on his arms in the dim light, his brown eyes blazing in anger. Picking a fight with a grizzly Shifter in the middle of the woods wasn't the best idea Gil could have.

"You want *me* to try it?" Gil asked. "I'll probably die if I get through, but hey, you'll know it worked."

Cristian reached for the silver talisman, careful not to close his fingers around it until Bowman released it. He held it up, letting it wink in the dawn light. "It is unmistakably Fae, but perhaps not magic. An ordinary pendant, I would have thought. The most interesting thing about it is the place in which you found it."

"Not far from here," Bowman reminded him, impatient.

"Exactly. Why should a Fae brooch fall in the woods near Shiftertown? With no sign of any Fae attached to it?"

"I told you, it's magical," Bowman said. "I think Turner used it to pay off the sniper, but it wanted to stay around here, close to something Fae, like one of the gates."

Cristian slanted him a glance, opened his mouth to argue, then closed it again. He tried to hand Bowman back the pendant, but Bowman shook his head.

"Keep it," Bowman said. "You're better at figuring out Fae crap than I am. If it has anything to do with Kenzie, tell me. If not, I'm not interested."

Cristian raised his brows, but nodded and slid the talisman into a pocket.

"Dad," Ryan said, so sharply that Bowman jerked his attention to him. "Is that him?"

Bowman spun to where Ryan was pointing. The Shifters around him came alert, and Bowman moved in front of Ryan.

The mists cleared, and Turner stepped out of them.

Jamie shifted and went for him. The cheetah sprang fast and hard, with Cade, still human, just behind him. Doing their jobs, fighting to protect Bowman and bring down an enemy.

Something buzzed in Turner's hand, and Jamie's Collar went off in mid-leap. Lighting licked all the way around his neck, surrounding him in a blue nimbus. Jamie tumbled swiftly downward, his mouth open in a furious snarl, and landed hard on the dirt.

Cade moved into the opening Jamie left, growling as he reached for Turner, but another buzz, and his growl turned to a shout of pain. The big man went to his knees, arcs of electricity snapping into his human skin.

The others were already moving forward, Pierce's sword ringing as he drew it. The primary purpose of the Sword of the Guardian was to release souls to the Summerland, but on any other day it was simply a damn sharp weapon. The runes on the blade gleamed in the gray light, as though they wanted to join the fight.

Turner shot a look at the sword, the only thing that seemed to frighten him. He showed no fear of the attacking Shifters.

Bowman decided to change that. He charged him, not bothering to shift, and grabbed Turner by the lapels of his padded jacket. Bowman jerked him from his feet. "What the fuck have you done with my *mate*?"

Turner's eyes were icy behind his glasses, with absolutely no feeling in them at all. Bowman had never seen anything like it. Though Cristian could be cool and calculating, the man had fire inside him. Turner had nothing.

Bowman's Collar went off. Turner jabbed something into the top of Bowman's thigh—a knife? A Taser? Whatever it was, it hurt like hell, and Bowman's skin crackled with the shocks from his Collar.

He transferred his hold to Turner's throat, no longer interested in keeping him alive. He let his claws come to cut into Turner's flesh, but felt his own body weakening as the Collar kept up its punishment. Blood ran hot against Bowman's leg, and he heard something crack.

The Sword of the Guardian swooshed past Bowman's head. Turner's eyes widened, and he shoved Bowman away as the blade came down.

The fire high in Bowman's thigh left him, though clenching pain remained. He heard Gil's shout.

"Grab the—" He said a strange word Bowman didn't understand. "Aw, damn it!"

The mists swirled, and Turner was gone. Bowman fell to his knees, his Collar still sparking.

"Dad!" Ryan was at Bowman's side, his small hands reaching for him. Cristian came to him as well, his touch surprisingly gentle as he steadied Bowman.

The mists thickened. Bowman reached for them but felt only moisture on his hands.

Kenzie! he called silently, then collapsed into the arms of his son and his archenemy.

"Bowman!" Kenzie leapt to her feet. Brigid lifted her head from where she lay and regarded her quizzically.

All was silent.

Kenzie had heard Bowman's voice; she knew it. A call across distance, mists, worlds . . . Wherever the hell she was.

Another trick? Kenzie turned slowly in a circle, searching. The vision she'd had earlier had shown her Bowman and Ryan smiling, happy, beckoning her to join them.

This time, she'd heard only Bowman's voice, which had been filled with rage, pain, and anguish. No smiling illusion. Desperation, hurt. Emotions that had grabbed Kenzie and wouldn't let go.

"Bowman!" she shouted back in the same desperation. "I'm here!"

The echoes of her words died, and silence descended.

"Did you hear him?" Brigid asked, her voice gentle.

Kenzie nodded, her eyes wet. "Like he was standing next to me. Shouting in that crabby way of his." She gave Brigid a shaky smile. "Have you heard your kids or sisters calling to you?"

"No." Brigid shook her head. "They only stand where I cannot reach, tempting me to go to them, but I cannot hear their voices. They are demons in fair guise."

"This was different." It had been Bowman's true voice; she was certain of it.

Kenzie's chest ached, her breath catching. She turned from Brigid so the Fae woman wouldn't see the tears rolling down her face.

Bowman, Kenzie called silently. *I'm here.*

I love you.

Bowman's eyes jerked open. He was lying, of all places, on the bed in Turner's wrecked trailer house. The bedroom ceiling was still intact, but the walls were full of holes from where Shifters had torn away wallboard, searching for anything Turner might have hidden. The bed had been shoved into the middle of the room, with Bowman spread out on it.

He sat up straight, which stabbed pain deep through his middle. "Kenzie!"

She wasn't there, of course. But he'd heard her voice, loud and sweet as a bell. *I'm here. I love you.*

Bowman tore the sheet from his lower legs and swung out of bed. He was naked and had bandages wrapped around his chest and thigh, the cloths stained with dried blood.

Jamie filled the doorway, now minus a door. "What are you yelling about?" Jamie growled. The man looked taller than ever in the doorframe, his head touching the top of the opening. He appeared to have recovered from his Collar shock and his fall, though his face retained a greenish tinge. Collar hangover was a bitch.

Bowman grabbed his clothes from the bottom of the bed. "You couldn't leave my underwear on? You needed to see everything I had?" His heart was pounding, his voice harsh. Sentimentality right now would finish him, so he stuck with temper and gibes.

Jamie, true to form, flipped him off. "Get over yourself. You were stabbed by a knife—a Fae dirk, Cristian called it— and it barely missed your junk. Pierce had to stitch you up. He wasn't thrilled about it, by all the swearing he did."

Bowman looked down and saw white tape over a line near the base of his cock. He shuddered. "Too damn close."

"Be grateful. Now when you find your mate, you can still show her how happy you are to see her."

"I intend to." Bowman drew a long, agonizing breath, realizing he had a few cracked ribs. "She's alive. I know she is. I just don't know where."

Jamie's hard gaze softened. "We'll find her, boss."

"Damn right we will. Where is Gil? Whoever or whatever he is, I need him to give me some answers."

"He's still here. You haven't been out that long."

Bowman winced as he leaned over for his boots. "What did Pierce sew me up with? A machete?"

"I don't know. I just hope the dirk wasn't poisoned. Fae weapons tend to be."

Bowman went cold, though a quick assessment told him he felt normal for recovery from a stab wound. Which was to say deep pain, soreness, and anger. "Thanks, Jamie. You're good at making your patients feel better."

Jamie shrugged. "I'm realistic. I came to help you get your ass up to show Cristian you're all right, before he tries to take over."

"You said I haven't been out that long."

"An hour or so. That's enough time for a Dimitru to decide it's his turn to rule. I don't feel like taking orders shouted in Romanian, so get out there."

Bowman gave him a tight grin. "You're a shit. I appreciate it."

"I live to serve you, boss."

"The hell you do." Bowman pressed his side and groaned softly, but he knew he was already starting to heal. He was good at it; he'd had a lot of practice.

He and Jamie went out together. The sun was up, the woods cold, the ground filmed with frost. His trackers and Cristian were continuing to sift through Turner's things. Pierce lay on a piece of tarp, eyes closed, his sheathed sword lying next to him. He was their combat medic and a good healer, but he always needed to rest afterward.

"Kenzie's alive," Bowman said from the doorstep. The others stopped what they were doing to look at him.

"How do you know?" Cade asked, his dark eyes hopeful and skeptical at the same time.

"I heard her." Bowman shook his head and stepped down to the ground. "Maybe I dreamed it. I can't tell. But . . . I *know*."

He saw the uncertain looks, but he didn't care. Ryan was right—it didn't matter about the mate bond. He and Kenzie had a connection they'd formed the moment they'd first seen each other. They belonged together, and nothing could change that.

"Hey, Dad," Ryan said, strolling to him, Gil behind him. "Feeling better?"

Bowman growled at them both. "What are you doing with *him*?" he snapped at Ryan.

"You always tell me we should keep our friends close and our enemies closer," Ryan returned calmly. "Did you come up with that saying?"

"No." Bowman couldn't remember who had coined the phrase, though Kenzie no doubt would know. "But you were supposed to stay with Afina."

"I know." Ryan shrugged off his father's orders. "But I had an idea, and I had to come out here to test it. Gil thinks it might work. I just need to . . ."

Ryan turned around and darted to Pierce. Before Pierce could come awake, Ryan had the Sword of the Guardian in his hands, struggling to unsheath it.

Pierce opened his eyes, blinked, then got to his feet with Feline speed. "Hey, don't touch that."

Ignoring him, Ryan ran with the sword to the place where Turner had come out of the mists. Gil, closest to Ryan, went after him and caught him.

"Whoa, slow down there," Gil said. "You don't know exactly what it's going to do."

"So?" Ryan struggled from Gil's grasp and finally managed to pull the sword out of the sheath. "It's worth a shot."

"What is?" Bowman demanded, his voice thundering. "Ryan, put that down."

A beam of sunlight broke through the clouds and thick trees and landed on the sword. The blade glittered brilliantly. Or was the sword itself creating the light? The lit runes seemed to dance.

Mists suddenly boiled up around Ryan. Bowman shouted and leapt forward. Gil seized Ryan and held him tightly as the sword shot forward, trying to pull Ryan with it.

"Damn it," Bowman yelled. "Stop!"

Pierce was right behind him, shouting as well. Cristian came running, but Jamie bound past them all and reached Ryan and Gil before the others could.

Ryan cried out as the sword pulled at him. Gil held him, but the sword tugged hard, lifting Ryan's arms straight out. Jamie reached them and wrapped his arms around both Gil and Ryan, trying to pull them back.

The mists whirled, and a wave of thick fog poured into the clearing, obliterating everything.

Bowman waved his hands in front of his face in the sudden whiteout, calling for Ryan. Cristian, beside him, yelled for him too, as did Cade.

"Aw, shit!" Ryan's voice rose high and shrill above them all.

The fog shrank back, as though Ryan's cry had slapped it apart. The dense whiteness lessened until it was nothing more than a dampening mist, and trees, Shifters, and Turner's trailer swam back into view.

Ryan kept swearing, using words Bowman hadn't known he knew. Bowman reached his son as Jamie and Gil set him down. Pierce was standing over Ryan in a towering fury.

"You *dropped* it?" Pierce yelled. "You dropped the Sword of the Guardian into an unknown, out-of-reach, magical world?"

The sword was gone. Ryan didn't have it, Jamie didn't have it, and Gil looked as baffled as the other two.

Ryan stared up at Pierce without flinching. "Not on purpose," he said, meeting Pierce's gaze. *"Obviously."*

"Shit!" Pierce swung away, fists clenching, his face draining of color.

Cade scrubbed his hand over his short hair. "This can't be good."

"We must retrieve it," Cristian said. His scowl was fierce, the man more troubled than Bowman ever remembered seeing him. "There is too much magic in the sword for it to be safe there."

"No kidding," Bowman said. "But how the hell do you propose to get it back?"

"Aw, *crap*." Gil's exclamation dragged Bowman from his irritating uncle-in-law.

Bowman's impatience turned to fear a second later. Gil was standing by swirling mist, and Ryan was gone. A sweep of the clearing showed that his son was nowhere in sight—the others were looking too.

"He was standing next to me," Gil said, stricken. "And then he wasn't. Bowman, I'm sorry. I *had* him . . ."

The mist cleared again, revealing the trees beyond, as they'd stood in that woods for centuries. Tall, serene, silent, dripping as the sun began to dispel the early-morning frost.

The mists had taken Ryan, and now he too was lost.

CHAPTER THIRTY-FOUR

"**M**om!"

Kenzie lifted her head, which she found difficult. Grief was tugging her, profound grief, wanting to embrace her in its darkness.

Don't give up, not yet, she told herself fiercely. *There is a way out, a way back to Bowman. You'll find it.*

Shifters found grief debilitating. Loss was something they'd had to learn to live with, but getting through it was tough, and sometimes the Shifter didn't make it.

Kenzie knew it could not be Ryan's voice she heard. She'd seen the vision of Bowman and Ryan three more times, both of them waving madly to her and looking puzzled when she didn't run to them. Each time, it had broken her heart.

Turner was dead meat.

"Mom! Hey! Help me!"

Kenzie closed her eyes. There were bad things in the mists, Brigid had told her—bloodsucking vampire-like creatures and other evils she'd never heard of.

"Geez, Mom! You can't be *that* mad at me."

Kenzie's eyes popped open. Sure sounded like Ryan.

Brigid was alert, peering into the warm darkness. "I hear," she said. "Resist. Do not go to it."

"I'm stuck!" Ryan yelled. "In lots of mud. Sucking me down. I need someone with longer arms than mine. Mom, what is *wrong* with you?"

Kenzie took a few steps into the trees, the darkness closing around her like a glove. She heard things out there, faint snarls, saw a flash of red eyes.

Ryan's voice cut through the night. "Shit, what is *that*? I thought Dad said zombies weren't real."

Kenzie's heart pounded as she quickened her pace.

"Aw, man, this would never happen to Harry Dresden." Ryan coughed. "No, wait, this would *totally* happen to him."

Kenzie ran forward. "Ryan! Keep talking. I'm on my way!"

Brigid dashed after her. "No. Kenzie!"

The Fae woman, surprisingly fast, seized her by the arm. Kenzie shook her off, and the mists closed around them both.

Kenzie almost fell into the bog that opened at her feet. Only Brigid grabbing her again kept Kenzie from plunging straight into it.

Ryan was up to his neck in mud and goo, both hands wrapped around a low-hanging branch. His eyes were round, his face frozen with fear. When he saw Kenzie, tears trickled down his cheeks, cutting through black filth.

"Hold on to me," Kenzie said swiftly to Brigid.

Not waiting for Brigid to answer, Kenzie threw herself on her belly and inched forward into the bog. Brigid's strong fingers gripped her ankles, the Fae woman cursing in her Celtic-sounding language.

"Let go of the branch," Kenzie commanded Ryan as she began to sink into softer ground. "Grab my hand."

Ryan didn't want to release his desperate hold of the over-hanging limb. He was terrified, and the distance between it and Kenzie's hands was a stretch.

"You can make it," Kenzie told him. "It's like jumping up and grabbing the zip line as it goes down. Don't think I didn't see you do that."

"Sorry, Mom," Ryan said, voice breaking. "They dared me, and I'm leader's son. I had to."

"I know. But I saw you succeed. You jumped up and grabbed that bar and rode it down. This is the same thing."

It wasn't at all the same, but Kenzie didn't know what else to say to him. If she inched any farther, she'd be diving face-first into the bog. Then Brigid would have to find a way to haul them *both* out before they drowned.

"Come on, son," Kenzie said, voice shaking. "Let's get out of here, find your dad, and then kick some anthropology professor ass."

Ryan sucked in a breath, coughing when mud came with it. He threw himself forward, let go of the branch, and scrabbled frantically for Kenzie's hands.

He missed one; Kenzie caught him with the other. Her arm jarred with the impact, her aching fingers wanting to jerk open.

Kenzie made herself clamp down on Ryan's wrist. She swung her other arm around and fixed her hold on the back of his neck, his scruff if he'd been wolf. She hauled him up, the bog releasing him slowly, slowly.

The mud sucked at him greedily, not wanting to let go of a life. Kenzie didn't think a patch of mud could be sentient— then again, around here, who knew?

With a boiling, sucking sound, the bog abruptly released Ryan. The sudden lack of resistance sent Kenzie rolling backward, Ryan in her arms.

She sat up, clinging to him and bawling like a baby. Kenzie rocked him, her son, her precious cub, who was real, filthy, and stinking like rotting vegetation.

"It's okay." Ryan patted Kenzie, though he was sniffling back tears himself. "I'm all right, Mom. We're all right. What took you so long?"

Brigid was down on one knee next to them. "She thought you were an illusion. This place is full of them."

Ryan lifted his head and stared at Brigid with wet eyes. "Hey, did you know there was a Fae next to us? I've never seen one before." He wrinkled his nose. "Do they all smell this bad?"

Brigid frowned, her long braids touching Ryan as she leaned to him. "You have no room to speak, young offspring."

"You don't, you know," Kenzie said to Ryan, holding him close again. "You stink something terrible."

Ryan looked offended, and Kenzie started crying again. This was her son; he was alive and with her. Hope broke through her despair, and her heart warmed anew. They'd get through this. And home. They had to.

Bowman kept moving because he knew that if he stopped, he'd die. Having both Kenzie and his son ripped from him had made the world grow surreal, outlines flowing and blurring into unimportant shapes.

Voices around him were hollow as his Shifters continued to search for a way into the mists.

Gil, horrified: "I couldn't hold on to him. Something yanked him from me. I'm so sorry."

Cade: "Eric called. His trackers are en route."

Bowman had heard his phone ring but hadn't had the strength to answer it. Eric would know to call Bowman's second if Bowman didn't respond.

Jamie: "What do you want us to do with all this stuff?"

There was a pile of Turner's crap everywhere. "Keep going through it," Bowman heard himself say. "There might be something to tell us how to get in to save Kenzie."

He was running out of belief. All he knew was that Turner had somehow managed to trap his mate and cub, and he might never see them again. Bowman couldn't face that—everything in him wanted to stop and howl, unceasing, until he died.

I'm here. I love you, her voice had called in his dreams.

I love you, *Kenzie,* came his answer, fierce and from his gut. *I love you with everything I am, everything I have.*

Why the hell *didn't I tell you that before?*

Because he was dumb-ass stupid, that was why. Bowman had been so fixed on the fucking mate bond, and on proving that he and Kenzie could hold Shiftertown together without it, that he had never acknowledged what she truly was to him.

Everything.

"I think I know why Ryan so easily went in." Cristian stood next to Bowman, his voice way too calm. "He picked up the sword and understood its connection to the mists. When he dropped the sword inside, it called to him, compelling Ryan to it." He fixed Bowman with a steady gaze from his wolf-gold eyes. "Ryan is very special. It could be that he will be picked at the next Choosing."

Bowman swung on him. "Screw that. No way is my son going to be a Guardian."

"If the Goddess touches him, he will have no choice."

Pierce gave a Feline growl. "Yeah, but Choosings only take place when the former Guardian dies. I'm not that old yet. You don't have anything to worry about, Bowman."

Cristian shrugged and didn't argue. Bowman knew damn well that it wouldn't matter what he wanted, or what Cristian wanted, or even what Ryan wanted at a Choosing. If the Goddess decided that Ryan should take up the sword and become the Guardian, there was nothing any of them could do about it.

Bowman hoped Cristian was wrong—Guardians were revered, but they were also, very politely, shunned. Pierce took it in his stride, but Ryan wasn't cut out to be a loner.

"Besides," Bowman said out loud, "he's going to be leader, not Guardian."

"*If* we can find him," Cristian answered.

Bowman swung on him. "If you say that like it's a question again, I'll take you apart. We're finding him. And Kenzie. Now stop standing around bleating like an old woman and get on with it."

Bowman expected Cristian to respond with anger, maybe even issue a challenge, but the older man only looked at him with understanding.

"You are right," Cristian said. "We must first find my niece and grandnephew and cease speculating on what might be. We will find them." He didn't touch Bowman, but his eyes held both strength and compassion. "This I promise you."

Brigid looked pained when Kenzie used the Fae cloak to wipe the mud from Ryan's face and hands. Ryan succumbed to the cleaning with poor grace.

"Why don't you turn to wolf?" Brigid suggested as he fussed. "Then you could lick yourself clean."

"Because, ew," Ryan said, giving Brigid a disparaging

look. "Anyway, what if the mud is poisonous? Could be, in a zombified place like this."

"You still haven't told me how you got here," Kenzie said as she wiped.

Ryan looked embarrassed. "My own fault, I guess. I thought the Sword of the Guardian might have enough magic in it to open the way through the mists. So I grabbed it and tried. The stupid sword flew in here like it wanted to lance something. I let it go, and Pierce yelled at me. I thought I'd reach in and see if it was, you know, like lying on the ground right inside, and I got sucked in too. I mean, really fast, like the sword did. I don't know why I ended up falling into the mud, but I did." He looked stricken. "Oh, man, I hope the sword isn't at the bottom of that bog. Pierce would be seriously pissed off at me."

"Sword?" Brigid asked with interest. She perked up at the mention of weapons of any kind.

"Of the Guardian," Ryan said. "Magical. They were made seven hundred years ago by a Shifter sword smith and a Fae woman who put the spells in it. The Shifter and the Fae were mates, believe it or not, and created swords to make sure Shifter souls didn't linger to be enslaved by the Fae. Fae were still trying to make Shifters their slaves, back then, alive or dead." Ryan shrugged. "Still are."

"So I have heard," Brigid answered, disapproving. "Foolish endeavors. We no longer need Shifters."

"Some Fae are fanatics about it," Kenzie said. "And those are the ones Shifters have to deal with."

"You have my sympathy." Brigid folded her arms. "Not that any of this helps us depart this place."

"That's true." Kenzie had never dreamed she'd a) meet a Fae; or b) agree with one so much. "Ryan, you said the sword came in here easily. From what I understand, it's pretty self-preserving, so I'd be surprised if it ended up in the bog. Let's look for it. Maybe it can help us get out." She allowed her hope to rise. "Turner said he needed a talisman to come and go through the mists, and you know, the Sword of the Guardian is one big magical talisman."

"Yeah," Ryan said, leaping to his feet. "You're pretty smart, Mom. Sometimes."

Brigid laughed, a surprisingly beautiful sound. "Offspring have much in common everywhere, do they not? My own daughters have said the same to me." Her laughter died, sorrow entering her eyes. "Yes, let us search."

Brigid helped Kenzie to her feet, and they started to look through the mud and reeds at the edge of the bog for the elusive sword.

A tingle of dread signaled Kenzie before the mists grew dense, wrapping clammy tendrils around her. Ryan shrank to her side as the mists thickened, then parted, revealing Turner standing not ten feet from them.

His outline was darker than before, and from this shadow, his blue eyes shone with cold light. He raised a tranquilizer rifle and shot first Ryan and then Kenzie, who leapt at him to keep him from her son.

Brigid's hands automatically reached for weapons she no longer carried, but Turner invoked the binding spell. She froze in place, bracing herself for a third dart to come for her.

It never did. Turner lifted something that glinted in the half light and the mists became dense. When they thinned again, Turner, the Shifter woman, and the Shifter woman's cub were gone.

CHAPTER THIRTY-FIVE

Brigid checked the perimeter of the place of their captivity, but Kenzie and Ryan were nowhere to be found. Turner had taken them.

The darkness was nearly complete by the time Brigid returned to the place she considered base camp—the large, flat boulder she used as a seat, the soft pile of leaves that was her makeshift bed. Kenzie still had the cloak, which meant Brigid would have no cover tonight. But this place, wherever it was, was far warmer than her home in Tuil Narath—what the Shifters called *Faerie*—so it scarcely mattered.

The emptiness that smote her as Brigid seated herself on the rock surprised her. She didn't like sentimentality, and she didn't like Shifters. Or so she'd thought before meeting Kenzie.

Kenzie had proved companionable. The Shifter woman understood, the same way Brigid did, about love and loss, hardship and happiness. Brigid didn't like to think about what Turner would do to her, or to Ryan, the cub.

Turner was a madman. Brigid had assessed that as soon as she'd looked into his cold, emotionless eyes. He cared for nothing and no one. He'd coerced Brigid into her labors, not to help his people, but for his own glory. To show everyone he'd been right that Shifters existed, and that they'd been wrong to shun him. Being right was important to him, and he was willing to hurt others to prove it.

Turner needed to be eliminated. That was the most efficient way to restore Brigid's life, as well as the lives of the Shifter woman and cub she'd decided to like.

The conviction rang like faint strains of music in her ears. It felt good to have a purpose. Brigid had always planned to kill Turner when the opportunity arose, but now she had to make it arise.

All very well, Brigid told herself, deflating a little. But she had to figure out how. She was stuck here, unable to leave but at his choosing. He had weapons, including the one that shocked, as well as spells and magical talismans. She would have to take away a weapon and turn it on him and hope she picked out the correct talisman to let her out of here.

After sitting some time in contemplation, Brigid realized that the music she'd begun to hear on the edge of her awareness was not in her head.

It was a humming sound, sweet and ringing, somewhere in the woods. Strangely, she thought she recognized the tune—a song her daughters liked to sing, perhaps? But that wasn't quite right.

Brigid wasn't one to sit still and wonder. She came to her feet and walked into the darkness, searching for the music's source.

About twenty yards to the right of base camp, she spied a light. The night was starless—if this place even had stars—and the light was a harsh beacon in the darkness. Its source lay on the ground near a clump of small trees, light spangling branches that leaned over it.

Brigid approached with caution. The light didn't move or change; it simply waited for her.

She brushed back a tendril from a fernlike tree and found herself staring down at a long-bladed sword with a thick silver hilt. The sword itself didn't contain the light; the runes etched into it did, and Brigid knew the music came from them.

Deep magic had forged this weapon. Fae magic.

Brigid studied it before she reached for it. That she could touch the sword, she didn't doubt. She was as Fae as the magic inside it. She hesitated only because of what Ryan had said, that a Shifter sword smith had forged it. Shifters could use iron, and iron was poison to her.

Another assessment told her that the entire thing was made of silver, no iron or steel involved. Brigid could smell the silver, taste it in the air.

She leaned down and closed her hand around the hilt.

The music crescendoed into a wild symphony. The sound grew so loud Brigid wanted to drop the sword and clap her hands over her ears, but she made herself stand fast.

"I will wield you, Fae weapon," she told it. "I will use you to find the Shifters and slay their enemy. And my enemy," she added. "In this instance, they are one and the same."

The symphonic roar softened a little, becoming gentler, but also a little bit smug, as though the sword approved. Odd, but Brigid was not going to argue with her good fortune. A weapon was a weapon.

Thinking over Ryan's story of how the sword had behaved in the mists, Brigid walked back to her camp. Had the sword been seeking Kenzie? Or Brigid, sensing a Fae? Or something else in this world?

No matter the cause, the weapon could penetrate the mists. What had Kenzie called it? *One big magical talisman.*

What had she to lose? If it didn't work, Brigid would simply find herself back at her camp.

She concentrated on the nearest patch of mist, shimmering white in the darkness. She held the sword in front of her, point forward, and walked.

Damp air closed around her, and the fog thickened. Brigid took another step, and another. She expected to bump against the large trees she'd seen on the other side of the mists when she started, but she did not.

The air grew colder. Bone-cold, making her regret the loss of her cloak. But the darkness receded, showing her light.

It was the crisp light of natural sunrise. Brigid looked up through tall trees to a patch of sky flushed with pink, gold, and darker red, beautiful blue beginning to ease past all other colors. The trees surrounding her were massive, the air smelling of pine, the floor of the woods covered with a carpet of long brown needles and fallen pinecones.

She was out. Brigid lifted the sword and gave a shout of triumph.

In the next instant, a pair of strong arms wrapped her from behind, an equally strong hand closing on her wrist below the sword's hilt. Brigid was pulled against a very tall man, who smelled of pine, musk, and a hint of wolf.

She looked up into a pair of deep golden eyes in a tanned face as the man said in thickly accented English, "And what are you, Fae, doing with the Sword of the Guardian?"

Bowman decided he couldn't be surprised anymore by anything Cristian did when the man walked out of the woods into the clearing at Turner's house, not only holding the Sword of the Guardian but towing a Fae woman by her bound hands.

Pierce came running. "What the hell?"

"I found her," Cristian said. "Carrying the sword, if you please."

The woman gave Cristian a cold look, betraying no fear. "I told you what happened, Shifter. What you believe is up to you."

"Oh, I believe you," Cristian said. "I am simply angry at you for not saving my niece."

"I tried." The haughty light in her gray eyes faded a little. The woman had long, white blond braids that hung past her waist, clothes of tattered brocade and fur, and thick boots for a cold climate. "He took them away."

Bowman brushed past Cristian to put himself in front of her. "You know where Kenzie is?"

The woman looked up at him fearlessly. "Your mate, as you call each other? And your wee one?"

Bowman's chest felt as though someone crushed it. "My son? You saw him?"

"I did. I—"

"Where?" Bowman leaned to her. Dimly he realized Cristian was trying to hold him back from her, a fact that might surprise him at any other time. "Where are they?"

"The man called Turner has them." The Fae woman sounded sad. "He took them, I know not where."

"How did you get the sword?" Pierce asked. He reached for it, and Cristian relinquished it to him.

"I found it. Or it called to me. The runes—"

Bowman straightened, and Cristian stepped in front of the woman as though protecting her. "Her name is Brigid. She is of a Fae clan called the Hunting Warriors, translated from her language."

"I don't care if it's called the Dancing Clowns," Bowman growled. "Why were you able to find the sword, and why were *you* able to get here, when Kenzie couldn't?"

"I don't know," Brigid said. "I started to explain that the runes called to me." She gestured to the sword, her hands tied with a thin piece of clean leather—Bowman didn't want to know why Cristian had been carrying tethers around with him.

The sword in Pierce's hands was quiet now, simply the Sword of the Guardian as it always was.

"She might be telling the truth," Pierce said, sheathing the sword and slinging it on his back. "I've carried this thing around for thirty years, and I still don't understand all it can do."

"She speaks the truth," Cristian said. "I can scent lies, and she has not made any so far."

"Then where is Kenzie?" Bowman demanded.

"I do not know," Brigid answered, unhappy. "Why not use the sword and try to part the mists again to find her?"

"That might not work," a new voice said.

Bowman swung around to see two men striding toward them. He recognized both, but Cristian and Pierce came alert, and Jamie and Cade stepped behind the newcomers, blocking their way out of the clearing.

The speaker was a tall man with a wiry runner's build, black hair, and eyes like pits of night. Brigid stiffened as she saw him, her nostrils flaring. She took a step closer to Cristian.

The other man was a Shifter. He was big, almost as big as Cade, but he was all Lupine. He had flame tatts down his muscular arms, buzzed black hair, and hard gray eyes that looked upon the world and dared anyone in it to mess with him.

"She is right that the sword called to a Fae," the dark-eyed man continued. "It knew danger, and it sought one who could wield it against a powerful, magical enemy. It might not be able to go beyond the mists again now that she is here, not there."

The Lupine, Graham McNeil, growled. "He's been spouting shit like that all the way across the country. Just my luck I get holed up with a crazy Fae in the cargo hold of a tiny plane. I *hate* airplanes."

"I am *dokk alfar*," the dark-eyed man corrected him. "Not Fae."

"Yeah, whatever," Graham said, making a dismissive shrug.

"I'm Stuart Reid," the dark-eyed man said to the others. "Eric told us you had a problem with the worlds in the mists."

"Whatever the hell that means," Graham rumbled.

Bowman was as impatient as Graham. "My *problem* is that some asshole has taken my mate and cub and hidden them behind these mists. What I want you for is to help me get them out."

"And kick some evil human ass," Graham said. He grinned, his harsh face softening. "That's where I come in. I get the fun part."

The Fae woman said, "If you let me loose, I can help in the, as you say, ass kicking. Find me a weapon to wield, and I am as good a warrior as any of you. This Turner has stolen my life and my work, has taken me from my children and my sisters. He must die."

Graham gave her a look of grudging respect. "I like her. Huh. Never thought I'd say that about a Fae."

Cristian studied Brigid as though examining a new species of insect. "She is intriguing. If I decide we can trust her, she might be useful."

Brigid shot him a withering glance. "How kind. I would say, as my daughter does, *bite me*, but I fear that you, wolf, actually would."

"Hmm," Cristian said seriously. "You never know what I might do."

Brigid turned a wary eye on Reid. "This one, he is . . ." She spoke a word that sounded like a lawn mower crushing metal.

"She means I'm an iron master," Reid said. He raised his hand, showing them a straight piece of rebar he'd held by his side. "The *dokk alfar* have always been able to wield iron, I more than most. And so the *hoch alfar* fear us."

"It is not fear," Brigid returned, though Bowman heard the lie. "It is disgust."

"I see the Fae are at each other's throats again," Gil said, stepping out of Turner's house. "Typical . . . Ah . . . Whoops."

He started to hurriedly retreat, but Graham leapt forward and grabbed him by the back of his neck, hauling him off the steps and around to face them.

"What the hell are *you* doing here?" Graham shouted into his face. "Misty's been worried sick about you. She's driving me effing crazy."

Bowman abandoned Cristian and the Fae woman to move to Graham in sudden swiftness. "You know Gil?"

Graham stared at Bowman. "Gil?" Graham's face flushed with anger, and he shook Gil by the back of the neck. "His name's not *Gil*. It's *Ben*. Ben Williams. He's some kind of species—a gnome, he calls it—that got kicked out of Faerie a thousand years ago. He's magical, he's a total shithead, and Misty says he helped her save my life."

CHAPTER THIRTY-SIX

Bowman studied Gil in great distrust. He'd known some-thing was off about him, even before Kenzie's discovery that he wasn't really Gil Ramirez, police officer.

"Your name's not Ben either, is it?" Bowman asked, amazed at how steady his voice was. "Who are you?"

Gil abruptly stood taller and shook Graham's hold off with ease. His appearance didn't change, but his nice-guy helpful-ness faded, and something old looked out of his eyes. He had a strength that had nothing to do with physical prowess; it was the strength of a boulder that had endured centuries of wind and rain.

"What happened to your prison tatts?" Graham growled at him. "You look the same, but not exactly the same."

"As I explained to Misty," Gil said in a firm voice, "I have learned to alter my appearance and blend in with the human world over the centuries. In Las Vegas, I was an ex-con. Here, I am a police officer when I need to be, or the beloved hired hand who became the bed-and-breakfast ghost in Fayboro."

"And what is a gnome?" Cristian asked. "I have not heard of this outside human children's stories."

"It is what my race called itself," Gil answered. "We've

also been called goblins. The Fae killed and banished us long ago, exiling us to this world, where most of us didn't survive. We hate Fae as much as Shifters do." His gaze went to Brigid. "I see that you caught one. What does she know?"

Bowman leaned to him, barely containing his rage. "Don't fuck with me, whoever you are. Kenzie was following *you* when she vanished, and you were with Ryan when he went. If any of this is your fault, you're dead. I don't care if you're a thousand years old; you won't live to see a thousand and one."

Gil met his gaze without fear. "I swear to you, I did nothing. I tried to stop them both being taken, but I failed. The gates won't work for me, as I said—the Fae saw to it that they work for none of my people. I can sense them when they appear, but not use them."

Bowman looked at Reid. "And you say the sword won't open the way again, not for me?"

Reid shook his head. "You can try, of course. I might be wrong."

The Fae woman broke in. "But Kenzie has been taken away somewhere by this man called Turner. She is no longer in the mists. I searched for her, and did not find her."

Cristian nodded. "She is correct, I think. Pierce has told me that Turner has made for himself a network of people to help him—such as the man who drove the truck with the beast, and the man who shot at us and the unfortunate Serena. He could have taken Kenzie and Ryan away anywhere."

"Then why didn't we see Turner come out with them here?" Bowman asked. "The Fae woman emerged in these woods."

Gil broke in. "As I explained before, the pockets have more than one entrance, and if one knows how to manipulate them, each entrance can go to several different pockets, which can in turn have many exits. Pockets are sort of like an interconnected hive, with passages and rooms going every which way. This is why Kenzie went in near Fayboro, when she was chasing me, and yet Turner could come out here, near his house—or wherever he likes. Someone with a talisman who has learned to navigate the pockets can travel anywhere, though it's highly dangerous. There are worlds out there far more deadly than Faerie or this one."

Bowman turned to his trackers and Pierce. "All right, then

tell me where he might have taken her and Ryan. You were tasked to find out all about Turner. What do you know?"

"If they're out in this world, he'd have taken her one of four places," Cade said without hesitation. "His lab at the university. His apartment in Asheville, but that's pretty public. This trailer, where he obviously isn't." He waved a large hand toward the torn-up trailer. "And a house in South Carolina, which used to be his mother's. His mother has passed, but he still keeps it."

"The university," Cristian said with conviction.

"How do you know that?" Graham asked.

"Because he hasn't played his end game yet," Bowman said before Cristian could answer. "He wants to be the foremost expert on Shifters, and he wants his colleagues to see that he is. Kenzie is a means to that end—I don't know how yet." His fear boiled up to mix with his anger. "I'm going to the university."

Cristian stepped in front of him. "Do you not think that he has taken Kenzie and Ryan in order to trap you? If you run to him, he will have his wish. You do not think he baited this trap well?"

"Doesn't matter. I'm going in to get her and my cub. The rest of you are coming as my backup—I'm not stupid enough to go alone."

"Bowman," Cristian said sharply. "This is my niece's and your son's life you play with. Do you not believe that a contingent of Shifters arriving at a human university and killing a professor there will bring the wrath of the humans down on every Shifter in Shiftertown?"

Bowman shrugged, though his heart was pounding, and the whole of him needed to find Kenzie and his son. "We'll be stealthy."

"I'll suck at the stealth part," Graham said. "But if you need to take this guy down, you should let me do it. I'm not from around here. I can disappear with him and do him far, far away, to keep the blowback from you."

Logical, and probably why Eric had sent Graham in the first place. Too bad Bowman wanted to taste Turner's blood.

Graham must have sensed this, because he gave Bowman a look of understanding. "We'll find her. And finish him." He cleared his throat and looked suddenly uncomfortable. "Oh, yeah. Misty said to tell Kenzie and Ryan she sends her love. You know females like stuff like that."

"I know," Bowman said. Kenzie was generous with her love and her friendship, not hiding her passion for life and for others.

Graham was talking again. "Misty also said . . . She said to trust in the mate bond. That the mate bond will know what to do."

Bowman stopped. Graham was watching him, and Bowman shook his head. "Misty knows Kenzie and I never . . ."

"Yeah, she does. But she doesn't agree that you don't have it."

Graham looked as though he'd say something more, then he closed his mouth, his cheekbones reddening. If Bowman had been in any other state of mind, he'd be amused watching the warrior Lupine grow embarrassed.

"Misty also sent a big flower arrangement for you," Graham finally said. "You know she still has the florist shop." He growled. "You know what I felt like holding that on my lap all the way across the country and then riding in from the plane? Don't worry, I left it at your house. Kenzie can enjoy it when she gets home."

The university campus was quiet this early in the morning, between semesters. Classes didn't start again, an electronic sign at its main entrance informed them, until mid-January.

Even so, there were enough people around to make Bowman's expedition perilous. Groundskeepers and maintenance workers moved about the campus on foot and in electric carts, department secretaries hurrying in to open offices. A few students trickled into the just-opened library, and one academic walked to a brick building, a briefcase in hand, head down against the cold.

The Shifters didn't resemble anything but Shifters, and one had a broadsword on his back.

Bowman had considered leaving Pierce behind—for about three seconds. Bowman knew he needed Pierce near, in case it became necessary for him to do his job as Guardian.

The Fae woman, Brigid, accompanied them, though she'd started to feel ill as soon as they'd left the woods. The Shifters had parked their motorcycles and trucks at the arena—the arena's shored-up beams had iron in them, as did the waiting vehicles.

Gil had stepped forward and solved the problem. He gave Brigid a necklace with what looked like a coin hanging from it, which, he said, would protect her from the worst of the iron sickness. Brigid took the necklace distrustfully, but when she put it on, the greenish cast to her skin disappeared, and she breathed better.

Gil handed another necklace to Bowman. "This will help."

"Help me what?" He was as suspicious as Brigid.

"Cut through any spells Turner has laid on to keep you from Kenzie. He knows a lot of Fae magic. Half the crap Cristian and I found in his trailer is about Fae spells and how to find the power, as a human, to work them. He's figured out a lot—how to tap the ley lines; how to use sympathetic magic— blood, hair, the like—to control people. He's dangerous. This is a fairly general spell, but it should help."

Bowman would have preferred him to say, *Here's the perfect weapon that will take out Turner and free Kenzie without her and Ryan getting hurt,* instead of *It should help.* But Bowman had learned to take what he could get.

They rendezvoused at a coffeehouse outside the university, a place that didn't mind serving Shifters. The clientele was young, mostly students and newbie executives. They gave the Shifters curious glances, though Brigid stood out still more than the Shifters. She'd look otherworldly even without the tunic and breeches, with her pale hair, long braids, and black eyes. She gazed coolly back at the men who stared at her in wonder until they pretended great interest in their coffees.

Bowman sipped his brew in the parking lot, for once having no enjoyment of the rich, bitter liquid. They'd decided to keep the penetrating team for the university small—Bowman, Pierce, Graham, Reid. Gil, who Bowman wasn't going to trust by a long way, would stay with Cade. Cade had orders to sit on him if he tried anything.

"I'm here to help," Gil said, undaunted. "Believe me, I owe Kenzie."

"Damn right you do." Bowman snarled at him. "But you take orders from *me,* got it?"

Gil raised his hands. "All right. It's your show."

"We don't even know if Turner's at his office," Pierce pointed out. "He could be at his house in South Carolina. The university is only a guess."

"Simple enough to discover." Cristian took out his cell phone and tapped numbers. "Hello, is that the Department of Anthropology?" he asked when a woman's voice answered. His accent became thick. "I am a colleague of Professor Turner, an anthropologist from Romania. Is he in? May I speak to him?"

Bowman heard the woman on the other end. "He's here, but he's over in his lab. He doesn't like to be disturbed there. I can leave a message with your number, or send you to his voice mail."

"It is no matter." Cristian managed to sound cheerful and bumbling, and somehow stooped and elderly, though he stood next to Bowman as taut and dangerous as a naked blade. "I take a chance. I call him again this afternoon, yes? Thank you, young lady. You have a nice day."

He tapped the phone again and dropped it into his pocket. "He is there."

"I heard," Bowman said tightly.

Graham gave Cristian a look of reassessment. "You're a devious bastard. Why haven't I met you before?"

"Bowman does not let me attend the meetings of Shifter leaders," Cristian said calmly. "He keeps me, as you say, in reserve."

"And you just happened to know the guy's phone number?" Graham asked.

"Of course. When we began to research Professor Turner, I learned everything about him—where he lived, where he worked, and who he worked with, and I stored it here." Cristian tapped the side of his head. "Better than a computer."

Pierce tried to hide his snort and didn't succeed. Cristian gave him a chilling look, and Pierce quickly drank coffee.

Jamie, Cade, and a few other trackers broke from the main party, Gil in tow, as they left the coffeehouse. They would keep watch, alert Bowman of any trouble, and be ready to assist when needed. Cade grumbled that he didn't like it, but he acknowledged that secrecy, not a direct attack, was the answer here.

Cristian accompanied Bowman's group with Brigid back

to the campus, then he and Brigid walked away together.
They'd been assigned the task of distracting campus security
while the other Shifters and Reid slipped inside the building
that housed Turner's lab.

Cristian, with his salt-and-pepper hair and tall body, and
Brigid, nearly as tall as he was, her white braids brushing the
backs of her knees, were certainly distracting. They drew the
gazes of not only the lone security man in his cart, but also
every other person they strolled past.

Bowman signaled the others. They opened the unlocked
door of the small building Cristian had told Bowman housed
Turner's lab and walked inside, one at a time. Following the
directions Cristian had given them, they went down a flight of
stairs and through another heavy door at the bottom.

The basement of this building was silent, dim, and empty,
and made Bowman's wolf growl in unease. The place, as Ryan
would say, creeped him out.

The scent was wrong, a strange combination of dry, steril-
ized air and dust. The hall was long, the tile institutional white,
the walls painted off-white and needing a touch-up. No pictures lined the corridor, though bulletin boards hung outside
each door. These boards were filled with photos, photocopied
articles with circled paragraphs, and small posters with sayings
like *You don't have to be crazy to work here, but it helps*.

The metal doors between the ordinary ones unnerved
Bowman most of all. These were stainless steel and massive,
like the doors of giant refrigerators. Large chains hung across
them, locked with padlocks.

Reid touched a door. "Ordinary metal," he said. "Not
spelled. But it makes you wonder what they're keeping in there."

Bowman sniffed but caught no scent. The chilled, dry air
dampened all smells.

They walked on in silence.

Turner's lab lay right where Cristian said it would. The
word "lab" conjured in Bowman's mind rows of test tubes and
flaming alcohol burners, but then, he'd never seen one outside
of TV or movies. This lab was nothing more than a large room
of tables, a desk and chair, a ton of dusty books on shelves
scaling the walls, and trays that held shards of pottery or
skulls and bones.

The Shifters tightened at the sight of the bones. Most were human, and ancient—any life that had clung to them was long gone. Even so, these humans should not have been disturbed from their rest.

Reid stopped before one glassed-in tray that sat by itself. "These are Shifter," he said.

Bowman went quickly to him, and the other two Shifters closed behind Bowman. Three skulls and several piles of bones occupied the case. Unlike the bones in the other trays, these weren't labeled.

"You see," Reid said, pointing, "the shape of the skull is slightly different, the bones a little thicker than those of a human. These bones that look animal are the right size to be Shifter."

They eyed the remains in disquiet. "How do *you* know what Shifter skulls look like?" Graham asked in a low voice. "We don't let people look at them."

"People, no. Fae, yes. Some of the *hoch alfar* still have Shifter skulls as trophies in their halls. Passed down through the generations."

Bowman felt sick. Whoever those ancient Shifters were, he said a prayer to the Goddess for them, hoping their souls had managed to escape.

"Pierce," he said.

Pierce knew what Bowman wanted. He drew his sword, went to the case, and brought the hilt down, shattering the glass.

Reid and Graham helped Pierce clear the shards away while Bowman stood a little apart, his heart thumping. The skulls were very old, he could tell by the scent, or lack of it, but the fact that they existed at all infuriated him. Turner could only have acquired them from Shifter hunters or from Fae.

Once the pieces of glass were out of the way, Pierce flipped the sword over and thrust the blade through the first skull.

The runes on the sword flashed, and a hum broke the silence. The skull disintegrated at the touch of the blade, a little sigh flowing into the room. One by one, the bones and skulls became dust, the little whisper as each was released making Bowman's throat tighten.

When Pierce finished, he let the sword's point touch the floor while he bowed his head and said a prayer to the

Goddess. Graham joined him, murmuring the words. Reid only watched, but his face was somber.

Bowman's cell phone pealed. The others snapped around at the sudden sound. Bowman clicked on the phone and held it to his ear. "What?"

"Leave your friends and exit the lab through the door at the end. It will be unlocked for you. I want you alone, or they both perish."

Bowman said nothing, only ended the call and dropped the phone into his pocket.

Graham, Pierce, and Reid had good enough hearing that Bowman didn't have to repeat the caller's words. The three followed him to the indicated door, which was another stainless steel one, but this one's padlock hung open on its hasp.

Bowman gave the others a quiet look, and they nodded. Drawing a breath, Bowman removed the lock, squared his shoulders, and reached for the door handle.

"Take this," Reid said, handing him the iron rebar he'd brought as a weapon. "Plain iron is best against Fae spells."

"It's good for whacking people too," Graham said. "Good luck, O'Donnell."

"It's not me who will be needing it," Bowman said, then he opened the metal door and walked inside.

CHAPTER THIRTY-SEVEN

The first thing Bowman knew was icy chill. That and the door clanging closed behind him, an electronic lock clicking into place.

He had entered not a room but a narrow hallway about twenty feet long. To his right was what looked like a radio control booth, the top half of its wall clear glass that reached to the ceiling. No door led from it to the hall Bowman stood in, though a closed door was on the booth's back wall.

Two smaller booths lay side by side at the far end of the hall, or else it was one booth divided by a partition. Each had a door, their top halves glass.

Turner sat in the booth on Bowman's right at a control board. Several cameras were fixed to the walls in the hallway, and Bowman saw himself on monitors inside Turner's booth.

Behind one door in the booth at the end was Kenzie. Behind the other was Ryan.

Bowman rushed to them with Shifter speed, raising the rebar to pound through the glass. Kenzie, bound to a chair with chains, lifted her hands, wrists in cuffs. She said something he couldn't hear, the booth soundproof, but her gesture was apparent enough.

Stop.

Bowman halted, the bar uplifted, and peered inside at her then at Ryan. Ryan was likewise bound to a chair. They both looked whole and unhurt, if grimy. In each booth, a shotgun had been positioned on a stand, the barrels pointed directly at each of them.

Even through the glass, even over Kenzie's and Ryan's fear and anger, Bowman could smell the weapons, gunpowder and metal packed into lethal barrels.

Bowman heard a *click* and then Turner's voice. "I study Shifters, you know. Everything they do intrigues me."

Bowman swung around and made for Turner's booth. "I don't care, asshole." He slammed the iron rebar into the glass.

The bar bounced off, jarring Bowman's arm. The glass didn't even scratch.

"I am quite safe," Turner said. He looked fresh and clean, as though he'd showered, while Kenzie and Ryan were filthy. "I am very interested in the decision-making processes of the alpha males. It is of great importance to understanding Shifters and how to deal with them. I have watched you try to defend your friends single-handedly; I've watched you delegate responsibility when you were hurt. I also watched you drag yourself up and attempt to save those in your care when you could barely walk. You use strength but also great cunning. Yes, I have observed you very carefully."

Bowman glared through the glass. "What does that prove except that you're the sick, twisted bastard I already knew you were?"

Turner continued as though Bowman hadn't spoken. He was dictating, Bowman realized, into a microphone.

"The familial bonds interest me most. The alpha Shifter must not only lead his pack but take a mate and continue his authority through his male offspring. Which is the more important to him? This experiment will study which he has the strongest instinct to protect. My hypothesis is that the alpha male will always choose the heir, in his need to keep his gene pool intact and continuing. A mate, who does not share his genetic material, on the other hand, will prove to be expendable, once she has born a living male cub."

Bowman slammed the rebar into the glass in front of

Turner's face again. Futile, but he needed to lash out, to pound at something until he could think.

"I have devised the experiment thusly," Turner went on, unworried. "The alpha male is placed into a situation in which he must make a choice. I have divided the far chamber into two rooms with a temporary wall. In one sits the mate. In the other, the offspring—the cub."

Bowman swung back to the two doors. Kenzie's look was pleading. *Don't.*

Turner was still speaking. "If the male opens one door in an attempt to free whoever is behind it, that door will activate a solenoid that completes a circuit to fire off the shotgun in the other chamber, destroying the Shifter confined there. The alpha male thus can make only one choice—saving his mate will kill his offspring; saving his offspring will kill his mate. Which will he choose?"

Kenzie watched Bowman's expression dissolve into fury and horror. She could hear Turner fine, because he'd made sure the speakers came into her booth and Ryan's. She could hear and see Ryan as well, because the partition between them was only a piece of hard plastic with holes in it.

Ryan was terrified, she knew. He didn't want to die. But equally, he didn't want to watch his mother be killed either.

"No choice is also a choice," Turner's loathsome voice droned on. "If the alpha male chooses neither, then I will fire off the guns myself, one after the other. Which will *I* choose to kill first?"

Kenzie could just see Turner's hands hovering over a computer keyboard in his booth. She kept herself still, knowing that any hint of aggression would likely end with her watching Ryan and Bowman die.

Bowman's eyes became red with his rage. His Collar let off a single spark, bright even under all the fluorescent lights.

"Bowman, no," Kenzie shouted, though she knew he wouldn't hear. She raised her bound hands and pointed both forefingers at Ryan. "Save our son," she said, mouthing the words as precisely as she could.

"Mom, no way!" Ryan turned to her, his agitation making her want to cry. "You can always have more cubs."

"Don't be stupid," Kenzie snapped. "I don't want more cubs. I want *you*."

"He has to pick one of us. I want you to be with Dad."

"No." Kenzie's voice sharpened even as she wanted to be gentle. "You're more important. This way, your dad can maybe find someone he can form the mate bond with." She wanted to rip out her heart even as she said it, but she had to acknowledge the idea.

That's bullshit, and you know it.

Kenzie's eyes widened as Bowman's voice sounded inside her head. *Bowman?*

His eyes went just as wide. *Kenz?*

She sucked in a breath. *What . . . ?*

Bowman, with minimal movement, touched a pendant on a necklace that hung just below the Celtic knot of his Collar. *Your friend Gil gave me this thing. Maybe . . .*

From the look on Bowman's face, he didn't think the pendant was doing anything, and neither did Kenzie. Whatever the talisman was, she'd be surprised if it made people suddenly telepathic.

First things first.

Sit tight. Bowman's voice sounded again.

Where am I gonna go? Kenzie gave him her usual impatient look.

At the same time, her heart sang. They were in sync, as always, looking at danger and deciding what to do. She and Bowman made a kick-ass team.

Turner had them by the balls, though. He'd explained the setup to Kenzie. When one door was opened, a switch would be sparked, carrying a charge to the solenoid on the other side of the partition. That solenoid, in turn, would trip another switch, pulling back a wire wrapped around the hammer of the shotgun in that booth, firing it.

Turner also had controls in his room that could fire off either weapon whenever he chose. Bowman couldn't break through the extra-thick glass and kill Turner before he could punch a button. Kenzie knew Bowman would never have come here without backup, but his trackers wouldn't be able to get inside in time to stop Turner either. Turner held all the cards.

Bowman held a rebar. He had a talisman that did

who-knew-what around his neck, and the ability to become wolf. That was it.

Kenzie went through the setup in her head, hoping it conveyed the situation in detail to Bowman. He wasn't looking at her, however, but at Ryan, who was speaking carefully.

"Dad," Ryan said, shaping the words so Bowman could read his lips. "The *latch* is the *switch*."

Bowman frowned at his son, unenlightened. Kenzie repeated Ryan's words in her head, hoping Bowman could hear them.

Bowman continued to frown, then he snapped his gaze to Ryan's door.

Turner's voice clicked on. "I will give you another thirty seconds to make your choice, Shifter," he said. "I have other things to do today."

Can you get out of those chains? Bowman asked Kenzie in her head.

I think so. She hadn't wrested herself free yet, though, because Turner had threatened to kill Ryan if she didn't behave.

When I move, you move, Bowman said. *I'm not sure this will work.*

Kenzie tensed. *Good to know.*

Ryan's got an interesting idea, but your gun might still go off. I can't see the wiring.

Kenzie had no idea what that meant, but she dragged in a breath, ready for whatever he was going to do.

Bowman, she said silently, sending every bit of caring and love she could through whatever link they were sharing.

Bowman's hard gray eyes softened for a brief moment. *Yeah, I know,* his whisper came back. *Love you too.*

He stood absolutely still for a few seconds longer. Turner waited, his fingers poised over the keyboard.

Then Bowman leapt forward and smashed the rebar through the wooden bottom half of Ryan's door. A moment later, Bowman dove for the hole he'd made and let his Collar go off.

Electricity sparked and exploded. Bowman's body jerked with it, a howl of pain escaping his throat. The door broke, but the frame remained connected to the wall, the latch in place, and Kenzie's shotgun stayed silent.

For now. With something as strong as Bowman smashing through it, the door could fall out of its frame any minute. Kenzie understood that Bowman had tried to short-circuit the wiring with his Collar, to disrupt electricity going to the switch Turner had put into the door, but a stray spark might set it off anyway.

Turner, red with anger, brought his hands down on the computer keyboard.

But he wasn't as fast as a Shifter. Bowman leapt through the wreckage of the door, shifting in midair, to catch Ryan and his chair and slam both out of the way as the shotgun in Ryan's room boomed.

At the same time, Kenzie shifted, letting herself linger in her between-beast state—a formidable cross between wolf and human, with the advantages of both. The form was difficult for most Shifters to maintain for long, but it got the job done in the meantime.

The shotgun in her room went off, pellets scattering everywhere. Kenzie ducked the worst of it as her chains broke, though shot grazed her, embedding in her fur and skin.

She didn't care. She only saw Bowman's wolf form light up with electricity as he landed with Ryan, the arcs from his Collar and the wall's wiring zapping him over and over again.

Kenzie burst the partition in two, becoming wolf all the way as she dove through. She dragged Bowman by the scruff away from the spaghetti-like live wires flailing on the floor and landed on top of him, using her weight to smother the sparks in his fur.

Ryan's face was wet with blood and tears, but he didn't break down as he struggled with his chains. "Dad, you are *awesome*! Mom, I can't get out of these, and Turner's coming!"

Kenzie changed to her half-beast again, her brute strength breaking the links of Ryan's chains. He shifted to wolf at the same time she did, the cub climbing onto his mother's back for protection.

"So," Turner said. He had come through a back door in the booth Kenzie had sat in, which must lead to his main control room, his face scarlet with rage but his voice still too calm. "The instinct of *Canis lupus shifterensius* is to preserve the entire pack. That gives me much to write about. This symposium will be interesting."

He brought up a semiautomatic, aimed it at Kenzie and family, and shot.

Bowman heard Kenzie's shriek inside his head as a bullet caught her. She had turned and slammed herself backward, protecting Ryan, which had exposed her belly and throat. Blood blossomed on her soft fur, paler on her stomach than her back.

Bowman's reason left him. He felt the bond between himself and Kenzie lessen, and the pain of that was unbearable.

I love you, Kenz was Bowman's last coherent thought. Then the world became a blur.

Bullets whizzed past him. Some of them struck him, but Bowman didn't notice. He ran at Turner, his claws ripping into the man's skin. He bit down and tasted blood.

Pain burned his side, and Bowman's own blood flowed. His Collar shocked him, agony streaming through every nerve, but Bowman ignored it. He bit, tore, and shook, and blood sprayed.

Turner's gun slipped out of his hands to clatter to the floor, but the man kept fighting. He was strong, and Bowman was losing blood. Turner managed to slide away from Bowman and try to run back the way he'd come, through Kenzie's booth. But Kenzie was there, ready to kill.

Turner had just enough time to turn and race down the hall to the steel door Bowman had entered through. He pounded four numbers into the keypad next to it and yanked it open.

He found two Shifters, one with a sword, one with massive fists, waiting on the other side. Behind them stood a tall *dokk alfar* with fire in his eyes.

Graham grabbed Turner, but the man had a few more dirty tricks in store. He Tased Graham, ducked under Pierce's reach, whipped his Fae dirk across Reid's face, and sprinted through the lab and down the main hall.

Reid was the fastest after him, with that weird Fae speed, but Bowman wanted Turner for himself. He bounded past the others, even as blood poured out of him, chasing Turner the length of the hall.

At the door to the stairs, Turner had to halt, confronted with Cristian, who was supporting a shaking Brigid. She was indicating, with wild gestures, one of the chained refrigerated rooms.

"It is here," she said, her dark eyes wide. "I know it. I remember the aura of it."

Bowman knew exactly what she meant. He ran for the steel door she was staring at and broke its chains. He had no time to howl a warning, but Cristian was already pulling Brigid out of the way.

Bowman brought his weight down on the door's giant handle and released the beast within.

CHAPTER THIRTY-EIGHT

A monster similar to the one they'd fought at the roadhouse
filled the hall. This one was a little bit different, with a
Feline body; huge, taloned paws; a face that was so distorted
it was difficult to tell what it was supposed to be; and a tail that
could only belong to a dragon.

Manticore was the word that flashed through Kenzie's
head, but it didn't matter what it was called. It was big, powerful, and very, very angry.

The thing struck out, its flailing claws and tail catching
walls, ceiling, doors, Shifters, Turner. Turner screamed as a
huge paw smashed him in the stomach.

"Whistle," he yelled at Brigid, who came at him. "I control
it with a whistle . . . !"

"Do you mean this one?" Brigid straightened from Turner's
fallen body with a silver object in her hand. "What a pity. It
appears to be broken."

Turner gasped as he scrambled up from the floor. "You
stupid bitch!"

He went for her. Cristian stepped in front of Brigid to protect her, then Bowman's charge caught Turner, and they both
went down.

Kenzie, human again, shoved Ryan back inside the room with the booths, ignoring his "But, *Mom!*"

Bowman was fighting Turner, but Bowman had been hit worse than Kenzie had. Though fiery pain seared her stomach, she could last long enough to get Turner. She snatched up the piece of rebar Bowman had dropped and ran to help.

Bowman was all over Turner, and the monster beast was all over Graham, Reid, Pierce, Brigid, and Cristian. Help was barreling down the hall in the form of Jamie, Cade, Gil, and other trackers, but there wouldn't be enough of them to stop it, Kenzie realized. She'd had twice as many Shifters fighting with her against the first monster, and they hadn't been able to make a dent in that beast. Only Bowman's quickness with the truck had saved them, and even then, the monster had chosen to run off. Or perhaps Turner had summoned it back with his whistle, now in pieces in Brigid's hand.

Bowman's Collar was going off as he fought Turner, and that and his injuries slowed him. Turner took advantage and drove his Fae dirk blade under Bowman's foreleg, deep into the fur and skin there.

Bowman's snarls turned murderous, but blood bubbled out of his mouth. Kenzie shrieked and smacked Turner with the rebar.

Turner dropped, but the next moment, Kenzie was flying through the air, the beast batting her aside. The thing grabbed Bowman as well, tossing him the other way, its tail sending him sliding across the floor to slam into the cement wall. Bowman lay still a moment before he climbed unsteadily to his wolf feet, shook himself, and stumbled back toward Kenzie.

The beast had Turner. Its claws ripped into him, spilling out blood, guts, bile. Turner screamed and screamed, alive and in agony. The sound burst into Kenzie's skull, and even with all the horrible things Turner had done, Kenzie started to crawl to him, to help.

Bowman reached him first. He shifted to human, got behind Turner, seized his head in his strong arms, and broke his neck.

Turner fell dead at his feet. Bowman's throat was lit up with his Collar, and the beast, deprived of its victim, attacked Bowman instead.

* * *

Bowman heard Kenzie shouting, but he was too busy to call out to reassure her. Giant arms came down to crush him, claws bigger than any Shifter grizzly's raked across his stomach.

Speaking of grizzlies, one filled the hall, Cade's roar a match for the beast's. Cade jumped onto the creature's back, teeth and claws deadly, but he barely slowed the thing down.

But there was Jamie, leaping with his cheetah's speed. Cristian was darting in and out as wolf, Pierce came in with his sword, and Reid was fighting with twin iron-bladed knives. Brigid had retrieved Turner's dirk and fought alongside Cristian, stabbing and dodging with incredible speed.

Kenzie was hurt. Her body was covered with blood and mud, her face streaked with cuts. Her stomach was a mess of black blood, and the way she staggered told Bowman she wasn't doing well.

He wasn't either. The beast came at him again, and Bowman fought with madness that kept him on his feet. The charm on the necklace Gil had given him flopped uselessly against his chest, below his crackling Collar.

Where *was* Gil? Bowman distractedly saw that the man wasn't fighting with them, but he was battling too hard to see what he was doing.

No, there he was, supporting Kenzie, taking her out of the way of the fight. Kenzie leaned against the wall, her face paper white, too much blood on her skin.

Bowman saw Gil stop a little way from the beast, hold up both hands, and start shouting in a strange, phlegm-clogged language.

The beast stopped. Turned. Cade and Jamie fell from its back, as did the huge wolf that was Graham. The beast swung all the way around, its bizarre face moving as it sought Gil.

Gil didn't look happy to be skewered by that gaze, but he kept chanting, hands held high. The beast began swaying back and forth, following Gil's voice as though mesmerized by it.

Pierce took the opportunity to shove the Sword of the Guardian into the creature. Deep into it. Pierce's hands remained around the hilt as he struggled to pull the blade out again.

The beast blinked. It shook itself away from Gil, turned and caught Pierce with one giant fist, sending him flying, then fixed on Bowman again.

Rage lit its eyes. It pulled the sword out of its side, raised it in clumsy paws, and plunged it toward Bowman. Bowman rolled to keep the sword from hitting his heart, but he felt the blade go into his abdomen and all the way through him, down into the floor.

He lay there like an insect pinned to a board, blood running from his torn body. The beast roared and raised its fists to strike him again.

Kenzie leapt up the monster's arms as they came down, climbing it as though it were a giant, animated tree. She slammed onto its back, her strong legs clamping its sides.

"Mom!" Ryan shouted to her from below, and tossed her the rebar she'd dropped.

Kenzie raised the iron bar, her other hand locked around the creature's head.

"Stay the fuck away from my *mate*!" she yelled, and drove the bar straight through its throat.

The beast roared. It thrashed, gurgled, sprayed blood, caught the others with its tail as they tried to get out of the way. Ryan sprinted back inside the lab, disappearing from the hall.

Walls cracked. The steel door the beast had come out of bent from its hinges and fell to the floor with a loud clang.

Kenzie was thrown off of the monster, landing on her back on the hard floor. Cristian grabbed her and hauled her out of the way. Bowman, stuck to the floor by the sword, could only thrust his arms over his face as the beast fell.

It struck the ground with a wet slap, like a giant water balloon. Blood sprayed everywhere with a stink that made Bowman start to fade into unconsciousness.

The great tail hit him, dislodging the sword and a good chunk of Bowman's flesh with it. Bowman rolled, every movement torture, and rescued the sword before several thousand pounds of dead animal could smash into it.

Bowman staggered to his feet, covered in his own blood and the beast's, struggling to stay upright.

"Here," he said to Pierce, shoving the sword at him. "Go for the heart."

Pierce, his face so pale freckles Bowman never knew he had stood out on his skin, closed his hand around the hilt and moved to do his job.

Bowman limped to Kenzie. Cristian held her in his lap, and Kenzie fought to breathe, blood trickling from her mouth. Ryan was with her, his small hands squeezing hers. "Mom," he whispered.

Bowman took her gently from Cristian, cradling the mate he'd loved from the first moment he'd looked at her. Kenzie's eyes, the ones that had arrested him from across the crowded, cold gym, opened, warming when she saw him.

"Did we get it?"

"You nailed it, baby," Bowman said. "We kicked its sorry ass."

"Good." Kenzie smiled, the sexy, sly smile he adored. She touched her chest, over her heart, then put her hand on the center of his chest. "I feel it," she whispered. "Do you?"

A burning sensation seared him where she touched. Bowman went utterly still as wild hope flooded him. "Yeah." He pressed his hand, covered with blood, over hers. "I feel it, right here."

"Good." Kenzie smiled again, looking so happy that Bowman's whole body hurt. She reached out her other hand and pulled Ryan to them. "Good," she repeated, then her grasp went slack, and she fell, limp, against Bowman's chest.

CHAPTER THIRTY-NINE

Kenzie peeled open her eyes. She took a breath . . . and spent a long moment calming herself down from pain. Her body pounded, her side burned, and her legs felt as though someone had broken them and glued them back together.

A quick downward check showed her lying in bed in a hospital gown, her bare legs free of any kind of splints, though bandages tightly wrapped her middle.

She opened her mouth to call out. Ryan—was he all right? And Bowman? What had happened to everyone? Her last memory was falling against Bowman, safe and content in his arms, but he'd looked as bad as she felt.

The only thing that came out of her throat was a groan. This was bad.

Something rattled. "Kenz?"

Her heart raced, which hurt, then settled into warmth. Bowman. She turned her head.

Bowman was in the hospital bed next to hers, the two of them separated by a few feet of space. Above each of them were machines that beeped, and tubes snaked from bags on stands into their arms.

The moment she saw Bowman and his stormy gray eyes,

the quiet warmth behind her breastbone flamed into white-hot heat. It cleansed rather than hurt, humming like an electric current, filling the air with a clean scent like a breeze after a grueling storm. Kenzie gasped for breath, but found it flowing sweetly into her lungs, erasing the aches of the fight.

Along with those hurts went the despair of long years of watching, wondering if she and Bowman would ever be complete.

"Bowman," she whispered.

Bowman gazed back at her, the quiet joy in his eyes matching her own.

She swallowed. "Ryan?"

Bowman nodded, answering in a low voice. "Is fine." He grinned, which turned up the warmth, the corners of his eyes crinkling. "He looked after us while we lay on the floor in pools of blood. They cleaned him up, checked him out, and let him go home with Afina."

Kenzie sank back in relief, ready to bask in the new feeling of contentedness. And yet it was more than contentment. A vibration deep in her body promised good things to come.

Bowman was here, whole. They were together. She thought about the way the two of them had shared thoughts during the danger in Turner's lab, and excitement blossomed inside her.

Then she blinked, as Bowman's words clicked, one by one, into place. "Let Ryan go home? Who did? Where the heck are we?"

Bowman's smile grew. "Hospital. After you passed out, campus police and town police were all over us, but they were nice and brought us to the hospital instead of taking us to jail."

"Jail?" Kenzie asked in alarm. "They wanted to arrest us?"

"They *did* arrest us." Bowman lifted his left wrist, which was attached by a handcuff to his bed. That explained the rattling noise. "You were so far gone the doctors wouldn't allow them to cuff you. They were afraid of circulation problems." The look in his eyes showed her the worry that had caused him.

"So after they patch us up, they're taking us in?" Kenzie asked. "Who? You and me?"

"Everyone. You should have heard what Cade called the officers who shock-sticked him into submission and shoved cuffs on him."

"Crap on a crutch," Kenzie said indignantly. She, Bowman, and their Shifters had saved the day, kept a dangerous creature from escaping, and got rid of a man who was a sociopathic nutjob, and *they'd* been arrested. "So after this . . . we go to prison?"

No. Kenzie needed to explore this new feeling, this connection with Bowman. She had to know . . .

"Maybe not." Bowman looked way too calm as he lay back on his pillows. Bandages wrapped his abdomen, but he'd either refused the hospital gown or slung it off. The thin sheet was draped over his lower body in a way that made Kenzie regret all the pain she was in. If they both felt better she could slip out of bed, climb over him, move the sheet, and . . .

Not being able to jump her own mate made her restless. "Why not? What's going on?"

"Your uncle Cristian is busy explaining everything to the police. Brigid is helping him." Bowman glanced around the room as though looking for listening devices, and spoke carefully. "Cristian is telling them how Turner contacted Brigid, an anthropology professor from Romania, begging for her help. How she phoned Cristian, a Shifter she knew, who rounded up a group of Shifters to help contain Turner's experimental creature. Unfortunately, Turner was killed in the melee, but we managed to put the beast down. Which was still lying dead in the hallway. Pierce's sword had no effect. The newspapers are having a field day."

"Oh." Kenzie relaxed again. Uncle Cristian had a silver tongue; he was the best negotiator she'd ever met. The fact that Bowman lay here, confident, letting Cristian handle it, told her better than words that everything was going to be all right. They'd made it through another crazy week in Shiftertown.

Kenzie reached for him. The movement took way too much effort, but Bowman stretched his hand toward her as far as he could in the cuff. Their fingers touched.

The contact sparked all the way up Kenzie's arm to her heart. Heat blossomed in her chest, and she swore she felt her wounds start to close.

"The touch of a mate," she said softy.

Bowman's smile warmed her again. "And maybe the mate bond?"

Kenzie caressed Bowman's blunt fingertips, loving their familiar roughness, his strength. "Do you think so?"

"I felt you," Bowman said, his smile dying. "When you were in the mists, when you were so far from me." His Adam's apple moved with a swallow. "I heard you calling out, in my dreams."

"I heard *you*." Kenzie remembered the clammy touch of the mists, her fear, her anger, her need to be next to Bowman. Then she'd heard his voice, shouting her name.

"And then we could talk to each other, in Turner's lab," Bowman said, his deep voice awakening every need inside her. "We could speak without words."

"Can you hear my thoughts now?" Kenzie asked.

Bowman stilled a moment, then shook his head. "No. But it's different now."

"I know," Kenzie said softly.

Their touching fingers brushed each other's again, a tingle of warmth. Kenzie had expected an explosion of incredible emotion when she and Bowman finally found the mate bond, but this quiet awareness was no less intense.

They were bound together. Bowman glanced from their caressing fingers to her face, and Kenzie caught the storm in his eyes.

She wet her lips, longing to spring across the chasm that separated them and into his arms.

"Is it real?" Bowman asked quietly.

"It's burning me all over," Kenzie answered, her cheek pressed to her pillow as she locked her gaze with his. "What do you feel?"

"Fire," he said. "And love. The most incredible love for my hot, golden-eyed, kick-ass goddess of a mate. It hurts with every beat, but damn, it's the best thing I've felt in my life." Bowman's look turned dark, a feral smile spreading across his face. "And I can't stop thinking how amazingly sexy my mate looks in a hospital gown and nothing else."

Kenzie closed her fingers around his middle one, letting her fingertips dance suggestively. "If I could, I'd get out of this bed, pull down that sheet, take you in my mouth, and show you what I want to do when we get home."

"Yeah?" Bowman leaned down and licked across her

fingertips, his tongue hot and wet. "And if I wasn't handcuffed to the bed, and could actually move, I'd be pushing you back into that bed. Maybe turning you over, because that gown ties in the back. Wouldn't even need to take it off you for what I have in mind."

"Mmm." Kenzie flicked the tip of his tongue with her finger. "I'm starting to feel better."

"Touch of a mate," Bowman said.

"We'd heal much faster if we could touch each other all over," Kenzie pointed out.

"We should make them push our beds together." Bowman's eyes sparkled. "And see how much we can touch with me cuffed. Might be fun."

"Sure, challenge me, Bowman." Kenzie gave him a saucy look as her heart cried out in gladness. "See what you get."

"Little devil." He drew her finger into his mouth, suckling, and heat squeezed deep in Kenzie's body.

A cleared throat made her jump. Bowman's teeth closed on her finger, not releasing her, as he shot an irritated glance at the intruder.

"I'd tell you to get a room," Gil said. "But . . ."

Bowman pretended to ignore him, but Kenzie looked limply at the man. She was still angry with Gil, but too wrung out from the fight, and much too interested in reveling in the mate bond, to bother.

"I see you two have finally figured it out," Gil said.

Bowman released Kenzie's fingers and turned a growl on Gil. "I want to know why you're the only one not chained to a bed," he snapped.

Gil shrugged. "I'm a police officer. I was investigating Turner's activities and happened to be on the spot when everything went down." He winked at Kenzie.

"Shit." Bowman sank back to his pillow, but he captured Kenzie's fingers again and didn't let go of her. The touch made Kenzie's strength grow.

Kenzie skewered Gil with her gaze. "How do you know about the mate bond? What was all that shit about me feeling it for you? I still want to gut you for that."

Gil approached their beds, and Kenzie wondered how she'd ever thought him simply a human cop. There was an ancient air about him, of a being who'd seen much, suffered much, and become wise instead of broken.

"I don't know," he said, losing his smile. "I felt something, Kenz." He pressed his hand to his chest. "I'd been feeling it for a while—a long time—seeking the other side of my heart, I guess. And the first time I saw you, I saw the mate bond in you." He put his hand in the air between Kenzie and Bowman, near their joined hands. "Very faint, but it was there. When you sat in the patrol car with me, you almost glowed with it."

Kenzie stared at him. "What the hell are you talking about? I didn't feel it until later, and only figured it out when I was trapped in the mists."

Gil shook his head. "I'm sometimes amazed at the things I can see, but I've stopped letting it bother me. I wasn't completely sure what I was looking at when I saw the sparkling threads coming out of your chest. When the warmth inside me built . . ." He again pressed his hand to his chest. "I thought about how you and me seemed to connect so well, and I let myself believe . . ."

"Oh." Kenzie had been wanting to gut him for making her think they shared the bond, but her anger turned to sympathy. Remembering the anguish she'd felt, she could imagine Gil's dismay when he discovered he'd been mistaken.

Gil's eyes held a sadness. "I saw the threads in Bowman too, when I met him. But neither of you seemed to notice, so I let myself believe. A thousand years is a long time to be alone."

Bowman had gone silent, but Kenzie looked at Gil in compassion. "When did you figure out you were wrong?"

"When I saw Bowman after you got trapped. The threads around him were—I don't know—desperate. They were stretching out, looking for you, crying out for you. It was heartbreaking. I knew then that you two had always shared the bond—that you had a powerful and profound connection. It was such a natural part of you that you didn't even know it." Gil shook his head. "It took both of you being in terrible danger for you to realize it. You two were trying so hard to feel what ordinary Shifters felt, that it didn't occur to you that the pair of you are *extra*ordinary."

"Oh," Kenzie said. She glanced at Bowman, remembering every encounter with him since the first, her constant awareness of him, her need to tease and dare him, the way she'd so easily accepted that they would be mates. She'd made him persuade her the day he'd come to mate-claim her, but Kenzie had already known, in her heart, that she'd go home with him.

Bowman still had to growl at Gil. "And it took you, oh wise one, to show us the way?"

Gil grinned, his humor returning. "Nah, you would have got there. Eventually. Goddess, but you two are stubborn."

"And *you* are a pain in the ass." Bowman gave him a growl. "Are you sure you're not some kind of Fae?"

Gil held up his hands, and deep pain flashed in his brown eyes. "Don't ever call me a Fae. Those bastards wiped out everyone I held dear—don't ever confuse me with *anything* Fae."

Kenzie gentled her tone. "Or a ghost?"

Instantly, Gil's rage departed, and his amusement returned. "That's just fun. That family really did adopt me a hundred and fifty years ago and left me the house. And everyone loves a ghost."

Bowman said nothing, but looked slightly less angry. Kenzie looked Gil over. She didn't understand him, and thought she might never, but he'd helped them every step of the way.

"Is your name really Gil?" Bowman rumbled at him. "Graham called you *Ben*."

Gil shrugged. "Neither." He winked at Kenzie again. "You couldn't pronounce it."

"And why didn't you tell us?" Kenzie asked. "Why pretend to be the cop? Why the glam?"

Gil let out a breath. "Well, to be honest, gnomes or goblins—whatever you want to call me—are not that good-looking to humans. And I've lived in stealth mode so long that it's my natural state. I don't know how to open up and be myself. When I heard about the attack of the beast, I knew I needed to investigate. It smacked of Fae. And if I'd told you I was from Faerie, you'd have gone for my throat first and asked questions later. Don't tell me you wouldn't. So I used a persona you'd find agreeable. When the creature turned up dead real quick, I planned to move on. But then . . . I thought I had a connection to you, Kenzie. I wanted to stick around and see what was going on, and I wanted to help."

"Do you still feel it?" Kenzie asked him softly.

"Yes," Gil said, his eyes quiet. "But I know it's not with you."

Kenzie's anger had gone, and now she felt sad for him. "That means she's still out there," she said to Gil. "The other half of your mate bond."

"If it even is a mate bond," Gil said. "I'm not Shifter; I'm not even human. What I am feeling, the person I need—it might not be that simple." He shrugged. "I guess I keep on looking. Maybe someday . . ."

Kenzie was still curious about the enigma that was Gil, but at the moment she was restless, wanted to go home, and wanted to see her cub. "When can I get out of here?" she asked.

Gil took a step to the bed and touched the handcuff around Bowman's wrist. The locks clicked, and the cuff fell away from him and the bed, Bowman jerking in surprise. Gil caught the cuffs before they hit the floor and tucked them around his belt.

"You've got some healing to do first, young lady," Gil said sternly to Kenzie. "Do that, then have your fun with Bowman. Maybe once you feel better, I'll tell you my life story."

Bowman rubbed his wrist and gave Gil a hard stare. "Can't wait."

Gil laughed. He turned away and beckoned to someone outside the door. "Another person to see you. She's been hoping you'd wake up soon."

A woman in a white coat breezed in, her eager smile in place. "Remember me?" she asked. "Dr. Pat, the vet?"

"Nice to see you again," Kenzie said, wondering that she had ever been jealous of the woman. What Kenzie had with Bowman left jealousy and anger far behind. Those were surface emotions, while the real ones were deep, deep down. "Don't tell me they called you in to work on us."

"Afraid they did," Dr. Pat said. "Some of your Shifters were injured so much in their animal forms that they couldn't shift back. Gil told the hospital to call me, and here I am." She looked pained. "That grizzly bear sure is grumpy."

Kenzie grinned, her heart light. "Cade doesn't like to admit when he's hurt." She gripped Bowman's hand again, his warmth flowing through her. "Thank you, Dr. Pat. I mean that."

"Don't mention it. While they were fixing *you*, Kenzie, something came to light, and I asked to be the first to tell you. And you," she added to Bowman.

Bowman half sat up, his eyes narrowing. "What? What's wrong?"

"Nothing at all." Dr. Pat's smile widened. "Kenzie's pregnant."

Kenzie blinked a moment. "*What?* How can I be?" Her hand went to her abdomen. "Seriously?"

"Seriously." Dr. Pat held up a file folder. "I have the proof right here if you want to look."

Kenzie gaped, while Bowman's hand clamped down on hers. Kenzie knew she'd never understand a single thing on a doctor's chart, so she didn't reach for it.

Then worry washed through her. "But I was hurt. Shot, for the Goddess's sake. How could . . . How could the cub survive?" She swallowed, fearing the answer.

Dr. Pat looked cheerful. "Shifters have an amazing physiology and sense of self-preservation. Even cubs inside their mamas, it seems. The bullet went nowhere near it, and even though you lost a lot of blood, your tissues healed fast, and your blood count is already back to normal. Your uncle Cristian told me that pregnant females become even more robust— they have to be, he said. The doctors checked you and the cub inside you thoroughly. So far, you're fine."

"But I thought I couldn't conceive again," Kenzie said in a rush. "I thought Bowman and I would never . . ."

Her words were choked off as tears flooded her eyes. Bowman was out of his bed, naked except for his bandages, heading for her. He never let go of Kenzie's hand.

Dr. Pat made a squeaking noise and spun and faced the door, her face flaming. Gil stood behind her, his grin wide.

"Maybe, ah, we should leave them alone," Dr. Pat said. "They just got life-changing news."

Gil gallantly offered his arm. "Sure thing. How about we go grab some coffee? We can talk about them behind their backs."

"Right." Dr. Pat, flustered, took his arm, and the two left the room. Gil thoughtfully closed the door behind them.

Bowman yanked the IV out of his arm. He lifted Kenzie

carefully, got into bed with her, and pulled her against him. The bed was narrow, Bowman taking up most of it, but Kenzie thought it a perfect fit.

"A cub," Bowman said, voice breaking, his hand on her abdomen. "Kenz . . ." His eyes were wet.

"She and Ryan are going to drive us crazy," Kenzie said shakily. "They'll gang up. We'll be outnumbered as soon as she's born."

Bowman kissed her forehead, the touch incredibly gentle. "How do you know it's a she?"

Kenzie smiled at him. "I know."

Bowman gave her a serious nod, believing her. She'd known Ryan was a boy as soon as she realized she carried him.

Bowman's kiss soothed the rest of her hurts. Kenzie rose to it, her heart beating faster at the rough feel of his tongue, the rumble in his throat, the way his fingers bore down as he held her. The promise of things to come.

They'd been through so much, and yet, it had been just one more adventure in the lives of Kenzie and Bowman. They fought side by side, they protected Shiftertown, they argued, they made love, they came together with Ryan as a family. Now that family would be larger, and, if Kenzie had her way, would grow even more.

The way Bowman rolled her down into the mattress, his bare body all kinds of good, she thought it wouldn't be long before they filled their entire house with cubs.

The mate bond wrapped them in its strands, humming in the silence. Kenzie twined her arms around her mate, who growled into her throat, opened herself to his kiss, and welcomed him home.

EPILOGUE

Bonfires danced all over Shiftertown. Music blared in the darkness, pulsing beats that led to dancing, or sex—usually both.

It was February, and the celebration of Imbolc. Spring was coming, winter would loosen its hold. Shifters danced in the circles to celebrate fertility, coming growth, new birth. Kenzie and Bowman's unborn cub was being celebrated, as was Marcus and Bianca's, the newly mated pair already expecting.

But really, Bowman reflected, Shifters loved any excuse to light fires, get drunk, dance around naked, and run off with one another into the darkness.

Not that he didn't enjoy it himself. He sipped beer as he watched Kenzie laugh with her friends. Her female cousins and girlfriends surrounded her, chattering with her, excitedly touching her abdomen.

Every once in a while, Kenzie would shoot Bowman a glance, and then burst out laughing. Her girlfriends would giggle with her. They were making fun of him, he knew, and Bowman was fine with that.

The night deepened. It was cold, but bonfires glared heat, and Shifter frenzy was rising. Cristian was the calmest, as usual. Right now, he leaned against a tree, talking with Brigid.

The Fae woman was trying to find a way back into Faerie so she could get home. Cristian was setting things up for her to go to Austin, where there was a known and navigable gate. They had to proceed slowly if she was not to be stopped by the humans, but Brigid seemed to trust that Cristian would get her there in the end.

Graham and Reid had departed before the cops had shown up at the university, knowing Graham couldn't be caught outside his state of residence. Bowman hadn't been able to say good-bye, but a call to Eric let him express his gratitude for their help. Graham had apparently said, *When Bowman needs someone to get him out of the deep shit he digs himself into, tell him to call me.* Reid had not passed on a message, but he'd kept Turner's Fae dirk.

Gil had been invited to the party tonight, at Kenzie's insistence, and now he was talking with Dr. Pat, who was smiling, as usual. Bowman still wasn't happy with Gil, though he had more sympathy now that he'd heard the man's story. Eric had confirmed that the Fae had driven Gil's people out of Faerie centuries ago, and most of them hadn't been able to adapt to the human world. Gil had lost his family, his friends, everyone he'd cared about. The Fae had put him through hell, and he'd led a lonely existence since.

Ryan, on the other hand, showed no sign of being lonely. He was dancing with his friends, the cubs being goofy, waving their arms and jiggling their bodies, before bursting into riotous laughter. Bowman enjoyed watching his son, thinking of the new cub who would soon join them, their little family increasing.

"Hey, Bowman." Kenzie's dusky voice came out of the darkness. She sashayed up to him, laid both arms on his shoulders. "Want to dance?"

Jamie, who'd been talking with Cade next to him, said, "Watch it, Bowman. Fertile females can be dangerous stuff."

Cade laughed, his rich voice surrounding them. "Like Bowman cares. I caught these two going at it in the hospital bed. Kenzie's machine was beeping like crazy."

"Bite me," Bowman said softly. Cade laughed louder, clapped Jamie on the shoulder, and the pair of them moved off into the darkness.

Music floated from the speakers in the trees, the beat sultry. Kenzie loved to dance, and Bowman loved to watch her.

She lifted her arms, her dress clinging to her belly, which didn't show much of anything yet. But Bowman knew his cub was there, could sense her tiny heartbeat.

Kenzie swayed against him, her body brushing his. He supported her in his arms while she leaned back in complete trust, moving her hips to the music.

I love you, Kenzie. My light. My life.

Kenzie smiled lazily, her eyes half closed. She hadn't heard him, he knew. Their ability to communicate inside their heads had vanished when the danger had gone. Maybe the thought connection would return when they had to fight again.

Didn't matter. The mate bond was true, twining them together. Always.

Kenzie trailed her hand through his short hair. "Anyone ever tell you that you were sexy, Bowman?" Her smile deepened. "Oh, wait, a lot of women have. That's why you're so conceited."

"You love giving me backhanded compliments," Bowman said. "That's why you're such a shit."

Kenzie stuck her tongue out at him. Before he could follow up with an interesting response, she kissed him on the mouth, spun out of his arms, and grabbed his hand.

"Come on. I know somewhere we can be alone."

"Home?" Bowman asked hopefully.

"Can't go there yet. Not when we're guests of honor. But if we slip away for a little while, they won't blame us."

Kenzie cast her gaze on Ryan, surrounded by his friends, carefully watched by Afina and other older females. Their son had taken being nearly drowned in a bog, captured by a madman, subjected to a cruel "experiment," and helping fight a battle with a monster in his stride. He was very proud of his part in the adventure and hadn't tired of telling the story yet, though his friends were starting to tease him about it. Ryan would be all right.

Kenzie took Bowman's hand and led him, at a run, through the darkness.

"Where are we going?" Bowman asked as they climbed hills. Perfectly cured and whole, Kenzie ran on light feet, loosening her dress as she went.

"To the zip line," Kenzie laughed. "We missed the zip line streaking last time."

"What?" Bowman pulled her to a halt. Their breaths came fast, fogging in the cold night. "We won't be alone *there*. Cade's friends will already be lining up."

"No they won't." Kenzie broke free of his hold and kept moving. "I told them they had to stay the hell away for a while."

Bowman sprinted after her. His body grew hot, his frenzy rising, as Kenzie's dress slipped off, leaving her in nothing but a patch of black silk panties, the ones he liked best.

She reached the top of the hill and climbed up to the zip line platform, loosening the straps that held the bar in place.

"Kenz." Bowman caught her wrist. "You can't go zip-lining. You might fall. You could hurt the cub."

Kenzie gave him her sexiest, most smart-ass smile, her golden eyes gleaming. "Oh, *I'm* not riding the zip line naked. *You* are."

Bowman stopped. "Say what? The hell I'm stripping down to ride that thing in the middle of February. A good way to chap every bit of skin on my body. Especially in the important places."

"Aw." Kenzie gave him a sly look. "Are you scared?"

"Gimme a break. Damn it, Kenz, you drive me crazy."

"Good. My work here is done." Still holding the bar, Kenzie rose on tiptoe and pressed a long, promising kiss to his mouth. She thrust the bar into his hands as she backed off. "Bet you I can make it to the bottom of that hill, on foot, before you can ride down."

Bowman growled. "Doubt it."

"Yeah? Want to put money on it?"

"No." Bowman took hold of the bar. "I want a better payout than money."

The smile Kenzie gave him made his insides molten. He felt himself grow hard, even in this cold.

"Tell you what," Kenzie said. "Whoever reaches the bottom of the hill first gets to have the other do to them whatever they desire."

Her emphasis on the word *desire* made Bowman's cock jump. To hell with the bet. He wanted her *now*.

Kenzie took the bar again. Holding it made her breasts thrust out toward him, and Bowman started sweating through the chill.

"I'll even wait here until you get undressed. So it will be a fair match."

Bowman leaned down and licked across her full lips that spoke the sassy words. "You *are* crazy." He tapped the tip of her nose. "But you're on, sweetheart."

Bowman got out of his clothes faster than he thought possible. He enjoyed Kenzie watching his body come into view, liked the way her gaze traveled down his torso, healed again, to his jutting hard-on.

"Give me that." Bowman grabbed the bar from her. "You are so screwed, my mate."

Kenzie laughed. "Off you go," she said, and pushed him away from the platform, swatting his ass as he went.

The world dropped out from under Bowman's feet. Cold wind smacked him, cutting through his need, and his arms felt as though they were coming out of their sockets. He heard Kenzie laugh. The little shit, he was going to . . .

Love her for the rest of his life.

Bowman's first shock fell away, and exhilaration took its place. Cade wasn't such an idiot after all.

Bowman threw his head back and howled in pure enjoyment. The line rushed him down the hill, freezing wind whipping around him, his naked skin tingling with the crazy-ass thing he was doing.

Far away, in the rest of Shiftertown, howls echoed his, and snarls and roars. Shifters celebrating joy with their leader.

Bowman saw the landing place coming up. It was empty, and he tasted his triumph.

He lifted his feet, ready for the impact. He let go of the bar, just as Kenzie stepped out from behind a tree, her smile in place. She wasn't out of breath; she was simply waiting for him. She seemed to have lost the black silk panties somewhere along the way.

"Damn it," Bowman bellowed as he dropped.

Kenzie caught him in her arms. He let the impact of his landing take them both down, falling to the pine needles that carpeted Shiftertown, his home, where he belonged.

The mate bond surrounded them, twining them in a warm net Bowman would never fight himself free of. He'd let it tie him up forever, with Kenzie, his mate, his love.

His everything.

Turn the page to read an excerpt from
the first book in the Shifters Unbound series

PRIDE MATES

A girl walks into a bar . . .

   No. A human girl walks into a Shifter bar . . .

The bar was empty, not yet open to customers. It looked normal—windowless walls painted black, rows of glass bottles, the smell of beer and stale air. But it wasn't normal, standing on the edge of Shiftertown as it did.

"You the lawyer?" a man washing glasses asked. He was human, not Shifter. No strange, slitted pupils, no Collar to control his aggression, no air of menace. Well, relatively no air of menace. This was a crappy part of town, and menace was its stock-in-trade.

Kim told herself she had nothing to be afraid of. *They're tamed. Collared. They can't hurt you.*

When she nodded, the man gestured with his cloth to a door at the end of the bar. "Knock him dead, sweetheart."

"I'll try to keep him alive." Kim pivoted and stalked away on her four-inch heels, feeling his gaze on her back all the way.

She knocked on the door marked "Private," and a man on the other side growled, "Come."

I just need to talk to him. Then I'm done, on my way home.

A trickle of moisture rolled between Kim's shoulder blades as she made herself open the door and walk inside.

A man leaned back in a chair behind a messy desk, a sheaf of papers in his hands. His booted feet were propped on the desk, his long legs a feast of blue jeans over muscle. He was a Shifter all right—thin black and silver Collar against his throat; hard, honed body; midnight black hair; definite air of menace. When Kim entered, he stood, setting the papers aside.

Damn. He rose to a height of well over six feet and gazed at Kim with eyes blue like the morning sky. His body wasn't only honed; it was hot—big chest, wide shoulders, tight abs, firm biceps against a form-fitting black T-shirt.

"Kim Fraser?"

"That's me."

With old-fashioned courtesy, he placed a chair in front of the desk and motioned her to it. Kim felt the heat of his hand near the small of her back as she seated herself, smelled the scent of soap and male musk.

"You're Mr. Morrissey?"

The Shifter sat back down, returned his motorcycle boots to the top of the desk, and laced his hands behind his head. "Call me Liam."

The lilt in his voice was unmistakable. Kim put that with his black hair, impossibly blue eyes, and exotic name. "You're Irish."

He smiled a smile that could melt a woman at ten paces. "And who else would be running a pub?"

"But you don't own it."

Kim could have bitten out her tongue as soon as she said it. Of course he didn't own it. He was a Shifter.

His voice went frosty, the crinkles at the corners of his eyes smoothing out. "I'm afraid I can't help you much on the Brian Smith case. I don't know Brian well, and I don't know anything about what happened the night his girlfriend was murdered. It's a long time ago, now."

Disappointment bit her, but Kim had learned not to let discouragement stop her when she needed to get a job done. "Brian called you the 'go-to' guy. As in, when Shifters are in trouble, Liam Morrissey helps them out."

Liam shrugged, muscles moving the bar's logo on his

T-shirt. "True. But Brian never came to me. He got into his troubles all by himself."

"I know that. I'm trying to get him *out* of trouble."

Liam's eyes narrowed, pupils flicking to slits as he retreated to the predator within him. Shifters liked to do that when assessing a situation, Brian had told her. Guess who was the prey?

Brian had done the predator-prey thing with Kim at first. He'd stopped when he began to trust her, but Kim didn't think she'd ever get used to it. Brian was her first Shifter client, the first Shifter, in fact, she'd ever seen outside a television news story. Twenty years Shifters had been acknowledged to exist, but Kim had never met one.

It was well known that they lived in their enclave on the east side of Austin, near the old airport, but she'd never gone over to check them out. Some human women did, strolling the streets just outside Shiftertown, hoping for glimpses—and more—of the Shifter men who were reputed to be strong, gorgeous, and well endowed. Kim had once heard two women in a restaurant murmuring about their encounter with a Shifter male the night before. The phrase "Oh, my God," had been used repeatedly. Kim was as curious about them as anyone else, but she'd never summoned the courage to go near Shiftertown herself.

Then suddenly she had been assigned the case of the Shifter accused of murdering his human girlfriend ten months ago. This was the first time in twenty years Shifters had caused trouble, the first time one had been put on trial. The public, outraged by the killing, wanted Shifters punished, pointed fingers at those who'd claimed the Shifters were tamed.

However, after Kim had met Brian, she'd determined that she wouldn't do a token defense. She believed in his innocence, and she wanted to win. There wasn't much case law on Shifters because there'd never been any trials, at least none on record. This was to be a well-publicized trial, Kim's opportunity to make a mark, to set precedent.

Liam's eyes stayed on her, pupils still slitted. "You're a brave one, aren't you? To defend a Shifter?"

"Brave, that's me." Kim crossed her legs, pretending to relax. They picked up on your nervousness, people said. *They know when you're scared, and they use your fear.* "I don't mind telling you, this case has been a pain in the ass from the get-go."

"Humans think anything involving Shifters is a pain in the ass."

Kim shook her head. "I mean, it's been a pain in the ass because of the way it's been handled. The cops nearly had Brian signing a confession before I could get to the interrogation. At least I put a stop to that, but I couldn't get bail for him, and I've been blocked by the prosecutors right and left every time I want to review the evidence. Talking to you is a long shot, but I'm getting desperate. So if you don't want to see a Shifter go down for this crime, Mr. Morrissey, a little cooperation would be appreciated."

The way he pinned her with his eyes, never blinking, made her want to fold in on herself. Or run. That was what prey did—ran. And then predators chased them, cornered them.

What did this man do when he cornered his prey? He wore the Collar; he could do nothing. Right?

Kim imagined herself against a wall, his hands on either side of her, his hard body hemming her in . . . Heat curled down her spine.

Liam took his feet down and leaned forward, arms on the desk. "I haven't said I won't help you, lass." His gaze flicked to her blouse, whose buttons had slipped out of their top holes during her journey through Austin traffic and July heat. "Is Brian happy with you defending him? You like Shifters that much?"

Kim resisted reaching for the buttons. She could almost feel his fingers on them, undoing each one, and her heart beat faster.

"It's nothing to do with who I like. I was assigned to him, but I happen to think Brian's innocent. He shouldn't go down for something he didn't do." Kim liked her anger, because it covered up how edgy this man made her. "Besides, Brian's the only Shifter I've ever met, so I don't know whether I like them, do I?"

Liam smiled again. His eyes returned to normal, and now he looked like any other gorgeous, hard-bodied, blue-eyed Irishman. "You, love, are—"

"Feisty. Yeah, I've heard that one. Also spitfire, little go-getter, and a host of other condescending terms. But let me tell you, Mr. Morrissey, I'm a damn good lawyer. Brian's not guilty, and I'm going to save his ass."

"I was going to say *unusual*. For a human."

"Because I'm willing to believe he's innocent?"

"Because you came here, to the outskirts of Shiftertown, to see me. Alone."

The predator was back.

Why was it that when Brian looked at her like this, it didn't worry her? Brian was in jail, angry, accused of heinous crimes. A killer, according to the police. But Brian's stare didn't send shivers down her spine like Liam Morrissey's did.

"Any reason I shouldn't have come alone?" she asked, keeping her voice light. "I'm trying to prove that Shifters in general, and my client in particular, can't harm humans. I'd do a poor job of it if I was afraid to come and talk to his friends."

Liam wanted to laugh at the little—spitfire—but he kept his stare cool. She had no idea what she was walking into; Fergus, the clan leader, expected Liam to make sure it stayed that way.

Damn it all, Liam wasn't supposed to *like* her. He'd expected the usual human woman, sticks-up-their-asses, all of them, but there was something different about Kim Fraser. It wasn't just that she was small and compact, while Shifter women were tall and willowy. He liked the way her dark blue eyes regarded him without fear, liked the riot of black curls that beckoned his fingers. She'd had the sense to leave her hair alone, not force it into some unnatural shape.

On the other hand, she tried to hide her sweetly curvaceous body under a stiff gray business suit, although her body had other ideas. Her breasts wanted to burst out of the button-up blouse, and the stiletto heels only enhanced wickedly sexy legs.

No Shifter woman would dress as she did. Shifter women wore loose clothes they could quickly shed if they needed to change forms. Shorts and T-shirts were popular. So were gypsy skirts and sarongs in the summer.

Liam imagined this lady in a sarong. Her melon-firm breasts would fill out the top, and the skirt would bare her smooth thighs.

She'd be even prettier in a bikini, lolling around some rich man's pool, sipping a complicated drink. She was a lawyer—there was probably a boss in her firm who had already made her his. Or perhaps she was using said boss to climb the success ladder. Humans did that all the time. Either the bastard would break her heart, or she'd walk away happy with what she'd gotten out of it.

That's why we stay the hell away from humans. Brian

Smith had taken up with a human woman, and look where he was now.

So why did this female raise Liam's protective instincts? Why did she make him want to move closer, inside the radius of her body heat? She wouldn't like that; humans tried to stay a few feet apart from each other unless they couldn't help it. Even lovers might do nothing more than hold hands in public.

Liam had no business thinking about passion and this woman in the same heartbeat. Fergus's instructions had been to listen to Kim, sway her, then send her home. Not that Liam was in the habit of blindly obeying Fergus.

"So why do you want to help him, love?" he asked. "You're only defending him because you drew the short straw, am I right?"

"I'm the junior in the firm, so it was handed to me, yes. But the prosecutor's office and the police have done a shitty job with this case. Rights violations all over the place, but the courts won't dismiss it, no matter how much I argue. Everyone wants a Shifter to go down, innocent or guilty."

"And why do you believe Brian didn't do it?"

"Why do you think?" Kim tapped her throat. "Because of these."

Liam resisted touching the strand of black and silver metal fused to his own neck, a small Celtic knot at the base of his throat. The Collars contained tiny programmed chips enhanced by powerful Fae magic to keep Shifters in check, though the humans didn't want to acknowledge the magic part. The Collar shot an electric charge into a Shifter when his violent tendencies rose to the surface. If the Shifter persisted, the next dose was one of debilitating pain. A Shifter couldn't attack anyone if he was rolling around on the ground, writhing in agony.

Liam wasn't sure entirely how the Collars worked; he only knew that each became bonded to its wearer's skin and adapted to their animal form when they shifted. All Shifters living in human communities were required to wear Collars, which were irremovable once put on. Refusing the Collar meant execution. If the Shifter tried to escape, he or she was hunted down and killed.

"You know Brian couldn't have committed a violent crime," Kim was saying. "His Collar would have stopped him."

"Let me guess. Your police claim the Collar malfunctioned?"

"Yep. When I suggest having it tested, I'm greeted with all kinds of reasons it can't be. The Collar can't be removed, and anyway it would be too dangerous to have Brian Collarless if he could be. Also too dangerous to provoke him to violence and see if the Collar stops him. Brian's been calm since he was brought in. Like he's given up." She looked glum. "I hate to see someone give up like that."

"You like the underdog?"

She grinned at him with red lips. "You could say that, Mr. Morrissey. Me and the underdog go back a long way."

Liam liked her mouth. He liked imagining it on his body, on certain parts of his anatomy in particular. He had no business thinking that, but the thoughts triggered a physical reaction below the belt.

Weird. He'd never even considered having sex with a human before. He didn't find human women attractive; Liam preferred to be in his big cat form for sex. He found sex that way much more satisfying. With Kim, he'd have to remain human.

His gaze strayed to her unbuttoned collar. Of course, it might not be so bad to be human with her . . .

What the hell am I thinking? Fergus's instructions had been clear, and Liam agreeing to them had been the only way Fergus had allowed Kim to come to Shiftertown at all. Fergus wasn't keen on a human woman being in charge of Brian's case, not that they had any choice. Fergus had been pissed about Brian's arrest from the beginning and thought the Shifters should back off and stay out of it. Almost as though he believed Brian was guilty.

But Fergus lived down on the other side of San Antonio, and what he didn't know wouldn't hurt him. Liam would handle this his own way.

"So what do you expect from me, love?" he asked Kim. "Want to test *my* Collar?"

"No, I want to know more about Brian, about Shifters and the Shifter community. Who Brian's people are, how he grew up, what it's like to live in a Shifter enclave." She smiled again. "Finding six independent witnesses who swear he was nowhere near the victim at the time in question wouldn't hurt either."

"Oh, is that all? Bloody miracles is what you want, darling."

She wrapped a dark curl around her finger. "Brian said that

you're the Shifter people talk to most. Shifters and humans alike."

It was true that Shifters came to Liam with their troubles. His father, Dylan Morrissey, was master of this Shiftertown, second in power in the whole clan.

Humans knew little about the careful hierarchy of the Shifter clans and prides—packs for Lupines—and still less about how informally but efficiently everything got done. Dylan was the Morrissey pride leader and the leader of this Shiftertown, and Fergus was the clan leader for the Felines of South Texas, but Shifters with a problem sought out Liam or his brother Sean for a chat. They'd meet in the bar or at the coffee shop around the corner. *So, Liam, can you ask your father to look into it for me?*

No one would petition Dylan or Fergus directly. That wasn't done. But chatting about things to Liam over coffee, that was fine and didn't draw attention to the fact that the person in question had troubles.

Everyone would know anyway, of course. Life in a Shiftertown reminded Liam very much of life in the Irish village he'd lived near until they'd come to Texas twenty years ago. Everyone knew everything about everyone, and news traveled, lightning-swift, from one side of the village to the other.

"Brian never came to me," he said. "I never knew anything about this human girl until suddenly the police swoop in here and arrest him. His mother struggled out of bed to watch her son be dragged away. She didn't even know why for days."

Kim watched Liam's blue eyes harden. The Shifters were angry about Brian's arrest, that was certain. Citizens of Austin had tensely waited for the Shifters to make trouble after the arrest, to break free and try to retaliate with violence, but Shiftertown remained quiet. Kim wondered why, but she wasn't about to ask right now and risk angering the one person who might help her.

"Exactly my point," she said. "This case has been handled badly from start to finish. If you help me, I can spring Brian and make a point at the same time. You don't mess with people's rights, not even Shifters'."

Liam's eyes grew harder, if that were possible. It was like looking at living sapphire. "I don't give a damn about making a point. I give a damn about Brian's family."

All right, so she'd miscalculated about what would moti-
vate him. "In that case, Brian's family will be happier with
him outside prison, not inside."

"He won't go to prison, love. He'll be executed, and you
know it. No waiting twenty years on death row either. They'll
kill him, and they'll kill him fast."

That was true. The prosecutor, the county sheriff, the attor-
ney general, and even the governor wanted an example made
of Brian. There hadn't been a Shifter attack in twenty years,
and the Texas government wanted to assure the world that they
weren't going to allow one now.

"So are you going to help me save him?" Kim asked. If he
wanted to be direct and to the point, fine. So could she. "Or let
him die?"

Anger flickered through Liam's eyes again, then sorrow
and frustration. Shifters were emotional people from what
she'd seen in Brian, not bothering to hide what they felt. Brian
had lashed out at Kim many times before he'd grudgingly
acknowledged that she was on his side.

If Liam decided to stonewall her, Brian had said, Kim had
no hope of getting cooperation from the other Shifters. Even
Brian's own mother would take her cue from Liam.

Liam had the look of a man who didn't take shit from anyone. A man used to giving the orders himself, but so far he
hadn't seemed brutal. He could make his voice soft and lilting,
reassuring, friendly. He was a defender, she guessed. A pro-
tector of his people.

Was he deciding whether to protect Brian or turn his back?

Liam's gaze flicked past her to the door, every line of his
body coming alert. Kim's nerves made her jump. "What is it?"

Liam got out of his chair and started around the desk at the
same time the door scraped open and another man—another
Shifter—walked in.

Liam's expression changed. "Sean." He clasped the other
Shifter's arms and pulled him into a hug.

More than a hug. Kim watched, open-mouthed, as Liam
wrapped his arms around the other man, gathered him close,
and nuzzled his cheek.

M1594T1114